D1168506

This book is part of the
DML Eisenberg Humanities Collection in honor
of
Dr. John M. Eisenberg, MD, MBA

Chair of Dept. of Medicine and
Physician in Chief

Dahlgren Memorial Library
THE HEALTH SCIENCES LIBRARY AT GEORGETOWN UNIVERSITY

BREAK AND ENTER

BREAK AND ENTER

BY

COLIN HARRISON

CROWN PUBLISHERS, INC.
NEW YORK

Copyright © 1990 by Colin Harrison

All rights reserved. No part of this book may be reproduced or
transmitted in any form or by any means, electronic or mechanical,
including photocopying, recording, or by any information storage
and retrieval system, without permission in writing from the
publisher.

Published by Crown Publishers, Inc., 201 East 50th Street,
New York, New York 10022

CROWN is a trademark of Crown Publishers, Inc.

Manufactured in the United States of America

Library of Congress Cataloging-in-Publication Data
Harrison, Colin.
    Break and enter / by Colin Harrison.
    I. Title.
  PR6058.A69225B7   1990
823'.914—dc20   89-28119
                                                                    CIP

ISBN 0-517-57281-8

10 9 8 7 6 5 4 3 2 1

First Edition

For Kathryn

# ACKNOWLEDGMENTS

Several individuals helped me gain access to the world of the Philadelphia prosecutor. Charles Gallagher, deputy for policy and planning in the Philadelphia District Attorney's office, and Joseph Wolfson, a former Philadelphia Assistant District Attorney now in private practice with Morgan, Lewis, & Bockius, both shared with me their impressions and experiences. My conversations with these individuals did not involve specific, attributable identification of any living individuals, either attorneys, defendants, or political figures in Philadelphia. In fact, our discussions were predicated upon this limitation by these men *and* by myself. Similarly, although the lawyer protagonist of this novel has the surname of Scattergood, no relation to or characterization of any living person named Scattergood is meant or implied.

Mr. Wolfson and Thomas Schindler, an Assistant District Attorney in the Chester County (Pennsylvania) District Attorney's Office and a friend for more than twenty years, checked the manuscript for legal and procedural accuracy. Their corrections and suggestions were invaluable. Any and all errors should be attributed to the author, however. A nod of thanks goes also to the men and women of Philadelphia City Hall, official and distinctly unofficial, who shared with me information about the building and the courts.

The "Eternal Truths" are derived from a list originally written by Richard Donelli, D.D.S., and modified by Ann Satterthwaite and the author. For several details about historical Philadelphia, I have depended on "Once Upon a Time," an article by Stephanie Grauman Wolf, Ph.D., which appeared in *Bryn Mawr Now*.

Finally, I wish to express my gratitude to James Michener and the Copernicus Society for their generous fellowship in support of the writing of this novel.

And thou Philadelphia, the virgin settlement of this province named before thou wert born. What love, what care, what service and what travail have there been to bring thee forth and preserve thee from such as would abuse and defile thee. O that thou mayest be kept from the evil that would overwhelm thee, that faithful to the god of thy mercies in the life of righteousness thou mayest be preserved to the end. My soul prays to God for thee, that thou mayest stand in the day of trial, that thy children may be blest of the Lord, and thy people saved by His power.

–William Penn's Prayer for Philadelphia, 1684,
inscribed on North Archway, City Hall

ONE

Guilty. The man's as guilty as they come, Peter Scattergood argued
to himself, nearly speaking out loud. He needed to get back to the
courtroom but tried, even as he hurried along—a big, black-haired
man in a dark, expensive overcoat—to look up at the sky, to catch a
piece of pale lunchtime light bouncing around up there between all
the new skyscrapers. There was no time to stop and stand. Peter
moved faster through the crowds, cold air slipping under his wool
scarf. Awaiting him was another appalling common case of sex
murder—premeditated, first degree. No need to think about it. But
because murder marked the outer limits of human depravity, reminding him that he stood at the opposite end of the continuum, there was
a small pleasure in its contemplation, a certain grim comfort. And he'd
take what comfort he could get, for lately it had been in short supply.

 He turned the corner onto Market Street, bent red-faced into the
January wind. A block east stood Philadelphia City Hall—six hundred rooms, thirty years to build, walls twenty-two feet thick, once
the largest and tallest public building in America, the colossal statue
of William Penn reaching five hundred and forty-eight feet above the
ground. He'd first been awed by it as a schoolboy. The edifice stood
before him in all its marble-scrolled splendor, gray from pollution,
with pigeon shit dripped around the cornices and columns and window ledges, but still it was a godawful magnificent building and filled
with the offices of government; the Mayor and his entourage—corrupt
bureaucratic pinheads all, the ever-bickering City Council, the social
services offices, the Pennsylvania Supreme Court, the city property

1

office, and jesus christ, of course, forty-nine courtrooms, and even, he had heard rumored (from Berger, who knew everything), a small janitor's closet where you could get a blowjob any hour of the working day. A girl sat there on a wooden stool. Five minutes, thirty bucks. But lately City Hall bothered him. It was the many figures sculpted in stone on the outside, the lion gargoyles who grinned maniacally at him, the bearded old tyrant perched over a window lintel five stories up who watched below, and the marble-cheeked virgins who stared wistfully from the top of porticoes. He told himself not to look at their stone faces.

Peter crossed at the green light, walked beneath the arch, and inside, past the Register of Wills office, toward the elevator to the fourth floor. He was working out of Courtroom 453 these days, and Judge Scarletti was not above scolding an assistant district attorney for being late to the afternoon session. He passed judges' offices, jury rooms, and other doors open wide enough for him to glimpse fleets of tired secretaries and wooden, ceiling-high shelves stuffed with files brown with age. The halls were subterraneanly gloomy; silhouettes advanced through light and shadow, shadow and light. He nodded silent hellos to other attorneys, court officers, judges. At the elevator door stood a couple of cops reading the *Daily News* on the taxpayers' time. On the fourth floor a group of jurors wearing yellow and blue "Juror" buttons bustled by, imperious in their fleeting importance. Somewhere a K-9 German shepherd barked. Peter hated the dogs; they were preternaturally huge and trained to terrify with crazy brown eyes and a quick bite. He passed detectives waiting to testify. Each was large, well-groomed, and overfed. They laughed amongst themselves. In City Hall, everybody knew everybody.

On the bench outside Courtroom 453 sat a man in his thirties sucking at a cigarette, the smoke lost in the dimness of the hallway. Long curly hair, motorcycle jacket, deep chest. A big man. Peter recognized him as one of the older brothers of Robinson, the defendant.

"Mister prosecutor," the man grunted in a hoarse voice. He stood and sized up the vertical sweep of Peter's Brooks Brothers gray pinstripe, maroon tie, and crisp white shirt. They stood out of earshot of the two policemen at the courtroom door.

"What can I do for you?"

"You from Philly?" The man flicked his cigarette at the floor. "Just asking."

2

"Born," Peter said. "And raised."

"How old are you?"

"Thirty-one."

"*Shit.* Punks sending up punks." He stepped closer, quite fearlessly. "If my little bro's found guilty, what will it be?"

"Life, probably life."

"He's a kid. You gotta go easy, man."

"The jury will decide that, not me."

"It's *you* who keep saying how guilty he is."

Peter remembered the murder victim, Judy Warren, and the hours spent consoling her family, swearing to her parents he'd put the killer away, explaining each step of the maddeningly slow legal process, from the charging to pretrial hearings to, finally, a jury trial. For months the family had been consumed by the monstrous energy of grief; the fine points of prosecutorial strategy meant nothing to them. The family wanted justice, the purge of their outrage. Judy's severed left thumb had been found in her vagina.

"That's what you wanted to tell me?" Peter replied in a cold voice.

The defendant's brother stared at him, then smiled.

"No. I wanted to tell you to go fuck yourself."

Peter pushed past him and was waved through the door by a cop with a metal detector wand. The familiar gloominess of the courtroom comforted him, with its faded carpeting, faulty lighting, and the wooden paneling on which hung grim portraits of long-dead judges. Gladys, the fat black court clerk, watched him make his way to the table and put down his briefcase.

"Mr. Scattergood, your wife called," she said sternly, stacking her records. "She don't seem happy with you."

"You know something I don't, Gladys?"

"Don't mess with me, Mr. Scattergood. She's a good woman."

"She leave a number?"

"Yeah, she did."

"Well, that's a start." He took the pink message slip from Gladys's smooth black hand and folded it into his pocket. "And without a start in life, where are we, Gladys?"

She gave him a sober look. "You tell me, Mr. Scattergood."

We're dead, he thought to himself. He fingered the slip, thought about calling. There was no time to worry about Janice now, no time to ponder what latest piece of his marriage had crumbled away. His chest was bothering him again, a dull pain right under the breastbone.

3

The doctor said too much caffeine and *entirely* too much stress. It was chest wall pain; there was no need yet to run an EKG—he had the heart of an ox, and low cholesterol, too, thanks to Janice's vegetarian meals.

Judge Scarletti came in and sat behind the bench with the obliviousness of a man boarding a bus. He fussed with a computer printout of cases, checked his watch, then looked up.

Two beefy sheriff's deputies entered with the unhandcuffed defendant, William Biddle Robinson, who sat down next to Morgan, his counsel. Robinson was a brash young man who looked as if he had just stepped out of an American Express card commercial. But despite a staid wool suit and tie, Robinson was entirely unpredictable— perhaps it was his habit of smiling inappropriately and raising his eyebrows several times a minute. His parents owned a controlling interest in the holding corporation that owned one of the city's private hospitals. Young William had murdered a girl whom he had seen romantically and then been dumped by. As cases went, it was typically horrific and had received little attention, perhaps because the murderer was from an outlying county and the girl, whose family shunned reporters, was lower-middle-class and without media-lustre. There had been some minor, obligatory attention to the case—page three of the B section of the *Inquirer*, the usual write-up in the *Daily News*—but basically not much, due also to the fact Philly was undergoing yet another periodic paroxysm of massive public scandal, with Common Pleas judges dropping regularly to corruption charges and organized-crime bosses being trapped by undercover operations. The swarming clot of cameras and reporters was down on the second floor reporting on this week's story of the decade—the prosecution of one of the crime bosses, a gentleman given to gold tie clips and tidy mob hits— and that was fine with Peter. Although this case was more gruesome than many, it would fall into the hopper of history with all the others. He was eager to get the trial done, in and out, no fuss. The roving, insatiable eye of the media—it could suck the energy out of a man—was just what Peter didn't want now, not with the trouble he already had.

Actually the newspapers and television stations had missed a good story. The defendant was twenty-two, brilliantly articulate at times, disturbingly disoriented at others, with a preppy Main Line education—the local brand-name private schools. A graduate of Yale, with one year at Columbia in the MBA program. He'd been arrested with no fewer than eighteen credit cards in his wallet and wearing

4

L. L. Bean duckboots, green wide-wale corduroys, and a button-down oxford shirt.

Through the interconnected world of Philadelphia's private schools, clubs, and summer camps, Peter had known vaguely of the Robinson family for over a decade, even once been to their home. As was often the case, the crime by one member of the family reflected the reality of the rest of its members. The Robinsons lived on a huge, Revolutionary-era estate twenty miles out of the city in Chester County, with a long driveway that led to the thick stone walls and simple lines of the old mansion. A pool in the back—in which Peter had swum, the most modern of kitchens, old Kashmiri Oriental rugs on the wide, pegged floorboards, Chinese jade on the bookshelves in the study, an expanse of bedrooms above. The parents had, over the years, smiled into the society columnist's photographer's flashbulb, drinks in hand, dental work gleaming. Sad, polished wealth. Covert facelifts, the Devon Horse Show, the shingled old summerhouse tucked away in the dunes of Nantucket, the signed Ansel Adams hung in the foyer, the quarterly trust fund check from a Manhattan bank. Peter had known such people all his life. Their children sometimes went mad, despite fancy funny farms in New England at eighty thousand dollars a year, psychiatrists, etc. What was worse? To have all of life's advantages and be a complete failure, or to have all of life's disadvantages, fight like hell, and still be crushed by your circumstances? Robinson's parents, shamed and angry, had made certain funds available for their son's defense and then absented themselves from North America for an indefinite period.

Thus neither parent of the defendant had appeared at the trial once, which the jury had probably already noted without sympathy. The fact was that the parents had given up long ago. Dr. Robinson made immense, unnecessary sums as a surgeon and used some of this money to indulge his avid desire for fly-fishing in remote regions of Canada, South America, and northern India. He was rarely home. His wife had suffered the unfortunate fate of raising four sons in isolation and wealth, and with minimal interest by their father. The sons went to the best of schools, and thus any tendency toward cunning was strengthened by a superior education. Complicating matters were their natural physical strength and courage (all of them ran on the large side, with the wide-jawed handsomeness of their father) and their proximity to all manner of disconnected males floating around the quasi-rural landscape: drug dealers, motorcycle gang members, gas station attendants, semi-pro mechanics, volunteer firemen, small-time organized-crime members, and out-of-work truck drivers. They were used to doing whatever they pleased and as boys ran amok over their parents' property in packs with their friends, occasionally setting fires, motorbiking across what once had been a rolled croquet lawn, torturing small and lost animals, holding deafening parties in the barn at the edge of the property, and, as they got older, manufacturing drugs in one of the outlying buildings, hiding stolen cars, and keeping small harems of disaffected local young women of little self-esteem or prospect. Each son knew that he would inherit at age thirty the principal of a trust that each year grew in magnitude—an arrangement their parents were wholly unable to avert, due to the trust details drafted by the long-dead grandfather—and thus there was no incentive for the boys to work toward anything.

William Robinson, the youngest son, had deviated from the pattern set by his older brothers to the extent that he actually pursued the semblance of an acceptable life. Propelled by the sums at his disposal and a restless intelligence, he progressed through college and into graduate school with little apparent trouble. But the stress of straddling too many worlds had finally broken him, or perhaps—Peter didn't know, didn't care, ultimately—Robinson had glimpsed the immense lovelessness within the center of his family.

"Ready, Counselor?" Judge Scarletti pulled the microphone to his mouth. Peter nodded and skimmed his notes. Someone had refilled the water pitcher on his table. Judy Warren's family came in and huddled together in the chairs behind the prosecution's desk. The women held one another's hands, fingered handkerchiefs. The men, unable to grieve openly, stared hatefully at the defendant, then assumed a look of strained dignity. Peter had seen it more times than he knew, and yet always he worried that he would fail them. Rightly or wrongly, he'd become dependent on those tears of gratitude that came with a verdict of guilty; it couldn't bring people back to life, but it did deliver a form of catharsis to the decedent's family. Now the defense counsel came in, then a few straggling spectators, the jolly retired men in cardigans who drifted from one trial to another for daily entertainment. For them, the drama was entirely academic, and they clicked their dentures happily at any mention of blood and whispered loudly as they questioned legal strategy. Then a stray law student, as Peter had been almost a decade prior—alone, quietly watching from the back, yet eagerly attentive, fitting the thick law books to courtroom reality. And now the jury filed in and found their numbered seats.

Last, the brother Peter had encountered outside the courtroom entered, looked around angrily, and took a seat in the back. They all knew what was coming next.

As the prosecuting attorney, Peter had already presented nearly his entire case and was now about to conclude with the examination of his final witness, the detective who had questioned Robinson after he was arrested. On the cross-examination, Morgan would do as much as he could to destroy this testimony. But Morgan's problem was that Robinson had confessed to the crime—or, at least, to a version of the crime. There had been no violation of the defendant's rights, perhaps because he was a white, college-educated male from the upper class, and so the confession was ruled as admissable evidence in a pretrial hearing. But there were certain minor inaccuracies in the confession, due perhaps to Robinson's excitable sense of irony and manipulation when talking with police officers. Forced into a corner by overwhelming evidence, Morgan had sought the bold stroke of genius and only come up with the improbable: In his opening statements he promised to create an alternative scenario of events in order to prove that Robinson could not have committed the crime, *even though he had confessed to it*. The strategy was as absurd as it was dramatic.

Peter flipped over the next page of his legal pad. It read:

> Detect. Nelson—questioning at 8th and Race:
> 1. procedural stuff—orientation
> 2. defend. statement.—lamp, knife, gasoline

The court officer swore in Detective Ralph N. Nelson, using a Bible with an uncracked spine and the courtroom number scrawled irreverently on the closed edges of its pages. Peter and Nelson understood each other perfectly—or as best they could given their different lives. Nelson was about fifty, black, and had been a cop almost as long as Peter had been alive, testifying in hundreds of cases. He'd been through the Rizzo, Green, and Goode administrations. Peter hadn't even pretended to instruct him prior to testimony; he would just lead the detective to all the right places and let him do the rest. Nelson was a piano of a man, and his size lent him the air not of unassailable strength but of titanic weariness, a superhuman burden of the knowledge of the ways human beings brutalized one another. Nelson settled in the witness chair, gave his badge number, and lifted his bloodshot eyes in patient expectation.

Peter moved quickly through procedural questions. Defendant

taken in for questioning. Unmarked squad car. Was he handcuffed? No. Where did you go? Room C, police headquarters, Eighth and Race Streets. Nelson sat completely still. His eyes barely moved, blinked occasionally; his voice bore the weight of cigarettes, radio crackle, methodical note-taking in the homicide division office, a three-year-old Buick, two slug scars in the lower back, a heavy-assed wife whom he loved loyally and deeply, season tickets to the Eagles, and a baby granddaughter born with spinal bifida.

"Did you read the defendant his rights?" Peter asked.

"Yes. I told the defendant, 'You have the right to remain silent. You have the right to a lawyer. If you cannot afford a lawyer, the Commonwealth of Pennsylvania will provide you one at its expense. Anything you say can and will be used against you.' "

"From what did you read this?"

Nelson held up the card.

"It's a police form. Standard form seventy-five dash miscellaneous three."

"What did you do next?"

"On the other side of the card are questions, which I then read to the defendant: 'Do you understand that you have the right to remain silent?' And the defendant said yes. 'Do you understand you have the right to a lawyer?' And the defendant said yes. 'You sure you understand that you can have a lawyer here if you want?' 'Yes, you motherfucker.' 'Do you understand . . .' "

Morgan sat at his table, intently listening, waiting to leap up with an objection, picking at lint, collecting paper clips in a pile, and watching his case die. Peter had selected this jury to believe a man such as Nelson. And listening to his words be repeated, Robinson kept his head bowed and smiled to himself, gripping the table with both hands as if he were about to fall backward.

"Was any force used in this interview?" Peter asked when the detective was finished. He would steal some of Morgan's standard questions, undermining the cross-examination that would follow.

"No."

"Was the defendant drunk?"

"No."

"Eyes glazed? Speech slurred?"

"No."

"Any sign of using narcotics?"

"No."

"Was the defendant ill?"

"No."

"Deprived of sleep?"

"No."

"Deprived of water?"

"No."

"Was he verbally abused, shouted at?"

"No."

"Did he appear to be oriented as to time, place, identity, and situation?"

"Yes, he appeared to be oriented as to the time. The place. His identity. And to the situation and gravity of being questioned by two detectives, Counselor."

He appreciated Nelson's tight, corrective testimony. It was a rare thing; most witnesses and even an occasional policeman slopped around within the vagaries of memory.

"And you took a statement?"

"Yes."

"Do you have that statement here with you today?"

"That is correct."

"Please describe the manner in which the statement was taken."

"I asked him questions and I typed each answer as he said it."

"Are you a good typist?"

"About ninety-five words a minute."

The detective smiled thinly, perhaps embarrassed about his secretarial prowess. Peter knew how to redeem him.

"Learned to type in the Army, is that right?"

"Yes, sir."

"So the statement is a fair and accurate transcription of your conversation?"

"That is correct."

"Why wasn't the confession videotaped?"

"We were waiting to use the camera, but he started talking before we even got into the room and had the camera set up, and he just kept going, so I started typing as fast as I could."

"Is there anything particularly unusual about that procedure?"

"No. We've used typed confessions a long time." The detective allowed himself a tired opinion. "They work."

"Okay," Peter said. "Did the defendant sign the statement?"

"Yes. He signed every page."

"Did the defendant read the statement first?"

"Yes."

"Can the defendant read?" A dumb question in light of Robinson's education, but necessary.

"I had him read the first couple of paragraphs aloud."

"I would like this marked Commonwealth's exhibit."

"Does counsel for the defense have a copy?" the judge asked.

Morgan searched his papers. "Uh, I had this a minute ago. . . ." Morgan, a man who possessed an excited explosion of wiry black hair that lifted off his head, was as disorganized as he was righteous. Waiting, Peter put his hand in his pocket and felt the slip of paper with Janice's number. Where in hell *was* she? Maybe the number was good for only a little while.

"With the court's indulgence, Your Honor, while he's looking for his copy, I'd like to take a quick break."

Judge Scarletti sighed; another delay in a career of delays. He glanced at his watch.

"I have no problem with that, Your Honor," Morgan said, the epitome of strategic graciousness.

"Gentlemen," the judge said, smiling wearily, "just remember that you are younger than I am. I'm due to retire in a few years and I'd love to see the end of this trial." He looked at Peter. "Ten minutes, Mr. Scattergood."

He slipped into a phone booth at the end of the hall and dialed the number on the paper.

"Hello?" came her voice.

"Hi, it's me." He stared at the slip in his hand.

"I called the courtroom during the lunch recess. They said you'd be back soon."

"What's this number?"

"Just where I am right now."

He ignored her answer. A good prosecutor got his information sideways when necessary. He wasn't sure anymore what a good husband did.

"What's up? How's the new place?" Too upbeat; she'd slaughter him.

"I've been busy. Adjusting, you know."

"Good. You okay?"

"I'm *fine*, Peter. You don't have to worry about me."

10

He did worry about her, but he also worried about what he heard in her voice, which said, *Keep your distance.*

"There wasn't any mail for you, but when I get some, what—"

"It's already being forwarded to me at work."

"Not to the apartment?"

"No."

She was slipping away quickly, changing patterns, leaving him confused.

"Can we talk tonight?"

"I'd rather not, Peter. You know that."

"I'm just hanging in space, Janice."

She didn't reply.

"Will you be at this number tonight?"

There was a long pause, and he knew she was considering the effect of her answer.

"For a while. Bye."

Down the hall, he saw Berger schmoozing with a couple of detectives.

"Hey!" he called, seeking relief.

Berger, a small stick of a man with the temperamental energy of a squirrel, hurried over.

"You talking to Janice? You have that look."

The call had made things worse. "Nobody else."

Berger's eyes bulged at this information, as they bulged at everything.

"You on for racquetball tomorrow night?" Peter asked.

"I have to depose this woman out in Harrisburg. Your basic hospital bedside deposition—saw the murder in Philly, got scared, moved to Harrisburg, and her bad heart caught up with her. My train's at five-thirty tomorrow."

Peter shook his head. "You just can't take my serve."

"What are you on?" Berger asked, indicating the courtroom.

"Robinson."

"Yeah. Nice guy, my kind of guy. How's Morgan doing?"

"He's nervous in there."

"Get him to jump up. Scarletti hates it when they jump up."

Back in the courtroom, he started with Nelson again.

"Okay, the next question," the detective replied into his microphone, reading from his statement sheet, dipping his head slightly

11

toward the microphone, readying himself. "Question: 'After pushing Judy Warren onto the couch, what did you do next?'

"Answer: 'I told her I knew she was giving it out on the side. She said I was insecure, that I had to be kidding. I'm not insecure. I'm amazingly secure, more than practically anybody. Most guys who say they're insecure are trying to make you think they're actually secure enough to admit their insecurity. Reverse psychology. You could even argue that because I'm pointing that out to you that I am in fact doing the same thing, just with another layer of subterfuge.'

"Question: 'Spell that last word.'

"Answer: 'S-u-b-t-e-r-f-u-g-e. So, see what I mean? I wasn't kidding. I told her I knew she was spreading her legs for about ten new guys a week. She laughed. I told her I knew about the other guys. I gave her a chop. Judy started looking at me funny. I told her not to scream, so the fucking bitch screams. Maybe she was doing it through the television, she had these tricks—I learned them all. I had to hit her to shut her up, and then I held her down to change the TV channel. I got the sports on Channel Three. They got that guy—Why don't you fucking say something? Just *sit* there . . . like my father, getting old, shriveling up, both of you preparing for the next step—a swift slice to the prostate. You and my dad, ha! That's good. I like that. I know this will be part of the police record. You can put in there that my father, Dr. James Covington Robinson the Third, majority stockholder of—'

"Question: 'Do you remember the question, Mr. Robinson?'

"Answer: 'All right, so I wanted to watch the sports guy, the guy with the helmet of hair—shiny, you know, shiny with hair spray. The guy, what's his name, who's totally into the *genre* of being a sportscaster in a major market—one of the lesser American arts. So Judy was on the sofa and she had her heels up and was kicking me in the balls. Nobody kicks me in the balls. I guess I was pretty pissed, especially since she was trying to use radiation on me. I got her again and she grabbed this lamp and jammed the light bulb against me. It was goddamn hot. She was fighting—you know what I'm saying? Not screaming. She knew I was serious. I got her once in the leg with my knife, but she kept kicking like she didn't feel it. Then I jumped on her . . . I got . . . I was completely fucked in the head because of all the radiation that was going around. This is totally scientific. You should see the crystal therapy research going on in California. The Western rational mind just can't *see* this radiation. And she was flipping the music at me with her eyes—you know what I'm saying? Sort of Madonna, but better. You're gonna find this out anyway, what the fuck. I mean you got the damn prints already. Right?'

"Question: 'I can't comment on that, Mr. Robinson. I can't say what will happen to you.' "

Benita, the good-looking court reporter, filled the sudden silence with her soft clacking. The roving jurors whispered among themselves at the back of the room. Peter glanced at Judy Warren's family. Her mother sat, head bowed, twisting her wedding ring around her finger, thinking what? That she should have protected her daughter, a young girl studying part-time to be a dental technician? Judy had possessed a sort of sleazy appeal—given to tight dresses and moussing her hair into a frenzy—but was no wiser than what she was, a twenty-year-old still living at home who inhabited the circumscribed world of drifting young people who hang out at malls and bars on the weekends, pass through one minimum-wage job after another, get married, and generally lead dissatisfied, materialistic lives repetitive of their parents'. Judy had been passively promiscuous, without any real desire for men. It was all probably a little boring, and so she began to hit some of the yuppie clubs and restaurants downtown. Peter guessed that she'd learned that a great set of tits helped a girl change crowds easily. She liked what she'd seen, and that had only accelerated her desires. It hadn't taken long, maybe a couple of months. A change of wardrobe, recreational drugs, quick mastery of the right topics of conversation. People find each other, and Robinson had found her and she him. Seeing that he was rich, she became more than willing to overlook his queer behavior. He had helped her move into an apartment out by the Art Museum. Then she'd dumped him, and he couldn't take it. When Peter was choosing the jury, he had been sure to eliminate anyone who might decide Judy Warren had been a cheap fuck waiting for trouble and had gotten what was coming to her. It wasn't *that* simple. He glanced at his notes, not wanting to make the confession any harder than necessary on the family. But he had to get the majority of it into the jury's heads. Nelson sensed the necessary lull, and shut his eyes.

"Please continue," Peter said.

"Okay, uh, repeating the question: 'I can't comment on that, Mr. Robinson. I can't say what will happen to you.'

"Answer: 'You fucking cops don't have any prints. I didn't kill Judy. I don't have the kind you found.'

"Question: 'Do you wish to continue your statement, Mr. Robinson?'

13

"Answer: 'Fuck you. Fuck you. All right, I'll give you what you want to hear. I stabbed the shit out of Judy. I jumped on her—' "

The sound of the defendant laughing interrupted Nelson. Robinson swiveled his head around and smiled brazenly, nodding enthusiastically to the jury.

"Ha! Ha!" he cackled, addressing the court. "Ready for this?"

Morgan quickly bent toward Robinson to silence him. It was no wonder that he decided to keep Robinson off the stand.

"I can say anything I fucking want," Robinson whispered loudly.

"Mr. Robinson, you will be held in contempt of court if we have any further outburst!" the judge bellowed. "Is that understood?"

"Yes." Robinson bowed his head. "Oh-ho, yes."

Morgan was rubbing his forehead in discouragement.

"Continue," Peter told the detective.

" 'I jumped on her and kept stabbing at her neck and she had her fingers in my eyes, but you don't fucking need your eyes to stab somebody. I was cutting at her neck and she stopped making those noises and fell sideways on the sofa, and I had to pull her by the hair to get her to sit up so I could keep cutting her. Cut, cut, cut. She was warm. I was getting a lot of the radiation from her now, especially because the television was on Johnny Carson. It was better than coke. I'm talking about L.A. coke, not this lousy East Coast shit. The kind the Bloods and the Crips sell, man, right? Wait till they get to Philly, kill those Dominican dudes. Anyway, I cut her open, right in the heart—it was harder than I thought. I'm telling you this because I'm going to transport myself out of here. I've got the technology, that's what you cops don't understand. I saw the security camera in the lobby, what goes in can go out. . . . She was all limp and her tongue was hanging out and that gave me a hard-on, her tongue, you see. But I wanted to put it somewhere different—see where I'm coming from? I had the big knife in my coat—'

"Question: 'Where is this weapon now, Mr. Robinson?'

"Answer: 'Both the knives are in the water over by the Art Museum. I practically ruined the blades. It was pretty fucking hard, too. Took about five minutes. I got this flap open and stuck myself in—'

"Question: 'Can you be specific, Mr. Robinson?'

"Answer: 'You fucking know what the fuck I mean. I put my cock in there against her heart 'cause it's warm and wet just like it's supposed to be, you know, and there's a lot of fucking ways to get fucked. Then she was pretty dead and a car commercial came on. "Make your best deal!" Balloons, small-town America, and you know—family values, and there I am fucking a corpse. Amazing society we live in. Amazing culture. Got a cigarette?'

"Question: 'Here. Go on.'

"Answer: 'Well, it was the usual shit, what do you do with the body. Typical cliché situation. Then I remembered that the television is full of crystals, all those solid-state components. I thought about sending her on to Johnny Carson. I was going to make her walk on to the show and sit down and talk with my man, Star Search Ed Mc-Mahon. But she was pretty bloody. I had the gasoline in the car and got that and came back in the building and poured it around with absolute care and took the phone off the hook. I turned Johnny up and then lit it—'

"Question: 'Were the lights on or off?'

"Answer: 'This was smart. I was smart. I kept them on, so you couldn't see the fire for a while. All the lights in the place. I got in my car and put on the Hendrix tape. That man was before his time, he knew about the crystals first. That's why he died, he came too soon before his time.' "

Peter made notes on his pad as the detective finished. The confession showed that Robinson had no legal claim to the insanity defense. Peter could argue that anyone cogent enough to: (1) make sure the phone was busy; (2) attempt to burn the evidence; and (3) throw away the murder weapon was plenty sane enough to understand the gravity of his acts and to be convicted of first-degree murder. The attempt at concealment indicated knowledge of wrongdoing before, during, and after the murder—which fulfilled the M'Naghten Rule test that the Commonwealth used to decide sanity.

"I don't have any more questions." He looked up. "Thank you, Detective Nelson."

Robinson now stared into space, like a man hypnotized by the sound of his own heartbeat. Perhaps he was remembering his own verbiage, perhaps the confession had penetrated his brightly sick confidence, and he finally understood how ludicrous was his defense. Even Morgan, who had long waited for this moment, seemed stunned. But he forced himself up and, like a small, pesky mutt snapping at a huge, immovable bulldog, began to pepper the detective with questions, trying to get him to admit that the defendant was obviously lying. Since Robinson had been arrested the next day, wasn't it plausible that he had driven by the burned apartment and seen what had

15

happened? And heard about it on the news? Wasn't it true that the police often received false confessions? Did it occur to the detective that Robinson might be familiar with some of the details of the apartment because he had been there so many times? Such as the location of the lamp and of the television set? Wasn't it true that the arresting officers had babbled details about the crime scene? Hadn't Nelson really told Robinson how the crime had been committed first and then "gotten" the confession? Wasn't it obvious that Robinson was highly impressionable and intelligent and, with some slight coaching, could sing out just about any version of events the detectives wanted? Didn't the rambling, associative character of Robinson's sentences demonstrate someone who was not in control of his faculties? Yes or no, sir? Did the detectives really know if the defendant was under the influence of drugs? Did they have a blood test to prove that he wasn't? Wasn't it true that no videotape was made because Robinson was so obviously sarcastic and spontaneously creative in his responses that the tape would have been a liability to the detectives? Wasn't it true that many key statements in the confession were wrong, such as the way the body was mutilated, and wasn't it true that those points that were more or less correct were easy facts to infer from all that had previously been said? Did the police immediately look for the knives that the defendant mentioned? Wasn't it telling that no knives were found? Wasn't it possible that Mr. Robinson included such a detail in order to convince the police and to please himself with his own manipulating intelligence? Wasn't it true that the entire confession was just a confabulation of this detail and of that hint and proved only that the detectives had arrested the wrong man?

It didn't work. Nelson disagreed with each question firmly, and Morgan began to look ridiculous. The detective, a tired man with no vanity, stank of credibility, and the questions came to an end.

Morgan then began his defense, introducing witnesses who would try to prove that the defendant had an alibi. Morgan had assembled a group of Robinson's local bar buddies who then grunted out various lies about spending much of the night drinking. One by one they seemed sullen and uncomfortable in the chair, dullards who could be bought. It was slow going, and, as was happening with frighteningly increasing frequency, Peter's mind floated around the room. It was dangerous to do this, he could lose the thread of questioning, but he couldn't help himself; the conversation with Janice was plowing him under. Perhaps he'd sounded foolish and pathetic to her. He was gripped these days—in court, in the office, anywhere—by the occasionally recurring worry that he might be a clown, a great glutinous-brained clown capable only of honking courtroom verbiage, who in the great scheme of things was as guilty and as doomed as those whom he sent to prison. Society had a way of spreading around responsibility. Laws and punishments and institutions were a thin overlay on the fact of ubiquitous guilt. And, in this brief, too-honest moment, he saw the court and clogged legal system as pathetic, absurd, and that he was, too. The ruffling of documents, the somber, pressed suit, the silk tie, the hours of preparation—it was very little, nothing really, and this depressed him, for without the accoutrements of the prosecutor, he was not even a clown but another cowering hairless monkey. His skeptical pal Berger saw this, but did the other lawyers on both sides? Didn't the women attorneys realize how pompous they looked, strutting around in women's business dress, spouting accusations? The men—getting fatter every year—enjoying the tightness of their pants and shirts, as if they would burst their armor with righteousness. He was tired of the legal scowl, that set of the jaw and eyebrows that carried with it an entire combative outlook.

And yet, neurotic relativist that he was, every time he walked into court he felt pride—inflated by his own cheap ego, no doubt—that he was prosecuting the worst crime a human could commit. The Philadelphia District Attorney's office handed down a murder charge with great reserve, and usually when the evidence was convincing beyond all reasonable doubt. To be a prosecutor was to have enormous power over the lives of individuals. To charge someone—even a nut like Robinson—with murder was grave business. Whether defendants were convicted or not, the murder charge changed their lives—if not in their own eyes, then in the eyes of those who knew them. Even the innocent were terrified by the power of the prosecutor's office. The Philly D.A. would never sell out a murder case, *never* plea-bargain down to a major felony in return for dropping murder charges. Such an act would be blasphemous, destroy the victim's family and police morale, and make a mockery of the public trust, which, all fashionable cynicism aside, was enormous, elemental. You have a fire and call the firemen; you expect them to show. Your daughter is murdered, you call the police, they catch the murderer; you expect that man to be put in prison, preferably for as long as possible. There was a precious covenant between the victim and the victim's advocate in the courtroom confrontation of a murderer. It was a responsibility he humbly hoped he could uphold, it was a responsibility he cherished.

*　　*　　*

Later. Time had passed and Peter could not remember his cross-examination of Morgan's witnesses nor what his thoughts had been, except that those thoughts had circled back to Janice. He wanted to get out of his suit and felt sleepy in the dry, hot air of the courtroom. He would call Janice in the evening to find out where the hell she was hiding. Judy Warren's father was watching him, and he worried suddenly that he'd missed something. From habit he scribbled notes on the pad while floating in and out of attention, relying on his instinct to follow the rhythm of drama, even a drama so worn and ritualized and predictable as a third-rate murder case. But the case was airtight. Morgan had nothing. The office had been scrupulous about the discovery procedures, not only because it was the law, but because the more you told the defense attorney about the stuff you were digging up on the defendant, the sooner he would angle toward a faster, potentially lenient resolution, usually a negotiated guilty plea. Morgan, who was now summarizing the defendant's movements on the night of the murder, was going for complete acquittal; it was a real waste of city resources. Deputies, support personnel, court reporter, court officers, and judge; each case that went to trial cost the taxpayer hundreds of dollars an hour. Peter would have preferred someone who knew the courts, an ex-A.D.A. perhaps, who, in the face of the overwhelming evidence, would have pled guilty pragmatically and never taken the case to trial. On the other hand, it would be another conviction. Peter was thirty-six and three on homicide, one of those three lost on changed testimony, one on a runaway jury, and one on his own stupid evidenciary mistakes—not that he kept score, which, of course, he did, and not that he saw himself running for public office, which, of course, was always a possibility.

Then—already—it was past five o'clock, and the judge told the jury not to discuss the case with anyone—no smart criminal lawyer ever assumed they all complied—and they filed out. The spectators stood up. The victim's family, drained from hours in court, floated toward the exit, a day farther from the death of their Judy, a day closer, Peter hoped, to some sort of emotional release. Usually he chatted with the family about how things were progressing, but he was too tired now to talk with them. And felt guilty about it. He spread his papers on the table and searched for his calendar. It was under the black-and-white glossies of Judy Warren's corpse.

He rode the elevator down, pulling even further into himself, too tired and anxious about Janice to nod again to the detectives and cops in City Hall. Outside, he headed home, his loneliness made worse by the empty beauty of the dark office buildings with their random patterns of lighted windows high above the street. The new towers kept going up, sheathed in granite, glass, and metal. It used to be that by custom the immense statue of William Penn, the patron Quaker of Philadelphia, looked over all buildings in the city from atop the clock tower of City Hall. In a plain hat—his curling hair falling to his shoulders—waistcoat, knickers, and buckle shoes, Billy Penn could see everything in the city he founded and designed and loved. This was no longer true.

Their townhouse stood on the south side of the two hundred block of Delancey. It was a narrow street, with two- and three-story brick homes, none newer than the early 1700s. Tourists who had tired of the Liberty Bell or Independence Mall often wandered down it, taking pictures, marveling at how well preserved the street was, how *historical* it felt. Peter had heard them on Sunday mornings, outside the window, reading the dates of the houses aloud, wishing *they* lived there. Janice had loved the shutters painted bright black, the worn granite steps, the iron railing and antique bootscrape set into the old brick sidewalk. And so had he, for this small, lovely street and their house on it had suggested an order and happiness, a certain classic domestic perfection. The area, the oldest in the city, contained some of its most expensive residential real estate. That he and Janice owned the house was testimony to their ability to work together. He had done all the restoration work, tearing up linoleum, sanding floors. They had been extremely lucky, buying just before the real-estate boom at a decent interest rate, but still sacrificing vacations, restaurants, and a car for several years to pay the mortgage, which was still sizable. Even now, on a combined salary of eighty-two thousand, they had more or less signed their life away on this house. But, oh, what satisfaction they had enjoyed, walking home from a movie or dinner down the quiet street, the soft light of gas lamps hinting that they had reached a point of near perfection, an aesthetic culmination of their desires—security, happiness.

Inside, Peter sorted through the mail. Bar association stuff, a flier from the Pennsylvania District Attorney's Association, the United Way, alumni mail from Penn, Visa and American Express bills, a mail-order catalog for Janice, a letter from Bobby, who had opted out of the East Coast mentality and become a geologist in Arizona. Married a beautiful woman, too. He set his brother's letter aside for a time

19

when he could enjoy it, and continued flipping through the stack. One of the hunger organizations had gotten his address. All of those outfits bought mailing lists—lawyers were supposed to have plenty of cash. They didn't know about underpaid A.D.A.s. He ripped the envelope open and read the computer-personalized appeal:

> Mr. Scattergood, your gift of $15 will feed a starving child in Bangladesh for a month. $30 will help two children. $74 will help an entire family. Please give today to help save lives!

Next to this was a picture of a starving boy, maybe four years old. His head was huge, his arms like sticks and his belly swollen balloon-big. On the reverse, it said:

> A RACE AGAINST DEATH IN FAMINE–STRICKEN BANGLADESH . . .
> · Almost fourteen million lives are threatened by drought.
> · More than 720,000 could die from hunger and related diseases in the next sixty days.
> PLEASE SEND WHATEVER YOU CAN—NOW!

He looked long at the photograph, wondered what it was like to starve to death, and resented the manipulation. He tore the return envelope in half and went through the rest of his mail. Should he put his coat back on and walk to South Street, maybe troll through a couple of bars, act the lonely fool with some cosmetically florid executive secretary?

He called Janice at the new number and she answered.

"How's business?" he asked, searching for neutral territory.

"We got three more women today. One was a police referral. So," she sighed, "we're full, but with two discharges tomorrow. A couple of the women were fighting over what their children could watch on television."

"Tiring." His attempt at sympathy.

"Yes. But we got the state grant renewed. I'm encouraged."

"All this other stuff between us is wearing you down."

"Yes," she said dutifully, not allowing his sympathies to register. "Peter, I need some more money."

20

"I get it coming and going, don't I?"

"We agreed—"

"I agreed to be coerced into agreeing that you can't stand me." This was nasty but felt good.

"All you're doing is proving I was right."

True. He was tired of her being right. He was even more tired of agreeing that she was right when in fact, in the mud of his soul, he believed he was right.

"I'm sorry," he said more kindly. "When shall we meet?"

"I don't want you to come to the apartment." A pause. She had made some mistake. "No, we better meet."

"I'll come over." She had moved to one of the apartment complexes not far away. He hated them, big ugly towers that overlooked the Delaware River, products of poor 1960s urban planning that clashed entirely with the neighborhood of Revolutionary-era architecture. But the towers were near enough so he and Janice could visit and talk to each other during the separation, and far enough away that she felt autonomous.

"Let's meet in town," she said. "Tomorrow."

"My office?" He knew Janice wouldn't go for that. She'd been up to the seventh floor and remarked each time how dirty the place was, the coffee stains on the floor, the tiny cramped offices where the staff worked, the boxes of papers and files stacked in hallways and along office dividers due to lack of space and funding. Neither did she like the detectives walking around with pistols in shoulder holsters, belt holsters, ankle holsters, even stuffed into the back of their pants.

"You know how much I hate your office," she said.

"So why don't we meet in your apartment? I can bring some more of your stuff if you need it. I spend so much time downtown I feel like a subway rat."

"You, a rat?" she teased.

"I said that so we would be able to agree that I was an evil, dirty, scummy rat of a guy and then you would see how agreeable I actually am."

"We can have breakfast, at that little place off Chestnut."

No apartment summit meeting. No fledgling pride at her new environment (the cost of which they were splitting, so it ran him an extra five hundred dollars a month), no intimate discussion about their problems with the possibility of a bedroom finale.

"Peter?" Janice sounded exasperated. "Eight o'clock?"

"Okay. Janice, why can't we just—"

21

"Because we *can't*. I don't want to go into it. You need to hear me. You're more interested in your work than in me—"

"That's not true. Janice, the issue is—"

"The issue is *not* my past, Peter. You're so quick to make that the cause of our problems. You don't love me, Peter. You think you love me, you *feel* love, but you don't act it, you don't do it. You promised me change and for a while I believed you. I don't believe anymore. I know I have problems, but I think you have a lot of things to process."

Process. Fast food was processed, due application of law was, God knew, processed, but not love. Janice's use of the word—entirely conscious and a professional trademark—was a way of keeping him at a distance.

"It's a matter of prioritizing what you care about, Peter," she said, speaking as she were talking to a four-year-old. "When you don't want to talk and do things together, that's emotional deprivation. If you want to work and be a hermit, fine. But I need—"

"I thought you didn't want to get into it."

"We're better than this. Okay, see you tomorrow at eight. Bye." She hung up.

He stood there and let the words drift out the room, his mind attempting to figure out how Janice had evaded him. One thing about sticking your hands into everyone's shit each day, you learn how people operate. Probably it was all part of dismantling a marriage: You begin to cultivate secrets, new regions of yourself, let old elements die off. He called the number at Janice's apartment, hoping he was wrong. He wasn't. A click, a whir, and the death tone of disconnection: *"The number you have reached has been—"*

His wife, with whom he had last unhappily made love a month prior, had moved out of her new apartment and he didn't know where she was.

The bad time came when he was ready to sleep and set the alarm. Janice had always woken early and meditated downstairs and then awakened him. He was never good at waking, because he never got enough sleep. He set the radio to KYW-1060, all news. Janice hated all news. "How can you make love at night and then wake up to all news?" she used to ask him, back when they made love each night. "It's too *hard*."

"Well, we're hard people," he had said.

"You're the one who's hard."

22

He flicked off the light and swam through the sudden darkness to the bed. Under the covers, he felt a little more of eleven years' worth of Janice leak out: the last year of college together, she at Penn on scholarship, he on the parental ticket, then living separately, then shacking up—his parents had been relaxed about it—then marriage in the three-hundred-year-old Quaker Meeting his family belonged to, saying their vows in the simple pale room with their friends silently watching. *In the presence of God and these our friends I take thee Janice to be my wedded wife.* He had been faithful, made a decent living, been a good lover. But he had overworked himself and been too tired on Sundays to go out for a picnic in Fairmount Park when she suggested it, and he had shown only a shabby interest in her struggle to define herself. He'd been noncommittal when she brought up children, not because he didn't care, but because increasingly he'd felt like such a failure with her. Janice had looked to him for the elemental affirmation her parents had never given her. After all, he was the one from a good family, the life of privilege. He'd enjoyed advantages that made him believe his needs were not as significant as hers, which was a good thing, for she had been unable to reach beyond her own decimated family history. She had needed to *feel* loved and hadn't found it. Not in him, not in herself. He seemed only to torment her through his deficiencies; and so he had started to withdraw, dry up a little more each year. Janice was increasingly flush with the social-work jargon; sooner or later, he'd long hoped, she'd stop looking for issues in their marriage to "work on," like a mechanic tinkering with an engine, and realize he was a regular, decent guy who loved her in a mundane, unconditional way. Was that so bad?

Wondering where the hell she was, he rolled around the bed in frustration, then forced himself to lie flat on his back. It was impossible to remove the sensation of bed from the sensation of her. His penis, trained dog that it was, hardened. He lay beneath the blanket giving it a bit of incidental attention, thinking about how Janice used to kiss him and jump up from bed to go put in her diaphragm and on her way to the doorway he could see that little sweet curve right inside between her thighs, and while she was in the bathroom he would loll around the sheets letting the day disappear, feeling swollen and satisfied and happy. She'd come back in, with the faint medicinal stink of the goop, and even this smell was mildly aphrodisiacal, by association. She'd never gone on the Pill, although her gynecologist had suggested it. Peter and Janice used to fight good-naturedly and then

23

not so good-naturedly about who would buy the fat white tubes of the stuff. He hated some of the looks he got doing it. Janice thought his buying it was "sharing." The least *he* could do, considering all the mess *she* went through. She was right, yes, but still it embarrassed him. He was tired of being slimy afterward and had always half-consciously resented her for not using the Pill. It seemed like cruel and unusual punishment to be forced to purchase birth control you hated to use, though the irony was, of course, that it was Janice who wanted children. Finally one Saturday morning he'd driven to a drug-store and bought twenty large-size tubes, hoping he would get Janice to clam up that way and not have to buy any more stuff for maybe three years, figuring about thirty pops to the tube. She had only smiled.

Janice had kept the supply under the bathroom sink, stacked neatly like firewood. As a man with nothing better to do than to wander through the wreckage of his marriage, Peter pulled back the covers, padded into the bathroom, and opened the cabinet door under the sink. She'd left one solitary, curled, used-up tube there, strangled and dead. A note was taped to it.

I KNEW YOU WOULD LOOK, said her wry, tight script.

Back in the darkness, the blood pooling in his brain, already for-giving her for her little cruelty, since as a dark-humored jest it ac-knowledged his torment, he suddenly and quite against his will recalled the ritual he and Janice had performed a thousand or more times when he put her to bed on the nights he worked late. He would lie next to her and ask, "Hey, you, whisper-woo, how many kisses do you want?" She would turn a sleepy face toward him, enjoying his sticky sentimentality, and be able to say any number that came to mind, knowing that even if it took all night, he would give her that many kisses; it was like money in the bank, and she derived great pleasure from making very small withdrawals, since they implied by inverse proportion all the love she had from him. So she would dream-ily say, "Seven," or "Nineteen," or even, in a rare mood of profligacy, "Thirty-two and all of them *good* ones," whereupon he would indulge her, knowing in his heart that it was one of those rare acts that was easy and meant so much to her.

Then they would snuggle and maybe talk a little happy nonsense and she would fall asleep, her breath evening out; at the same time he would snooze for ten or twenty minutes, just let the first layer of sleep wash over him. Then he would get up and prep a case in his study, his eyes burned out by the lamp, and finally go downstairs and putter around, get a couple of things done. If he had any energy left, he'd do the dishes; if not, he would at least take the garbage out to the cans in their tiny backyard. Walking over the moist rug of grass toward the yellow square of the open kitchen door, he might look up, able to see a couple of stars under the bright Philly sky. If he was lucky, he picked out the Big Dipper, but beyond that he was lost.

But that was then and this was now and he lay back in bed, empty except for him, and wondered about his heart. There was pain in there, some ventricle too tight. His grandfather had died of a massive coronary in his father's arms. These things skip generations. He took a deep breath and his chest muscles seemed to flutter, faster than a spasm, as if trying to squeeze out all the caffeine, Nutrasweet, MSG, and other daily poisons. Janice would live to be one hundred. He probably already had early arteriosclerosis, the gunk clogging his pipes.

The pain receded. He wanted to sleep but his mind pulled up the day one last time. Robinson slept now on prison-issue sheets, waiting. And only twenty-two. On *his* twenty-second birthday, Peter was already in law school, starting the slave years, which were better forgotten except for the good times with Janice. He always worried about whether the verdict actually matched the reality. With decent evidence, anybody could convict the obviously guilty person; it took real skill to convict somebody who was innocent. He had that skill. Therefore, it was his habit now, after seven years, to ask himself quietly before a trial began if he was sure of a defendant's guilt. He could not and should not convince a jury if he was not sure himself. Of course, this sentiment had little to do with the truth. The law dealt with evidence, not with proof. Once Robinson was convicted, his youth would be squandered within the concrete walls of prison. Peter pictured Robinson wiping Judy Warren's quickly coagulating blood on his shirt, tracking it over the floor of her apartment with his shoes. Peter did not like blood. When he and Janice had sex during her period, he'd withdraw and see himself slick and glistening and erect, and though Janice hastened to mop up, he'd be stunned by the sight of himself—felt strangely and powerfully guilty, as if he had wounded her.

There remained one last thing to do before sleep. He forced himself up and went to the bathroom to get his glasses. They had toothpaste crud on them from the sink. He put them on anyway, and little pale

25

stains blurred his vision, making him feel dazed and clumsy. Downstairs he retrieved the two halves of the hunger envelope. He found a roll of tape and carefully rejoined the envelope, aligning its bar code so well that the post office optical scanner would be fooled. His checkbook was in his desk. He'd be paid at the end of the week, but money was becoming a problem. Virtue was not attainable by doing what he planned to do, but he did it anyway, quickly wrote out a check for three hundred dollars—after taxes, about two days' work—and put it in the envelope. He sealed and stamped the envelope and pulled on his coat and boots. Outside, he hurried through the cold toward the corner mailbox as the PNB clock tower twelve blocks west gonged midnight. What was Janice doing now? Dreaming? Her feet tended to flutter as she slept, and sometimes she called out. So often she had woken to nightmares about her mother and he had woken, too, to hold her. She suffered the free-floating fear of an orphan—that she was not worthy of love, that those who might love her would abandon her. His reassurance had its limits, beyond which Janice ventured alone. The cold metal handle stung his hand as he pulled open the mailbox. Tomorrow was already today. He slipped the envelope into the slot and walked quickly back—a big, hunched, hatless figure in pajamas and dark coat—shut the door, turned the heat down in the house to save money for his estranged wife's rent, and found sleep.

TWO

Peter stood in the cold and through the restaurant window suffered an intimate view of his wife. It was the first he had seen her in twelve days, and time was slipping past too quickly. Was she getting used to being without him, liking it? These, the dead days of January, when daylight seemed to last only a few hours, were the absolutely worst time of year to launch a reconciliation, but here he was, doing his best.

Janice wore her burgundy dress and her hair was up, and she only put her hair up when she had time to fuss around before a mirror. It occurred to him that she would pick a place to eat that was more or less on the way to work at the women's crisis center in West Philly and not far from where she was staying. So maybe she had an apartment around the corner, or a few blocks away. She wore the pearl earrings he had bought her in San Francisco. Peter squinted and saw Janice had on eyeliner. She never wore makeup to the shelter; she was a good-looking woman unadorned, and the women who came in there were so distraught and ashamed and suspicious that the last thing they needed was to feel they were competing with silk and tastefully applied makeup. How many women would choose careers in which their beauty could work *against* their effectiveness? And that wasn't all. The shelter's support community included a few hard-core lesbians who chopped off the hair on their heads, grew it under their arms, went unashamedly fat, picnicked on the solstice, and dressed in overalls and flannel shirts. Some of these women looked at Janice with disgust, and others with longing, as he did now. Her lips moved a little as she read the menu written in colored chalk on slates. He knew her breath tasted of the natural toothpaste she used, that because she had on the black hose with the little white diamond design, which he could see, she also wore the black heels, which he couldn't see. They were beautiful calfskin shoes and she saved them for special occasions. He liked it when she wore heels; they were unabashedly sexy, and Janice had beautiful legs. He and Janice had made love last November in a Club Med swimming pool in a desperate flight to the Caribbean to inject something lost into their lives. In the lapping chlorinated water, she was remiss at first but he convinced her that not only was it anatomically quite possible but that no one could see them. They had laughed about it later, and for the rest of their vacation she kept bringing glassfuls of cloudy pool water up to their hotel room.

Now Janice was checking her watch but in a casual way, which meant she expected him to be late. People walking into the restaurant were staring at him but he didn't care—I don't care what you think, that's my wife in there, mister, don't touch her, he thought, don't look at her, don't even think about it.

He yanked off his hat, ran his hand through his hair, unbuttoned his coat, and opened the door.

"Peter," she said softly as she turned around, offering her large blue eyes to him, whispering his name with such disarming and conspiratorial love for him that it was as if they had booked a room at the old Bellevue-Stratford Hotel three blocks away for a tryst, something they had never done but which the tone of her voice allowed him to imagine—heavy blankets, champagne, high view of the city, snowy rooftops, the color of the winter dusk across her breasts. Of course, the old Bellevue-Stratford, once one of the finest hotels in the country, rivaling the swanky New York hotels—faux marble and thick red carpeting in the lobby—had been chopped up into offices, stores, restaurants, and a parking garage, and was called something else now.

They went silently through the cafeteria line, sliding bright green trays along chrome rails, aware of the distance between their shoulders. By habit he leaned close to her, then corrected himself when he saw her stiffen. He ordered an omelet with ham. She looked at him in surprise.

"Eating meat again," he said.

She smiled at him tentatively and paid for herself before the cashier could ask whether their orders were together. He watched her hold her wallet, believing he could name from memory nearly every paper and card inside it.

28

"*But*, I still put that brewer's yeast in my cereal."

They found a table. The artwork on the wall was a collage of President Bush with a big grin. Instead of teeth, the President flashed a row of miniature white space shuttles. On the left upper incisor—Peter knew the term from forensic dentistry testimony—was a tiny picture of a homeless black man. Thus, the smile wasn't complete.

"What's up?"

"Oh, just busy. I told you we have a full house. We're working with the next group of volunteers," Janice said evenly.

"New crop?"

"Half will burn out by the third session. Too invested in their own issues to help others. One woman is so mad at men she can't be nurturing of others now. She's on a kick to warn women away from men." Janice nodded at him. "Pretty unfortunate."

"What did you tell her?"

"I had to bring her into my office and say maybe she had to work out some personal issues before helping other women."

"Did you point out the fascist similarities between radical feminists and the neo-fundamentalists?" he asked, trying to sound amusing.

"Peter, she *means* well—"

"We all mean well."

"Everybody does, Peter," she said softly before taking a small, precise bite. "You know that."

"Yeah." He needed to hide his bitterness. "Can't you at least tell me where you're living?"

He knew her secret and now she realized that. She stared at him, thinking.

"No, I can't."

"Why? You found some guy?"

"*No.*" She angrily dug her spoon into her grapefruit.

He didn't expect another man yet; not at all, actually. He knew Janice better than that. And neither did he expect himself to be involved with another woman. He didn't *want* another woman. All that had happened thus far was that they had lived apart for a couple of weeks; not so bad, really. But where the hell was she sleeping? A friend's house? Possibly, but Janice had a lot of pride—too much, in his view, though not enough self-esteem. Besides, she had moved out, she said, to lose her dependence, not transfer it. It was possible she was still in the apartment but had her phone disconnected, meanwhile taking and making calls somewhere else. He had called Information and she was not listed anywhere, nor listed as "unlisted," so the phone number she had given him earlier was just a number among millions and wasn't tagged with her name. It wouldn't be too hard to get the address of the phone number through the police, but that was illegal. But all this was the wrong track, perhaps. It was *unlike* Janice to live somewhere without a phone. She needed one—she received calls from the women's house at all hours of the night from staff members and women who couldn't control their children or who were feeling suicidal or angry, or who wanted to complain about other women in the shelter, or worst, and common enough, had a husband who had discovered the address of the shelter and had threatened to come harm them or steal the children. Occasionally men showed up at the shelter—drunk, pissed off, explosively angry—and yelled the house down; it was not for nothing that the building had a police call alarm.

He watched Janice inspect each bite of fruit as she ate. He admired her; she had pulled off some pretty spectacular stunts in helping wives hide from battering, angry husbands. He was certain she wouldn't disconnect herself from the shelter, and thus, she *did* have a phone, was reachable somehow. He knew, too, that there was no way for him to work through the shelter, to call up casually and ask for his wife's number. The shelter staff had always been quite pleasant with him— indeed, he knew most of them by name—but he was certain that by now Janice had told all of them of her situation—if only as an act of solidarity—and they would steadfastly refuse to reveal her whereabouts. This, after all, was what they were trained to do, and he was no longer an ally; in their terms he had crossed over to the other side. The easy methods of locating Janice wouldn't work.

"You won't tell me or you can't tell me?" he finally said, squeezing the words out in anger.

"Both. Stop cross-examining me. Let go of this now, Peter. If we can talk, I'll stay. If you badger me, I'm leaving. It's really pretty sad that you have to sit there trying to figure out where I'm staying. Like we're playing a game. I can see it all happening on your face."

"I don't see this as a game—"

"You *approach* it like it's a game, something to be *solved.*"

He didn't respond, for suddenly he worried he had lost his notes for the trial that morning; he had spent an hour early that morning prepping the case.

"Your briefcase is by your leg." Janice smiled at him, and at the way she knew him. "What's happening?" she asked, changing the subject.

"You don't want to know. A lot of sad cases."

"For once I want to know," Janice said, leaning closer and smiling. Her blue eyes shined at him with cost-free affection. He'd take it, a chance to let out a little tension.

"Okay . . . Last week I got a third-degree plea all worked out. A guy got in a fight with another guy outside a bar, two witnesses saw him hit the deceased with a section of a broken door that was in the street. We had it all arranged. Then three days after he pled, he changed his mind. You can do that, up to sentencing. So we'll redo that in the spring. Now I got a case where a guy got jealous and killed his old girlfriend. He wouldn't leave her alone, went after her. Very sad. The victim's family is destroyed. We have a legitimate confession. Usually in a murder case with a confession, the defense will argue that the confession was obtained illegally, in a way that violated the defendant's rights, or they'll admit that the defendant is guilty but argue that he is insane. In this case, though, the defense is saying, 'Yes, this guy is crazy but he's also innocent.' His confession, the defense says, is the result of leading questions by the police and has nothing to do with the murder. The defense is trying to show that the defendant could not possibly have been at the scene of the murder on the date in question."

"How will they prove he's crazy enough to offer a false confession?"

"They'll trot past old school counselors or a shrink—you know, the usual. The guy does *say* crazy things, but the police psychologist says he's oriented. Has functioned at a high level, no involuntary commit record. *Believes* in his pathologies more than is actually controlled by them. I mean, of course he's insane—you have to be insane to kill somebody—but under the M'Naghten Rule, uh, in legal terms—" This kind of self-involved rambling was exactly what she always bitterly criticized him for, saying he had more passion for his work than for her.

"You're tired." Janice pursed her lower lip and nodded. "I can see that."

"You know," he went on, wanting and yet not quite able to accept Janice's sympathy, "I talk to witnesses and read the police file, work out the case and so on, and in a certain respect you understand what has happened." Lives fell apart and behavioral patterns tended toward a situation which resulted in murder. "I mean, when was the last time you read about a murderer who had a happy childhood and progressed normally into full, healthy adulthood?"

31

"You're saying love, self-perception—"

"*Whatever* that is."

"—whatever that is, by definition, limits destructive behavior," Janice agreed.

"Exactly. Right. It *should*. I read the file and see how it all was coming. You've told me a million times you see this with the men who beat their wives and children. You and I work the same vector of behavior, just at different stages."

"I know." She shook her head.

"Chance situations being repeated until the odds catch up," he continued.

"Those people scare me," Janice said.

He mumbled agreement and checked his watch, feeling the day's pressure begin. Right now the gargoyles and maidens and rams and lions carved into the outside walls of City Hall were rolling their eyes in delight, waiting for the morning's influx of lives and flesh and drama.

"We've got a tremendous backlog of cases. And we keep losing judges." He shook his head in disbelief, for he was genuinely amazed—even given the normal high level of corruption among city officials—at just how rotted out the system was. "You read about the three judges who resigned because of the payoffs from the roofers' union?" He worried that she was bored or that he was bullying her with the tone of his voice, half-aware that the rhythm of their inter-action was moving back toward conflict. "Enough of that agony. Why did you take the Ortho-junk?"

"Do you need it?" Janice dodged this sudden lunge.

"Yes, I brush my teeth with it. The *Harvard Medical Journal* rec-ommends it. Can't get pregnant from oral sex."

"I *took it*, Peter, okay?" When he didn't say anything, she leaned back, pushed at her food. "It's *representative*. Don't pretend to be stupid."

"Where are you staying?"

"That's not your business."

"Please tell me where you moved, Janice. I need to know."

She shook her head.

"I need to know. A lot."

"The apartment was just an extension of us, Peter. I mean, you helped me find it, you helped me move—I needed a *break*." She looked around the restaurant. "I have a place where I feel some space. For the first time since I can remember. My life is changing and it feels good.

I need space from you, Peter. I feel like you're going to come after me."

He thought of a childish response and said it. "I always came after you did."

"Get a *grip*." Her eyes flashed at him. "What I really mean," she said, her tone earnest again, still hoping he would hear her, "is that I need to feel separate for now, completely separate."

He glanced at the President's smile in the artwork. The man had surfed into national office on a wave of toothless campaign promises and a shocking disregard for the truth. As Peter got older, each President seemed less mythic, more pathetic.

"Any more separate you'll be riding the space shuttle."

"Peter, *stop*."

They were silent for a minute. Janice had left much of her hot cereal uneaten. He finished his omelet, watched the other people in the restaurant, wondering if their private lives were equally upset.

"Jesus, you're being a bitch about this, Janice."

"That's it, I'm leaving. Good-bye."

She rose to leave, lifting her bag from the floor.

"I'm sorry, Janice. Please."

She slowly returned to her seat. He felt lucky. Usually such scenes required his chasing after her, and a truckload of retroactive admission of wrongdoing. But this time Janice did something unexpected. She took his hand and looked at him, pushing her lips together, eyes watering slightly.

"You're having a hard time, aren't you?"

This was the truest thing either one of them had said to each other yet that morning.

"I know I'm acting like an ass . . . I know it." He bowed his head in confession. "I can't believe this is happening. I mean, we go back so far. I wander around the house . . ."

Her eyes became unfocused, contemplating the conflicted mystery of things. It was the same look she got when she talked about her mother's suicide when she was sixteen.

"Please come back, Janice." He regretted saying this.

"I can't, Peter."

"I love you, you know." This he didn't regret. "I'll do anything for you."

"Yes, I know, but basically it's irrelevant." She was starting to cry, darting her eyes around and trying to blink it away, but her face got soft and screwy and she was crying.

33

"Let me go, Peter."

"I can't."

"Please just let me *go*." Her voice was bitter now.

"I did."

"No, you *haven't*. You made me pull away. If you really love me, you'll let me have the space. You'll *see* me."

"I can't talk to anybody else."

"You're going to have to learn how."

They looked at each other, seeing only loss. And one of the things that was lost was her nakedness, which he craved. Lately when he thought of Janice naked, he could picture her neck and stomach and her modest pubic triangle, but he couldn't picture her breasts as well as he would have liked. This was mysterious and disturbing to him; he loved her breasts. He could not remember *exactly* how large her nipples were, the size of a quarter or a half-dollar. A small, crucial fact had disappeared. It pained him to know that his visual record of Janice was fading, even a little, even as she sat before him poking at her grapefruit rind. And, too, he hated himself for the stupid distractions his mind now threw up like flack in order to avoid the devastating reality of the conversation. He could, for instance, picture Janice in a swimsuit or a bra or blouse but not naked. Stupidly, inexplicably, his wife's breasts had always been important to him. He remembered the morning when he was about twenty-six and the moment he realized Janice's breasts had just started to fall—seen the beginning of the inevitable move downward of those pert, buoyant globes to something a little closer to earth, each now-invisible nipple lower, farther down her chest by maybe a quarter of an inch. It had been in the early morning, the sun streaming horizontally into their bedroom as Janice came in from the shower. "What're you looking at?" she'd said, seeing him stare at her from the bed. "Nothing," he replied. "Nothing in particular. I like watching you dry yourself off." She had smiled at this and come over to the bed, given him a toothpasty kiss, and sweetly called him a liar. He had always depended on her ability to know he was lying. It was one of the things that kept him honest.

"Peter?"

"You've always been much stronger than me, Janice," he muttered distractedly.

"I hate being strong." Her gaze passed him, looked at other things. For Janice, life had been marred by more than the usual disappointments. Strength was brought about by occasions of loss. And Janice had lost plenty. She had found her mother in her parents' bedroom,

34

staring deadly at a never-finished letter to Janice's father. Years ago, she had told Peter she wondered how someone could calmly read while bleeding profusely from arteries severed lengthwise in each wrist, which first had been placed on a white towel so as not to create a mess. Her father, a man with expansive depths of bitterness, had torn the letter up without reading it, perhaps in some evil way feeling tricked. These were things Janice had known intuitively at age sixteen, and yet were only articulated as she and Peter talked through the years. As Janice's past cooled, they could dissect and understand it. Yet always, she had been set apart from him by it. Now he watched her eyes cloud in awareness, telling the story of her own life to herself; this sad scene in the restaurant would become just one of many moments, past and future. The look on her face—the judgment of time—had always scared him.

"Hey," he began, wanting to bring her back to the present, over which he might have some control, "I'm sorry I hassled you—I've been an ass, Janice. A total ass."

She relaxed visibly; it wasn't going to get worse. He checked his watch. He had to get to City Hall soon.

"You don't want me to call you, right?"

"Not for a while. I'd appreciate it if you just didn't."

"Right. What about the apartment?"

"I'm not going back."

"Good-bye to security deposit," he groaned.

"Good-bye to security deposit," she said, nodding.

"Good-bye Columbus."

"Good-bye, Mr. Chips."

She looked away sadly, her eyes drifting distractedly over the ebbing breakfast crowd.

"Neither one of us is dealing with this very well."

"What about rent at the new place?"

She did not answer him directly. "I still need money."

Peter didn't want to see her beg. Her job didn't pay enough to really live on. A woman helps other women, listening to the same problems week in and week out, gluing lives back together, wiping their kids' noses, making sure there was food in the cabinet, and gets paid nothing. And scouts watching dropoff corners for crack gangs made five hundred dollars a day, tax free.

"Here." He pulled out his checkbook and ripped out ten checks. "Write whatever you need."

"This is a pretty messy way to do things."

35

"You still have your little bank machine card, don't you?"

"Yes."

"Take the checks, and make a couple of deposits into your separate account," he directed. "Make it as much as you need. Use the other checks for food or whatever, the divorce lawyer—"

Janice looked up at him quickly.

"Just a lucky paranoid guess." He smiled as steadily as he could. "Put the money in your account and you can still use your card."

"I wouldn't ask if I didn't need it."

"I know." This was true. "Car okay?"

She nodded.

He had tried to dilute his anger with affection; the result was righteous stoicism and made him think of one more thing.

"I guess, then, I'll need the other key."

Janice hadn't been expecting this. But he had been returning from work to find pots missing, small plants, books, clothes, her favorite things. Items he loved. A jewelry box, her Patsy Cline tapes. This was intolerable, a kind of guerrilla warfare on his psyche. Her closet was emptier, the rooms of their house larger, full of new echoes. Getting the key forced Janice to call if she needed something from the house, and with her being coy about her whereabouts, he'd take whatever contact he could.

She fumbled through her purse, found a key chain with about eight keys on it—front door of work, office, file cabinet, the Subaru, plus the key to the townhouse. He watched her twist the key off the chain. There were a couple he did not recognize, house or apartment keys. Janice handed him her copy of their house key and put the chain back in her bag.

"Difficult," she said softly, blinking and searching his face for tenderness. "Necessary but difficult."

"You gave the key back already, Janice." He rose and put on his scarf. "This is just a formality."

Janice buttoned her coat, then dutifully squeezed his hand. He wanted to hold her fingers, so much smaller and finer than his. As she politely pulled her hand from his, he saw she had removed her engagement and wedding rings.

"Good-bye, Peter."

She turned and left.

Outside, people rushed by him, hunched over, hurrying toward jobs, conquests, conflicts, joys, and the grave—they were the unknowing blur, the smudge of movement, inside the great grid of stone. The city was so old, and in mysterious ways he was old with it, for the ancient Scattergoods had lived here, long before City Hall was an idea, no more than a deep pit in the bedrock where, oddly enough, a small deposit of gold was later found and plundered. He knew the city so well, felt its seasons, the drift of years.

And now it was time to pump up today's righteousness. Morgan had come to court that morning to do battle on this, his final day of presenting witnesses, and Peter could see in Morgan's busy movements—the scribbling of notes, the constant whispered statements to the defendant—the rising energy of a man who has departed from rationality in the service of a ludicrous goal. Morgan had probably ingested too much coffee that morning, and Peter remembered Berger's advice from the day before to get Morgan as agitated as possible.

Now Morgan began with Mrs. McGuane, the Robinsons' housekeeper, in his attempt to prove Billy Robinson's innocence of the murder of Judy Warren. Mrs. McGuane was a fiftyish woman wearing glasses with heavy designer frames and a rosary around her proud, bullish neck.

The opening questions established that Mrs. McGuane had been in the employment of Dr. and Mrs. Robinson since the late 1960s, serving all of that time as their housekeeper on the estate, that she had completed the ninth grade, and was once briefly married, long ago. These were easy factual questions, which Morgan lingered over in his attempt to have the jury know and like and trust her. The man's job was to attack the facts, as presented by the prosecution. Yet he could not focus on the method by which the police had gathered the facts— the evidence, including yesterday's confession—for that information had been ruled admissible in court. Instead, Morgan would attack the *perception* of the confession by carefully building the fabric of mundane details upon which to base an alibi. Mrs. McGuane was essential to this task, and Morgan's toothy, predatory smile went on and off like a light as he worked Mrs. McGuane with the control of a puppeteer, nodding reassuringly as she sang out the predetermined answers, rephrasing a question slowly if she became flustered. Morgan was the kind of man who became more irrational the closer he came to large sums of money, and no doubt he viewed this case as entry into the Robinson vaults. Usually he was quite happy to slobber all over the reporters' microphones outside a courtroom, but this time he had been strangely quiet. Such a change, which was another reason the media

37

had ignored the case, could only be due to some explicit instructions from whichever faceless, high-powered firm oversaw Dr. Robinson's affairs. No matter how little or ineptly the parents actually cared for their sons, they had their pride to maintain, and that was worth whatever fee Morgan might charge. If Morgan won this unwinnable case, many similar ones would come his way. The incentives to get witnesses to lie were enormous.

The defendant—hair still slick from the shower—was particularly motionless and attentive as the housekeeper described herself. For though Robinson had not received a mother's unquestioning love, he enjoyed the fierce, doglike loyalty of Mrs. McGuane, who, it became clear, was a well-intentioned yet limited woman who ran the household and knew more about the sons than anyone. She possessed the conviction of the wholly self-deceived and thus was a hostile witness, one whose testimony Peter had to tear apart.

". . . I heard Billy come in downstairs in the front—or rather, I should say I heard *somebody*—and so I walked out of my room and saw him over the balcony and talked with him a minute and that's how I knew it was him," she was saying, her voice loud and emotional. "I saw Billy and that's how come I say he was home that night. He ain't guilty of nothing, that's why I'm here to tell it to you."

"Objection," Peter said matter-of-factly. "Witness's answer is not responsive to the question."

"Sustained." Judge Scarletti nodded. "Please restrict your answers to the questions, Mrs. McGuane."

Mrs. McGuane had spent a lot of time putting on makeup that morning, and now, as she was unable to avoid crying, her mascara started to run, dripping over the foundation and blush applied so heavily on her cheeks. Peter saw that the jury was buying it, the eight women understanding completely the humiliation of running mascara, thereby empathizing with her, and thereby more likely to believe her story. In fact, Peter thought angrily, nearly everyone was tortured by this bit of melodrama, and Mrs. McGuane, perhaps sensing her advantage, carefully refused to dab at the inky tear of mascara clinging to her cheek.

She made a show of controlling herself and nestled into the witness chair to describe in her earnest, self-interrupting manner the evening in question. She explained the nature of the radio show she'd been listening to and how she remembered she was listening to it when Robinson came into the house. The time of the radio show fixed the time of his entrance, which *of course* was exactly the victim's approximate time of death, as fixed by the city medical examiner, a time known to Morgan, who now entered into evidence the published programming format of the radio station. On it was listed the radio show Mrs. McGuane described. All this testimony was designed to dovetail with the statements made the previous afternoon by Robinson's drinking pals. Mrs. McGuane, prompted by Morgan, even admitted that William Robinson might have driven home a little drunk—the strategy, of course, was to admit a bit of wrongdoing and thereby humanize the defendant, trade down on sins. Mrs. McGuane was doing her part well.

And Judge Scarletti, seeing this, glanced at Peter. *How are you going to counter this?* his lifted eyebrow inquired. The judge, a prosecutor back in the days when the American public erroneously believed it had reached the zenith of cynicism, was a fair man with a good legal mind who nonetheless generally despised defense counsel for representing such scum of the earth and disliked prosecutors for their inevitable mistakes—thus, he was a man who had only predilections, not favorites.

Morgan stood close to the witness stand throughout the examination, which was unusual behavior for a man who liked to pace around, lean on the jury rail, fuss with his notes, twist his gold pinkie ring, and dispel as much nervous energy as possible with such bad courtroom habits. No doubt Morgan had decided to slow his movements. The jury saw everything that courtroom lawyers did, their mumbling and shuffling, their herky-jerky karate chopping of the air to emphasize a point, their surreptitious scratching of testicles, their yawns jammed with a fist. As Morgan quizzed the housekeeper about meaningless things—how she'd put water in the dog's bowl before going to bed—Peter wondered where Janice was right now. Helping or comforting someone besides him. That had been the pattern a long time now and he'd always been jealous, wanting so badly a few minutes' worth of affection, guiltily hating the women in the shelter who got his wife's best energies. The house key was just gratuitous knife-twisting and they both knew it, and she was too hurt or too good to make something out of it. He hated his pettiness. If she had walked into the courtroom and said, *Peter, let's get out of Philadelphia, just go somewhere,* he might actually leave and never come back. She'd take off those beautiful black heels and place them side by side, toes touching, in her closet in the house. He'd find the highway maps in the third kitchen drawer, and they'd go camping in West Virginia, sing songs, and eat apples in the car.

Morgan finished up and it was Peter's turn. Attacking the alibi testimony of a weepy woman before a jury was tricky; he could find that he had dismantled the alibi yet won the jury's reproach. Peter stood up and walked over to the witness stand.

"Now, Mrs. McGuane, we are interested in justice here," he began evenly, looking in her eyes.

"Yes, sir."

"Did Mr. Robinson ever tell you about Judy Warren?"

"He mentioned her."

"It's true they saw each other for almost six months?"

"Well—for a time," she agreed reluctantly.

"Isn't it true he brought her home a number of times and that they stayed in his room?"

"I can't say, exactly."

"Where did they sleep?" Peter asked.

"In his room."

"And where is that?" he said.

"On the second floor."

Peter remembered the layout of the house from a detective's diagram.

"And where is that room?"

"All the boys have their rooms over the kitchen, either on the second or third floors."

"Miss Warren left Mr. Robinson last July, isn't that right?"

"Sometime. I think he was glad to see her go."

"I didn't ask you to tell me your opinion of her. Now then, did he ever say that he was jealous of her new boyfriend?"

"No, certainly not."

Peter turned, to check the jury's attention. Robinson was watching raptly, his sharp nose pointed up and his eyebrows lifting repeatedly. He seemed almost happy—perhaps the defendant was getting the attention now that he needed when he was young. Peter turned back to the witness and decided to change the tempo of the questions so that Mrs. McGuane would not have time to remember everything that she had said.

"Did Mr. Robinson ever complain that he knew that Judy was having sexual relations with another man?"

"No."

40

"Isn't it true that you and Mr. Robinson are good friends—old friends, one might say?"

"Well, I've known him most of his life."

"You have done a great deal for the defendant and his brothers, haven't you? They have come to depend on you."

"I guess you could say that."

"And you don't mind? You don't mind working for them all the time?" he said sarcastically.

"I love these boys. I'd do anything for them and they know it."

"Would you lie for one of them?" he snapped.

"No!" Mrs. McGuane spat, leaning forward.

"Do you receive pleasure from the fact that you are so willing to wait on them hand and foot?"

"Well, sir," she bristled, "I suppose I care a great deal for those boys."

"Is the defendant close to his parents?" Peter followed.

"I would say that they are reasonably close."

"Does he kiss his mother from time to time?"

"I couldn't say."

"When was the last time you saw it happen?"

"Well—"

"Does he kiss you sometimes, like a son would?"

"He might have, he and his brothers."

"Did he kiss you on the night of August sixteenth?"

"No, I spoke to him from the balcony above the front door."

"Is it fair to assume the Robinson sons are closer to you than they are to their mother?"

"I could never say that was true."

"You are here, now, testifying for the defense."

"Yes."

"Do you see the defendant's mother here in this room?"

"No."

"We're talking about human emotions here, Mrs. McGuane. About a young man, and I'm simply asking you to characterize your relationship with the defendant. It seems that you've done so much for him, that you've cared for him in so many small ways."

"Yes," Mrs. McGuane admitted softly. "I guess you could say that."

Peter paused, surprised that Morgan hadn't objected to the questioning, which was meant to convince the jury how unreliable a wit-

41

ness Mrs. McGuane was. Perhaps Morgan was saving his objections.

"You say you heard Mr. Robinson downstairs on the night of August sixteenth?"

"Yes. I lay in bed listening to the radio. I always do, right next to my bed, it is. It relaxes my nerves, see." Mrs. McGuane smiled in seemingly genuine embarrassment. "I saw the lights in the window and then he came in and I talked with him for a little while."

"This is what you told the police after the defendant was arrested?"

"Yes."

"And you say you remember the radio show?"

"Yes. As I just got done telling, it was this show where mentally ill people call in and tell about being crazy."

"Well, I'm certain none of *us* in the courtroom today were calling in that night."

"Oh, yes," she agreed tentatively.

"We have heard a description of the Robinson estate already. Now, would you describe the security arrangements?"

"Objection," Morgan said. "Your Honor, this information is confidential, for the protection of the defendant's family."

The judge looked at the housekeeper. "Just answer in a way that will not compromise your employer," he instructed.

"Yes, sir," the woman said.

"Would you say that crime is bad in your neighborhood?" Peter asked casually. The old country estates were easy pickings for motorcycle gangs looking for antiques to fence.

"It's not real bad, but you have to keep your doors locked, if you see what I mean. Even with the neighbors."

"Can't trust them?"

"Even people you think you know."

"Someone ever break and enter that house?"

"Yes, they took some of the silver and the big rug in the dining room. Then Mrs. Robinson had the new system put in. About two years ago."

"Your Honor," Morgan barked from his table, "I fail to see how the general patterns of crime in the suburbs of Philadelphia can have *anything* to do with this witness's testimony."

"What are you getting at?" the judge growled at Peter.

"Behaviors, Your Honor. I'm interested in behaviors here."

"Proceed," the judge replied after a moment's thought. "Let's find out what behaviors you mean."

42

Buried deep in the police report was a brief description of the workings of the Robinson alarm system. Peter had seen it and realized that it weakened the defendant's alibi. He knew, too, that if he had subpoenaed the company that had installed and programmed the security system, and thus conveyed this fact when listing his probable witnesses, then Morgan would have been tipped off to Peter's interest. Mrs. McGuane had originally told the police Robinson had come in through the front door—apparently blurting this out before thinking clearly—and had been forced to stick to this testimony all along. By not calling the security system representatives in to testify, Peter had *appeared* to indicate to Morgan—if Morgan had in fact considered it—that he, Peter, had either missed the information in the report or deemed it of no importance. Thus Morgan had not adjusted Mrs. McGuane's testimony. Morgan may have just missed the fact. After all, the man had other things to worry about, namely Robinson's boastful, sick confession. But there was a gamble here. A good prosecutor didn't ask questions to which he didn't know the answers. And Peter didn't intend to depart from that rule, except that he didn't know if Mrs. McGuane would provide the answers. He was betting that the housekeeper had intimate knowledge of all the workings of the house, from the number of best-silver spoons to the schedule of when to turn the mattresses around, to this, the routines of the security system. She did not seem bright enough to spontaneously amend her testimony if Peter could jar her out of her rehearsed version of events. He had spent many hours flipping through the police reports, sorting and discarding facts, trying not to think of Janice's departure, and even though he had mastered those facts, he knew now that he needed to feel his way toward the right order of testimony—set bits of information in the jury's minds without tipping off the witness. He checked his notes and looked up. Morgan, seeing the direction of the questioning, and perhaps realizing that he might have made an oversight, was nervous now, eager to fend off Peter's questions with objections. The defense attorney compulsively tapped a pencil against his pants leg while waiting for another chance to object. Peter looked at the witness. Mrs. McGuane smiled to the court, appearing helpful. "Now then," he said, "I would like to turn the questions to what happened that night."

"Like I said," she repeated without being asked, "I was in bed listening to the radio and the lights of the car went past the window, and then after he parked he came in the door and we spoke and then said good night. As simple as that. It was a regular night, you know what I mean? No big deal. Just a regular night."

"It had rained that evening, right?"

"I think so."

"Yes, there was a summer storm. Now, let me ask, there are a number of cars on the estate?"

"Yes."

"Do the boys—the Robinson sons—drive them all?"

"Yes."

"So the sound or appearance of one car doesn't signal a particular son?"

"That's right."

"And the cars are generally parked where?"

"Around the side of the house."

"Where, exactly?"

"The wider part of the driveway."

"Where is that?"

"The driveway comes up toward the front of the house and then goes around the side by the kitchen and there's a little lot."

"It's a big house."

"Oh, there are bigger houses in the neighborhood."

"Is it an average-size house, would you say?"

"Perhaps a little bit larger than usual." She shrugged.

"How many rooms?"

"Maybe, uh, about thirty rooms."

"That's a very large house—that's a mansion."

"I've lived there so long it seems normal."

"Well, it's certainly not normal in a city where some people live on top of one another like rats, right?"

"No, I suppose—"

Morgan shot his hands into the air as if he were receiving a long touchdown pass. He beseeched the judge: "Your Honor, what are we talking about here? The prosecution is going on and on about general crime patterns, how big or small the house is—all, I protest, absolutely meaningless issues, meritless in regard to the issue at hand."

"Mr. Scattergood," the judge said, "please demonstrate, if you would, that your line of questioning has some apparent intent to it."

Peter turned back to the witness.

"So Mr. Robinson had to walk a very far way from where he parked to the door where he came in, isn't that right?"

"No," she protested, "it's not far."

"How far?"

"I'm not good with distances. . . ."

"The depth of this courtroom?"

"Perhaps."

"So at least fifty feet."

"I guess so." She shrugged. "I don't see what difference it makes."

"Perhaps none at all. Now then, when Mr. Robinson came into the foyer and then the living room, you spoke with him?"

"My room," she sighed, clearly having lost patience, "is just off the master staircase, over the front door. The car came up the drive, the lights shine right into my room—"

"You sleep in that room so you'll know who is coming and going?"

"Yes."

"Please continue."

"So the car went by the room and then a minute or so later he came in and I got out of bed and looked over the balcony and we talked."

"Tell me about the foyer."

"It's just a place where you come in."

"Double set of doors?"

"Yes."

"Does it have any special features, like a little Oriental rug, or artwork?"

"There's a very fine jade dragon on the hall table that Mrs. Robinson loves, as a matter of fact."

"So this is the formal entry of the house, the entry used on special occasions, dinner parties, etcetera. Right? When the plumber comes to fix the sink, he doesn't use this entry, is that right?"

"Yes," Mrs. McGuane said with unmistakable pride.

"Is there a carpet underneath?"

"It's wall to wall in that part of the house."

"What color, if I may ask?"

"Oh, I'd say it's an off-white, a bone white."

"Okay, what did you two talk about?"

"I think we talked about whether or not his parents were returning from Nantucket."

"Their summer home?"

"Yes."

He'd wage a little class warfare on behalf of the jury: "Is that home also a spacious mansion?"

The housekeeper bristled. "No."

"And what was the conclusion of the conversation regarding the plans of Mr. and Mrs. Robinson?"

"I think I told Billy that his mother had called to say that the boat needed something, it needed a sail repaired, and so they were going to be delayed by a day."

"You have a good memory, Mrs. McGuane."

"Thank you," she said, bustling in her chair, eager to answer the next question with similar competence.

"So this was normal, mundane news," Peter summarized. "Just information that you were delivering as you might do any day?"

"Yes."

"What else did you talk about?"

"I think that was about it."

"How many sentences did you exchange?"

"Maybe five."

"It was a brief conversation?"

"Yes."

"You probably spoke to each other about a minute once he was inside the front door?"

"Yes, not much more than that."

"And did anything remarkable happen thereafter that evening?"

"No, I went back to bed."

"I repeat the question: Did anything unusual or traumatic occur then?"

"No, I just went back to bed."

"That is correct? You're sure of it?"

"Yes, I heard him come through the front door, I got up and saw him, and then I went to bed. How many times do I have to say it?" she concluded, taking her glasses off to clean them—a common and unconscious mannerism of bad witnesses; unable to see their questioner's face, they lied more easily, and thus more convincingly. Peter waited while she cleaned and recleaned her glasses. When she realized he was waiting for her, she put them back on.

"You are speaking the truth?"

"Yes," Mrs. McGuane said, hinting irritation. She pursed her lips and lifted her eyebrows innocently.

He walked over to the bar and faced her down.

"Do you swear it?"

"Yes," she snapped.

"I'm just trying to get things straight here. You say you are telling the truth? You are telling the *absolute truth* to this court?"

"*Yes.* I maybe didn't finish my schooling, but I'm *not* ignorant, Mr.—"

"Scattergood."

"Yes, I may seem that way to you, but I assure you I understand everything we say here and that I'm telling God's truth. May he strike me down if I'm lying."

"I am glad to hear you're so certain of that, Mrs. McGuane—"

"Objection!"

Morgan jumped to his feet, arms up, and executed a small angry dance around the table. "Your Honor, I absolutely object to the treatment of this witness. I move for a mistrial on the grounds—"

"I'll be happy to demonstrate why, exactly, I am skeptical," Peter interrupted.

"The motion is denied," the judge said. "Go on, Mr. Scattergood, but get to it. This is not yielding much, as far as I can see."

Robinson, who was smarter than his attorney, looked at Peter and suddenly smiled, perhaps now understanding Peter's strategy. Peter turned back toward the witness. "Would you tell me the first thing that you do in the morning?"

"I get up and go down to the kitchen."

"Are you usually the first one up?"

"Yes."

"What about the sons?"

"They usually sleep until ten on the weekends."

"And what do you do?"

"I make the coffee and go outside and get the paper."

And now Mrs. McGuane looked toward him with sudden concentration, her eyes unblinking, seeing past him, past the room and the assembled people, and into her habits of the morning. She knew now what the prosecutor wanted from her.

"The paper is delivered to the kitchen door?" Peter pressed.

"Yes," she said in a quieter voice.

"Because that's the door where you or the Robinsons like to have it delivered?"

"Yes."

"Is there a nice, big breakfast table where people spread out the paper?"

"Yes."

47

"The paper comes to that door and not the front door?"

"Yes, the boy brings it around."

"And why is that?"

"Because that's the door that's easiest," she said vaguely.

"What's so easy about it?"

"Well, I'm there in the morning."

"Now then, you have told us about the remarkable security system the Robinson house has. I am certainly no expert on such systems, but I do know that generally speaking there is a control box or a numeric keyboard where the homeowner—or in this case the housekeeper—can turn the alarm on or off. For example, the alarm must be turned off before a window may be opened. Does that sound like your system?"

"Yes."

Peter had priced a system for his own house last summer, what with the crack addicts getting bolder by the month, using hacksaws and hydraulic tire jacks to get through window bars. He had researched several options, even. But then he and Janice spent the money on a Caribbean vacation, hoping to get closer.

"The alarm is on at all times?"

"Yes." The housekeeper kept her eyes downcast, toward Peter's feet.

"The company that installs these systems usually programs them. The electronics are very complicated. Is that the case with your system?"

"Yes."

"Would it be a fair statement to say that once the installation was complete, it was not changed by you or anyone else in the household?"

She nodded.

"Let the record show that the witness nodded in an affirmative manner," Peter directed toward Benita, the court reporter. "And, as the person who runs this household, is it true to the best of your knowledge that the company installing the service would keep a record of when and how that was done?"

"Yes."

"The Robinsons would want a first-rate alarm service company that kept scrupulous records, is that true?"

"They wanted the best, yes."

"Is it a correct statement to say that in order for you to go get that newspaper each morning you have to turn off the alarm?"

"Yes."

"You turn off the system by punching in a password or a code?"

The witness looked at the judge. "I don't think I should tell the answers to these questions."

The judge leaned forward. "Don't tell the court any special codes, but otherwise please answer all questions."

"All right," she agreed. "Yes, you punch in a code."

"Just for the kitchen door or the whole system?"

"I can do either."

"But you must do this to turn off the alarm?"

"Yes."

"For any of the doors or any of the windows?"

"Yes."

"And where is the control box?"

"In the kitchen."

"Where?"

"In one of the cabinets."

"In the kitchen proper?"

"Yes."

"And this is the only way the alarm system is deactivated?"

"Yes."

"So if someone comes in the kitchen door using a key, the alarm immediately goes off?"

"No."

"And why is that?"

"Because that door is set to wait a little bit so that you can get to the box and punch in the code."

"And how long does the timer wait? Five minutes?"

"Oh no," she said. "It's only thirty seconds."

"Is this true for all the doors?" Peter followed quickly.

"No, just that door."

"Then why and how in the world would William Robinson park his car next to the kitchen door, the door that he would know was the only door that would allow him to go in without making the alarm go off, and then walk fifty feet out of his way, come through the master entry in wet feet on a white rug usually used only for formal occasions, stop, see you and talk about this and that, without the alarm going off?"

Mrs. McGuane glanced anxiously toward Robinson, and in this Peter nearly felt remorse for what he was forcing her to do.

"Oh, maybe I made some silly mistake," she blurted out, "but I *know* Billy was home that night."

49

Peter waited for this statement to dissolve harmlessly. It was plausible that the housekeeper genuinely believed in Robinson's innocence or was, at some level, lying to herself, unable to accept his guilt. Billy Robinson was, after all, one of the children she never had. Addendum to a tragedy: a mother's heart broken. Peter let the witness and the court pause silently for a moment. He liked the feeling he had. It was not smugness, but a better form of satisfaction. He had done his job well and it was about to pay off, for this was the sudden quiet moment, he knew from seven years' experience, in which the jurors would find themselves realizing the defendant was guilty. He paused, drank some water from the glass next to the pitcher. The radiators clanked, the water cooler hummed. The three court officers, men and women who had heard it all, had returned to their self-involved rituals of time wasting: fondling their watches, cleaning lint off the cuffs of their blue nylon blazers, chewing gum. Peter ordered his points in his mind, making adjustments for the testimony he had just heard. He wished Janice were there to see him work. He seemed to have lost all her respect.

"The mistake you have just alluded to *appears* to be in your whole story, Mrs. McGuane, and I'm going to point it out to you so that you may *clarify* yourself. From what I understand, the sons all sleep in a different part of the house, over the kitchen. They each drive all the cars. So you cannot tell which son is which by the sound of the car. The cars are usually parked next to the kitchen. You wanted the police to believe that you saw Billy come in that night and so you told them when they questioned you that you had seen him come in the front door. But there is no reason, by your own testimony, for him to do that. Why in the world would Billy Robinson park there, then walk fifty feet across wet grass or gravel, avoiding the kitchen door, which leads directly to his bedroom, and enter through the formal entry if the front-door alarm would go off? I submit that this version of events doesn't make sense, not to me, Mrs. McGuane. There seems no reason to do that. Why would William Robinson, Billy Robinson, set off the alarm on purpose, especially if he knew you were resting comfortably in bed? Right? See what I'm getting at? You said it was a normal night. The kitchen-door alarm timer is set so that people can go in and out without setting off the alarm. It's next to where the car was parked, by your own description. And for good reason. Either he goes in the front door and the alarm goes off, or he does what he always does, goes in the kitchen door, and the alarm doesn't go off.

Those are the only logical options, based on your testimony here this morning. And yet your version of the events doesn't match either one of those. What really happened, I submit, is that he came in that night, sometime after you went to sleep, and he came in through the kitchen and out of habit punched in the code in the thirty seconds before the alarm went off. That seems to be the only possible chain of events, Mrs. McGuane. And since that is so, you cannot truthfully say exactly when William Robinson came in that night, whether at the time in question or an hour or two later. Wouldn't you agree?"

"I . . ." She paused.

"I am asking you whether you agree with what I have just said or whether, instead, you can explain the contradictions in your testimony here this morning."

"Well, Billy . . ." Again she stopped, and again she began to cry, this time in uneven gasps, ugly and sad. "Billy . . ."

"We must have truth here," Peter continued. "A young girl has been *brutally* murdered, and this is a court of law. I ask you once more, Mrs. McGuane, I ask you before the good ladies and gentlemen of this courtroom, who have taken time away from their regular lives to attend to this serious matter. Can you explain why your testimony conflicts with itself?"

She was unable to speak, and lowered her smudged and blurry eyes. No one in the courtroom despised her for her lies, for they all knew she had only tried to protect a boy she had raised. She glanced worriedly at the members of the jury. They stared back. In the tired, eternal gloom of the courtroom sat a woman whose testimony would convict the young man she had loved like a son. There was no mistaking her private agony, but he could not worry about that. He need worry only about destroying her.

"Can you explain your testimony?" he asked sharply.

Mrs. McGuane shook her head.

"No explanation? Should this court disregard what you have said?"

She was silent.

"Your testimony was only a story from the beginning, right?"

She made no response.

"No more questions, Your Honor."

It was his intention to slip quickly, peaceably, out of City Hall for lunch, but suddenly here was the short, thick body and florid face of

Hoskins, Chief of Homicide, standing at the elevator door on the third floor. Peter nodded silently at his boss, a man of undependable friendliness who favored bow ties and had once been a promising pianist, according to rumor. Nothing important was ever openly discussed in the elevators of City Hall, and those who rode in the tight boxes—cops, detectives, lawyers, witnesses, family members— invariably stared intently at the floor buttons, the ceiling, or their shoes. Hoskins was no exception, and tipped his eyes downward over his stomach to inspect his polished wingtips in satisfaction. Hoskins, Peter knew, prided himself on knowing everything about the cases within his responsibility, but that was of course impossible, and so he had to *appear* to know everything by badgering each of his subordinates into spewing progress reports at any moment. And yet, during trial-planning meetings, it was always clear that Hoskins was a brilliant if ruthless schemer. If you questioned his strategy, you were probably wrong. A tale still went around about Hoskins's early days as a prosecutor. In a rape case a defendant took the stand to testify on his own behalf, hoping to clear his name before the court, which included his family, all devout Roman Catholics. Hoskins shamed and bullied the man into admitting his guilt, and, suddenly weeping great remorse, the defendant bolted toward a courtroom window that opened onto City Hall's inner court four stories down. He dived headfirst through the window to his death. Peter had never been able to forget this about Hoskins. Now the elevator opened at the first floor and the two men stood to the side of the doors.

"How's Robinson?" Hoskins demanded, looking up at Peter and inspecting him for doubt.

"This morning, it went pretty—"

"Just make sure that housekeeper doesn't bullshit everybody." Hoskins grimaced in disgust. "You go hard on her, got it?"

"I have already," Peter said dully. Hoskins frightened him, but not so much that Peter couldn't hide his fear.

"Good, then. That's what we planned. You worn out?" Hoskins jabbed him with a steely forefinger, as if testing a piano key. "Where's the fire?"

"Inside my chest," he said. "Roaring like hell."

"Good." Hoskins nodded affectionately. "Keep it there."

Peter walked out of the east arch of City Hall, past the polished black sedans the Mayor and other high officials used. It was easy to remember the point of Hoskins's finger: A man such as Hoskins was

quite obviously kept at a boil by the power he held, and though Peter
had once admired his boss's drive, he had come to fear its intensity,
the bullish righteousness of the maestro that could overshoot its mark
and abuse power. No one got power who didn't want it, and no one
kept it without undermining others' attempts to steal it. Hoskins himself always appeared to be a man just barely held in check, and Peter
had seen that it was *not* the common good that Hoskins burned so
brightly for; it was, instead, the steady accretion of privilege and
influence. And, over the years, Hoskins hid this desire with greater
care, displaying an ever-shifting paternal affection for his young prosecutors, graciousness toward reporters, and a restrained public identity. But at the same time he sought the next handshake, the next
connection that might pull him forward. Hoskins would never be a
politician—he was too gruff and looked bad on television—but as an
operative, he had a future. Ten years older than Peter, Hoskins had
fattened into and then past that golden moment when one stood ready
to run for elective office and so he had been forced to buy a tuxedo and
learn to grin and guffaw his way through all the right dinner parties,
schmooz and booze with all the other schmoozy people, pretending he
loved his wife, a tiny, rather frumpy woman with an uneasy smile and
too much lipstick who was obviously incarcerated within the personality of her husband. Hoskins, Peter reflected, was a man who
believed—or wished to believe—that in the conquest of ever-higher
positions lay adulation. The man had become a choke-point for others'
destinies. If you admired him, and if he knew it, you swore your
allegiance to his abusive leadership. If not, you tried to get your work
done and keep your head low, and not become a chess piece in
Hoskins's master-level skirmishes with the public defender's office,
the U.S. Attorney, the local political machines, the Mayor, the media, the civil-rights organizations, and the black community.

At the other end of the spectrum was Berger, the skeptic, who felt
no fear when Hoskins tossed around threats, who prosecuted in a
detached, analytical way, seeking to do a professional job but realizing
the powerlessness of being so powerful, seeing power as relative,
fleeting, and often illusory. Whatever altruism Berger had was kept
behind a glib detachment from the petty strivings of men. Essentially,
being a prosecutor confirmed Berger's worst suspicions about everyone, including himself.

Peter ate a sandwich in a luncheonette on the crummy section of
Market Street, having no lunch appointment that day and having

forsworn the trendy lunch places, where the attractive professional women would remind him that he hadn't had sex in a long time— weeks. He thought about slipping into one of the porn theaters tucked into the crumbling brick buildings behind the Reading Terminal Market—duck past all the other lunchtime perverts in suits and ties, and maybe even enjoy beating off inside the little booth, which is what they were designed for, while on the screen some guy fucked a girl in the mouth. The guilt would be worth it, would burn off some of the tension for a few hours, but there was always the chance he'd run into somebody he knew. There were services you could call up and a girl would come over and have sex, but that held little interest— the girls were probably pathetic and ugly and drug addicts, and he'd end up feeling sorry for them and ask them their life stories. Besides, he wasn't so desperate as to screw a whore. So, instead, he read the paper, turning first to the sports section. The Sixers had lost three in a row and their star, Charles Barkley, was petulant and critical. Peter missed Dr. J. When the Doctor retired, the whole city lost some grace. The newspaper headlines floated across his view of the moment: Ragged street people were fighting over the steam vents, a sixteen-year-old crack dealer had been shot in the head at the corner of Eighth and Butler. Was it really so different from the time when the Irish were the city's poor, living eight to a room, working in the Baldwin locomotive works or in dress factories, children trapped inside the steam-driven looms, the grandmothers scavenging for coal? He was mumbling again, nearly aloud. Through the luncheonette window, Philadelphia was a hellscape of ashy snow and frozen trash, and spring seemed an unlikely prospect. The noon sky was pale, with an early evening on its way, and he couldn't remember the time of his racquetball appointment after work. A worm of pain twisted in his chest. It was for this that he had put in years shuffling through thousands of plea-bargained cases, scheduling witnesses, battling against continuations, cutting deals with defense attorneys who believed him to be cruel-hearted. He wished for some kind of deliverance, a brain balm that would make him forget that Janice hated him and that before him stretched a never-ending array of murder cases. The twenty-odd lawyers in the homicide trial unit handled almost five hundred cases a year. Maybe if an interesting case came along, he'd stick it out awhile. There was always other work—insurance-claim work or politics or some other carnivorous art. Lots of young prosecutors got fed up with the jammed, corrupt court system, dumped their ideals in the river, and skipped out to the private firms to pull down an easy one hundred thousand. But he was too tired to consider changing jobs now. He'd just ride everything out, just juke and float and cut past the pressures like the new, young guard of the Sixers moved toward the basket past lumbering seven-footers. No problem, *no problem*.

And hours later, thousands of words later, he was done for the day, having argued with and contradicted and undermined the defense's witnesses and convinced everybody that Robinson was guilty. For his part, the defendant had stared at Peter the whole afternoon, and there had been a moment when Peter had realized that Robinson was not thinking about the case, but about Peter—examining him with that same rabid intelligence, searching for a point of recognition. When the defendant was taken away, he saluted his prosecutor knowingly.

Now Peter sat in his chair, pushing his papers together, waiting to be released until the next day, which would bring the closing arguments. The courtroom emptied, and he knew as the hallway sounds echoed within that he was waiting for something. Dusky snow began to fall. The building got cold at night. Benita was quietly marking her paper tape. After eight hours of work she still looked fresh, and it took little imagination to picture giving her a quick pop. Ask her to lean over. She folded the tape and wrapped a rubber band around each stack. The tape was used to repeat testimony to the court but was actually a backup record. She flipped the cassette from her machine and slipped that and the tape into her briefcase. Tonight, he knew, she would put the cassette into her computer system, which would read the magnetic coding on it and screen up a rough transcription that she would correct.

Meanwhile, he was due to walk to the club for an hour of racquetball. Did he want to go, since Berger couldn't make it? He watched Benita. She was maybe twenty-two, twenty-three. He wondered if she played racquetball, but was afraid to ask.

THREE

Peter paused outside in the cold, piss-stenched shadows of the City Hall arches. Office workers hurried toward the subways and commuter trains, and nearby, handcuffed defendants drained out of the courtrooms and through a special door into the gray Philadelphia Prisons Transport bus. They were the lucky ones. The bus went to the county prison, which housed convicts whose minimum sentence was less than twelve months. The small van parked not far away would head out to the state prison, where the long-timers and lifers were sent. An emaciated black man in a ragged coat appeared, and Peter shrank back, sick of being harassed for money wherever he walked in the city. Nevertheless, perhaps more from guilt than from true concern, he reached for his pocket. The man was compulsively flipping a nickel.

"Hey, *yo*! What's it going to be?"

"What?" Peter snapped.

The man's face was wildly animated as he waited for the coin to fall. Rheumy eyes and rotted teeth.

"What'll it be?" he demanded again. "What will happen?"

"I don't know."

The man laughed wickedly, tossing his head back, then yanked a bottle of Thunderbird from within his coat and gummed the lip of the bottle. He flipped the coin again.

Peter escaped, unwilling to join anybody's madness. Usually he enjoyed the walk to the club, the night air against his cheeks, the muffled warmth of his wool coat and winter suit, but now he covered the long blocks quickly, ignoring the massive silhouette of City Hall looming behind his back.

The freezing air eddied out of his coat and gloves while he stood in the club's chrome-and-mirror elevator. A couple of muscle mutts— the grossly overdeveloped men who hung out all day at the club— stood around the lobby pretending they were not displaying themselves. What are they compensating for? he wondered. Little dicks? Little minds? Were they just scared, adding flesh in a flesh-eating world?

The mirrors on the four sides of the weight room reflected an infinity of men and women pumping away on gleaming weight machines. Janice still had her membership. He wondered if she had stopped working out there in order to avoid him. It seemed likely. On one of the machines you sat and opened your legs quite wide, then squeezed them shut. He'd heard a couple of women laughingly call it the Yes/No Machine. These were the hard-driving professional women who hung out at the gym, subsuming and converting sexual hunger into sleekness and muscle. Yes—open. No—shut. It had been too long since he'd had any Yes, and jerking off was the same as shaving—a necessary habit to remove stuff the body kept producing. Next door, the aerobics class. Gaudily dressed women and a few very slender men jumped, kicked, and gyrated. No Janice there, either, just a crowd of panting, sweat-drenched women, all of whom wore shimmering leotards and tights. Some were legitimately gorgeous. Each year such women looked younger to him, receding from view. It had been ten years since he ceased being younger than centerfold models, though of course the fourteen-year-old in him lived on, alive as ever, acutely sensitive to the ink smell and thick-paged feel of a new *Playboy*, a world of airbrushed fantasy made new each month. His typical piggy male lust had been subjected to the most stringently purifying feminist inquisitions over the years, and had emerged un-scathed. Amazing how men continued their resistance and women their complicity: pornography, advertising, clothes, movies, breast implant surgery—entire subsections of the national economy and culture were based on the male desire for the perfect tit.

In the locker room, he pressed his hand to his forehead, smoothed back his hair, and bent close to the mirror. His hairline was holding out, and no gray yet. Hell's bells, he was a young man, thirty-one is *young*, guys still play pro sports at thirty-one. He undressed and weighed himself naked. The digital readout said 202, twenty-two

57

pounds heavier than he'd been at the end of high school, twelve pounds heavier than the end of college, four pounds heavier than the end of law school. Not bad for six-foot-two. He wondered if he could still dunk a basketball, could still experience the lovely light scratch of the rim as his hand jammed the leather ball through, then dragged over the metal on the way down. Penn Charter against Episcopal, 1976 Inter-Academic League Championship. P. Scattergood, starting forward, five for nine from the field, one for two from the charity stripe, six rebounds. A good contribution to a losing cause. He still had the yellowed three-inch *Philadelphia Inquirer* column somewhere. He tied his court shoes, gave a quick hoist to his jock, and wished Berger weren't on the Amtrak to Harrisburg.

He found an exercise mat and stretched the way he used to when he had time to exercise properly. With mirrors in front and behind him, he saw a million diminishing versions of himself—saw the fat creeping around the thighs and belly, the ass sagging ever so slightly. Berger kept his weight down but he did it the illegal way. Peter carefully worked each muscle group in his legs, stretched his back, neck, and finally his shoulders. He rolled over and did twenty-five push-ups and then fifty sit-ups. The loud exercise music filtered into his veins.

Minutes later, on the racquetball court, he was enjoying practicing his shots—crisp, triple-ricochet shots that came off the front wall nearly impossible to return, center-of-court blasts, and tactical, dead-dropping touch shots—when a face, a woman's, appeared in the small observation window. He was unable to see the face well; the woman—not Janice, unfortunately—stood a foot away from the window, a porthole of thick polyurethane scarred from errant racquets and slightly opaque. But it was a woman's face in the window, he could see that, and she was watching him.

He was tempted to open the door and inquire if she was looking for someone, but some small irritation kept him stroking the ball as if he had not seen her. He'd dealt with people all day and his voice was ragged from talking. He concentrated on his shots. Once, digging the ball out of the back corner, he saw her eyes draw back from the glass.

The racquetball court was simplicity itself. Four white walls, a wooden floor, one man with a stubby racquet and a blue rubber ball. Simplicity. Smash the fucking ball. All the tactics and strokework were an overlay on the sheer pleasure of powering the ball as hard as he pleased. He settled into the stroke rhythm, working up a good sweat. Berger tended to be slow at times and to jabber between serves to catch his breath. Hit the ball. Peter would give the closing argument the next day, then wait for the conviction and sentencing—most likely first degree—and meanwhile be prepping the next case. Ball. Hoskins pissed him off. The worst kind of friendliness—Peter didn't know whether to trust it. At the same time, Hoskins had been pressuring the hell out of him lately, being overly intrusive about his strategy—ball—crowding his judgments with pointed questions in the weekly meetings, as if he doubted Peter's competence. Ball. It was hard to tell with Hoskins, though—sometimes his abuse was a form of affection, a vote of confidence.

Hit the fucking ball—now. And then there was Janice and the marriage slain by an overworking husband and a wildly insecure wife. Get it, ball. When she'd moved out she was beyond anger, cool and tough. Ball. Mouth tight and determined. Three suitcases, her papers, some kitchen utensils, as much stuff as could fit in the Subaru. Ball. She hadn't called a lawyer, and didn't know where she was going that night. Ball. The next day they found an apartment for her. He didn't blame her, completely. After months of hellish arguing, something—ball—had quite obviously snapped her slender faith in the two of them. Perhaps it had been—ball—his obsequious, impossible promises that he would revamp his entire personality. Ball. She had not been cruel, ever. Livid, certainly, and even—ball—ugly, but never cruel—ball—and even to the end, constantly—ball—reaffirming—ball—that she loved him, which made it all the more—ball—difficult.

The face was back. He snatched the ball out of the air and turned to the door. A woman in shorts and a black T-shirt stepped into the court holding a racquet. Her eyes were dark and her hair swept low across her forehead. Her belly was flat, and her breasts sagged fully against her narrow torso.

"You have a partner?" There was a husked-out sexiness to her; what remained implied what had been, and she had lost that slight layer of flesh that keeps a woman soft-looking. Instead, she appeared burned away to a tough and stringy essence. He noticed her arms hung easily at her side and were corded with muscle. Wide in the shoulders, almost bony.

"No." Peter waved her in and wondered if he would have to pansy the ball so as not to embarrass her too much.

"You serve first." She faced the front wall. "I'm warmed up." She stood on her toes, with her knees bent, leaning forward and swinging the racquet back and forth in concentration.

Peter thought for a moment. Medium-hard serve, something that would force her to react but would give him enough time to get to center court. He bounced the ball and gave it a good whack. The ball jumped off the front wall right at the woman. With a graceful yet quick stroke—a chop, really—she sliced a tight backhand, and the ball grazed the side wall, touched the front wall, and dropped dead, unhittable.

"I'm Cassandra." She touched him on the shoulder with her racquet. "Nice to meet you."

She won the first game 21–16. Cassandra had certainly played a lot of racquetball. She knew all the angles and anticipated the ball. But, he muttered to himself, he had the speed and power and the youth on her. He would serve now with all his strength, and try to whisk tough low serves into the back corners where she would have to scoop them out, giving him a chance at the kill shot.

They started the second game, and he felt the sweat really coming now, the deep breathing. His legs felt full of striated strength, his right shoulder pumped large. He gave his all to each shot, scuttling quickly into position, blasting, slicing, cutting the ball, anything to get the angle. Cassandra moved assertively across the court. At 15–15 he dug her serve out of the backhand corner and looped a drop shot off the wall. She got to it and swung a bit too hard on a drop shot of her own. Sprinting toward the front wall, he figured on a low blast that would pass her on the forehand side before she had a chance to reach it. He set up and blasted, knowing full well she could not return the shot. The ball exploded off the front wall. He turned to admire its placing, and as he spun his head, a speeding blue circle appeared inches away from his eyes, and then, before he knew it, he was flat on his back, his head ringing, the blood high behind his eyes. His forehead stung.

"Hup."

She stood over him and helped him up. Her grip was strong.

"How in fucking hell did you get that shot?" he said.

She did not answer and they stood before each other in the whitewalled box, breathing deeply, skin flushed and sweaty. Peter looked down into Cassandra's face. A pumped, sweat-gleaming vein snaked over her temple. She had a thin, sharp nose, and her mouth was set with devouring intensity; her face was that of a person who had outlasted many others. Cassandra swung her racquet back and forth unconsciously.

"I think we may be out of time," he said, checking his watch. "My hour's nearly up."

"I bought the next hour." When she smiled, the tip of her nose bent.

"Ah. You like racquetball."

"I like you."

Her thigh muscles lifted as she walked to the back of the court.

On the third point of the third game, while lunging at the ball, Peter knocked Cassandra to the floor, hard.

"I'm sorry." He was uneasy at his sudden violence. "Here, let me help you."

"I'm fine." She jumped back to her feet. "Go. I'm ready."

She won the game.

In the fourth game he decided to resort to strategy—pure strength was not working. Try to force her into his rhythm. But she caught shots before they bounced, halving his time to react, and knew what it was he wanted to do and was able to do it just that much more. If he carved deadly touch shots, she carved them back, only a slice more accurately. If he countered with wicked ricochet shots, then she used them, too, weaving a blue blur around him in the white box. She possessed deadly accuracy. She was doing everything he was doing, and she could do it better, and exactly when she wanted. With practice he might get to be that kind of player, but not soon. It took years to be able to achieve this devilment with the ball.

They began a long rally and worked closer to the front wall until they were lunging desperately for each shot, slapping the ball as hard as they could, back and forth—lunge, dive, slice—unrelenting, moving only on reflex. He threw himself into the game, trying to crush the ball with each stroke. He sensed Cassandra adapting to his higher level of intensity. He madly flailed his racquet and slammed himself from wall to wall while she coolly maneuvered each point. He gripped the racquet handle with both hands like an axe and waited for the serve. At 19–17 in the fifth game, her lead, there was a knock on the window. A couple stood ready outside the court. The time was up. Cassandra turned to him. She was hardly winded.

"We didn't get to finish."

Outside the court, Cassandra picked her towel off the waiting bench and wiped her forehead.

"That was *good*," she nodded.

"Where did you learn to play so well?"

"Tennis is my base, though it's such a different game."

He found himself staring at the corrugations of muscle in her forearm. "Did you play a lot of tennis?"

"Enough to pay for business school way back when."

"You were pro?"

"A couple of years. Best I did was the quarterfinals at Forest Hills. A freak string of tournament victories. I was ranked something like one hundred and eighty-sixth in the world that year, my zenith." She laughed, revealing receding gums and extensive dental work.

"What happened at Forest Hills?"

"Chrissie Evert, who was a *kid* then, burned the panties off me, that's what. I couldn't match her ground strokes. It was over in forty-nine minutes. I decided to go to business school full-time, and that was the end of the tennis."

He responded with an appreciative silence.

"Hey," Cassandra said without hesitation, putting her hand tightly on his shoulder. "Let's have dinner."

She suggested a small place ten blocks away, and numbly he said that was fine. They'd meet outside the locker rooms in twenty minutes, which was enough time, he decided, for him to grab a few minutes in the whirlpool. There he rubbed his forehead and tried to enjoy the swirling, bubbling heat that surrounded his body. The whirlpool was near the club pool, and a man and a woman splashed in the shallow end, laughing and surreptitiously nuzzling under the water. Apparently the man's foot was between the woman's ankles. Their desire depressed him, and he sank down into the water, thinking of Janice.

What had happened to her so long ago lived with him. If it was possible to be driven by a wrong done to another, then he had been driven, and for a long time now. Each time he prosecuted a crime, it was, in a private way, done for her, because the man who had hurt her was free. Secretly he believed himself to be lazy and selfish; Janice had provided him the righteousness he had needed to face down one criminal after another. Without her, his ire ebbed.

He hunched lower until only his head was above the steamy, frothy water of the round pool. For a confused moment he felt as though he were within his own churning cranium: a head within a head, the mind endlessly looking at itself endlessly looking at itself. But soon he felt limber and momentarily relaxed, his body rubbery and pink, his thoughts cooked out.

Before stepping into the shower, he lingered before the mirror, mentally subtracting the slight softness at his hips, flexing his stomach muscles to test for definition. He continued his inspection. His shoulders were firm, his legs in excellent condition. No way would he end up screwing this woman tonight, he thought; she had too much class and he probably wasn't interested. He tested his stomach again. In his junior year in high school, a million years ago, he had once done four hundred sit-ups holding a twenty-five-pound weight behind his head. He could fuck like a machine when he was seventeen.

Peter showered, picked at his nose in the mirror, toweled off, dressed. The odds were infinitesimal that Janice might be in the restaurant Cassandra had picked. It would be too expensive for her current condition, unless some guy were taking her out. He felt guilty for having dinner with Cassandra, and blamed Janice for it—a convenient psychological device, he realized. On the other hand, he need not feel guilty, since all it *was* was a dinner. If Cassandra were some sweet young fox, he might be getting some mileage out of his guilt. He was glad he wasn't very strongly attracted to her—physically, at least. He looked around, feeling vaguely miserable. Men came into the locker room in their overcoats and suits, stripped themselves, and became pale, blobby boys in shorts and T-shirts. A few men, in much better shape, were obviously cruising. He could tell in a lot of small ways, from two decades' experience—the locker-room code: Basically, one didn't *present* oneself to another man. But the rest, just regular guys like himself. How many had cheated on their wives?

Cassandra waited for him outside. She had changed into a blue wool business suit and carried a slender leather briefcase.

"You look like you make more money than I do," Peter said.

"Probably." Her eyes were bright. "So I'll buy dinner."

They reached the restaurant in her car. What he really needed to do, he decided, was go home and prepare for the summary argument. The waiter appeared and Cassandra ordered.

"You've barely spoken since we left the club. Tired?" she asked. "Or a complicated silence?"

"Both."

"You complicated?"

"I'm simple." He felt like arguing. This was all happening too easily. "I'm like anybody else. I want certain things and don't get most of them. I make a lot of mistakes."

63

"You're acting like I'm one of them." Her voice was even, almost amused, and he realized by her tone that she had experienced plenty of men and knew how they worked.

"You're not a mistake, Cassandra, and you're right to point out what a complete, multifaceted ass I'm being." He pushed back from his chair, let the first sip of wine sift through his brain. All he did anymore was apologize to attractive women in restaurants. "This sounds ridiculous, but I had a tough day and even though I want to talk, I'm having a hard time being witty and interested and all those things that I'm supposed to be"—he looked at her pointedly, almost aggressively, despite his apology—"in such a situation."

"What do you do, Peter?" she asked, charming him out of his distraction. "You still haven't told me."

"I'm a priest."

She laughed, looked at his hands.

"C'mon."

"I'm a butcher."

"Somewhere in between?" She lit a cigarette, watched it burn, then sucked on it deeply. He hated the smell of cigarette smoke, wondered why people insisted on killing themselves. But it was human nature to be self-destructive. Cassandra watched him. As on the court, he felt she knew his moves, and was willing to play any version of the game he could come up with.

"I'm an Assistant D.A. for the city," he told her. "My current specialty is homicide. I worked my way up through assault and the rape unit."

"Sounds messy. Maybe righteous, too."

"Yeah. I used to think the work was important. Now I'm not so sure."

"Burned out?"

"Every prosecutor, almost, burns out sooner or later. For me it's the grief," he said, just wanting to tell it to anybody, and maybe piggybacking his own grief over Janice onto others. "You look somebody in the face and you see they knew the victim all their life and loved them and then some idiot comes along and—like we had an old guy who was a retired fire fighter, worked as a security officer for a little extra money, and some kid with a machete can't get past the caged security area and so he kills the old guy and leaves. Doesn't even take his wallet. Sometimes you do the best you can to get the guy put away for a long time and some fine point of law stops us from getting the verdict we seek. You try to explain to the family. It pisses me off. No, it just makes me tired."

"You don't look tired." She smiled. Her nose bent at the tip again and despite his feeling of guardedness, his instinct to distrust, he liked her. She was being perfectly obvious, just perfectly obvious.

"Well, I feel it. Worn down. I'm not cynical, just have that eroded feeling, you know? You got babies being killed when a drug deal goes bad and the shooting starts, the kid's on the sofa—stuff like that. It's beyond tragic, it's stupid, absurd. If we could get the fucking hand-guns outlawed, that would be half the battle. Anybody can buy a gun in this town, anybody, anytime. Or a semi-automatic assault rifle, for that matter."

"How?"

"Go to a street corner and stand around for a few minutes. Or any bar in town, or places down by the river. Your favorite deli probably has a fence going."

"You like this job?"

"I can sleep at night. I do an honest day's work."

Confessing his thoughts to a stranger wasn't something he usually did. There was, however, no one else to talk to now. "I figure I have to decide in a year or two if I'm a company man. Once that happens, you start to move into the upper management. I've got seven years on the job."

"Do you want to stay?"

"Who knows?" He wasn't quite ready to tell her what he wanted. "What about you? What do you do?"

"I'm at First Philadelphia Bank. Ten years."

"Hey, that's where I bank. You have ten years' worth of author-ity?"

"No, more like twenty, unfortunately," she told him.

She was, Cassandra said, Vice President for Operations. She appeared genuinely unimpressed by herself, and this intrigued him. He wondered what the price of her success had been—not every woman wanted to get married and have kids, so maybe it was something else. They talked further about climbing the managerial ranks, the constant assaults on her authority from above and below, her mentoring of younger women, the tiresome corporate code of dress and behavior, the office warfare for bonuses and raises. Cassandra spoke in complete sentences with precise objectivity about the structures of the bank corporation; she would be quite adept at dictating letters. He realized, in an accidental way, that she was probably quite rich. And yet, ultimately, her career seemed like a faraway land of passionless stratagems and manipulations and hierarchies into which she had ventured on a long, dry tour of duty. Her voice held no enthusiasm for the hours or the responsibilities. He wondered if she might be a bit lonely, and as the wine eased his own tensions, he saw a fleeting look of quiet desperation in her eyes, and it answered his own current emptiness. They were strangers, and yet, he suddenly believed, he knew just who she was. By the time dessert was served, he had slipped easily into his questioning role, careful to appear interested, even more careful to maintain the conversation at a distance from any possible mention of Janice. And yet, while striving to do this, he again sensed Cassandra knew what he was doing.

"Which means," she was saying after he had asked her about her specific duties, "that when you use your little bank card in any of our eighty-six Philadelphia locations or four hundred affiliate locations, I'm responsible, ultimately, for making sure we get a computer record of the transaction and you get a printout receipt, the cash you ask for, and nothing less or more."

"Especially not *more*," he frowned mockingly. "Mustn't get more than we ask for."

"What are you asking for?" she asked, staring boldly at him.

"I'm asking you to drive me home because your Audi is a hell of a lot more comfortable than the subway."

"It might not be any safer."

It took them ten minutes to get to Society Hill, about half the usual time. Cassandra stopped the car in front of his home on Delancey. All the windows in his house were dark and he was aware of the statement this made about his life. He smelled the new leather seats of the car, wondered how much a bank vice president made.

"Did you plan this?" Peter asked, feeling like a small animal snared in a trap.

"Yes. But I think you know that." Her voice was frank. "I saw you at the club a week ago, with another man, and I checked the court reservation book and decided to be around the next week when you showed up. It was just luck that you were alone."

"Seems pretty unusual, for a woman," he said.

"Does it?"

He had no answer. They sat silently. Then she leaned over and kissed him. He tasted the cigarette in her kiss, and he felt ashy himself, small, needing to be held badly. She put her arms around him.

"You were banging that ball around so hard, with such"—she searched for the word, laughed whisperingly next to his ear—"with such angry *contemplation* that I knew I wanted to get to know you. I wanted to know who was inside that face." She kissed him again. He smelled her perfume and their wine and felt confused, yet pushed it along, moving his hands over her, worrying that he appeared stupid and thick-fingered. She was the first woman beside Janice he had touched in over a decade.

"I like you, I like you very much," she said, slipping her hands beneath his jacket and rubbing his chest. "I like how big you are." He looked at her, figuring she was five or six years older than him, maybe more. How much more, goddammit? Women could be brilliant at concealing their age. Women over thirty-five lose their jawline, the skin starts to drop from the bone. He looked down, shamed. But he liked it when she kissed him. He heard her whisper, "I want to come inside, Peter."

His head was heavy with wine as they floated through the house. He didn't turn on any lights, barely bothered to wave an obliging hand here and there, not really saying anything. "Kitchen, dining room, den, there's a small backyard." Cassandra's perfume invaded the rooms. Despite his dizzyness from the wine, he guiltily made a mental note to air out the house the next day. Professional criminals leave no evidence. Cassandra took his hand and asked him where the bedroom was, and he appreciated her forwardness; it was not crass, but honest and matter-of-factly accepting that he was too tired and too ambivalent to be coy. He climbed the stairs to the bedroom and felt the two hours of racquetball in his legs. Cassandra used the bathroom. He left the light off in his bedroom and began to undress, tossing his underwear with his foot toward the laundry hamper, now overflowing. Strangely, he didn't feel especially self-conscious and this worried him. He was supposed to be worrying about getting it up, and instead he half-wished Cassandra would dematerialize like Kirk or Spock being beamed somewhere on "Star Trek" and he could just go to sleep. He had a load of work to do, and Hoskins, the man with balls as big as City Hall, was always looking for any indication that you were slacking off. He couldn't afford to be doing this. Maybe Cassandra would confess to a divorced husband, kids. They'd talk and he'd whisk her out the door. He wouldn't tell her about Janice. Keep that part inside. To cover the silence of his apathy, he asked her when she returned, "How many people under you at your job?"

She was sitting on the side of the bed, fumbling in her purse. "What? I've got four hundred people in my department." She threw her purse to the floor. "Peter, I didn't bring any contraceptive. I honestly didn't expect . . ." She looked at him. "I hope tonight you'll understand."

"That's fine. That's okay."

"I can still get pregnant, even at my very advanced age, and we certainly don't want *that*."

She found a hanger in his closet and hung up her wool suit. He noticed the veins on the back of her thigh.

"That's okay." He went over and kissed her but did not enjoy it. "We can work around it. Pardon the euphemism."

Meaning a blowjob. It had been particularly long since Janice had been in the mood for that, had pulled the pleasure from him, instead of having him force it out. They began to touch each other, and Cassandra pushed her tongue into his mouth and quickly moved her hands downward. He tried to reciprocate but his fingers were blind, stumbling over unfamiliar flesh. He remained abstracted, watching himself. He had purposely not washed the sheets since Janice left, maintaining the comforting familiarity of stray hair, old perfume, dried stains. The bedroom and whole house had quickly become a museum, with him as curator, guide, and until now, sole visitor. Cassandra's hand grasped him tightly, making him feel his own pulse. He wondered about diseases, take your pick: the traditional ones, the harmlessly incurable, the curable yet aggravating ones, the incurably fatal. He wanted to assume Cassandra was honest enough to tell him if she had some ugly viral evil floating around inside. But his work told him that you could rarely trust anyone completely.

"I need to ask you a question," he began, sitting up. "It's no reflection on you—I'd ask it of anyone in this situation."

"You want to know if I'm clean," she told him. "I can see that. It's okay. I'm being straight with you." She stared at him. "Everyone's afraid," she said.

He was just drunk enough that he didn't have to consider all the meanings of this statement.

"In that case, I have an idea."

"Yes?"

"About how we could still—"

"You have something? For you?"

Her high-voiced abruptness disturbed him.

"No. But I'll be right back."

In the bathroom, with the wine making his head feel as if it were set on well-oiled ball bearings, he fumbled under the sink. There was a lot of Janice's old stuff in a basket. She'd left it, probably forgotten it. Archaeological layers. Her hard contacts case, from before she got soft ones. Perfumed soap, the paper wrappers stained, Robitussin cough formula, outdated prescriptions, orphan hairpins, then what he was looking for—her old diaphragm. When she'd moved out, she had taken her new one and in her haste and tumult forgotten this one, unused in three or four years, and certainly of no use to Peter. It was stained, dusty even. He held it up to the light to see if any light came through. No. He ran water in it, and found no leaks. In the mirror he looked white, scared. His cock, hard as a broom handle a minute before, had wilted sleepily. It was nearly two A.M. He had to be at work in six and a half hours. He couldn't even remember the case. Temporary insanity, so many cases. Summary? Waiting for a verdict? *Voir dire* jury selection? He was tired of interviewing people. *Do you, sir, have any religious, moral, ethical, or conscientious objections to the death penalty such that those objections would prevent you as a juror from imposing the sentence if the defendant is convicted of murder in the first degree?* His ancestors, the Scattergoods, black-hatted Quakers who helped to found the city on principles of peace, tolerance, and profit, would twist in their graves—six feet deep in the small, crowded cemeteries in the old meeting houses around the city—if they knew their descendant enforced the death penalty.

He fumbled around and found the twisted tube of diaphragm gunk. The note was still on it. I KNEW YOU WOULD LOOK. Now it was his turn for fun. Ha. With determined squeezing, he forced out barely a teaspoon. Enough? No wonder women hated smearing this goo around with a finger. It better be enough. *The uterus may be imagined to be approximately the size of a pear.* Ancient rape testimony from the medical examiner. Half the women in the office wanted babies; it was all they ever talked about. The diaphragm spread an arcing barrier of death. The next case involved a defendant with a long bookie record. He'd shot his neighbor in the back of the head. It appeared to be a love triangle. If he picked the old black women for the jury, they'd hang the guy high and dry—they were very tough jurors, those Sunday-morning Evangelical screamers who didn't put up with bullshit street jive. White middle-class women could go either way. On the other hand, the black women often knew how capricious and unfair the police were and, understandably, resented the system that crushed so many of their men. America, in so many ways built upon the back of the black man, continued to exact costs. If he, Peter Scattergood, hadn't had every single fucking advantage in the world, then he too might be some wretched drugged-out, jobless, mind-blown coke fiend, scuffing a living selling stolen needles, courting AIDS and all the other evil that was killing everybody. He stood in the harsh light before the mirror, spreading and respreading the white goo. Janice wanted to have kids, dreamed of it, and he was ambivalent—they'd eliminated hundreds of little Janices and Peters with thousands of dollars' worth of birth control, and he wouldn't have had it any other way. You turn thirty, you know how to prevent kids better than how to have them. Maybe if he'd let Janice have children, she'd have stayed with him. Maybe, yes, but would it have been right? Some little dark-haired baby girl bouncing on his knee. *Daddy!* It was a godawful crime they had never had kids. Would have made his parents happy, too. Janice, I don't know why I'm doing this right now. She would have natural childbirth, he'd sit there and hold her hands, watch her face strain. It would scare all hell out of him to see Janice in such pain. He had been a goddamn coward all along—he had to find her and talk to her in person. Soon. He could get a trace on the number she gave him, but the phone company required a court order and that was a guaranteed impossibility. Too slow. He wondered if old black women screwed old black men. Black women ran the grass-roots Democratic political machine, the north wards. The money came from the state organization; with good weather and two dollars per voter, the machine was very effective. The new Mayor had all of them in his pocket, he was smarter than the last one, knew how to organize the women who needed some outlet for all that occupational frustration. The women who screwed old black men in North Philadelphia who kept their undershirts on and a bottle under the bed. *Be good to me, Mama. This called humping the stump.* And right now, in the dead of winter, small rooms in a big city. Sure, everybody fucks everybody.

"Peter?" The voice came from the bedroom. He had no idea whose it was. He returned to the dark.

"I thought you'd disappeared," Cassandra mused affectionately. "What were you *muttering* in there?"

70

"Hold out your hand."

She did.

"It's—" he began.

"No explanation needed." She felt it with her fingertips. There was an appraising silence as she tested its size, then she gave an amused laugh. "It'll do."

He sat down on the bed.

"You mind if I smoke first?" she asked a minute later, using a tissue to wipe her hands.

"Go ahead."

"It relaxes me."

A match flared in the dark, brightening the gaunt edge of her cheekbone. Her eyes watched the tobacco brighten. He hated cigarette smoke.

"How much do you smoke?"

"Not enough to damage my health. Just now and then."

"Right."

"Now listen to me," she said with grave amusement, wrapping a ropy arm around his chest, pulling him toward her, "*most* women, and I mean practically *all*, would never, *ever* do what I just did. Most would consider it a foul act."

"Do you consider it a foul act?" he asked the pin light of her cigarette.

"Yes," she exhaled. "But being alone is a whole lot worse."

They began to move. He did not feel the surge of sexual curiosity one is supposed to feel when beginning an affair; instead, for the first time in his life, he experienced the sensation of holding one woman while fervently trying to trick himself into believing that it was another.

It was later. He rested his head on her breast, his cheek against her skin.

"I'm going to rub your back." She blew in his ear. He had to admit she was more affectionate than Janice, for whom affection had become a balance-of-trade commodity. He remembered sleeping side by side angrily, two people hating each other, lying quietly within themselves, feeling a vast distance of inches between them. Cassandra, on the other hand, seemed genuinely unselfish. First-time courtesy? He'd been out of circulation for a long time. What did he really know about the manners of the American sexual marketplace in the waning years of the twentieth century? He was only some poor slob whose wife had

71

just left him. Cassandra's hands moved across his shoulders, kneaded his spinal column. She rubbed his back, his rear, the moist, tufty no-man's-land between his ass and balls, his hamstrings, the back of his knees, and his calves.

"Feels great."

"Good." The bedroom was dark.

"I'll do it for you."

"I'm happy. You just be."

"You like being vice president of a bank?"

"There're ten of us. It's not quite the position it sounds, but it gives me things I need. How's this?"

She pushed her thumbs into the deep muscle region of his rear.

"It's. Terrific."

She kissed his back and worked her fingers around his ribs.

"You able to determine people's banking habits from all those automatic tellers?" he asked into the sheet.

"What machine they get their money from and what time, things like that."

"Right." Janice typically used the machine often, after work, or on Saturday mornings before she shopped. Maybe he could locate Janice by finding out where she was using her bank card.

"What're you thinking?" she asked.

Nothing he was ready to tell her. "I'm trying to think up a joke about banking and sex. I've got the punch line but not the lead-in."

"What's the punch line?"

"Substantial penalties for early withdrawal."

She grunted a laugh and rolled him on top of her.

"That's pretty pathetic, Mr. Scattergood."

"I agree."

"What else, then?"

"I can hear your heart," he said.

"How fast does it go?"

He listened.

"It goes 'Uh-huh, uh-huh, uh-huh.' "

"Listen again," she told him. "I'll slow it down."

He pressed his head close. He could feel her breathing and the heat of skin. In the dark, this was the whole world.

"You did it." He lifted his head. Her hand moved from his shoulder to his neck. A slight pressure.

"Now listen."

This time her heart fluttered rapidly. Her body tensed and her skin warmed. His penis lifted in response.

"Yes?" she said.

"Yes."

Her heart slowed and she pulled him toward her.

"How do you do that?"

She locked her arms around him happily.

"Practice."

He drifted through a field of sleep until she spoke again.

"Tell me something I don't know," she asked playfully.

"What kind of thing?"

"Oh, I don't know."

"All right. Inside you right now is a substance called prostatic acid phosphotase. Only men produce it. If we were in court and you wanted to prove—"

"That's lovely."

"What did you want to be told?"

"What your wife is like," she responded suddenly.

He had forgotten Janice, if only for a moment.

"How did you know I was married?"

"Well, you happen to be wearing a wedding ring."

"Yes I do, don't I?"

"Also, it's in your face. You're used to being married, you don't have the approach single men have. Married men can be very attractive—they're trained."

"Am I being patronized?"

"Not against your will," she laughed.

He rolled over and she sat on him, his thick chest straddled by her slender legs. In the streetlight, he could see how skinny she truly was. Her breasts clung to a wall of ribs.

"You know," he said, "in five hours, or whatever it is, I have to be back in court, and after this I'm not going to feel like it."

"Yes?" She was rubbing his fingers.

"I mean in the morning, I'm going to wake up and just want to laze around, you know? Christ, who the hell wants to put on a suit and tie and march around a courtroom? It's a hell of a way to make a living."

"We could go out for breakfast somewhere," she said, lying down. "I love croissants. And good coffee."

He hadn't answered her question about Janice and they both knew it. He lifted his knee into her crotch, enjoyed its warm moistness. She breathed in his arms. His eyeballs rolled back under their lids, and for a time he floated free of his own thoughts and lived in some warm, safe place defined by the edges of the bed. Then Cassandra's hand touched his temple.

"Well?"

"What?"

"What's she like? Is she attractive, smart?"

"I'm not ready to talk about her."

"How long since you last saw her?"

This was too much. He opened his eyes. Before him rose one large inquiring eye, wide open, wide awake.

"What time is it?"

"Late. Early. Why? You going to kick me out?"

They lay there naked, aware of themselves.

"No," he whispered, "of course not."

And this was the truth. Part of his code was that as a man, he took care of women when they appeared to need it. It was probably patronizing, self-serving, and reductive of women—all the things Janice used to tell him—but it was his code, nonetheless. He found an old flannel shirt and some wool socks of his and insisted she put them on. Then he pulled up the covers and listened to her begin to sleep. The bedroom was dark but he moved easily. He felt solicitous of her. He was, however, he decided, under no illusions that he had fallen in love or otherwise become attached to Cassandra. The grim, small truth of it was that they were two adults who had talked, coupled, and treated the other decently. There was something pathetic and lonely in all this, and as the minutes passed, his time with Cassandra flattened toward a minimal interaction. He would disengage himself tomorrow.

This decided, he picked up her clothes and folded them neatly and put them in the chair so that she would see them in the morning. He could hear her breathing evenly. Already unconscious. Had he meant so little to her? Or was she simply tired and at peace? He found his bathrobe and put it next to the clothes. His radio alarm was set to ring in three hours. Tomorrow—*today*—he was due back in court. He'd have to prepare in his office early in the morning. In the bathroom he pissed, enjoyed the slight burning pleasure that came with cleaning out the pipe. He put out a fresh towel and wiped spots of dried toothpaste from the mirror. Then he cleaned the toilet seat and checked the bath drain, where he found a dry matted circle of Janice's

74

and his hair. He dropped it into the toilet, where it floated like a tiny woven wreath.

He wandered the house, not daring to fall asleep next to Cassandra—sleep being more intimate than sex. If he closed his eyes, he'd slide down the chute of unconsciousness, unable to walk. Only a few hours remained till dawn and the morning and noise and rush and all the nonsense that he depended on to keep him from thinking. He went into his study and turned on every light. His ghost sat working at his desk, hands blurred like a drummer's over a continuous white stream of paper. Paying bills. Trial notes. Internal office memos. Police reports. Peter's eyes burned with supernatural alertness, waiting.

FOUR

Somewhere in the night's exhaustion, he must have wandered back into the bedroom, for when the sound of the phone stabbed at his head, he was beneath the sheets in his underwear. That anyone was calling him now meant trouble, and instinctively he thought of Janice, that she might somehow need him. He reached toward the phone and encountered another body.

"Yes?" Cassandra spoke. "It's very nice to speak to you, and no, you haven't woken me. Here's Peter."

Cassandra held her hand over the receiver.

"You were so tired you *fell* on the bed about four."

"Who—?" he whispered.

"It's a Bill Hoskins—"

"My boss."

"He thinks I'm your—"

Peter nodded, cutting her off. He took the phone. Cassandra lay next to him, her knees tucked up under his.

"Yeah?" he croaked.

"Peter!" Hoskins boomed. "I wish *my* wife was up this early in the morning."

"Okay, I'm awake. What's the story?"

"Just got a call from the trailer."

The office maintained an office in a trailer by the Police Administration Building at Eighth and Race Streets. There, new A.D.A.s rotated shifts, receiving information on crimes and arrests from the police.

"Peter," Hoskins continued, "we got a young black guy named Darryl Whitlock dead in his apartment with blunt trauma head injuries in West Philly."

"If the young blacks in this city stopped bumping each other off, we'd have very little business." Peter felt Cassandra kissing his back. "Sounds pretty routine."

"That's what I knew you would say and that's what you won't say when I tell you three facts."

Hoskins was a man who loved to present facts like a boy lining up toy soldiers: carefully, and in a row. Peter was never sure if Hoskins's maniacal behavior was constitutional or a conscious strategy to put everyone on the defensive. He had obeyed Hoskins for so many years now, without trust.

"Make me curious enough to forget how sleepy I am."

"Peter, remember Wayman Carothers?"

Cassandra was trying to roll him over. He resisted. "No. Yes, a couple of years ago? Some guy who beat a charge because the evidence was screwed up. That the guy who broke into a house and the owner resisted and he got angry and killed him?"

"Berger prosecuted that case—"

"It was a weak case, we never had enough. The guy had a hell of a temper."

"Hang on a second, Peter," Hoskins said.

Peter watched Cassandra get out of bed and pad into the bathroom. She had stretch marks on her breasts, tiny grooves colored slightly lighter than the rest of her skin. Had she ever been pregnant? How drunk had he been? Had she been up while he'd been asleep? Did she go through the house, his papers? It was terrible to be so paranoid, but hell, he was paid to be paranoid. He knew almost nothing about her, including her last name.

"All right—" Hoskins came back.

"So it's Carothers, or might be," Peter said, jotting down notes on a pad he kept by his bed. "How'd you get him so fast?"

"Got an ID from a neighbor. We had him in the mug books, and the cops have already picked him up for questioning," Hoskins replied. "The second fact is that the newspapers know about the murder and that we have a suspect."

"If the newspapers *care*, you better say who the victim is."

"He's the Mayor's nephew."

"Oh, fucking great."

"Yeah, son of his sister who lives out on Baltimore Avenue in West Philadelphia. He had an apartment two blocks away. Lower-middle-class family, stable. Everybody loved him, a real prince. Want more? Straight-A student at Overbrook High, on full scholarship to Penn. He'd been accepted to Harvard Medical School. A smart kid who was going to be a doctor. Somehow got hooked up with Carothers. We think maybe Carothers cruises Penn, knows some of the people who deal to the kids. We don't know how they knew each other. Maybe they didn't know each other. Maybe Whitlock was buying from Carothers, which sort of tarnishes the image and makes it stickier for the Mayor, not that I care what people think about him. Maybe it was straight robbery. Everybody says Whitlock was clean. You're going to have to dig into that, very tactfully. The papers are going to be very interested. The black community is very interested. I understand there's been a call already from some of the black leaders offering 'guidance,' whatever the hell that is. The Mayor, for God's sake, is going to be very fucking interested. He hasn't been in office very long, so he'll try to squeeze every advantage he can out of this."

"Yeah, it's a mess."

"How's your caseload?"

This was not a genuine question, just one of the hurdles of protocol. Hoskins, unsympathetic to the difficulties of life, was never interested in how hard someone was working. He had it figured both ways, too: If you weren't working hard, you needed to be; if you were working hard, it was because you were stupidly missing something obvious, in which case you needed to work harder to find out what that thing was.

"Uh . . ." He had better remember what he was supposed to do that day. "I got final arguments in Robinson—"

"Shit, that's easy."

"Isn't this a special case—"

"Berger's somewhere the hell out in Harrisburg."

"Right."

"Besides, his concentration isn't good these days. I saw him sucking face with some—"

Cassandra returned, wet, a towel around her, another wrapped around her wet hair. She kneeled next to the bed and kissed his belly. He grunted, trying to respond to everybody at once.

"Right. He won't be happy about it. But you're at a point now to take something like this on. You got a wife who's awake in the morning. Good. Very good. How old're you, Peter?"

"Thirty-one last fall." Maybe Hoskins was on his side, after all. Now Cassandra had him in her mouth.

"Perfect. This case is at just the goddamn right time for you. It's a job for a guy who's got iron-fist control. This is a total-concentration, no-screw-up operation. This comes out right and so will you, fucking guaranteed. I had pressure already to put one of the other guys on it, make a more politically appropriate selection, but I say fuck 'em, let's go with the best iron-fist control we have. That's you. We gotta hit the ground fast. I'm officially assigning you the case and you should be goddamn glad to have the opportunity. Get the other work done—do it, do it well, but concentrate on Whitlock. This is the main dish now."

Peter was still too sleepy to pretend to be gung-ho. He wondered if by some freak of nature Cassandra had been impregnated by him last night. She was teasing him now, flicking with her tongue.

"You're ready?" Hoskins asked.

"Yes." He'd let Cassandra pay for the abortion, assuming the pro-life people hadn't bombed every clinic yet. He didn't have any extra cash right now, and besides, how could he be sure it was his?

"No distractions?"

"No," he grunted. Cassandra was working on him in earnest.

"You'll be dealing with the Philadelphia media, not the odd court reporter. The police will of course handle the basic announcements this morning," Hoskins barked, "then you'll take questions as the investigation progresses and you develop your case." Hoskins went on to say that the District Attorney, a tidy man who enjoyed a fine reputation despite the fact that coke traffic had tripled during his tenure, would be taking a low profile on the case, largely because he was too busy planning a run for the U.S. Senate and had already blocked out a heavy schedule during the next month for early fund-raising appearances around the state, plugging into the closed-door Washington connections. Furthermore, Peter knew, the District Attorney, an elected official, was a Republican; there weren't many more votes to be won in the city that had just elected a Democratic Mayor over a candidate the D.A. had endorsed, even though that endorsement had been lukewarm and delivered only out of loyalty to the Republican Party bosses whose support he needed later. The D.A. already had a record to run on, and was expected to have a strong chance at the Senate. He needed big money more than he needed a prominent trial. Additionally, if the D.A. went high profile on the case, then it might become politicized, a focus of rant by the new Mayor, whom insiders considered occasionally unpredictable. If the case went smoothly, the Mayor might not like the suffering of his family to benefit a political enemy's reputation—by removing himself, the D.A. removed the office's political lightning rod. Peter knew the D.A. couldn't afford to get mired in a stupid battle with the Mayor. Frankly, the man was distracted, and had probably dumped the mess into Hoskins's lap.

"So," Hoskins was saying, "you can expect extra pressure. Also, the Mayor will probably speak to you in a general way, offer his support and confidence—"

"He might be a good man beneath all that charisma."

Hoskins had expressed no liking of this Mayor, but of course he'd do a very professional job, if only to further his man-eater reputation.

"You're all go on this? Ready to run with it?"

"Yeah." He pictured Cassandra's mouth. Her wet hair lay against his skin. "Got it."

"Good," Hoskins concluded. "Stop by my office this morning and get the paperwork. All right—wait a minute! I almost forgot! I want you to get out to the crime scene right away—"

"What?"

"I know we don't usually do this, but the Mayor's *nephew* doesn't get beaten to death every day. Just go out there, have a look. Don't let the detectives hassle you. It'll piss them off a little, scare them— whatever, make sure they do a decent job. Might help later on. I want our office to have as strong a position as possible."

"What's—what's the condition of things out there?"

"They're taking their time. They haven't even—"

"What I'm asking about, to be honest," breathed Peter, "is whether the body will still be there."

"Yes, I think it may be."

Peter scrawled down the address, replaced the phone, and fell back into bed. Cassandra pulled and urged and finished him. She disappeared for a minute into the bathroom, then reappeared, wrapped in his bathrobe. She sat on the edge of the bed and pulled a comb through her wet hair, combing it in shiny, perfect rows.

"Well?" she asked.

"Uh, well, *that* was great," he breathed.

"No." She smiled. "The call."

"Another terrible murder has been committed." Peter caught his breath. "And the *entire* city of Philadelphia is going to know about it in approximately three hours. The crime itself is not unusual, but the victim is." It would be, he knew, on the front page of the late city editions of the *Inquirer* and the *Daily News*. Repeated on WCAU and KYW, the all-news stations, every fifteen minutes, most of the day. On the hourly newscast of the music stations, the noon news, the five-thirty news, the six o'clock news, and the eleven o'clock news on all three local television affiliates. It would be in the black community churches on Sunday. The Mayor will be on television talking about it, synthesizing it into his political position on crime. . . . He realized he smelled of wine and was too tired to suck in his belly as he stood up and retrieved his underwear.

"Ready for a speech? Okay. A family and a wider community who had great hopes for what sounds like a talented boy is going to feel crushed and disturbed, vengeful. The black community doesn't *get* that many kids like this. The man who commited the crime, as far as we know, has escaped prosecution for a similar crime in the past. This makes a family and a community extremely angry, and with complete justification, in my view. On a philosophical level, there has been an emotional and noticeable tear in a certain part of the social fabric. Somebody is going to carry the responsibility to publicly sew that tear up. He'll have help, but the *responsibility* will be his." It was going to be the case of his life—and he feared the pressure and the possibility of blowing it. "Would you want to be that person?"

Cassandra had pulled a white silk blouse over her muscular shoulders. Now, again, she was the professional woman. And he the professional man. When the sun rises, the expertise clicks in and the moments of shadow and silence of the night disappear.

"Peter, I think you're really great, but it doesn't sound to me—" she stopped. "Who am I to tell you how to run your life? It's just that you mumbled your wife's name last night before we finally went to sleep—" She smiled stiffly. "Don't worry, it doesn't bother me—I find it touching, though it makes me a little jealous, too. What I'm saying is that your house needs to be cleaned. You need *food* in the refrigerator—"

The phone rang again. Cassandra shrugged. "I'll be making breakfast." She left the room.

Peter picked up the phone, defeated by the truth of Cassandra's words. His mood was foul.

"Speak."

81

"Peter Scattergood?"

"Yes."

"My name is Gerald Turner, aide to the Mayor. Do you have a minute so that he may talk with you?"

"Yes, of course."

He was put on hold, and took the time to clear his throat. From downstairs came breakfast sounds. The sweat started to trickle down his armpits. He had glimpsed the Mayor in City Hall, heard a couple of speeches by him, and seen him on television myriad times. Successor to Wilson Goode, and as a former councilman, an excellent public speaker. A man who exuded power, even though he'd just taken office. Whereas Mayor Goode had left only a record of bumbling good intentions, the worst of course being the MOVE tragedy in which an entire city block was burned down by the police, the new Mayor was more magnetic a character, known for his constant schedule of appointments, moving always in a darkened limousine from this place to that—a business gathering in one of the new hotels, a renovated school building, a shelter for the homeless. He was hungry, he had said, to put the city back together. He was a man, he had told them—dabbing at the sweat on his brow—a man with ideals, a family man, someone who understood that the community must be *healed*. He and his wife, along with their four children, all in high school or college, attended church together each Sunday. He pledged to work with everyone—the police, the City Council, the private sector, the school board. While his rhetoric thus far had not translated into change, there was no doubt that the new Mayor was a man of action, given to appearing at impromptu press conferences outside City Hall, dressed always in expensive, conservative tailored suits, addressing reporters by name—the better to curry their favor, of course—and able to stare into the television cameras and whirring motor drives with impunity. Always he was attended by an entourage of handlers, not a few of whom looked as if they had been picked off the corner of 52nd and Market the previous day and given a new suit. Their presence gave the entrance of the Mayor to any event the sudden excitement of the appearance of a heavyweight prize fighter—the build of which the Mayor possessed, with the thick torso of Joe Frazier, another famous Philadelphian.

It was no wonder Hoskins disliked the Mayor—Hoskins was one of those people who couldn't quite believe that blacks had wrested so much political power from whites. Though the powerful businessmen and developers in the city were white, the governance of the city was controlled by blacks. Political corruption knew no race, of course, and thus continued to run through the local government like steam pipes in City Hall—everywhere, and where you least expected. The electorate, exhausted by betrayal, knew that the city could no longer pay for all its poor people and that each administration just gorged at the trough. The new Mayor had come in promising change. He had eased through the Democratic primary and then narrowly beaten the Republican candidate, a business executive who happened to be rich and nominally Catholic, a man who needed to pull over thousands of Italian and Irish Democrat votes to win but whose Main Line aura had alienated them. Hoskins, through the D.A., had strong social connections to the defeated candidate. But, Peter knew, as power concentrated at the top, unofficial relationships thickened, across race and party. Hoskins would play it by the book, if only for his own advantage.

"Hello?" a familiar voice said.

"Mr. Mayor? I'm terribly sorry about your nephew, sir."

"Yes, uh, Mr. Scattergood. I appreciate your sentiments. It's a tragedy, a family tragedy. His mother, my sister Lorraine, is in shock."

"We see that a lot, Mr. Mayor. The effect on the decedent's family is devastating." This was babbling, and he stopped.

"I understand from Bill Hoskins that you'll be handling the prosecution of the young man who allegedly murdered my nephew."

Careful wording, even for a confidential call.

"Yes," Peter said, not sure if he had heard a cold tone in the Mayor's voice. "I understand we have a suspect. If he's charged, if it's a good case, I'll handle the prosecution."

"I am glad of that," the rich voice said. "I understand that you're very proficient at what you do. I commend you for your service to the city and I want you to know you have my full personal support and that of my office. I will instruct one of my aides, Gerald Turner, to work out a communication scheme with you. It will not be necessary to work through your superiors. Just provide me, please, on an informal basis, with information on where your prosecution is going. I promise you I will not meddle, Mr. Scattergood. That is not my intent at all. It's simply for psychological ease, if you understand. Frankly, if you can talk to me for a few minutes regularly, I may be able to alleviate some of the typical family pressure you may feel in cases such as this. Above all I have no desire to interfere."

"Sounds reasonable," Peter agreed obligatorily.

"I do wish to add one more thing, and it has nothing to do with any desire on my part to impugn your integrity. I must say it because you are an unknown quantity to me and I want to be sure to say it to whomever runs this case. I want no funny stuff, Mr. Scattergood. Bear in mind that I have said this from the absolute start of our relationship. *I want this case to be clean going in and clean coming out.* I'm a lawyer. I want the discovery process to be full, I want the evidence procedurally sound, all of it. If it does go to trial eventually, I don't want the case leveraged in any way because the Mayor's nephew has been murdered—" An emotional pause. "In the long run, that won't help anybody. Run the thing by the book. Have your people run it by the book. Have them run their *lives* by the book if necessary, so we don't scare up some half-connected scandal. The papers love half-connected scandals, you may have noticed. Don't take any shortcuts. Is that understood?"

"I understand."

"The other side of the coin is that I want you to do everything possible to make sure this Carothers, this suspect—or whoever did it—gets salted away for a proper long time."

"Right," Peter said.

"One more thing," the Mayor said, the adjustable warmth coming back into his voice, the stern tone receding, "you understand, of course, that all communication between us is confidential, off the record, not to be alluded to when speaking to the press, not even to be mentioned to your colleagues. Our official communication will be on paper and through my aides."

"Yes."

"Any questions in respect to how I would like this tragic affair handled?"

"No, none."

"Thank you for your valuable time so early in the morning, Mr. Scattergood. Stay in touch."

After a quick shower and breakfast, he looked at Cassandra, whose dark wool suit now hid her thinness.

"You understand I have to run out. . . ." He tried to sound casual. "I appreciate you helping me this morning. Please pull the front door shut when you leave."

"That's okay." She smiled, replacing the orange juice in the refrigerator that Janice had picked out. "I understand completely."

"Something else, Cassandra. I'd appreciate it if you let me answer

84

my own phone. More than appreciate it, I really do insist you not compromise me again like that."

"You're serious?"

He let his silence answer her, and while he was silent he noticed something. He had been letting the dishes pile up in the sink, and here was Cassandra, standing in her eight-hundred-dollar outfit, still fresh from the day before, with her hands in sudsy warm water with bits of rotten vegetable floating in it. He glanced at his watch, thinking he did not want her to do his dishes for him; the act implied intimacy and cooperation and domesticity and all the things Janice had taken with her. Cassandra seemed to enjoy the washing—the *meaning* of it—and he almost asked her if she felt so comfortable as to do this, going to the trouble—he considered mentioning all this, but he remembered that a corpse lay in a room across town and that he had a responsibility to that corpse. He had better get moving. What was a sink of dishes compared to a Mayor's wrath?

He pulled on his coat. Cassandra turned and smiled at him.

"Hope it goes well."

"Yes." His voice was inconclusive. Her eyes waited for something from him, some acknowledgment, and he knew himself to be a small-hearted, selfish bastard. In the sunlight, she looked haggard. He wanted to scream at her to leave, for her presence implied his failure. Instead, he shuffled over and planted a meager but passably affection-ate kiss on her forehead.

"Busy today?" he inquired dutifully.

"The usual planning meeting. I give a presentation."

He didn't answer.

"Call me?" she said.

"Sure."

Outside his house paced a small woman in a blue winter coat. For a moment he thought it was Janice—and in that case they wouldn't be able to go in the house; despite the fact that she had left him, Janice would explode if she found Cassandra inside. The woman turned at the sound of the door shutting—not Janice. She had been waiting for him. He pretended not to see her and walked up the street.

"Mr. Scattergood?" she called after him.

He hurried to his car, thinking that all he had to do was get in and shut the door. Soon the coffee would mask his exhaustion, compelling him toward whatever it was the day held.

"Excuse me!"

She caught up and he stood staring unhappily into two blue eyes magnified grotesquely by thick glasses and framed by curly red hair. How could he ever have thought she might be Janice?

"Nice house," she said. "I love these old streets. The cobblestones and everything."

"Thanks."

"My name's Karen Donnell." She reached out a gloved hand he automatically shook. "With the *Inquirer*."

"Don't recognize you," he said.

She pulled out an *Inquirer* ID.

"The city desk assigned me the Mayor's nephew story. I'll be following the case. The desk wants to do an investigative piece, use it as an opportunity to get behind the workings of the D.A.'s office, see the way a case progresses, really put the whole thing under a microscope and see how it's done."

"Oh." Why, he wondered, would she tell him this? "Sort of a page-one feature?"

"Right," she answered. "I need to ask you a couple of questions." She produced a small voice-activated recorder and flicked it on. A red light appeared above the condenser microphone.

"Well, I really haven't had time—I heard about it just an hour ago." Backpedaling, thinking about what he'd already said, figuring how to say nothing more. "How'd you get my name, anyway?"

"Someone in the Mayor's office mentioned you might be heading the case."

Which meant events were now moving forward faster than he could keep abreast of them. The Mayor's office was not going to let him breathe.

"I see. Look, honestly, I really don't know much about the case yet."

The reporter's eyebrows flew up in interest. He distrusted her high level of energy. "Do you want me to say that the chief man is unable to provide the simplest details of the case? Is that what the taxpayers are getting for their money?"

Up to this moment he had been willing to give her the benefit of the doubt—most reporters were not so bad, just doing their job, all part of the adversarial system that made America throb—but this was unfair at five forty-five in the morning. It was too early to be answering fish-bait questions intended to produce snappy J-school lead paragraphs.

"All right, shoot," Peter said tiredly, setting down his briefcase and pushing his gloveless hands into the pockets of his coat, letting his mind glide away from the idiocy of the moment, instead, searching for distraction of any kind, enjoying the sound of the few long-dead sycamore leaves whisking along the cobblestones. The sound and the crisp air reminded him of the mornings when he walked to school, his hair still slightly wet from the shower his mother used to make him take each morning, the smell of milk and bananas on his breath, his bookbag in one hand and the square, secure lunch box in the other, the Thermos rattling a little as he walked. Blowing spumes of breath in the cold air. The many mornings of one's life. He and Janice had stood in this same spot a thousand times, deciding when to call each other, dawdling before leaving, exchanging last-minute information about bills, work, money, the car, arguing, arguing about arguing, kissing to make up, believing with all their hearts that their lives were something beautiful.

"First," the reporter asked, "can you tell me the circumstances of the murder?"

"I'll tell you what I know, which is very little. We have a homicide of a young black male last night or early this morning in West Philadelphia. Apparently he is the nephew of the Mayor. A full investigation is under way."

"Do you have a suspect in custody?"

"I have no comment at this time. Certainly the police will question all those involved with the case. You guys always get that info from your own sources over there anyway. But if you call my office in a couple of hours, I'll be able to help you out."

"What's the suspect's name?"

"If there is *in fact* a suspect at this time, I can have that for you at the appropriate time, long before your first copy deadline. Literally, Miss Donnell, I have just woken up."

In addition to the tape recorder, she carried a reporter's notepad and now paused to scribble something—what, he didn't know, having said nothing important—and in the lull he reminded himself that he had better deal with this and all reporters sensibly. Not let his irritation show. The reporter looked up, her lips precise instruments through which to mete out difficult questions. "Do you feel that a case of such public interest could be directed by an inexperienced prosecutor?"

"Of course not," he snapped. "You get experience fast in the D.A.'s office. I've handled thousands of cases and a couple of hundred trials in my time."

"Is the killing drug-related?"

"We don't know."

"I've been told crack was found on the murder scene."

"I couldn't say if that's true."

"Do you think drugs were the motive?"

"Again, no comment. We're just beginning our investigation, miss. I've only known about—"

"Who found the body?" she persisted.

"I don't know, but I'll make sure you're informed."

"When will the medical examiner issue his report?"

"That depends on the length of the autopsy. Sometimes tissue tests have to be run that take extra time. We usually get a turnaround on a preliminary report in about a day. These questions are a bit general."

The reporter shot her glance over his shoulder toward the house, as if she'd seen something in the window.

"Are you happily married?" she asked.

He looked at her. The reporter smiled blithely at him.

"What?"

"I asked you if you were happily married." The corner of her mouth was turned up in coy aggressiveness.

"What kind of question is that?"

She began to open her mouth. He felt the coffee flick on in his brain—finally, a surge of energy.

"Oh," she said, grinning, "I suppose it's the kind of question—"

"*No!* Don't answer that, I will. Turn off that recorder!"

Surprisingly, she did. He moved closer to her.

"Now, *strictly* off the record, Miss Karen Donnell. I'll tell you exactly what kind of question that is. It's the kind of question that comes out of the mouth of a rookie reporter who comes to the city for the first time and who, listening to the police scanner early in the morning—God knows why, since *normal* people aren't up at five in the morning—plays some sort of lucky hunch or gets some backdoor information while talking on her car's cellular telephone to somebody who knows somebody and who then decides to camp out on my doorstep and see if she can't get a story before anyone else. What are you? Banished to the Main Line society beat as a rookie and impatient or something? I *know* the *Inquirer* newsroom is a shark nest, everyone trying to outwork everyone else to win this year's Pulitzer. But I'll tell you something else I know, lady. You don't write investigative stories in one day—no, don't protest. *Investigative* is the word you just used,

Miss Donnell. It's my job to remember what people say—I think you can appreciate *that*, since it's your job, too. As for the city desk, the first news budget meeting doesn't begin for hours. The national AP wire has just started to dump stories in your computer system. I guarantee you that if Japan buys General Motors, then not much else will appear on the front page. So that leaves me with the conclusion that your line about some front-page investigative feature is a bunch of small-town bluffing, though let me tell you one more thing before you get the hell out of here—and that is I *was* willing to give you the benefit of the doubt. After all, you are standing out here in the big bad cold. But the *tip-off*, the absolute *dead truth* came flying home to me when, after all your transgressions of professional journalistic conduct, which most everyone else on your paper seems to practice admirably enough, after all *that*, most of which I bet was just showing off, given what followed—after all *that*, you have the fucking *gall* to jab your way into my private business? What do you *care* whether I'm happily married? I'm not a celebrity, I'm not famous, I'm some average, private guy. And who the hell are you to ask, anyway? What are you, greedy? Not only does the early bird want the *worm*"—the reporter winced—"but she wants the page-one story, too. Suppose I were unhappily married and your question caused me genuine mental anguish? That would be terrific, wouldn't it? You're a great human being, and a super reporter, cultivating the confidence of your sources. Why, I'd say that you're set for a brilliant career."

She was nibbling her lip, refusing to react.

"Okay." He was miserable now. "Just respect me and I'll respect you. Call my office in a couple of hours and I'll give you the straight stuff."

He stared at her, waiting for a response.

"I'd heard about big-city prosecutors—" she recovered.

"Don't mind me, Miss Donnell. I'm not myself."

A light rain fell. In his own rarely used Ford, Peter drove west over the wet streets to West Philadelphia, replaying the conversation with the reporter, still angry but worrying that he had been unfairly virulent. He passed the massive Thirtieth Street train station, then skirted through the University of Pennsylvania, over to Baltimore Avenue. He'd spent seven years living in this part of the city during his undergraduate and law-school days. The houses were large, three-story professors' homes, well-maintained Victorian structures, which then gave way to the student roominghouses, many badly needing paint and even basic repair, then farther west, the smaller homes of the slums, many of which had crumbling stoops, broken windows, rotting porches, and above all, the inescapable mark of deepening poverty. Out here the city didn't even clean the streets.

He parked his car at the police barricade at Forty-fifth Street and Baltimore. A TV camera crew eating breakfast slumped in the open back of a transmitter van. Not far away, a clot of officers and detectives from the Eighteenth District huddled under the leafless branches at the door to the brick apartment house. He wouldn't immediately be recognized, for as a trial attorney he usually had little contact with the local investigation of a case. The logic of Hoskins's directive kicked in, however; seeing the crime scene might well be helpful if he needed to recreate it for a jury, and he could be present for any legal questions the detectives had. The car was warm and he sat there a moment more for pleasure, tasting Cassandra's eggs and coffee in his mouth. There was no doubt, he decided, that she was a lonely woman fighting the demographics, scavenging affection where she could. He would have to find some humane way to let her know he didn't want to see her again.

The policemen in their rain slickers milled about, lit cigarettes, rocked on their feet. They had probably divided the area into sectors and now had teams looking for witnesses, poking through trash cans, scuffing for information he'd eventually decide was sufficient for a formal charge. The official police file would contain blue carbons of the police reports, with the defense attorney receiving the white copies. Through the windshield he watched a few gawkers slide up to the police and ask questions. The cops shrugged noncommittally. Peter dealt with cops all the time, reading their reports, preparing statements, checking testimony as to the way evidence was seized so it would be admissible in court, but he had never been able to know why cops did what they did, what they thought in the deep brain. Becoming a policeman was not quite the neighborhood patronage system it used to be, and selection procedures were monitored carefully. What fed them? The identity of the uniform? Service? Power? Gun-lust? He admired the resilience necessary to cruise a beat month after month, endure risk and scorn. They had a hard job. Each year the citizenry poorer, more dependent on city services and more violent. Under Rizzo, the cops were an invincible, if brutal, army. Now there weren't enough of them to go around, and the city was cutting back again. In some neighborhoods, like Spanish Kensington, the cops no longer had credibility. Peter did not love cops but he respected them—they did what had to be done, that which no one in his right mind would do. And yet, so often they were stupid men, too, clumsy, unforgivably brutal. Every year they looked younger to him. In Philly, you still didn't have to be a high-school graduate to be a policeman. Cops protected themselves and one another, and distrusted lawyers as a matter of policy. A small but steady percentage of cops were corrupt, got caught. He wondered if all versions of men were stupid at times. Ninety-three percent of all felonies were committed by men. Again and again, the biological imperative toward aggressiveness drove men—even men socialized to be peaceful—into stupid, violent behavior. Had Whitlock been that kind of man and lost?

He locked his car and walked over to the barricade and showed identification. A cop thumbed him through the door, past several reporters and two heavy black women who were crying and asking to be allowed in. The apartment house was a thirty-unit job, five stories high, each apartment renting for about three hundred a month. The elevator was broken. He walked up the staircase, the treads slippery from policemen tramping up and down it in the rainy hours since the murder had been discovered.

At the landing on the third floor he followed the scratchy sound of a portable police radio down a dim hallway and into an apartment foyer. The dispatcher's voice was garbled, punctuated by blasts of static; the city radio transmitter network was riddled with dead spots, and many of the police radios were worn out. Inside the apartment, two detectives sat on a sofa. A policeman stood inside the doorway.

"Yeah, who are you?"

"Scattergood, from the D.A.'s office."

"We know what we're doing here."

"Is that in doubt?" He pushed through, saw that he was lucky. He knew one of the detectives, Harold Jones, an older man who once had a bullet pass through his ear. He liked to show the dime-sized scar as proof of luck. The other detective, a slick-haired young man, was making notes. Labeled plastic evidence bags lay on the couch.

"Hey there, Mr. Peter Scattergood." Jones looked up. "We don't usually have the pleasure of the presence of a representative of the D.A.'s office."

"I know you're overjoyed, Harold."

"Berger's not on this?"

91

"No. I got called in. What do we got here?" Peter nodded hello at the younger detective.

"We're almost done here. The lab guys been through and got prints and fibers," Jones began. "They're taking pictures now." He jerked his thumb toward the hallway. "Be done in a minute."

"Find much?"

"Not a thing."

"No drugs?" Peter started looking around the room.

"We had a dog up here earlier, and nothing in the apartment."

He didn't want to see a dead body and was happy to wait.

"Has the place been cleaned up?"

"Same as when we got here," the younger man said. "They just finished vacuuming."

"Who was here when you arrived?" Peter asked.

"Patrolmen Phillips and Axsom. They're downstairs."

"What'd they have?"

"Neighbor called from upstairs, heard a fight."

"What'd he see?"

"She—never saw nobody—"

"So who saw this guy Carothers?"

"Somebody else, a woman emptying her trash in the trash chute—she's down at headquarters being questioned. The lady upstairs who heard the fight, she called nine-one-one, and when the car got here, she insisted they follow it up."

"How'd they get in?"

"They called for backup and broke it down," the younger detective said. "Fucking cheap door. The door was locked. It'll be in the report."

"Good," Peter shot back, feeling tired at this sudden petty antagonism. "Glad to hear it." Sooner or later the young detective would learn that it paid to humor the D.A's office. But there was no point in returning the hostility; it was smarter to bring the young detective around to his side. "Say, I didn't catch your name."

"Al Westerbeck."

"Al, what kind of weapon do you think it was?"

The detective scowled, Peter saw. Hell, he too had done a lot of dramatic scowling in his first few years.

"Whitlock was shot a couple of times. We don't have a weapon or shells—"

"Hoskins said he'd been beaten."

92

"No, the girl was."

"The girl?" Peter exploded. "Hoskins didn't mention a girl. And he said the boy was beaten to death."

The detective sucked in his cheeks and shrugged in judgment. "Hoskins's information is old."

The police photography team bustled down the hallway carrying their aluminum camera cases.

"We're done." One of the men nodded.

"Let's have a look," Jones said.

The three men walked into the kitchen, where a slender young black man in bikini underwear lay on his side on a linoleum floor. He had been shot in the head and, where bullets had entered his skull, a glutinous, dull-red mass had congealed. Inside, thought Peter as he kneeled to look more carefully, had been an authentically superior mind. Another bullet had struck him in the shoulder blade. The boy had voided his bowels as he expired.

"What did the neighbor hear again?" Peter asked. "Exactly."

Westerbeck checked his notepad. "A girl screaming and some gunshots."

"One of them women outside said this was a pretty smart kid," Jones said.

Peter worried stupidly that the body was cold without clothes on. The limbs were already waxen; the boy's fingers were straight and beginning to stiffen. His glasses had been dragged under his face and now rested beneath his mouth. Blood had stained the lenses red. He'd bled the way a healthy young man with a good heart would be expected to bleed. Blood had in fact flowed copiously on the floor, following the cracks and slight cant of the linoleum tiles. The edge of the flow had congealed with dust and floor dirt. A neatly constructed peanut butter and jelly sandwich with one bite gone lay on the floor next to Whitlock's head. Blood had seeped into the crust of the bread. Whitlock's eyes were open with a look of undiverted attention to the food six inches before his face.

"Burns," Peter observed with forced detachment.

"Yeah, but only from one shot," Westerbeck confirmed. "We got a powder pattern over by the bedroom door. I think the perp got him in the shoulder first, the head second from across the room, then gave him the last one close. That's why we got burns on only one head-entry point. Like I said, the perp picked up the shells."

"The boy left the library at midnight, but didn't get here until early

93

this morning," Jones began to narrate. "This is his apartment, but the girl basically lived here, too. We're only about ten blocks from campus. . . ."

Peter stared at the sweet beauty of the boy's body, trying to will him back to life. The boy had known he was to die for only several seconds at most and, thankfully, hadn't suffered.

"Where are the kid's clothes?" he asked.

Westerbeck pointed at a folded shirt and pants on a kitchen chair and a pair of shoes set beside it.

"He took them off here in the kitchen. There's a house key on top, next to his watch and wallet. The wallet has eighty-six dollars in it, so robbery wasn't the motive. My guess is he came in late, undressed in the kitchen so he didn't wake the girl, got hungry and made a sandwich—"

"Then he got it," Peter interrupted. "Boom."

A double homicide was big trouble; it created more pressure, and ran into the issue of the death penalty, which ran into a grab bag of related issues. It worried him that neither Hoskins nor the Mayor knew about the girl. How could they not know?

"But it's cold in here," he said. "Why would he take his clothes off in a cold kitchen?"

"I hadn't thought of that," Westerbeck admitted.

"It probably means the window wasn't open at the time," Peter said, feeling he was observing the obvious. "Where's the girl?"

The men walked into the bedroom, where a beautiful black girl lay on the bed. The covers were pulled up to her chin and her eyes were shut. Peter noticed how long her lashes were.

"Something blunt and in the bathroom, where she was hiding," Westerbeck reported. "Pretty sure at this point."

Peter turned his head toward the bathroom. The door was marred by a broken latch and a long, almost casual swipe of blood on the white paint. On the bathroom floor were pink stretch leotards and aerobics shoes.

"The perp kicked in the bathroom door and got her on the head and put her here, maybe after she died," Westerbeck reported earnestly. "The blood pattern in the bed is a seep. I don't think she was pumping it out of the back of her head. No thrashing pattern of blood on the sheets, no convulsions. Her face and eyelids are stiff and so are her limbs, so my guess is she died up to an hour before Whitlock."

Peter noticed on the floor a jump rope and exercise leg weights that attached at the ankle.

"The guy busted that lock and dragged her out's my guess. They didn't trash the room. Her name is Johnetta Henry."

There was something interesting in all this, some illogical nugget.

"Jonesy, you said the neighbor heard yelling, or something," Peter said. "A fight. And the responding officers showed up and kicked down the door. But it's obvious Whitlock was *surprised*. And the girl dead an hour before—"

He stopped talking, looked at the two men. They were watching him intently.

"What?" Jones challenged.

"Not sure," Peter lied, not knowing why, except that the detective seemed defensive. This was no time to create ill will by second-guessing the police. "Guess the perp waited and knew Whitlock would be home."

"Right," Westerbeck said.

"Course, that doesn't explain why the murders were committed differently, does it?"

No word came from the detectives.

"A man," Peter mused pointedly, despite his efforts to be diplomatic, "who has a gun will use it in favor of anything else, all other things being equal. A man who has no gun will use whatever he has. Got an answer to that, Westerbeck?"

"He killed *her* in a fight and didn't think he'd been heard, then he waited for the boy. Killed him with the gun and left. Pretty simple to me."

Ah, simplicity. For him, a charged word. It was one of the Quaker values, instilled in Peter his whole childhood: Live a simple, peaceful life that is socially useful. How few people actually did that. Peter stared absentmindedly at the girl's face. He half desired to bend over and gently, reverently, kiss her cheek as a benediction from the quick to the dead. He wondered if he were going insane, concluded that might be true, and forced himself to consider the information at hand: The neighbor heard the girl's screams, Jones had said, then called the police. The girl had died up to an hour before Whitlock had been shot to death—and Whitlock was dead when the police broke in. Therefore gunshots had sounded *after* the police had been called. And the neighbor, Westerbeck had just said, had also heard shots before calling the police. There was a logical fallacy in this account—the caller could not have done both these things unless *two* calls had been made before the police had come. That would explain why the neighbor insisted the officer break down the door. In fact, it was unlikely the police would

95

break down the door on the basis of anything less; they hated to deal with domestic fights and would rather let the minor skirmishes resolve themselves. What was apparent, based on the evidence the detectives had unwittingly divulged, was that the police took around *an hour* to show up—a fantastic, unbelievable amount of time—and in that period, the Mayor's nephew got his. Did the two police detectives realize all this?

"You said the neighbor mentioned gunshots in her call, right?" he asked casually.

"I said that, right."

"There was a second nine-one-one."

"Why?" Westerbeck said.

He wasn't going to be able to keep his mouth shut. "This is *your* speciality, guys, not mine. But you might as well listen up. Here are the order of events. First, you got a girl's screams, which are heard by the neighbor and results in, two, the call to the police. When the police finally show up *after* the sound of gunshots, they find the girl who was screaming dead for an hour—based on rigor mortis—and a boy dead of gunshots minutes prior. The girl died first, after the call but before shots had been fired, then shots were fired, which resulted in another call to the police and then they showed up."

The other men were silent and maybe angry.

Peter said, "Where's the neighbor who saw the guy, Jonesy?"

"Like I said, she's down at Eighth and Race. She made the ID and gave them a statement."

If the death of the Mayor's nephew could be associated with a slow police response time, then there was a perverse spin to this whole thing already. But he wasn't ready to make any conclusions. The 911 operator routed calls to a dispatcher while a computer assigned the call a priority value of zero to six. Fives and sixes were often never answered, and in the worst spots of the city the police sometimes let street fights—threes and fours—continue without response in order to avoid injury and hassle.

But, as if he were reading Peter's mind and wished to discredit the D.A.'s office, Jones muttered quietly, "Berger's into the junk, ain't he? That why he's not here?"

"Berger's in Harrisburg. He'll be back in the city around lunchtime. *That* is why he's not here."

Peter examined the girl's sunken eye sockets and the tautness of the skin around her temples and cheekbones. He looked around the room. "What do you think here?"

"I say the perp got out the kitchen window, up the fire escape, over to the next building."

"How do you know?" Peter asked. "That still doesn't answer the question why Whitlock took his clothes off in a cold kitchen. Unless the window was closed by the perp when he came inside, and re-opened when he fled."

"Right."

"Maybe—that assumes the perp came in the window in the first place, which could be wrong. Get somebody to rebuild that front door and figure out how the lock was constructed. See if it locked with a key from the outside or if it pulled shut locked or opened with a credit card through the crack."

"Right." Jones scribbled a note to himself. "You should see her body, and I'm not being a sicko, either."

He reached over and pulled back the sheets. The girl was naked and slender. Except for the matted red wool of her head wound, her body was untouched and possessed a supple, holy stillness. Her arms lay at her side, as if she were sleeping with no anxiety at being vulnerable, or peacefully submitting to an examination, which of course she was. Peter ran a fingernail over her stomach, feeling the lack of subcuta-neous fat and the tight corrugation of muscle. Her breasts were flat knobs of nipple, her navel a tight slit. He knew, without seeing it, that she had a terrific ass. And he knew what a pig he was for thinking about such a thing, too.

Now he took one finger and deferentially pulled up her lip, bending close to examine her teeth. They were perfect.

"Any signs of rape?" he asked.

"None, but the lab will tell us for sure. I think she must have been into the junk to get that thin," the detective said.

"That all you think about, who's into the junk?" Peter responded. "This girl was in great condition. Find out if she belonged to an exercise club, dance class, something like that."

Peter looked at her face. Lividity—the gravitational movement of body fluids to the lowest-lying portions of the corpse—had set in, but she retained much of the color of life. So often black women had such beautiful skin, even black women in their fifties, better than white women twenty years younger. He covered the body and for the first time looked around the room carefully. Preppy clothes, the boy's biology, chemistry, and anatomy textbooks in the shelves. A VCR, dozens of trashy rock-video cassettes next to it. Near that, carefully labeled notebooks and Polaroids of some spongy stuff probably taken through a microscope. In the closet were Air Jordans, L. L. Bean duckshoes, Gucci loafers. America: A person no longer lived a life-style, but bought it. He tried to piece it together. Where did the money come from? Why was the girl cowering in the bathroom? The dead couple had a future, were on their way up. Who would want to kill them? Who would dare?

"Did the crime unit get any kind of blood pattern?" he asked. "Flecks, drops?"

"You're going to have to check that with them."

"So you think he went up the fire escape?" Peter said.

"I think that's the way he came in, too."

"Why?" he asked.

" 'Cause the front door was locked."

"Maybe the perp came in peaceably and she locked it after him or he locked it himself after closing the door. Or locked it on the way out," Westerbeck suggested.

"That doesn't explain why she was in the bathroom."

"They had a fight and she ran into the bathroom."

"Or she suddenly heard him come in and locked both doors. I think that's it. She wouldn't have locked it if she knew he had the key—she would have fled. Which means he slipped the lock or came in through the window. Also," Jones reasoned further, "if she knew he had the key and if she was in trouble, she wouldn't stay here. She could have left through the window, too."

"Right, so if the door couldn't be slipped, then he had a stolen key or came in through the window," said Peter, thinking to himself out loud, at the same time vaguely tired at all of this circular logic nec-essary to play out every possible scenario. "If she did lock the two doors and hide in there, why didn't she have clothes on and why wouldn't she call the police? Maybe she did call and we don't know it. The girl's the secret to this. I noticed the phone has a long cord. Get whoever knows this apartment, her mother or somebody, to tell us where she usually kept the phone. This girl's neat as a pin. She's the kind to put the phone back in the same place after using it. See if the phone was always pulled into the bedroom like this."

The detectives weren't used to taking orders from an A.D.A. They just scowled and didn't speak.

"Did somebody check under the fire escape?" Peter asked. "Why couldn't he have gone down?"

"It's rusted shut. It would be something like a thirty-foot drop."

"So then we know he didn't begin his entry with the fire escape."

"Some of those black guys can jump pretty high," Jones cracked.

Peter ignored this. "What's above it?"

"The ladder leads right up to the rooftop," Westerbeck said. "And there are a couple of other buildings he could have gone down."

"All right."

Despite a little bungled logic, the detectives knew, of course, what they were doing. They could continue without him. He wanted to leave, anyway. He didn't like standing around with dead bodies.

"What's wrong?" Jones asked.

"I don't like standing around with dead bodies."

"You're an office man, what do you expect?"

"Keep in touch, Harold."

"Yeah."

"One more thing, okay?" Peter stood up, looked at the girl again. He'd see her many times again in the photographs taken that morning.

"Yeah, what?" Jones answered.

"If Berger's got his problems—and who the hell really knows what they are, anyway—the whole world doesn't need to know about them, what do you say?"

"I was talking confidentially, but I hear you."

"People have problems," he said, getting his coat from the living room. He looked at his watch: almost eight A.M. "Myself included."

"Tell me about it," Jones said, lighting a cigarette. "You're fucking golden in this city."

Back in his car, Peter heard the radio newscaster announce in somber, thrilled tones the death of the Mayor's nephew. He drove east on Baltimore, back to Center City. The death of the boy was the second leading story, just behind the new trouble in the Middle East. In the short run, it was a hot story. In the long run, almost nobody would care, because something else, some new happy disaster that sold newspapers and justified advertising rates, would come along. The grand design, the deep trends, the stuff that really mattered—well, he'd long since realized he was going to live without really knowing what was happening in the time and place of his life. History had a way of clarifying the essence of foolishness, and no one liked to believe themselves to be a fool.

He turned the radio off and parked behind the D.A.'s office at 1300 Chestnut. Inside the front doors, the detective on desk duty waved him through to the elevators. The homicide unit offices were on the seventh floor; the coffee-stained carpeting and hallways lined high with boxes of files belied the tremendous power hidden within the messy cubicles where the attorneys worked.

Cassandra had called him, and this surprised him, for certainly he had not expected to hear from her so soon. Didn't she have some meeting to attend? That she had called was a bad sign—it meant she had not reasonably considered the kind of day he was having. Cassandra represented a temporary weakness, a mistake he had made, and he told himself he would not make it again. He wanted to remember the sex as mediocre, which in fact it probably had been, given they didn't know each other, but what lingered unwanted in his mind was the absolute, animal pleasure of lying in bed with another warm body.

He sat at his desk fiddling with the papers and the stained Styrofoam coffee cups from the day before, missing Janice and staring vacantly into space, half knowing he was living now in the moment that came each morning at work before he lost himself, forgot who the hell he was, and plunged into the day, only to reemerge late in the afternoon a day older, a day more permanently tired. Seven hours ago he had been humping a strange woman. Two hours ago he had talked to the Mayor of the fifth-largest city in America. An hour ago he had stared at a dead woman's face. Ten minutes ago he was eating a doughnut with commuters just in off the trains, snapping their *Wall Street Journal*s as they turned the pages.

The phone rang, and a detective identified himself.

"We got Carothers."

"I know," Peter asked. "You got an ID and ran him in."

"Going to work."

"As he showed up for work?"

"Yeah. The paperwork should be on your desk in maybe an hour."

"You guys are working fast for a change," Peter said.

"Well, we got a call from the Mayor's office saying they wanted this done by the book. In *my* book," the detective complained, "that means he wants no fuckola bullshit screw-ups, so we did the paper right away."

"You prepared a warrant for Carothers's place?"

"That's what I was callin' you for, yeah."

Peter heard the details and gave agreement on the search warrant. With the form approved by the on-duty judge, the police would search Carothers's belongings that morning.

100

Outside, the traffic rose, the city rumbled into full motion, hundreds of thousands of cars streaming in from the expressway, drivers listening to morning drive programs on the radio. He stood at his seventh-floor window to watch the people hurrying along Thirteenth Street; there was no solace in his similarly infinitesimal position. He did not mind being one small, limited man, but it galled him to think that there were others who were living his exact life, give or take a few specifics, in Philadelphia and other cities all over America. Other promising young white men with good conventional educations who rose in the morning and put on a suit and went to work and lived. The pre-work scene this morning had been an aberration. A million men like him bought *USA Today* because of the good sports section, shaved their faces five mornings a week at the same time, knew at any moment exactly how many women they had slept with, and what their total worth was, could identify the local news station by the lead-in music on the telecast, knew by heart every door between their bedrooms and their offices. Men who as teenagers had measured their erect penises and occasionally wondered if it had grown any longer or shorter since then, who had read some of the great texts—Peter had once read every essay by Ralph Waldo Emerson—and had forgotten nearly everything that was in them, who all thought it would be great someday to take a couple of months and drive around America in a camper, who had started to watch their waistlines with morbid curiosity, who finally understood by dint of repetition of experience *who* their fathers were and what they had suffered, who didn't read the Op-Ed pages as carefully as they would have liked, who didn't know their world geography well, who guiltily thought racist thoughts from time to time, and who had never experienced any true form of material hardship or known few people who actually had, and who were not yet afraid of death.

Would he ever do something that was great, something that was in *any* way memorable? Would he live his life and when he died, the surface of time would close over him as if, for all purposes, he had never lived? No wonder people had children; a child was proof one had existed. Even these very thoughts, he knew, were hopelessly typical, the expectable thoughts had by other men. Perhaps his entire mind was largely similar to those of other men. For three years he had been trained to think in the conventional structures of the law. Grinding away in the law library, outlining cases, walking into his constitutional law class absolutely *ready*, confident that the professor could grill him and he would be able to respond perfectly. Nothing but

101

pathetic vanity. He'd been serviceable in constitutional law, a dullard in tax law, a wizard in criminal law.

By the third year, after a summer internship, he'd known he wanted to work for the District Attorney's office. He still had his framed letter of appointment in a closet somewhere, and remained glad he hadn't taken a regular private-practice job. While other freshly minted J.D.s were sitting in some twenty-fifth-floor law firm library, he'd been slugging it out with public defenders, sleaze-bag defense attorneys, the full palette of criminal personalities, judges on the take. He had worked with some great lawyers, too; top pros, like Berger. It was one of the few decisions of which he was proud. Janice had been proud of him, too, though in retrospect she may have wished he had gone into a big firm. The work would have been just as hard, the hours as long, but the emotional roughage almost negligible. If he had gone corporate, he would be making *deep* into the six figures. Could he have bought off some of Janice's unhappiness? Probably. He could have taken her on great trips, hired someone to come in and clean twice a week. But he would have achieved—he was certain of this, knowing his own weaknesses—the state of being a walking, talking dead man, deader than he was even now. He saw such men every day around town, their lives inescapably rooted in the transmission of wealth from others to themselves. They rotted invisibly from within, for their work had little to do with actual life. He hated them, and for some of the wrong reasons. They knew they were stuck in a system and had decided to get as fat as possible off of it; this did not seem entirely undesirable. They looked down on attorneys like him, who in their eyes did what amounted to unpaid dirty work. Of course, all other things being equal, in court none of them had enough experience to carry his briefcase. He hated them because of their greed and he hated them because, unlike him, they seemed to be absolutely safe.

So, Peter decided, kicking his feet onto his desk, wishing he could get away from the office, he was going to take a risk, like taking a good foul in basketball—it could hurt you but the potential cost was worth the potential gain. Janice's absence was driving him toward some sort of action, wasn't it? He was pissed off, wasn't he? Yes. And unable to see this whole unhappy episode as anything other than a *stage* of the marriage, from which they would emerge intact? Yes. He made sure his door was shut, then flipped through his Rolodex to *V*. He dialed and walked the phone to the window.

"Yeah."

"Vinnie, this is Peter Scattergood."

"Peter. It's been a long time," coughed a hoarse voice. "How's the hangman business?"

"A thrill a minute."

"I understand you guys been busy this morning. What can I do for you?"

Vinnie got right to the important question, with no time for falsely sentimental chitchat about shared boyhoods when there was business to attend to. As an Italian from South Philadelphia with forty years of family connections, Vinnie understood the city differently than Peter, had grown up in ward politics, and often knew at least remotely the men of Sicilian descent in good suits who from time to time were found dead in the back of new black Cadillacs. It was no accident he was situated in the police radio room. Vinnie's father had made enough money in the construction business to allow the family to spurn the Catholic schools and send their four boys to Penn Charter to get prepped for college, which Vinnie had decided he hadn't needed, much to his father's anger. Vinnie and Peter had traded off at the forward position for three years. Vinnie, a terrible shooter, would clog the lane with his thick, hairy trunk and foul unmercifully—a knee in the balls, a sudden elbow in the gut, and a look the other way. Vinne had tired out the sleek black wizard shooters the other Inter-Academic League private schools imported on scholarship like contraband from selected Philadelphia neighborhoods to beef up otherwise lily-white squads. Then Peter would come in, start setting picks, passing, hitting short bank shots. He had never much liked Vinnie but had always been compelled by his frank dishonesty, been amazed at the way he cut practices, cheated in scrimmages, claimed he had butt-fucked the coach's wife. By age seventeen, Vinnie was covertly arranging abortions for the knocked-up girlfriends of classmates. He and Vinnie saw each other at the alumni basketball game every couple of years.

"I need to find a car, Vinnie."

"Right. Say, I'm gonna be eating a late breakfast, Peter. Let me give you my deli number."

Peter waited five minutes while Vinnie left his office and, presumably, went to a public phone. Then he dialed.

"Vinnie?"

"Peter."

"You sound pretty paranoid."

"The phones are bad in my office. In my whole fucking department. An FBI guy is screwing a secretary down the hall. She doesn't
know we know, but we know."

"I'm looking for a car."

"Some cars are hard to find. We got over a million vehicles registered in the greater metropolitan area. Plus junk plus stolen plus
chopshop."

"I need it quickly and quietly." He hoped Vinnie was not taping
the conversation to blackmail him later. "All I want is a *pattern.* Where
it's parked and when."

"I can get it put on the teletype to the precincts," Vinnie responded.
"At each roll call, the men on patrol will be reminded it's one of the
cars they're looking for. One out of many, you understand? That's all
I can guarantee."

Peter stood at his window. On the corner below, a SEPTA bus
tapped the rear of a taxi. He told Vinnie the license number.

"What's it look like?"

"An 'eighty-eight Subaru wagon. Yellow, light yellow. Scratch
along the right side." Janice was a good driver, but somebody had
nailed her in the Acme parking lot. "There's a green NOW sticker on
the bumper."

"Now?"

"National Organization for Women."

"Never heard of it. Ha. Go on."

"It has jumper cables and a rocking chair in the back."

"A rocking chair?"

"It was on its way to be fixed. A slat broke."

"You know this car pretty well."

"Yes." The chair had belonged to his grandmother and then his
mother. He had been nursed in it. His grandfather had even died in
it, dropping his head to one side, spittle on his lips.

"How long will this take?" Peter hugged the phone with his chin,
and found his briefcase.

"Give me a place to start."

To answer Vinnie would be the first real transgression against Janice. Sleeping with Cassandra was wrong, but it didn't violate the
terms of the separation. Telling Vinnie to go ahead constituted his
first infringement on Janice's new autonomy. But he didn't see any
other way, short of hiring a private detective, who would take time to
find and who would cost more money than he was currently able to

pay. He himself could follow her home from work, but she would be wary that he would try that, and if he were caught, it would hurt his cause. What else? He could call up all Janice's friends and try to worm it out of them, but that would be embarrassing, not necessarily successful, and certain to get back to her. Her phone couldn't be traced. It had occurred to him that when the checks he gave Janice were returned to him by the bank, he might be able to figure out what neighborhood she was in, and then ask around a little. But that would be in a couple of weeks, and he didn't have the patience. He was beginning to imagine things about Janice that upset him—sex, namely—and beginning to fear his own desperate nature.

"Try around the forty-two hundred block of Spruce, around there, days," he finally answered. "Brick, three stories, side entrance."

"You mean the women's shelter."

"The location is supposed to be secret."

"Not to me." Vinnie sounded bored.

"Well, keep it to yourself. It's secret for a good reason."

"Right, right."

"Try there days." He emptied yesterday's paperwork from his briefcase onto the desk.

"Yeah. Am I looking for a car or a driver?"

"Just let me know where the car is nights."

"You can expect to hear from me shortly. And, Peter?"

"What?"

"Sorry your wife moved out."

"Don't fuck with me, Vinnie."

He hung up. The office felt too small. Everything felt too small, including each minute—he was due in court in an hour, and would be unprepared. He suffered a capricious urge to dump all his trial preparation reports out the window, to let the intimate trash of other lives flutter through the corridors of buildings. Maybe a couple of sheets—police charging forms, ballistics, medical examiner's report, any of it—would float up against Janice's door, her window, wherever the hell she was staying. She would wake up one morning and see little Judy Warren's picture blown flat against her window, and know that he, Peter, was not so evil, after all. Judy Warren's corpse, photographed with dispassionate expertise by the police evidence team, showed, by virtue of its roasted shanks, the scalp shaved and blackened by heat, the body sprawled on charred furniture, that he, Peter Scattergood, was not evil. He was many things—insensitive, emotionally sloppy, selfish—but he was not evil, and this knowledge gave him a queer sense of resolve. Vinnie could help him out. Calling Vinnie was neither bad nor good, it was inevitable. Did Janice think he was some kind of fool? You don't just let your wife run away, you go after her. He felt no ability to mediate on his own behalf. The only way through was to plunge as deeply and rapidly as he could. He was a very reasonable man, but reason was no longer relevant. He had lost control and now he must do anything he could to get it back. He was furious. Janice had left him and this he would never allow.

FIVE

One of the jurors in the Robinson case, it turned out, had a sick ten-year-old boy and would not be able to make it to court until the afternoon. Such a delay was typical, and thus he would have a reprieve for a few hours before the closing arguments, which he still hadn't outlined. But the Whitlock case wouldn't allow him to prepare; the detectives kept calling. Wayman Carothers was not talking, of course, not without a lawyer. According to the senior detective, Carothers was sitting down at the Police Roundhouse at Eighth and Race with folded arms and a bored, fuck-you expression on his streetwise face. He'd dealt with police before. His attorney was in St. Croix, he'd told detectives, and he was expecting to be formally charged soon—either that or be set free.

The neighbor, Wanda Douglas, who said she remembered him standing outside the apartment of the dead couple had identified his face in the large mug-shot books. Now the detectives were stalling for time, checking into Carothers's whereabouts on the night of the murders. Miss Douglas, a chronic insomniac, had decided to take the garbage to the apartment building's trash chute, she had told detectives. Why had she decided to empty the trash then? Because during the day the janitor fired up the incinerator and bits of ash and smoke drifted up the chute into her face, she said. She thought it was after three A.M. but couldn't be sure. A man had been standing at the door to the Whitlock apartment. Had he gone in? the police questioned. She didn't know, maybe. All she remembered was that he was breathing hard, a black man in his twenties in a long black coat. She thought

107

she'd seen him around the neighborhood from time to time—he looked the same in his picture as he had the previous evening, she could say that, all right. He had keys in his hand. She thought she'd heard steps in the hall earlier in the night but couldn't be sure. Miss Douglas had been sent home with strict instructions not to discuss the case with anyone, and to inform police if anyone threatened her or members of her family.

This was the beginning of a case, Peter thought, but not much. There were so many questions not asked, questions any defense attorney would seize on. How much light was there in the hall? How far away was the woman standing? Did she usually wear glasses and did she have them on? None of this information was there—the police had only asked the most cursory of questions. And for all anybody knew, the man letting himself into the apartment had only been there a minute. Maybe he hadn't even gone into the apartment or had nothing to do with the murder. That Carothers had been identified within hours of the murders seemed almost impossible to believe, a lightning bolt of luck. And there was something else, Peter realized privately. A girl such as Johnetta Henry would have no reason to open a kitchen window in the dead of the night—it was too cold for her fatless body. And it was unlikely the apartment was too warm, not for three hundred dollars a month. If Carothers had in fact entered and left the apartment via the hallway, which was logical to assume since he'd been seen standing there with a key, then why was the window wide open?

More paperwork and information arrived, including a report describing the detainment of Wayman Carothers at his place of employment, a moving company in northeast Philadelphia. He had been taken in for custodial interrogation shortly before five A.M. while gassing up the moving van at the company loading dock. He was headed out of town on a two-day run to Pittsburgh. He had gone peaceably. "Suspect cooperative, and said nothing," the typed report read. "Suspect appears to be alert and calm. Dressed in blue mover's overalls, with work boots."

Meanwhile, the preliminary analysis by the assistant medical examiner had placed the time of Johnetta Henry's death as between two forty-five and three-thirty that morning, based on the progression of lividity. Algor mortis—body temperature at the time of examination—was less accurate, the report said, due to the lack of body fat and the open window near the body in the apartment, but confirmed the lividity finding. The formal write-up would take a while to be transcribed and delivered, but for now, this information would be assumed to be accurate. Whitlock was still being examined. The cause of the girl's death was two severe blows to the head with a blunt instrument, but it was also clear that she had been strangled in the struggle; her hyoid bone, just above the Adam's apple, had been fractured. These injuries had occurred within at most a few minutes; it was conceivable that she lost consciousness while being strangled and then received the death blows to the head. There were no needle marks, no incisions, no deep bruises, no internal injuries. And though she was naked at the time of death, there were no signs of sexual abuse, no semen, no hair cuts into the vagina, nothing. She had not menstruated in at least several months, due to inadequate body fat. Though she was slightly anemic, the examiner concluded that she was quite healthy, with a strong heart and clear lungs. All internal organs appeared healthy and normal. Her muscle tone was excellent. The blows that killed her would have killed anybody and were meant to kill. Toxicology studies showed that the victim had no alcohol or narcotics in her bloodstream at the time, nor was there any evidence of chronic use of either. The examiner could find no blood, hair, or skin samples beneath her fingertips. There was a slight hematoma above one eye, but the examiner did not feel this was the result of a sharp blow; it was soft and shallow, more likely due to slumping forward against a wall or floor before her heart stopped beating. The victim had once given birth, not recently.

From detectives came the information that Johnetta Henry had last been seen leaving the University of Pennsylvania main library, where Whitlock had also been. Her fingerprints were all over the apartment, as were Whitlock's. Five other fingerprints had been found in the apartment, but none of them matched Carothers's. Friends said Johnetta often read in the library with Whitlock while he studied biology. They said she and Whitlock had been steady for over a year, though she was quite a bit older than he. She had worked at a variety of jobs—telephone sales, office support in the Mayor's election campaign—and most recently as an aerobics instructor at a local gym. The gym was a known distribution point of illegal steroids, but the police didn't feel she was involved. The consensus was that she was bright and determined but, until she met Whitlock, had received few opportunities for advancement. That she was devoted to him was unquestioned, and she had openly talked about the life they might have together as he climbed into the professional ranks. She planned to go with Whitlock when he attended medical school at Harvard. It was she who bought him the expensive clothes and dressed him well. Whitlock, for his part, was considered brilliant yet naive, a bit of a bookworm, well-meaning yet emotionally immature, outwardly idealistic but passive in most respects, and passionate only about science, but lost without Johnetta. She had been his first girlfriend, and it was probable he had been a virgin until he met her. There had been many men in her past but no one else in a long time. Friends remarked that the couple seemed mismatched; others said they thought she controlled him, or just knew what he needed. They had lived together about a year, with no apparent conflict. Friends interviewed by the police said he seemed happier than ever, and appeared comfortable with her coming with him to medical school the following autumn when he started his studies. His family agreed that he seemed happy but said they doubted she would have followed him to medical school.

How often these murders were lodged within the most mundane of details. One moment a girl is sitting in a library thumbing through *Cosmo* or some other magazine preying upon female insecurities, looking at the nail polish ads or reading about how to build a happy relationship, and a few hours later confronting her killer. Did the victim ever have a moment to reflect upon the sudden shift of realities? Or was the moment so elemental, so engaging of the instinct that such rumination was impossible? Johnetta Henry had left the library and gone home alone, to wait for a call from her mother. What could be more mundane?

And this was all they had so far. None of it, Peter saw, explained why the police had taken an hour to show up. Before he was due in court again, he decided to talk it over with Berger, who, back from Harrisburg, he found in the men's room baring his teeth in the mirror.

"Filing them down?" Peter said.

"Bad gums, same as my mother." Berger shook his head. "Destiny."

"Or bad flossing. How was your trip?"

"I got there. Her lawyer called last night and said her medication cycle meant she was most alert at five in the morning, don't ask me why. I got her to say what we needed and took the train home. If she dies tomorrow, her words live on."

Berger, Peter had decided long ago, had been a smart-alecky, jitterbug shortstop know-it-all kind of boy. Pesky sharp nose, quick to argue, with an eagerly destructive intelligence. The years in the D.A.'s office had worked their wear, however. As Berger grimaced before the mirror, Peter could see that Berger's face was shifting, dropping, the skin under the jaw heavier and thicker, the hair thinning to a sparse, unhappy bristle on top. In the seven years they had known each other, folds had appeared ever so subtly above Berger's eyes, and his cheeks had become lower and heavier by the thickness of a new legal pad. With this change had come a deepening of character toward melancholic sarcasm—Berger no longer cared how smart he was, for his intelligence had only made him see things he wished he hadn't.

"You have any idea what those operations cost?"

"I asked you if you flossed, motherfucker."

"Never. Who has time for preventive maintenance?" Berger asked, lifting his high freckled forehead. "Hey, incidentally, Hoskins pulled an LBJ on me about two minutes ago. He came in and sat on the can and started giving me orders—"

"What did he say?"

Berger turned around, his face grave. He checked the door. "He said not to give you any help on the Whitlock murder."

"What?"

"Maybe that means he *wants* me to help you. Maybe it means he doesn't want me to, and is making it sound like he's giving you a test to see if you can fly on your own. Maybe he's trying to split us up."

"You know what?" Peter said. "Fuck him."

"Exactly. Anyway, have you heard from Janice?"

"Bergs, I'm getting worried. I don't like this."

"Get a lawyer. That's all I can tell you."

Peter stared into the urinal.

"You got to protect yourself," Berger told him.

"I'm not convinced I need a lawyer yet."

"That's the problem, you need a dose of reality. Come on, I've got Tama in my office." Berger waved at the door, and they headed down the hall. "Anyway, I shit thee not, buddy. A good divorce lawyer will help you work it out so you aren't begging for change on your lunch break. You can be sure she's got someone already and he's telling her how to position herself for a fight. He has her writing down what your income has been, what the joint assets are. He's going to come at you with all kinds of requests for paper. They want to know the number of hairs on your ass. These guys are merciless. Every tax return.

Every check you've written for five years, and they're going to get it, too. It doesn't matter that no kids are involved, either. You two were married before you went to law school?"

"We married my last year." During the ceremony, he had kept his eyes open a second longer than Janice before they kissed, and so he had seen the trust in her closed eyelids, the implicit hope in her pressed lips.

Berger's office door was open and Peter shut it gently. Berger's daughter was playing on the rug and had pulled out a couple of law books.

"Hi, Tama," Peter said to the child.

"She supported you?" Berger went on, jabbing at him mechanically, thinking more like a lawyer than a friend.

"Some."

"How much?"

"Don't know." He turned to the child. "Why's she here?"

"My wife usually picks her up. We had a little—things are just a little hectic. . . . Say hello to Mr. Scattergood," Berger prompted his daughter.

"Hello," she whispered, barely looking up from her toys. Peter wondered if the child's hair had been brushed that morning.

"Well, I don't think it looks very good," Berger said.

"Past and future valuation of advanced professional degree as part of the settlement?" Peter responded absentmindedly. Tama was absolutely beautiful. How could such a beautiful child have been spawned by such a burn-out twitch like Berger? More to the point, how was it that beautiful children became wretched, burnt-out twitches? Peter was half in love with Tama. On the night she was born, Berger had called him from the hospital, saying words he'd never forgotten: "We're in the thick of it now."

"Of course that's what I mean," Berger went on, pursuing the divorce issue.

"She wouldn't do that, she has too much pride."

"Hey—I love Janice, too. Don't look at me like that, Peter." Berger pulled out a pen. "This guy's good." He scribbled a number. "Doesn't shit around—tells you what you're up against. He handled my brother's divorce. Give him a call."

"We'll see." About matters of love, he didn't trust Berger, whose own marriage had long been in famous tatters. Berger carried specially prepared business cards to use when he picked up secretaries in the Center City bars. On the reverse of the cards Berger had printed, I FIND YOU VERY ATTRACTIVE. He took the secretaries to the Hershey Hotel, always using the same room, if it was available.

"I suggest—Tama, *don't!*" he yelled, then softly, apologetically, "Those are Daddy's books. . . ."

Tama dropped her head and was quiet.

"Lot of good-looking women around, pal," Berger went on. "You should see—"

"I've seen them, all of them," Peter said. "Bergs, I want to *find* my wife."

"Yeah, wives . . ." Berger looked at his fingers, comparing the left hand to the right. He turned his palms up, examined them. His forehead glistened. "Things are very bad, Peter. Very. I'm, ah, thinking of—we're having some definite money problems. It's not that we're wiped out—"

Peter didn't answer. The other side of Berger, the side that swapped spit with women in public, also probably did a little recreational coke in his off time, just as Jones, the detective, had hinted. Maybe Berger was getting careless, making buys from people who had recognized him or who had sold that information to the cops. Peter had always half known, and in the last few months it was apparent Berger was beginning to drown. Should he say something? He loved Berger, as a confidante, a colleague, a fellow man of the world. He loved Berger's many despicable traits, even. Other than a chronic sniffling, Berger didn't show many symptoms. And there was no joy in looking for them—Berger was his best friend. They had a balanced relationship; Berger was smarter, but needed Peter's approval. As a lawyer, Berger was tops in the office. His in-court perfectionism was entirely unintentional, the by-product of a mind that worked like a man painting a white room white who never believes he has finished. And yet he was unlike so many of the attorneys in the office, especially Hoskins, who stormed and stammered and seemed to think that hours worked would *always* win out over brilliance. More than once, while all of them argued around the table in the two-hundred-year-old tavern behind the office, Berger occasionally let loose a remark that stopped Hoskins in his tracks like a spear hurled from across a room. Hoskins had an ego that functioned like an immune system; it flowed to any wound and absorbed and neutralized all alien information. Berger didn't work that way. He was habitually at the office at six A.M. handling the most difficult and publicized cases, often being interviewed, eloquent in a tired and dispassionate way, impeccably dressed, the epitome of well-prepared calm in the courtroom, able to wriggle out of the constitutional snares set by the private-practice defense attorneys—many of them former prosecutors. He could face down the most recalcitrant of witnesses, fluster them into betraying themselves, surprising the truth from them like a bird flushed from concealing underbrush. Berger, more than anyone, had taught Peter his job.

"So what about Hoskins? You have anything specific to say to me about handling this case?"

"Don't take it on Hoskins's terms," he continued in the same ruminative voice. "The pressure is too much. You think you can *manage* the pressure, but it adds up. You think you can handle it, that everything is under control. In fact, the more it's out of control the more excited you get about keeping everything under control—you have to go faster and faster, you have to start really flying to keep up with everything. I found myself—don't even get started, it gets to be—you get into it and then you're in trouble—" Berger stared at Peter as if he were trying to speak without the liability of words. Tama had stopped playing and was watching the two men talk. "Just don't make the mistakes I've made," he went on. "Avoid the obvious fuck-ups."

He didn't call Berger's divorce lawyer. Anyone Berger recommended would be wildly expensive and suggest aggressive techniques to squirrel money away from Janice. Besides, he'd wash his own dirty linen privately. The Philadelphia Bar was notoriously cross-wired and incestuous, and above all, he was a private man.

Instead, he did the stupidest thing one could do when looking for a lawyer. In the Yellow Pages, he found a couple of divorce lawyers downtown and called Phil Mastrude, Counselor at Law, Practicing Primarily in Family Law and Domestic Relations, No Charge Initial Consultation, Fees Available on Request, *Compassionate Advice Humbly Offered.* The last, questionable line of advertising intrigued him. Either Mastrude was a nut, or saw his work as a lot more than filing divorce papers. Peter spoke with the secretary and made an appointment for the following day.

It was later now, nearly noon. He should be preparing for Robinson. Already he was second-guessing himself about talking to Vinnie. Meanwhile, the detectives were trying to trick Carothers into talking—discussing sports, offering cigarettes, saying it would be easier on him now, etc.—but he sat quietly in his chair, not talking, now on the official advice of his attorney, a Mr. Stein, who had called from Miami and told the D.A.'s office in a firm voice they had better have some concrete reason to bring a charge against his client or he would sputter indignation to the press. The police had up to ten hours to charge him. With the approved search warrant, police had quickly combed Carothers's Philadelphia apartment and turned up nothing but a small bottle of gun oil under the kitchen sink. The gun oil tantalized the police—made them, Peter knew, cuss and look at one another in knowing frustration. Its existence, of course, proved nothing, and by itself was useless information. The neighbors questioned by the police said Carothers worked days as a furniture mover, came and went quietly, apparently didn't spend all his nights in his apartment, and spoke to few people.

Then, as the day had worn on, Carothers had suddenly gotten angry and protested that he was innocent and in danger of losing his job by being detained.

"He's fucking guilty," the detective complained on the phone.

That was not necessarily true, Peter told himself. Like many cases, this one was marred with niggling inconsistencies: a double murder with different methods, and police who may have been slow to respond to an emergency but who had identified and located a potential suspect within hours of the murder. All this information tended to strengthen the case for Carothers's innocence, or rather, to be exact, his inability to be charged. And yet, Peter wondered, how could an hourly-wage moving company employee afford a high-priced private-practice lawyer who would fly immediately from his vacation to defend him?

A few minutes after one, Berger walked in, carrying a portable radio.

"Listen to this." He turned the volume louder.

". . . who has been questioned as a witness in the slaying of the young couple, admitted upon confrontation by a newspaper reporter that she was a heavy drinker, and was drunk last night. A short time ago, Ms. Douglas admitted to our reporter that having been inebriated may well have compromised her ability to recognize—"

The door exploded open.

"What the *fuck* is that? I say, what in the goddamned fucking world is that?"

Hoskins, chief terrorizer of them all, stood in the middle of the office listening to the radio, his eyes goggling around in anger, face red, feet planted wide like a catcher at home plate waiting to block a runner heading home.

"That," Berger appraised, "is the end of that witness."

"Off! Off!" Hoskins waved at the radio while he wrapped his fingers around Peter's phone and dialed the detective unit that was handling the case. His stomach strained his shirt.

"This is Hoskins—yeah, *get* him for me. I don't care if he's—no, you don't understand, I mean get him, *now*." He looked at Peter. "What are *you* looking so relaxed for, buddy? This is your fish and he's slipping off the goddamned—what?" He turned back to the phone. "Yes, I just heard it. Who? Donnell? Never heard of the bitch—"

"The *Inquirer*," Peter said to Berger. "Short woman, reddish hair. The investigative sort."

"The *Inquirer*?" Hoskins hollered. "Never heard of her, ever. It doesn't matter . . . all right. Tell me, then."

After a minute, Hoskins slammed the phone down.

"This reporter, Donnell, whatever her name is, found out who the witness was. Somebody down there told her the woman lived on the same hall. All she did was return to the building! The simplest, easiest thing in the world. The apartment was sealed off, but not the *floor*. A radio reporter went with Donnell. This Wanda woman is dropped off by the detective and walks inside the building still smelling of booze. They never got her cleaned up. She *was* drunk last night. Donnell asks a question right in front of the policeman guarding the apartment door and the woman says, 'Yeah, I suppose I could have made a mistake'— into the fucking microphone! Goddamn dumb-ass witnesses don't have shit between their ears! Fucking reporters!"

"We got to let him go," Peter said.

"All you have is a bimbo witness who admits to two reporters she was drunk," Berger added.

Hoskins nodded and muttered as if he were biting off and eating their words as quickly as they could speak.

"We can't hold him for no reason, not with this kind of attention," Peter reasoned. "There are no outstanding warrants for him. It appears as if all he's been doing for three years is working at a moving company. His boss says he's a good worker and rarely misses a day. We haven't yet found anybody who can connect him to the couple. For all we know, he goes to church regularly. The papers will paint it as a setup. It'll look bad as hell that we arrested some guy just because some drunk woman thought she saw somebody in a hallway. As soon as this Stein guy steps off his plane in an hour and calls his office and finds out about the woman, he's going to be on the phone demanding we release Carothers."

"If only we could hold him another day," Hoskins mused angrily, "just to see what would come out of his mouth. Under that cool mask is a guy who's very upset. He's our guy, he's got a record as long as my dick."

"Not a long . . . record," Berger observed.

Hoskins shook his head, ignoring the joke, unhappy with the general configuration of the universe and his inability to change it. "The Mayor said to me when I told him we had Carothers that he was *very pleased* this thing looked so straightforward."

Hoskins stared abstractly toward the telephone, and for the life of him, Peter did not know what he was thinking or why he cared about the Mayor's opinion. Within the political constellation of the city, they were enemies.

"So what about the Mayor?" Peter countered. "You know what he told me this morning? He said run the whole thing by the book. If we charge some guy with no evidence, the Mayor's going to look like a bully. He should know that. You ready to build a charge *now* on that woman's statement and then find nothing else and *then* have wasted the time on the wrong guy?" Peter said. Everyone in the office understood such a course of action could publically embarrass the D.A. "Besides, that's not the point. We really don't have enough."

Carothers was in custody but had not been formally charged. The police had no statements by the defendant, no eyewitness account, no physical evidence, and, of course, no statement by the victims. The only shred of connecting information had been discredited. Nothing linked Carothers to the scene, and under law he had only to wait ten hours in custody without being told by a magistrate what he was charged with before going free. He'd been taken in at five A.M. and thus, even fudging an hour, they had less than three hours to the deadline.

"I fucking *know* he's the guy," said Hoskins.

"Oh, how?" Berger asked.

Hoskins stood up, agitated, looking like he needed to break something. "Look at my face! Am I smiling? No!" His bow tie appeared tighter than usual, and he pointed his round, fat forefingers like pistols at Peter's face. "And you better be right, Peter. You had better be right. Sorry is no good in this town when you fuck up. Sorry doesn't feed the cat."

The reporters had found him. Competing for the slightest piece of information, they wanted to know more about one of the main players in the Whitlock case, and had found Peter at the very hour he was to finish up the Robinson trial. As soon as he had turned the corner on the fourth-floor hallway, someone had looked up and said "Over here" and the lights had snapped on blindingly and microphones were shoved toward him and the questions peppered him. He'd moved tight-lipped through about ten reporters, gotten into court, and finally, trying to finish a bad dream, they had moved to the closing arguments. His head pounded in exhaustion. He listened to Morgan finish up his rant about the confession and add to that the usual wind about circumstantial evidence and inconsistencies in testimony for the prosecution, then finish his summary with a hackneyed emotional guilt trip for the jury: ". . . and do you really wish to convict a man—remove his freedoms, the very thing this country is based on—because of what the prosecution *purports* to be evidence, when in fact . . ." It was boilerplate, and it was bad.

Now Judge Scarletti nodded at him to begin his summation. Peter stood up and walked over to the jury, hands open before him like a preacher. A dumb trick, but it got their attention. He would speak for Judy Warren, who could not speak for herself, and his words would be the last the jury heard before the judge gave them the charge. Now he would impose a narrative on the testimony, remind them what they had heard, and what they should remember. His words would clarify, simplify, and bring order so that the jury would apply common sense to what it had heard.

"Ladies and gentlemen of the jury, thank you for your careful consideration of all the evidence you've heard, evidence which I suggest shows beyond reasonable doubt that the defendant, Mr. William Robinson, did on August sixteenth of last year murder intentionally and knowingly Miss Judy Warren. Now, I want to reiterate"—he didn't like the dull look he was getting from the old white-haired man, a retired barber who sat in the last row—"I want to review the important points of testimony for you, because, as I suggest you will see, this is a fairly simple case in which all the pieces fit together. That's right—every piece fits every other piece. They show just when, where, and how Mr. Robinson killed his ex-girlfriend after being seized with anger. He was frenzied with jealousy.

"Now then, the defense has chosen not to contend these facts directly. The defense, ladies and gentlemen, has offered to you what I suggest is an utterly improbable set of events. The defense"—the disgust in his voice was palpable now, he knew—"would have you believe that William Robinson was nowhere near Judy Warren last August sixteenth and that his confession is the result of mental illness and was elicited, planned, and coached by the police. The defense would have you believe that the confession is spurious, a hoax, a falsehood. The defense has brought in a couple of William Robinson's old high-school pals to say he was with them early that night when they went drinking. They are his friends and they want to be loyal to him, so they're telling a story they all agreed on. They testified he drove home that night. I want you to consider what kind of witnesses they were, and whether you can consider them as credible. Then the defendant's housekeeper has said she heard him come in the house and that she spoke with him. Yesterday we saw that this testimony doesn't hold water—she as much as admitted that herself.

"Mr. William Robinson did not come to the stand and testify in this case. That's okay. He doesn't have to. He has the right of protection against self-incrimination. You *may* be tempted to infer from the fact that the defendant did not take the stand that he is guilty. You may say to yourself, 'If he is innocent, then why didn't he come forward and say so?' " He paused just long enough to make sure they asked themselves this question, because he wanted them to answer it themselves. "But that is not correct. It's not the way our legal system operates. The defendant is presumed to be innocent, as you were told at the outset of this trial. However, I do wish for you to infer and decide from what you *have* heard, which I suggest is very conclusive evidence that William Robinson is guilty of murder. The defense's testimony rests on vague, inconsistent statements, not on demonstrable fact. We're looking for a true verdict, and what the defense has offered us just doesn't fit what a reasonable man or woman would agree with. Okay. Why do I say that? Because we've got so many pieces of proof that add up to an actual trail. Even though we have a constitutionally sound, properly administered, full and complete confession dictated by the defendant and then signed by him in the presence of two police officers, we don't need that evidence—we have enough physical evidence to convict Mr. Robinson. As I promised to present in my opening statement, we can track the defendant through the entire day. We have the Wawa food market receipt with the date and time on it, forty-one minutes before the approximate time of death of Judy Warren. This particular Wawa is about five minutes from where Judy lived. We have testimony from Mr. Keegan, the defendant's co-worker at the stock brokerage, that Mr. Robinson was always talking about the victim, about her appearance, about how she looked in a halter top she wore because of the hot weather. As Mr. Keegan described for us, Mr. Robinson was angered by the fact that Miss Warren was seeing another man. We have the friend of the victim, Miss Swick, who said that the victim told her that she believed Mr. Robinson had followed her home several times the previous week at five-thirty in the afternoon. There was testimony that Mr. Robinson was starting to harrass the deceased, that he wouldn't leave her alone. Miss Swick said she herself had seen the accused arguing with Miss Warren. Miss Swick was quite certain about that. As you saw, she was a little hazy about the time of day, but that's understandable. This happened about six months ago. But as to her identification of the defendant, Miss Swick remained certain, on direct questioning, cross-examination, and on redirect.

"We have the portion of Mr. Robinson's left thumbprint on Judy Warren's eyeglasses. His thumbprint *somehow* appears on her glasses. Were they still intimate enough that he would take off her glasses for her or would she let him hold her glasses? No. Miss Swick remembered the deceased being repelled by the sight of the defendant and not trusting him. The words she used, if I remember, according to Miss Swick, were 'Actually, I think he's a sleazy weirdo.' She was no longer attracted to him. She wanted to avoid him. He scared her. So, again, I want you to ask yourselves, why in the world would a fingerprint of Mr. Robinson's appear on Judy Warren's glasses? The defense has tried to discredit the expertise of Captain Docherty of the mobile crime unit, who's been with the Philadelphia Police Department for seventeen years and listed his certifications and continuing professional instruction at national forensic seminars on fingerprinting. Captain Docherty, you will remember, testified that the thumbprint on Judy Warren's glasses, matched to a reasonable degree of scientific certainty the left thumb of the defendant. I'm talking about a pattern, ladies and gentlemen of the jury. A *chain* of evidence that links the dead body of Judy Warren to William Robinson. It's very simple, there's nothing tricky, nothing fancy about it, because Mr. Robinson did a very poor job of covering his tracks. . . ."

He had to make sure the details stuck in their minds. Little red darts he lobbed through the dead courtroom air. Darts with suction cups that flattened smack on their eagerly solemn foreheads. Respect the juror but remember all the television he has watched. Make the event real, serve up a little trauma with professional reserve, stir the citizen outrage at such a carefully planned attack. He reminded them that Robinson had first raped his victim and that he was a secretor, which was a certain physical type of male whose blood appeared in all bodily fluids, including semen. He reminded them of the testimony about the rape sample points—vulva, vagina, and cervix, where semen containing minute amounts of the same blood type as Robinson's was found—and he reminded them of the hair cuts on the labia majora and minora and bruises on the thighs, both indications of force. This evidence, Peter admitted, contradicted Robinson's bizarre, grandiose claim that he had put his penis into the girl's warm heart. The jury had to envision the forced entry into the apartment, the attack and the rape, and then the stabbing; they had to see the knife cut into the poor girl's belly, and look back now at the pointy-nosed defendant, look at his wiggy expression and arching eyebrows and know—and *feel*—that this rich punk greased this poor girl after stalking her for more than a week. Robinson had fallen in love with the maternal abundance of her breasts—from the lab photos you could see she was stacked—and her refusal to see him anymore drove him crazy. The jury had to know that he merited a life sentence, care of Gratersford State Prison. Twenty or thirty years to think about it real hard.

". . . as expert medical testimony has shown, it was then the defendant took the larger of the knives . . ."

He was sure to remind them about the blood samples on the charred sofa that were an exact match to those found on the defendant's corduroy pants. The evidence technicians loved figuring out stuff like that down to the chemical level. Peter couldn't bring in the 439 porno magazines the police had found in Robinson's closet or the animal-cruelty charge at sixteen—blowtorching a cat—or the twice-failed polygraph test. He brought in what he could, though, and made sure that the jury—especially the eight women—were sold. The room, he felt, was his. But he kept his tone even and the summation under thirty minutes.

". . . confident," he concluded, "that you will return a verdict of guilty to the charge of first-degree murder."

Peter's voice hung in the large room for a moment, and like at a Quaker Meeting—strangely enough—he recognized the gathered silence of a group of people in profound contemplation of what they had just heard. Finally, Judge Scarletti cleared his throat and proceeded, asking the jury if any of them would be unable to deliberate on the sentence because of sickness or pressing need. No, everyone would be able to pass judgment. It was rare for a juror to quit at this point, having invested so much time. A verdict released the juror's tension, too. The judge asked the alternate jurors to leave the courtroom, and then gave his instructions to the jury, defining first-, second-, and third-degree murder. "You will have to de*cide*, based on your dis*cus*sion and inde*pen*dent judgment of the testimony of *every* witness you have heard," he started, and droned on, speaking patiently while everyone in the courtroom knew the boy's goose was cooked, "guilty as charged" practically dripping off the greasy lamp globes way up in the ceiling, where a veritable mausoleum of dead flies and moths revolved slowly in the dusty crochet work of a hundred spiders as the heat rose from the radiators clunking away in the corners of the courtroom. *Guilty.* The word dripped down each brass button of the court officers' uniforms and flitted across the smug, shiny faces of the sheriff's deputies, young men of little education who derived great sources of identity from a set of pumped-up arms, pressed blue uniforms, and polished black shoes. Yes, everybody knew. Peter could feel the sure verdict slip around the room like the ghost of the blowtorched cat nuzzling the jurors' socks.

At quarter to five, Peter combed his hair, straightened his tie, checked to see that no remains of lunch clung to his teeth, splashed water onto his face in order to wake up, and prepared on an index card a short statement for the reporters and television cameras assembled in the D.A. press room. Some had followed him over from City Hall and seemed excited to be with him, acting as if they had found a new player to push into the media spotlight. He saw Hoskins conferring with Gerald Turner, the Mayor's aide. Peter reminded himself to speak clearly, to look at the cameras, and to sweep his gaze from one side of the room to the other. He'd done it a few times before, the first time staring into those powerful TV lights like a scared animal frozen on a highway at night before a car. But now he delivered the announcement of Carothers's release coolly, calmly. It was a simple, quick matter, almost perfunctory. Hoskins stood at the back of the room nodding slowly. Peter glimpsed Karen Donnell. She smiled at him—guiltily? bitterly?—and resumed her note-taking. The press conference had been timed so that the television reporters had little time to ask further questions and just enough time to set up for a live report outside or to get videotape across town for editing before the local news broadcasts went on. The double-murder would compete with a subway derailment and the announcement that another city

122

judge had been indicted. On the way out, Turner beckoned to Peter. He ignored the Mayor's aide—what more could be said today? And besides, Turner was the worst kind of political operative, a moon eagerly reflecting the sun. He didn't want to be involved.

Outside, alone finally, with taxis racing the trash blowing along Market Street, Peter paused at a magazine stand, where his gaze wandered stupidly over the women's magazines with their fake awareness and hard sell, the exercise magazines (the new genre of soft porn), the usual straight and gay porn, both upscale and blue-collar, the news and business magazines, both mainstream and hip—in all, hundreds of happy photogenic faces bounced and sparkled and laughed in static beauty before him, competing for his dollar, for his emotional response, for his mind. And what was the quest for beauty but the quest for love? How much American culture twisted and squirmed and cried out—an amorphous choir of souls—that it wanted to be loved. People, people, people, driving and pushing and crowding and killing to step into the limelight of love, wishing to be declared a genius, a billionaire, an artist, a somebody worthy of collective attention. People equated fame with love and there was a great need for many famous people, more than ever before. Didn't anybody realize that history was choked with the lives of people such as this? Always there would be the ever-burgeoning numbers of people who wanted to be someone. It was a stupid world, and he was stuck in it.

So, after a long day that had dug its nails deep into his scalp, at least now there existed some prospect that he would find Janice. Maybe Vinnie would help him out. In the evening, at home, he glanced at the mail and turned on the most sensationalistic of the local news stations. At the top of the broadcast the Mayor told reporters he was disappointed the suspect had been released but that he had full faith in the District Attorney's office. Then the camera cut to a street interview, crowds of black teenagers smiling and goofing in front of the camera while an older man said: "I think they covering up who did it. Maybe it's some white guy—no black person would do *that*. They wanted to *get* that boy and they arrested a black man and then they realized they couldn't get away with it." Then the reporter turned to the camera and said solemnly, "And *so*, despite the many theories about what motivated this most tragic of murders, for the Mayor and for the families of Johnetta Henry and Darryl Whitlock, the hope that justice will be done . . . must begin again."

The real justice would be if television reporters and their solemn,

123

quasi-grammatical phrasings would disappear from the face of the earth. The news was followed by the opening music of an unbearably stupid show with a beautiful, leggy girl who climbed slowly out of a swimming pool and walked wetly toward the camera. The growing problem, of course, was sex. He wanted it, but without much else that went with it. In the absence of a loving wife, all that he wanted— what any man would want—was some stacked, gorgeous somebody whom he could fuck until the cows came home. The absolute lack of self-respect in such an idea was inversely proportional to the pleasure of it. Of course it was childish; that was what made it so terrific. He sat at the small writing desk in the living room and gazed at Janice's picture. Sex had become *remystified* to him lately—he seemed to suddenly desire it to the same improvident degree as when he was young—but it was attended now by dark reverberations of fecundity and death. Sex was no longer simple and fun, not as it was when he was fifteen and argued his high-school girlfriend into giving him what he wanted, however fast and fearful and awkward it had been. Subsequent encounters—many of them, most fun and easy—had taken him farther from where he had wished to go. By twenty he had slept with enough girls to understand he hadn't loved any of them.

The summer before his senior year he'd worked as a dishwasher on Nantucket for twelve weeks. Within the bright noise of bars and tanned faces, he became involved with a wealthy, divorced young mother who required only one thing, really, and with little attempt at concealment, either. Hers was the hunger of bitterness, and what she wished for most of all was an obliteration of the previous ten years of her life. In this he'd seen the true inconsequentiality of himself, and how their physical passion was both fraudulent and wasteful. One day, with her children at the beach with a nanny, they went to bed. He watched the clock by the bed, curious to see how long the human male could copulate. After nearly an hour, when she realized what he was doing, she saw her insult turned back upon herself and was furious. He'd sworn off all involvements then and began to spend his nights reading. It was then he realized how easy his life had been.

That fall he saw Janice. Her blue eyes stared out from beneath dark, inquisitive eyebrows, and he'd felt a sudden riotous calm. He lost all his glib confidence. She was nineteen and did not trust him. He suffered willfully and remained persistent. The vulnerability of his devotion won her over to him, and she conceded to talking. She was on full scholarship from a large suburban public high school.

124

Thus she had earned her chance at an excellent education, and not been provided it by birth. He saw in her an elemental loneliness, forged in her effort to escape a childhood that otherwise would have destroyed her. It was this childhood she described haltingly, shamed about her origins. Yet she displayed the surety of one who has decided to create her own fate, a young woman whose father had broken her arm when she was eight, who now attended class with girls who complained that they had not gone skiing during Christmas vacation.

When Janice had first undressed before him, he felt humbled by the trust implied by her. And, simply, she was beautiful, impossibly perfect, her breasts large and high, her skin slightly olive. She stated quite matter-of-factly that she did not *really* know what to do, a fact that amazed and thrilled him. His ache for her was complete, unfettered by memories of previous women, a reverent, clean want.

They became inseparable, and life seemed to hold a fierce clarity. It was, Peter supposed now, only the clarity of passion, an emotion doomed by its intensity, and perhaps he was a sentimental fool, but these memories were all he *had*. The warm spring night they'd driven down by the freight tracks to the Schuylkill River and undressed in the car—he remembered it perfectly. They'd slipped into the dark muddy water and swam out. He dove down, surfaced. She was a ways off, a dark head in the water. "You hear that?" he yelled. The sound rolled through the dark trees, the back-to-back diesel engines, rail ties creaking, couplers vibrating, wheels grinching the rails, clacking. They swam in, and he pulled himself up the bank and ran naked to the train. Hoppers and tank cars and box cars rolled past, big shadowed letters: READING RAILROAD, CONRAIL, UNION CARBIDE. A hundred cars, easily. The sound was enormous. His naked shadow wavered against the cars. Janice stood at the river's edge with a towel. Then she ran to him. The noise was around them and yet he felt the heart under her wet skin. He yelled as loudly as he could, to be heard above the freight train: *I love you, and I swear I always will.* She lay her wet head on the back of his shoulder and shut her eyes. *Always*, he repeated.

After college, they went to Europe for a month. In Nice they walked the streets and shopped for bread and fruit and fresh fish. They swam in the Mediterranean and laughed with the beach venders who hawked refreshments in a mix of languages. Janice relaxed, visibly, and wanted, like any first-time traveler to Europe, to see everything. He was happy to indulge her, and was thus transformed into a loaded, flapping pack mule bulging with maps, train tickets, Florentine paper masks, guidebooks, French T-shirts, Italian shoes, Swiss chocolate, postcards, and so on—whatever her eye fancied. In Venice, a city of soft light and softer lines, they walked the narrow, pestilential streets, pausing at the small bridges that arced over the canals. In the low hotel room off a crooked, wet alleyway, they made love like a man and a woman—that is, they took their time.

And on one of those evenings—he remembered this vividly—they bought a big bottle of cheap red wine and watched the crowds and gassy lights of the Piazza San Marco. Then, sufficiently drunk and removed from America to say it, Janice finally told him about how, after her mother had killed herself and before she had escaped to college, her father would come to her bed, once or twice a week. She had desired a father's love and got something else, worse than if she had been ignored. Peter was just old enough then to know she wanted to be told she was not disgraced or fouled or guilty; she had been exploited and abused, and nothing less. Hers was the kind of father, she said, who a girl will give anything to forget. The man, destroyed by the loneliness he had sown for himself, now drifted somewhere in the American Northwest, lost.

Outside their room, gondolas had glided through the canals. The long, glossy black boats sagged low in the water with drunken American tourists listening happily to third-rate tenors croon love songs. Peter and Janice sat naked on the sheets, ignoring the mosquitoes. She explained how she had wanted to tell him before but hadn't dared to, because she felt ashamed of herself, how as a young girl it had taken too long for her confusion and paralysis to give way to the horror of what was being done to her. She had wept while her father was on top of her, twisting her head from side to side, her hands pushing against his doughy chest, begging him to stop, saying she hated *it*, hated what he was doing to her. And then, after her father never responded to this, she had realized with a child's perfect clarity that her cries fed all that was sick in him. She resolved that he would receive as little satisfaction as possible.

In this moment something was destroyed in her and something else created. In the future it would allow her to leave anybody. It was not heartlessness, but a deeper desire for survival. And so when her father returned, as she knew he would, she mutely accepted him, her head turned to the wall, silent and rigid and abstracted, far away from his sweaty, ugly body, far away—for now—from the ever-mounting debt of pain. As Peter had listened that night in an old city, a critical intersection of vocation and love began for him; that anyone had raped or beaten someone he loved angered him and bespoke the incomprehensible cruelty visited on other innocent lives. They talked the whole night, gradually sobering into the strengthened vision that together they could forge a future and transcend a past. He decided he wanted to marry her, for her suffering and strength elicited the best of his nature, and this brought him to himself.

In law school that next year he had dutifully slogged through torts and contract classes. It was criminal law that awakened him. He skipped classes to visit City Hall and heard the stories told by the raped, the stabbed, the beaten. Because of Janice, he began to see the sanctity of life, and how it must be protected from the stupid, the vicious, the disturbed, the angry, and the uncaring. He saw, too, the elusiveness of justice. His love for her had brought him from cloistered privilege to a budding awareness of the human capacity for brutality. He was righteous, full of energy, and very bright. He had been alive for the first time, and known it.

And later, they sat on the west bank of the Schuylkill, watching the crew teams carry gleaming wooden shells from the boathouses. "Let's get an apartment," she'd suggested. And when they stood in the peeling three-room walk-up in West Philadelphia near the law school and looked at each other, the oppression and worry faded from her eyes. She painted rooms and found cheap furniture, joined a food co-op and stuffed the kitchen with vegetables and grains and fruit. She waxed the wooden floors. She was, she'd told him, the happiest ever.

Late in the evenings then she would put on her nightgown and get in bed. Then call to him. He would slip beneath the covers. Always it was good. Afterward he would rub her back and wait for her breathing to settle out, then dress in the darkness and go to the other room and read law. Civil procedure, constitutional law, advanced torts, domestic relations, execution of wills. The reading went slowly, and often he would repeat sentences, forcing comprehension into his tired head. ". . . state of mind often may be proved circumstantially from statements of the person whose mental outlook is at issue. Statements used in this way are not hearsay because the jurors are not concerned with whether the statements reflect reality; they are only concerned with what the fact that the statements were spoken implies about the declarant's belief. . . ." When his eyes wearied, he slipped outside to walk the sidewalks of West Philadelphia, by the student boardinghouses and apartments, where laughter and conversation drifted out to the street.

The night before his first law exam, Janice asked him when they would get married. He replied that he didn't know, but would be happy to discuss it after he took the exam. She responded that he cared more for the exam than for her. He said at the moment he did care more about the exam but of course in the large scheme of things he cared more for her. He was anxious to do well, he said. It was only natural. She started to cry and said she felt alone. He tried to reassure her. She said he didn't love her, not really. This seemed ludicrous to him, for he didn't understand what would make her say such a thing. Hadn't his pledge been enough? Then he told her he could not afford to indulge her that evening. They got into it from there, and when he finally left the apartment at two A.M., he walked with a cold, hateful resolve to an all-night convenience store and filled a bag with coffee, Pepsi, and chocolate bars. He found an open classroom in the law center and at his table built a fortress of heavy law books around him. After the exam, on which he performed well, they went out and saw *Casablanca* at a revival house. It was December and a light snow had dusted the city streets. They had, he recalled, a great weekend.

But in truth he had never been content in those days. He worried about her happiness, money, and his future, for the process of becoming a lawyer was narrowing and honing him, imposing architectures on his thinking, removing colors from his perceptions. Thought had become navigation by logic; he tacked back and forth in subroutines of inference when no tailwind of certainty carried him straight toward an answer. Increasingly, life appeared to be a series of planned manipulations and strategic intentions. This change was a matter of grief, for it implied not only the absolute death of childhood but of a way of thought, the murder of pure intuition. And yet the evenings he walked alone, there would come a moment when he'd turn the corner and see their darkened apartment window above the street and know she slept there waiting for him. This had been enough. Wasn't it she who would preserve in him the sense of wonder? When he returned to the bedroom, always he softly whispered reassuring noises. She needed to know it was him, for otherwise she might hear the creak of the bed and jump awake, terrified.

The phone rang. "Peter Scattergood," he answered dully, by habit.

"Hey, man, Mr. Scattergood, why'd you let that fucking nigger go free, man?" A heavy working-class, city accent. "You asshole liberal *pussy—*"

"Who is this?"

"Me? I'm a *taxpayer*. I pay your fucking *salary*. I bet you love niggers, let them fuck you up the ass. I pay *you* to fucking *lock up* them son-of-a-bitches, not—"

He hung up. Did these idiots know where he lived, too? He clenched his fists in the air, half wanting the chance to beat up the next person who crowded him.

The phone rang again. He grabbed it.

"Yes?" he demanded in anger.

"Oh, *Peter*, finally."

He hadn't spoken to his mother in weeks, at least. "I know I haven't called."

"I was thinking of you. I'd love for the two of you to come out to dinner one of these evenings. I haven't seen Janice in a couple of months, it seems."

"I'm pretty busy now, Mom." He heard the vulnerability in his voice, hated himself for lying to her. "So's she."

"I'm sure you both are. Why don't you ask Janice to look at the calendar and find a day next week? Any day's fine for me."

"I'll do that, call you back."

She hadn't mentioned the television. Having given up on local news and its mix of sensationalistic and idiotic filler stories, his parents adhered to the national newscast and its relatively prim journalistic standards.

"Here's Dad." Her voice faded. "It's Peter, honey."

"Peter? What's new?"

"Been playing some racquetball. I've got a new partner."

"Good?" His father loved to analyze sports; as he aged, his ability to remember the golden moments of his youthful athletic prowess seemed to improve, those moments becoming even more glorious and heroic. "I played tennis indoors twice last week. I can't serve the way I used to. I hate these new oversized racquets, but everybody has them. I tried to stretch my back out on the living-room rug—"

"Put heat on your back."

"Yes." His father changed his tone, father-son ritualizing done. "Look, your mother thinks you don't want to come home."

"No—"

"She's in the other room, so I'll get right to it. Mom doesn't want to mention it, but she's due to have a little surgery. We don't know why we haven't seen much of you lately. But that's not the issue. Your mother would like to see you and Janice before she goes into the hospital Sunday night."

"Dad, what's the matter?"

"The doctor wants her to have a hysterectomy."

"Uhh," Peter breathed. "Cancer?"

"The Pap smear turned it up and they ran some more tests. There's, uh, some abnormal tissue, in the, uh, cervix and uterus." His father, an overly modest man, stumbled along: "We don't know how extensive. Mom'll be in the hospital awhile."

"Tomorrow's Thursday." He pulled a commuter train schedule from a drawer. "I'll be on the eleven thirty-six Paoli Local Saturday morning."

He hung up, remembered his mother's voice, and wondered what a uterus meant to a fifty-eight-year-old woman. Nobody liked being cut open. He didn't believe his mother had cancer, but told himself he had to prepare for that possibility. His chest ached. He reached for the phone again, to call Janice. Only she would understand. They had to talk—he needed her reassurance. This kind of fear flattened other worries and he had faith Janice would set aside their troubles temporarily on behalf of family unity. Of course she would.

The phone line was busy. Good, Janice was home. The next time he called, five minutes later, there was no answer. He tried fifty or more times that night to reach her.

SIX

The next day, Peter Scattergood was alone in a mirrored elevator, rising soundlessly one hundred feet per minute up one of the new granite and glass towers, his feet deep in the wine-colored carpet, his face ruddy and abstracted before him, worrying about his mother, watching the floor numbers flick on and off, worrying about how much this was going to cost him, worrying about the Mayor, and, above all—like a knife in his chest—wondering where Janice had been the previous night.

Mastrude's law office looked respectable enough, but when the secretary waved Peter in, he had second thoughts immediately. The attorney was a bearded, clownishly obese man in his late fifties who had a few thin red hairs plastered to an otherwise balded, freckled scalp. His bifocals, too small for his fleshy head, rested below bloodshot blue eyes. Crumbs clung to his tie and a constellation of dandruff floated across the dark lapels of his suit. The office smelled unmistakably of Chinese food, and everything about the man bespoke a marginally competent, low-budget law practice. Perhaps he had made a mistake.

"Okay," Mastrude barked, pushing aside the files covering his desk. "My secretary said you called yesterday. How long have you and your wife been married, Mr. Scattergood?"

"It's been about seven years. Please call me Peter."

"I will. Children?" Mastrude scribbled on a pad.

"Nope. We talked about it."

"Well, it's a whole hell of a lot simpler without a custody battle." Mastrude rubbed his fingers across his belly.

"Right," Peter answered. "My wife isn't looking for a fight, anyway. She just wants out. I'm certain she doesn't want to take it to divorce court and will agree on a settlement with reasonable monthly alimony. So, uh, the divisible assets accumulated during the marriage—"

"You an attorney, Mr. Scattergood?" Mastrude looked annoyed, as if he was not being allowed to do his job.

"Yeah, as a matter of fact."

"Big firm in town?" Mastrude bit a pencil and inspected the tooth marks.

"No. Assistant D.A. down at City Hall."

"Have a specialty?" Mastrude's voice held more interest.

"I prosecute homicides," Peter said, feeling strange, as if he were guilty of one.

"Okay." Mastrude was not impressed. "In that case, you should already know that life is messy, unfair, fraught with irreconcilable conflict, and basically a long row to hoe. Most people are unhappy most or some of the time, and few human relationships are devoid of the most evil intentions and the most wicked and hateful of thoughts."

"Wow," Peter joked uncomfortably.

Mastrude leaned forward, ready to move on. "No kids. How about affairs while you were together?"

Peter shook his head. Cassandra didn't count, really.

"No?"

"No."

"We need the facts here." Mastrude sounded like a prosecutor.

"You have the facts."

"Why's she leaving you?"

"It's pretty complicated."

"I don't doubt it. What about her? Affairs? Flirtations?"

"No, not that I know of."

"Well, let's hope you know about *yourself* at least." Mastrude's massive red face crinkled in delight. " 'The cod-piece that will house Before the head has any, The head and he shall louse: So beggars marry many.' The Fool, *Lear*. In other words, take care of yourself first, your pecker second. You'll find I'm an irreverent man, Mr. Scatter—Peter. It's the only way I can cope. That's not to say I don't care about your situation. Now then, since it's sometimes an issue, what religion are you?"

"Quaker."

"Quaker? No kidding! There aren't that many left."

"Some, here and there."

"They *founded* this city, if you read your history," Mastrude exclaimed. "You look Presbyterian or Episcopalian, something typical. A Quaker, how about that? There're not many original Philly Quakers left. Like descendants of the Dutch in New York City. Can't find them. How strong is your practice?"

"I go to Meeting for Worship once in a while." Janice had usually wanted to go. She loved the silence.

"That's what Quakers call church, right?"

"Yeah—it's silent."

"I've seen the meeting houses," Mastrude remembered. "Scattered all over the state, right? Most of them are stone and look three hundred years old."

"Most of them are."

"The Quakers don't dress in hats and black—"

"No, plain dress went out about a hundred years ago," Peter responded; it was a typical question. "That's the Amish or the Mennonites. Quakers have been corrupted by the modern world along with everyone else."

"Is your family—"

"Goes all the way back. One of my ancestors worked for Governor Penn himself."

"Very few people know that the Declaration of Independence was based in part on the Charter of Liberties, written by Penn." Mastrude beamed. "Did you know the Liberty Bell was cast in honor of that document, and its inscription written by a Quaker?" he asked.

Peter shrugged. The Quakers had relinquished all political power by the nineteenth century. Somehow this was painful to him.

Mastrude pulled open a drawer. "You a pacifist?" he asked, producing a soggy cardboard box.

"Is this related to my marriage situation?"

"No, just curious." Mastrude nodded, his mouth suddenly full of pork and rice.

"I don't think force should resolve problems. I'm nonviolent, yes."

Mastrude made a sucking sound, half laugh, half scoff. "How do you square that with your work? Christ, man, you say you're a pacifist and yet you enforce the law via punishments! This state has the death penalty—"

"I'm quite aware of that."

"Well?"

"The death penalty does bother me—I consider it an awesome thing, *never* to be taken lightly. Perhaps I believe in the law more than I subscribe to the tenets of Quakerism. As dictated by reality," Peter said, not enjoying the exchange.

"Like a Catholic who uses birth control."

"Well, that's a pretty faulty analogy."

"And you're an argumentative fellow. Which is expectable. I like that in a man, but not in a client." Mastrude opened another drawer and brought out a beer. "Now, what does your wife do?"

"She's director of a safe house for battered women."

"You'd be surprised who beats up on whom—then again, *you* wouldn't, I suppose."

"There's not much money in it, though she's a licensed social worker."

"She could decide to go into private practice," the lawyer concluded. "All right, aside from the professional degrees, tell me about the assets accumulated while you two have been married."

There were, Peter answered, the equity in the house, the cash management account, the shrimpy savings account they plundered for vacations, the small but healthy stock portfolio Peter had built and was absurdly proud of, various furnishings, Janice's car, the Ford, the computer, jewelry, etc. With the appreciated value of the house, several hundred thousand dollars.

"The usual junk owned by the investing class," Mastrude summarized.

Their debts included a revolving two thousand dollars or so on the credit cards, the usual monthly bills, the endless years of mortgage payments remaining on the house, and the pesky remainders of student loans. The only way to get back all the equity in the house was to sell it, of course.

"All right, since you seem to know what your wife wants, why don't you tell me what's really bothering you?"

Peter opted for the truth. "Hell, I don't want to get divorced."

"As is often the case, one party doesn't want to do it." Mastrude nodded compassionately, as advertised. "Too weak, too scared, too sad, too hopeful, too dependent. Any of those words apply to you, Peter?"

"All, probably." He leaned forward. "But I think there's a chance we can get back together."

"Why do you want to do that?" Mastrude yanked open another drawer, as if it contained the answer to his question, and pulled out a roll of antacids.

"Because I love her, Mastrude, farfetched as that may sound. Jesus, you guys like to chomp on the jugular, don't you?"

The intercom buzzed and Mastrude asked his secretary what she needed, then motioned to Peter that he'd be a few minutes. Peter started to think of the work *he* was supposed to be doing. He had let so many things slip lately, not working as long as he needed to, nor as efficiently. So far no one had noticed, though you never knew; two hundred and twenty lawyers pushed through the front doors to the D.A.'s office every morning and many of the new youngbloods were sure to be plotting their professional rise from the municipal court unit to felony waiver to felony jury up to the cream of the office, homicide trial, just as he had done, an honored tradition in the office. He knew from basketball that there was *always* some maniac who would outwork you no matter how dedicated and obsessive you were—the guys who shot three hundred foul shots after practice and dribbled a ball while they ate breakfast—*always* one pathologically organized and methodical nut who cut through the mediocre masses of mumbling, posturing, paper-shuffling lawyers the way Michael Jordan had sliced up the Sixers two nights prior for forty-eight points. He was convinced Hoskins was watching him, waiting for him to screw up the Whitlock case.

Mastrude banged down the phone.

"Where were we? You don't want to split up." Mastrude inhaled the wheezy breath of the obese. "Okay, Peter, looking at you, I see you're young, ambitious, probably work too hard, which is what a lot of young lawyers do—I see it with *boys* of twenty-five, twenty-six, just out of Penn Law or Harvard or some other overrated place, and personally I think Temple and Villanova do a fine job, the graduates are less cocky and more dependable. Anyway, you all are kids aching to start climbing into your graves. Everyone thinks he can beat the system, beat the odds, beat life on its own terms. I hear it all the time. I talk to women and men, men and women. Peter, I'll tell you what they say, too. Ready?" Mastrude's eyebrows shot up like a curtain being lifted. "It's a list I've memorized. 'I want to be alone to be free to think and work, and I want to be in a committed relationship. I want to live forever, but I want to take drugs and drink and smoke to an excessive degree. I want children, but I want to be able to work

135

twenty hours a day. I want my spouse to have the most fantastic body I ever saw but none of the obsession, vanity, or values that go with it. I want to indulge the sickest, weirdest parts of my personality, and I want everyone to think I'm the most healthy soul they ever met. I want my wife to have a fulfilling, lucrative professional career, but I want her to give birth to a bunch of adoring, bright, perfect, happy kids and to have dinner waiting for me. I want to be free to meet new people and have great sex with them, and I want my spouse to stay faithful so that I can have great sex with him or her. I want the wisdom of getting older without losing my hair or getting crow's feet. I want to do everything I should feel guilty for doing but without the guilt. I want to be an artist or to help people and not compromise myself, and I want to make a huge pile of money any filthy, sneaky way I can. I want my subordinates to be loyal, productive workers, and I want my boss to give me all the credit for what they do. I want my aging parents to live out their lives in a healthy, happy way, but I want them to die quickly so that I can have all of their money. I want my kids to feel loved, but I don't want to bother helping them with their homework—' "

"Okay, I get it," Peter said, irritated.

"A childless divorce is *small potatoes* compared to some of the damage possible to inflict on another person. Good Christ, I hope you know that, you're the murder man. I always tell people, 'If you don't get everything you want, think of what you don't get that you don't want.' Now, to get back to the point, your wife is probably very intelligent and articulate. People tend to marry at their own level of looks, wealth, education, and so on. You're both attractive people. Nobody waves around a pistol or threatens suicide in your household, the bills get paid, and you subscribe to a couple of great publications like *The New Yorker* or *Harper's* magazine that you don't have time to read, or am I wrong?"

"No, you're right," Peter answered, feeling reduced by Mastrude's overview.

"Okay, that means you probably tried to talk this out. You can afford counseling, and it's the healing paradigm your wife subscribes to, no?"

"Two-on-two counseling, listening script, personality testing. Eighty bucks an hour. An expensive failure." Janice had insisted they get therapy. He had tried to be open and honest and a good listener. He had earnestly recounted all of his sins and shortcomings before complete strangers for twenty-eight weeks in a row. He had listened to Janice explain with deadly precision his inability to understand her and make her feel loved. The counselors had nodded their understanding while she spoke—after all, the three of them spoke the same language, grooved on the same buzzwords—and then, so conscientiously that it made him sick, asked how he *felt*. Like a fool, that's how he felt—for putting up with the inane false intimacy they were shoving down his throat. He had been unable to complain about her, even upon the counselors' prompting. Just sat there, the meter running, unable to weep or be angry or tell them that he hated himself for the way he was apparently torturing her. He looked up, saw Mastrude waiting. "The psychologists were pretty good," he said. "I just didn't want to be there."

"If they *were* good, they were helping you to break up instead of keeping you together." Mastrude contemplated his belly as if it were an unwanted appendage. "That's the danger, and that's the incentive, see? They want you to keep on coming in their office. Figuring out who you are is a goddamned national *industry*—"

Peter waved him past this topic.

"Right, fine." Mastrude nodded quickly, checking his coffee cup for a last sip. "I'm just trying to speed along your perceptions. I've done somewhere between four and five thousand divorce cases." He pointed at the thick files on his desk. "It's a messy business. Peter, you have to wake up. Your lovely wife wants a divorce and you're going to deal with it and eventually heal. Deal and heal. My guess is this is the first major blow you've ever had. Rational discourse will not solve your problem. Remember Pascal: 'The heart has reasons reason will never know.' Maybe real love is the least aggravation. Maybe it's pheromones—those things that come from a person's body that you smell unconsciously. Maybe it's having a sense of humor. I'll tell you this: It's not money or sex or children. I don't know what went wrong in your marriage. It's not my job to know. But it's your job to find out. *Listen* to me, son. What I'm talking about can't be taught but must be learned. You'll find someone else whom you'll love dearly and with whom it can work. And don't think because you spend all of your time prosecuting murders that you have lost all of your innocence," Mastrude warned him, waving a pointed finger. "You may innocently still believe that love conquers all. Often the most apparently jaded people are the most idealistic. And there's a lot to be jaded about. As a society, we have become all that we abhor."

Peter felt the way he did back in school when an opposing player hooked him a vicious elbow in his gut and knocked the wind out of him—it only made him jump back up feeling invincible and angry. He appreciated Mastrude's toughness; it was efficient and meant to be humane. But he didn't agree with everything Mastrude had said.

"I hear you," Peter answered. "But I want you to slow the thing down. Draw out the discovery process, lose the interrogatories, pretend we're going to trial, anything."

"It won't work."

"It might. I want her shock to wear off, to give her a chance to miss me."

"Don't prize yourself too highly. Don't prize *her* too highly."

"I won't. But I'm not selling myself short, and that's the intangible area that you are in no position to judge."

Mastrude sighed, the folly of youth apparently discouraging him. "Fine. I can drag it out. It'll cost you more, but you don't seem to care, particularly."

"Whatever it is you charge."

They discussed the financial terms of representation and Peter wrote out a check that delivered the death blow to the savings account. "Look, I just want you to quibble for a while, buy a day here, two days there. It can be done. Put things in the mail late on Friday afternoons so the mail isn't picked up until Saturday and delivered until Tuesday. Tell her lawyer I'm a mess and can't get together my tax stuff, anything. I just want some time, see if I can work it out with her."

"It won't pan out." Mastrude shook his head.

"I hope you're wrong, and I won't hold it against you that you have no faith in me." Peter smiled. "I'll be honest with you. The idea of losing her just kills me."

"Don't let it," Mastrude jumped in. "There's better theater down at the Shubert. I've seen a couple of husbands kill themselves. The last guy felt sorry for himself, he worked down at Philly International Airport and crawled into an unheated luggage compartment on a flight to Norway. It was a mess. The Norwegian authorities, the airline security, U.S. Customs, the city coroner's office. The wife got rid of him *and* got his entire estate. Homer, Shakespeare, and half the junk on TV to the contrary, love's not worth that."

"I'll remember it."

"I doubt that. I get the feeling you're not listening to a thing I'm saying." Mastrude's face reddened. "But I'll keep talking—that's what

138

I'm paid for. If it helps at all, fool around. Get a handle on it. Remember what Sophocles said."

"What? What did he say?"

"Marry well, and you're happy. Marry badly, and you're a philosopher. So, go out and rent all of Woody Allen's movies."

"Right, right." Peter looked at his watch.

"Son, maybe I'm not the lawyer you need."

"No, I like you. I'm listening."

"Then listen to this"—Mastrude bent painfully over his desk, so close Peter could smell the fried rice on his breath and even see a bit of scallion jammed between two tiny yellow teeth—"when it comes to knowing what love really is. . . ." Mastrude's bright greasy face loomed disturbingly near, his tiny eyes playing back and forth over Peter's face, searching for something.

"What?" Peter exclaimed. "What do you see?"

Mastrude leaned back suddenly, as if discovering an unfortunate answer to a difficult question, and concluded the consultation in a remote voice: "I'll be in touch."

"You were no help," Vinnie said hoarsely over the phone.

"What do you mean?" asked Peter.

"I mean the address where you told me to look was no goddamn good. But traffic division picked up the car this morning down toward the river, on Christian Street and Sixth. The car was parked on the wrong side of the street when they tried to clean it."

"Christian Street and Sixth?" This was an old, working-class Italian section of South Philadelphia, very conservative and one of the last places he expected to see Janice.

"It's been parked down there all day, all night."

"You have an address of the driver?" Peter asked, frankly amazed at how quickly Vinnie had procured an answer for him. Maybe the man was more powerful than Peter knew.

"You told me to look for a car, not a driver, as I remember."

"Yeah, Vinnie, you're right. But you wouldn't pass up the information if you could get it. I'm just trying to save myself a little time, so if you have the address, tell me."

"Actually, I don't have a driver, because traffic doesn't do that."

"Not far from the Italian market."

"Yeah," Vinnie said. "Got it?"

"What's this going to run me, Vinnie?"

"It's a favor," Vinnie said slyly. "It's always a favor."

139

"I'd rather it not be a favor. I don't want to worry about you collecting when I'm not ready to pay."

"You want to pay now?"

By any reasonable view, Vinnie was diseased meat who sooner or later would be regurgitated by the system. Peter pictured FBI sound technicians squatting over a tape recorder in an unmarked van. They could be on to Vinnie and catch him as well. The beleaguered Police Department and half the elected officials kept coming up with new ways to entice an FBI or Justice Department investigation. Commission after commission was formed to clean up the corruption, with little effect. And now, with his help, the District Attorney's office—about the only relatively clean office left—would be dragged into the mess. *Assistant District Attorney Indicted for Misuse of City Resources to Find Estranged Wife.*

"Where you calling from, Vinnie?"

"A pay phone," Vinnie answered. "How you think the Sixers will do against the Knicks?"

"They'll win."

"I doubt it."

"I'll make you a little personal bet," Peter said.

"What is it?" Vinnie asked, understanding. "Make it good."

"Sixers win, nothing. Knicks win, I pay you ten times whatever Ewing gets."

"He had thirty-two last time," Vinnie mused.

"He could go high or low."

"You got a deal."

Peter hung up, and checked to make sure he wasn't due anywhere during the next two hours. The Robinson jury hadn't come back yet. The press was badgering the police about new suspects in the double-murder—"the murder that has rocked the city," they were calling it—and the police were busy putting West Philadelphia through the sieve, searching for somebody to charge. Now that Peter knew where Janice was, the case seemed very far away.

But on his way to the elevator he passed the inspecting eyes of Hoskins, whose bow tie was tied so tightly it appeared ready to spring off his neck at any moment.

"Everything under control?" Hoskins called.

"Yes," Peter answered.

"Good. Keep it that way."

*   *   *

140

Outside, walking toward Broad Street, he decided not to take the #64 bus—it would take too long. Instead he checked his cash—each day there was less money in his account—caught a cab, and settled back in the cracked vinyl seat.

The cabbie drove down Broad Street before turning south, then stopped a couple of blocks away from the five hundred block of Christian Street. He'd go the rest of the way on foot. He had brought along his briefcase, so as to appear to have business in the neighborhood. The cab sped off. It was after two; Janice would have long since left for work at the women's shelter in West Philly. Vinnie had said the car wasn't being parked at the West Philadelphia address. She had to be taking a bus or the subway.

He walked the sidewalk, conspicuous in a good suit and shined shoes. The sun was high and bright, the radio in the taxi had said temperatures were running in the forties, warm for late January. It was a transitional neighborhood, the old Polish and Italian strongholds disintegrating as the unions lost strength and the newest generation yearned for the suburbs. The Vietnamese had moved in, and as the older generation migrated one by one to VA hospitals or Catholic rest homes, the tide of gentrification advanced. The buildings were all brick, variously restored and dilapidated, mostly the latter, places that sold for fifty thousand. All you paid for was the shell, and if you sanded down the wooden floors, patched the walls, and hung a decent-looking door on the front, the value skyrocketed, assuming enough other people were doing the same thing in the vicinity. A couple of barrels of trash sat at the mouth of the alley behind Christian, and an overloaded green dumpster sat on the street near the corner with FUCK ME DEAD spray-painted on its side.

He paced the street, risking being seen. The Subaru was parked near the corner exactly as Vinnie had said it was, tucked in between a VW and a vintage Cadillac with two flat tires. A couple of faded parking tickets were stuck under the Subaru's wiper. The car was registered in his name at his address and Janice had made him a scofflaw. Why was she so careless? Perhaps she was concerned with other things, maybe even another man.

Since neighborhood parking spots were more or less holy ground, the car had to correspond closely with the house she lived in. He therefore had his choice of the corner house and the two next to it on Christian Street. One had a pile of old neighborhood newspapers on the stoop. Janice, the queen of cleanliness, wouldn't allow that, except of course if she knew he would look for her and make the assumption—that she didn't live there—he had almost just made. In that case, she would leave the newspapers there. Or was this kind of reasoning as unstable as it sounded? Was he just paranoid and overanalyzing, seeing strategies and counterstrategies in every tiny fact? He had reached the point where he inferred Janice's feelings toward him from old newspapers on a front stoop.

The second house had a child's doll left on the top step. The third one, the rowhouse shell on the corner, was larger than the other two. The door had been stripped of paint and was being refinished. The first- and second-floor windows facing the street were boarded over with plywood. The recessed whine of a power tool worked its way through the front door. Hard to say which house she lived in. He needed a clue, and he looked in the back of the Subaru with curious trepidation, as if he were peeking into a coffin. His grandfather's rocking chair was still there. His grandfather, an old-school Quaker banker, had been the last one in the family to use the Quaker "thee" and "thou" privately. Twenty-five years back, from across the room, he had stated firmly as Peter complained about something: *Thou art an impatient boy, Peter. Thee must learn better discipline.*

Peter looked over the rest of the car. The inspection sticker on the window was expired. Somehow that and the parking tickets cheered him, slightly legitimized Vinnie's surveillance—good old bad-meat Vinnie, plugged into every computer search the Police Department ran. He wondered how many Patrick Ewing would get that night against the Sixers—twenty, thirty points? The Sixers had once been a great and proud team. Peter didn't even recognize all the names on the roster anymore.

The car would tell him nothing. On the opposite corner was a neighborhood grocery. Peter stepped across the street and went inside. A heavy man with the back of his hairline shaved two inches up the back of his head looked at Peter. Though he was in his late thirties, presumably past the age of foolishness, an earring the size of a fishing lure hung from his left ear. Janice probably shopped here for bread or a quart of orange juice. While she no longer ate or drank dairy products because of the link to breast cancer, she still drank the occasional diet soda, the caffeine of which had been linked to fibrocystic disease, which made detecting malignant lumps difficult. Janice had once wept at the prospect of losing a breast; she feared he would leave her. He had said no, of course not, but as the words came out of his mouth, he realized he'd be forced to find some private peace within himself, as would, of course, she. One in eleven women got breast cancer, and those who contracted it before menopause, as had Janice's mother, were more likely to die of it. Of course, Janice's mother had killed herself before the cancer finished the job. What do you think about when you find your mother has killed herself? *I decided right then that I would never make the mistakes that she did, that I would always have the courage to get free,* Janice had told him long ago. He hoped for her sake she would get off the caffeine, preserve her life. Having children before thirty was supposed to help out with the odds—that was another thing he had not done for Janice. She had started reading baby books furiously when she was about twenty-eight, bringing them home, peppering him with facts. So often when walking in the park, she'd see a mother with a child and clutch his arm and sing half-despairingly, "I want one!"

He had stalled for a couple of years, basing his arguments on money, time, personal development. He scrutinized young fathers out with their babies: Did they appear *really* happy? Every day parents beat children to death at the simple provocation of hearing them cry. He hadn't suspected himself of such violence but worried how impatient and aggravated he could become. Then, about the time the question began to ease in him, when he could picture himself as a father and had stopped considering all the things he couldn't control— birth defects and accidents and money—Janice began to back off, to freeze. The statute of expectations had expired. She became ever more involved at the shelter, piling up the hours, making presentations to foundations and agencies, counseling mothers, making an occasional guest appearance in a class at Penn or Temple. She appeared happy, so the issue faded. Then one day they saw a mother and her baby in the supermarket. Before a wall of sugary children's cereals, Janice faced him down: "I will never forgive you for not wanting to have children," she said. The grocery cart was left in the store, half-full, while he chased after a tearful Janice to the car, where they sat, stunned and silent.

Before him were rows of foodstuffs, magazine racks, fresh fruit. No doubt Janice had stood right where he stood now, figuring what she needed to buy, and a clerk would soon notice an attractive woman shopping there regularly. But he couldn't ask about her outright. People were tight-lipped in these neighborhoods, especially to strangers. He looked at the store clerk, knowing he had to open him up, hoping the clerk hadn't seen him on the local news the night before.

"Give me a lottery ticket," Peter said.

"Instant or Daily Number?"

"Instant. That's fine."

"And that's a buck," the man said, punching the cash register. "One dollar, U.S. of A. currency. Good the world over, best black-market money there is."

Peter tucked the ticket in his shirt pocket. He stepped over to the cooler.

"I'll take a bottle of orange juice, too." He decided to say something stupid to put the man at ease. "I'm thirsty enough to drink ten of these."

The other man liked this. "I got a two-hundred-milliliter bladder capacity. That's about half a can of soda. You got about twice that."

"What cut down your capacity?"

"The Cong fucked with a Claymore on our LZ perimeter and I had a little piece of our own mine zip in there and cut the thing in half. It brought me home, home to the absolute fucking paradise of South Filthydelphia."

"This your old neighborhood?" The trial attorney's credo: People talk about their life when they feel you like them.

"My mother's got a place a block down. She suffers from Alzheimer's, so I live with her. She walks the apartment. I finally had to throw out the rugs—she wore a track right through them. But she's physically healthy. Least I pay no rent. And rents are going up around here, let me tell you."

Peter nodded. "Looks like there's work going on across the street."

"Everybody's fixing their shit up," the man grunted in agreement.

"What's that big dumpster out there for? In the alley?"

"For the house they're rehabbing on the corner."

"How do the people next door feel about it?" Peter asked. "All that noise."

"Next door is a bunch of fucking neo-Nazi fundamentalists," the clerk spat out. "House full of them. They come in here and tell me we should have dropped the bomb on Hanoi. Kids, mostly. They think Satan's giving me a blowjob, so they put me on some mailing list. All those TV preachers send me shit. Hate their fucking guts. But they're moving back to Odessa, Texas, or whatever place spawned them. Most racist people I ever met."

One house down, two to go. "What about the rehab house?" Peter asked. "Owner doing a good job?"

144

"I don't know anything about carpentry. I was a medic, now I work in a grocery. The painters come over here all the time on their lunch break. All women. Bunch of lesbians. I see them hanging on each other at lunch, kissing and hugging and shit like that. A couple of them are pretty goddamn good-looking, too. Hell, I can deal with unshaved armpits, same as the women in Europe, right? You should have seen some of the whorehouses in Saigon. 'Course some of those places up in North Philly are pretty bad, dirty needles all over—"

Peter ceased listening, sipped his juice, and felt a sudden ease. That the corner house was being painted by a group of women painters was good evidence that it was where Janice was staying—virtually conclusive, knowing the socio-sexual-political spin of the governing ideologies of Janice, her friends, and the shelter. Perhaps the house belonged to the women painting it. He stepped out of the store and returned to the corner house, pausing at the front doorway to listen for the sounds of power tools or hammers or people inside. He heard nothing.

Would he do it? Yes, of course—he had to. He pushed his way in past the peeling doorframe, sliding his feet cautiously over the dusty floor of the vestibule. He could see the empty living and dining rooms, every wall in both pocked by smooth white stains of joint compound. Wires twisted from unfinished electrical sockets. He moved quickly into the kitchen, hearing his footsteps echo, aware of his escape route. The kitchen appeared to be in working order. Through the back window he saw the painting crew eating lunch at a picnic table in the backyard beneath a half-dead elm tree. The rest of the yard included some leafless forsythia bushes, an ancient cracked patio, assorted trash and rotten lumber and a jungle of runty, untrimmed ironwood trees at the back. One of the painters was unscrewing a Thermos, which meant, he figured, that they had just sat down. They were squinting happily into the oddly warm sun, chatting among themselves. He'd have a few minutes to look around. Dishes in the sink, a box of cereal in the cabinet. He pulled open the refrigerator. The old door stuck, but when he got it open, he saw a block of tofu soaking in a bowl and a pot of tabouli salad. Grapefruit, a jungle of veggies on the second shelf. Bottled water. Janice was here, in all her organically grown, vegetarian glory. Uncooked wheatgerm. Half a bottle of wine. Red wine unlocked in Janice a happy, celebratory lust. She was well moved in. Of course she slept upstairs.

Someone rattled at the door. Quickly Peter opened his briefcase and pulled out a legal pad. A short, powerfully built woman in a jean

145

jacket and T-shirt pushed open the door. She was lightly speckled with paint and her breasts bounced heavily beneath her thin white cotton shirt. She thrust an empty soda can under the faucet and filled it up.

"What're you here for?" she demanded of Peter, looking up into his face.

"I'm with the real-estate company." He clicked a pen.

"How did you get in?"

"The front door was unlocked," Peter replied. "But I do have the key." He smiled easily. From his pocket he drew out his ring of keys, and selected his own house key as if he were very patiently willing to demonstrate to her that he was legitimate. The woman barely looked at it.

"You know what this place is going to be used for?" the woman asked suspiciously, dumping the water from the can.

He didn't know why she was testing him.

"Yes," he began, "but I'm not sure if I'm at liberty to discuss it. The owners . . . have asked me . . . I, uh, hope you understand. . . ."

The woman found this acceptable, and even nodded as if she knew exactly what he meant. She refilled the can and opened the back door. Peter motioned to continue the conversation.

"Before you go, how's the upstairs coming along? The plumbing was one of the things we—"

"*That's* shot to hell," she interrupted agreeably. "They're going to have to tear up a lot of flooring under the tub. The plumber won't be back till three. Go see for yourself. I got to get back to lunch."

She closed the door and strode across the backyard. Peter watched to see if the other painters looked back at the house when the woman arrived at the picnic table. He decided he couldn't wait and darted up the backstairs through a hall past several empty bedrooms. Janice would take a room with morning sunlight. Hers was the last bedroom, a mattress on the floor—a single: That's a good sign, he told himself— and a telephone beside it. In the middle of the room sat an old kerosene space heater, the same device the Philadelphia Fire Department hated so much. Who would put that there? In overcrowded slum houses, the heaters had a tendency to be knocked over and start fires. He considered dismantling the heater and buying Janice a good electric one, but of course he couldn't do that, and instead offered a small prayer that she be careful around the heater. By the phone were stacks of file folders, all shelter stuff. A quick glimpse: funding proposal, architect's plan for renovation, contractor's agreement. The house

146

belonged to the women's shelter—what else would a renovated house being painted by women painters and lived in by Janice using a quasi-secret phone number be? Legal habit getting the better of him, he took his time with the funding proposal. ". . . need for the establishment of a satellite home, due to the eroding confidentiality of the West Philadelphia address and to our strong desire to serve women in a different part of the city. This unit will comprise temporary emergency facilities for 8 to 10 women and their children. Our effort continues to be crucial and inadequate in a city in which thousands of women live in crisis each day. Referrals and counseling will continue to be centered in the West Philadelphia unit . . ."

That explained the renovation, the untagged phone number, and Janice's new parking habits. He felt disoriented, suddenly full of grief, for Janice had not even mentioned the house to him, even though it must have been at least six months in the planning. She had been preparing to leave long ago, and he hadn't seen it coming. He wondered if she had thought about her plan while he had been on top of her, sawing away like a goddamned fool, fat-headedly believing she was half-dead with pleasure. Had she thought about her carefully planned stages of escape while they had breakfast? While he told her about office politics? While she chatted with his mother on the phone? While they gave their last dinner party three months back, smiling and making clever conversation with their guests? While she folded laundry, while they argued, while he told her—crying on a few occasions—that he loved her? That seemed impossible, yet it had to be true.

Sadly, he replaced the folders, pulling his hand away from the cardboard file separators with the strangely disturbing knowledge that he had just left his fingerprints all over them, probably several dozen already in the house, enough for a basic breaking and entering charge. Next to Janice's perfectly made bed was a clock radio, a ghetto box with a bunch of tapes—her tastes ran to the lyrical and rhapsodic—and a new journal. Oh, how he knew his wife! Janice's periodic decisions to completely reorganize her life were often accompanied by her purchase of a tiny spiral-bound notebook or a bound black-and-white-covered composition book, or, when the desire for sweeping change was most acute, a beautifully bound diary of blank pages. These she kept with her until sooner or later she forgot about them, until they migrated to the miscellaneous drawer of her desk, joining a pile of predecessors. Peter picked up the new journal.

He really must not read it. He really needed to read it. The first entry was dated about two weeks prior.

—Exercise—run, aerobics class, swim
—Eat right (950 cal./day), stay away from caffeine, dairy fats
—Watch money
—Don't expect too much too soon

Saturday: Moved into new unit house today. Needs a lot of work, none of it structural. I'll supervise renovation and keep the property lived in for the time being. Lorraine suggested this; she knows what's happened with Peter. And my ambivalence about keeping the apartment. She's wonderful, the only woman who gives me what I never got from mother, except for Mrs. Scattergood, the other Mrs. Scattergood . . . I'm going to miss Peter's mother. So, life will be simple for a while, just going to take care of myself.

Tuesday: Bad about keeping this journal. Told myself I'd do it religiously, that it would provide a backbone of personal time for the days and let me release emotion. Let me understand what I went through when all this is over.

Thinking about how Peter's doing. He'll grind himself down so that he doesn't have to deal with it. So annoyingly capable most of the time. He's been working so hard the last couple of years. I ask myself if he works so hard because he doesn't love me the way he used to, or is it that he works so hard because he is drawn to it and it just takes away the time and energy for me? It is something I do? Not worth trying to sort out. I'm just going to let it go. I decided today after meeting with Mr. Brackington to not write in my journal about the divorce proceedings, just put Mr. Brackington's letters in a file. He's kind, an older man who lost a leg somehow. Very protective.

Peter has been good about not calling me. I wonder what's happening to him.

Fucking good question, Peter thought.

He seems almost to despise the work. What stupid
irony; he worked so hard to get there, and gave up
so much to work for the D.A. I remember one night
when I was home early and looking for the checkbook in the den and I came across a stack of his
work files, just papers he had thrown on his desk
the previous evening—between the two of us and
our work, I sometimes think this city is one of
Dante's nine circles of Hell. So much suffering. I
guess he didn't need the files at work that day. It
was a trial prep report. I remember I felt curious. I
opened up the file and saw this photograph of the
young girl they found in the trainyards out by 30th
Street. The one who was found under the pile of
railroad ties. She and her boyfriend had been arguing, the boyfriend drinking. He killed her, hid the
body, was arrested after being questioned. I remember standing in the den thinking that *this* is the kind
of stuff Peter has to deal with each day and he
brings it into the house. How can a man think about
this stuff and also be thinking about love and raising
kids?

Sometimes I try to touch myself but it seems so
uninteresting, so *pathetic*. We always thought no
matter how badly we fought that it would bring us
back together. We could be screaming at each other
and it was as if we were actually *preparing* to make
love, the anger becoming incredible until either we
destroyed each other or made love, which sometimes was the same thing. Foolish. We tried to fill
up the emptiness of the other time by getting in
bed. The thing I finally understood about Peter was
that we underplayed his sexuality. He softened
himself, so not to threaten me. I think it scares him.
I think he doesn't understand his own urges. He
used to say that one reason he loved me was that I
let him go someplace and come back safely. That
state where it was all just in one direction, where he

couldn't think. I sort of understand—I translate to
my terms, just that warmth all over, feeling so full.
But sooner or later the sex goes. It has to.

More sad truth blasted from the coal mine, chunking its way to the
surface for him to inspect, the faulted facts on which he'd been standing. Peter put the journal aside. He'd tried to hug Janice and kiss her
and she would go rigid in his arms, like a high-school girl terrified of
getting pregnant. He got tired of reaching out and stopped trying to
warm her up. That had only made things worse. And as for Janice
thinking that he was scared of his own urges—well, he had to hand it
to her, she knew him down to the cells in his marrow. Yes, so often
he needed either to have sex or to break something or fight. That's
why he loved being in court. *You were allowed to fight,* to escape from
all that pacifist Quaker stuff! The combat was verbal and stylized and
played within rules, but you were still fighting, fighting to put somebody away, fighting to soothe the victim's family. And just fighting
for the pure pleasure of disagreeing and slicing up the other guy and
generally scaring the shit out of the defendant. How pleasurable it
was to fight, to push against an invisible wall of existence, the searching that is sex, just pushing and shoving and trying to drive toward
whatever was on the other side. . . . He glanced at his watch, decided
to read a few more pages.

> I'm 30 and Mother had a miscarriage at 33. It hap-
> pened in her bed—she only mentioned it once. I see
> young mothers and I just *want* that baby. Almost a
> hurt.

> Wednesday: The house is coming along. The car-
> penters rehung the windows on the first floor today.
> They had to pry out the sides of the frames and get
> at the long heavy iron weights inside the wall that
> make it easier to open the windows. The furnace is
> still not working very well. Tomorrow the plasterer
> comes. It's exciting to recreate a house. It makes
> leaving Delancey Street easier. I just feel small and
> contained and autonomous here, here amongst the
> starkness.
> The police electrician came today and wired the

house for the police call button. The one at the other house gets used maybe five times a year. But we made a few changes. Instead of in the living room, we're putting the button in the upstairs office, which is my bedroom for now. It's done with the phone lines, somehow.

Thurs.: I weigh 118 pounds. The carpenters are men. We wanted all female crews but it turns out that getting work at the best price means we should hire a contractor who has a crew of men. The foreman's name is John Apple. He has a marvelous beard, reminds me of a pirate. I trusted him immediately and asked him if he knew the purpose of the renovation. He said he guessed it. I told him to please not inform his crew, and he said this was fine. I wish we could just keep the location an absolute secret, but that's impossible.

Friday: Today a woman came in. We did the intake. Twenty-four, never finished high school. Three kids. Kept saying she wanted to return to her boyfriend because she loved him. In the past I've tried to give a non-directive response in such a situation, though inwardly thinking the guy is probably a jerk, and hoping she would see that. But today I felt for her. I wanted to cry for her and for myself and for all the screwed-up, best-intentioned love that chokes so many hearts. Why is it hard? I'm not stupid or insensitive. I'm strong and good and Peter is a good man and would give me anything and it didn't work.

Had another dream about Mother last night. Following her along a path and trying to keep up. I was young. I remember the espadrilles she used to wear in the summer and the shoulderless summer dress with the big square pockets. I loved that dress. I could bury my face in that dress. I wanted so much to hold her hand. I reached out but her hands were so small I couldn't hold them. It was like they were far away even though I was almost touching them. I called to her. Mother turned around on the path and looked at me. Her face was perfectly made up, a mask. I always thought Mother was beautiful and now she was so beautiful it hurt me. I said something to her and I could see she was trying to talk. But her face was *stuck*—I could see the face under her face, I could see her weeping and the contortedness of her brow and yet I was looking at a perfectly calm smile at the same time, like those trick 3-D pictures that flick back and forth. She opened her mouth, to speak, I thought. She stuck out her tongue and there was a razor blade sticking in it, straight up and down. She looked at me. Did she hate me? Then she pulled her tongue back in and smiled at me. Eyes crinkling, lips pursed daintily, hating everything so prettily. I woke up feeling confused, scared. I looked out the window until the streetlights went off. I do miss Peter.

Saturday: John Apple carried a heavy trash can outside today. He was wearing only a T-shirt and heavy work pants. I like the way his armpit hair stuck out from under his shirt and was sweaty-wet. I started a letter to Mr. and Mrs. Scattergood this evening but I couldn't finish it.

Sunday: One of the women at the shelter ran into her estranged husband in front of her child's schoolyard and he pulled her into his car. She jumped out at a traffic light and pulled her daughter out of the car. A taxi cracked into the car and the child suffered a concussion. The father drove off when the police came and now the child is in University Hospital and her mother is in the shelter, more or less hysterical. All because some jerk yanked her into his car.
Today 450 calories. Wasn't hungry.

Monday: Almost called Peter last night but told myself why? What is the point? We'll just rehash.

152

Maybe there's a chance for us, but for now I'll continue to go ahead with the divorce. I guess.

Tuesday: Last night was such an amazing time that I want to get everything down before I forget. I didn't think it would happen so quickly—

This was what Peter had worried about. Janice's handwriting was small and unusually controlled, which meant, he knew, that she was writing slowly and thoughtfully.

—I was in the kitchen, just back from my run and had taken my sweatpants off. I was sweaty. John came downstairs from the second floor and said, "Miss Scattergood, I'd like to show you something." There's something boyish and shy about him. I was all hot from my running and I felt sort of self-conscious in my shorts. He didn't seem to notice. Maybe I was noticing him. Probably. His back is so wide. I'm used to Peter's face, which is so fine and sharp. But John has a simpler kind of face, kinder looking, actually. He looks at me and I can tell he feels kindly toward me.

We went downstairs, me first. I felt sort of sexy in my shorts. Don't usually feel that way. John said he'd found something in the basement he wanted me to have a look at. We went downstairs and he took his flashlight over to a big stone oven built into the wall. He said that often the old houses had an oven in the basement. The chimney system was attached to the chimney of the fireplace above, in the living room, he said. In winter the heat of the oven would rise and warm the house above. In the summer, the basement was a cooler place to work. He made me lie down inside the oven and look up. He opened the flue and I could see a tiny square of daylight very high up. So it was a working oven.

Then he told me to look at the *back* of the oven. I did. He removed two bricks from the oven wall by slipping a screwdriver between the cracks. You would never know the bricks lifted out. Behind the bricks were hinges. They were only a little rusty. He told me to push on the wall. I did and nothing happened. Then he pulled the flue lever next to the oven and told me to push again. I did. The wall swung back and there was a little dark room. You could fit maybe three people in there, all curled up. I asked how they could breathe and he said there was an air vent that went to the upstairs closet. He said the flue was a fail-safe system so that the wall could only be opened when no fire burned in the oven. No one would build a fire without checking the flue, and if they did build one with the flue shut, the fire would draw poorly, not burn, and fill the basement with smoke. Then somebody would open the flue. I said who in the world would build a fake back to an oven? "The Quakers who smuggled slaves," he said. I told him that my former husband was a Quaker. John said he didn't realize I was divorced. I said I'd been divorced a year. He said he didn't mean to be asking such personal questions. Actually I didn't mind letting him know I was sort of available. I don't really think of myself that way. John asked me what my ex-husband did. I just said he worked in Center City. We got back to the oven—the neighborhood used to be a mercantile area and, of course, back in the early eighteen-hundreds, the city was run by the Quakers. I knew all this but didn't say much. The neighborhood was close to the river and that's where many of the merchants originally lived.

Get to it, Janice, Peter thought, hating her for her need to recount every detail of what could only be a seduction, pained by and admiring of the earnestness and care with which she lived. He heard noises downstairs but kept reading.

He said he'd recommend that he brick up behind the oven then, not brick up the trap wall but behind

154

it. I said that was fine, keep the wall so we can look at it, but make sure the rats stay out.

Later after all the workers had left, John knocked on the door. He had a bottle of wine and a bag of groceries and said he wanted to make dinner for us. Also he had brought a kerosene space heater and showed me how to use it. The house will be warmer now! He had gotten some fish and vegetables from the Italian market. So I said yes and we made dinner.

I told myself I wanted nothing to do with any men for six months at least, maybe a year. Janice, a fool for love. John and I went to bed. On my crummy narrow mattress and it was the most romantic thing in the world, just the two of us and a bare room and the wineglasses on the wooden floor. I did everything I could to please him and I liked doing it. Afterward he slept on the floor next to me, using his pants as a pillow and with one arm draped over my back. I really didn't sleep much. I think he's about twenty-six. Younger. I lay there with one hand on my breast. The light came into the room about five o'clock. The walls lightened and the shadows moved over John's back. He slept very still. Peter always plays basketball in his sleep. John lay there so peacefully, so beautifully. About six o'clock, John woke. We made a joke about the painters, how they would lose faith in me. He understood and slipped out before they came. My world is different now. Things change, spin forward, happen. I'm learning. I'm free—

"Find what you needed?" a voice hollered up the stairs.

Peter quickly tossed Janice's journal back into the spot where he'd found it and darted into the bathroom. He flushed the toilet.

"Yeah, they changed the float valve—the thing that cuts the water off," said the painter he had spoken to earlier. He pretended to inspect the old porcelain toilet, and, leaning over, saw his face reflected in the water and read the words AMERICAN STANDARD.

"Looks good," Peter stalled, his universe rearranging itself inside

155

his head. "Let me ask you about the carpenters. You're around during the day. Are they overcharging?"

The painter liked being asked a question of expertise.

"Well, they could work harder, if you know what I'm saying. The foreman hangs around, could do more. But they're doing a decent job. You see the floors downstairs yet?"

He needed to escape.

"Please show me," he responded weakly, remembering to get his briefcase from Janice's room, even stealing a last superstitious look at the bed as if it were a place somebody had died or where a terrible accident had occurred. They clumped downstairs and he inspected the tightness of the floor, heard how each board had been hammered in. He looked at his watch in front of the painter, and said he really had to see another property. He walked casually through the front door and fled.

When Peter returned to the office, he had a stack of calls and fax reports waiting for him. "They got that guy," a detective from North Philadelphia hollered on the phone. "That guy Carothers isn't going anywhere *now*." The information had come in sudden bits and pieces, and Peter stacked the reports on his desk in chronological order: Late the previous evening, a Kensington police stakeout team had observed four armed men knock over a supermarket. They waited in an old van parked forty feet from the store's bright windows and watched the men drive up, get out, walk stiffly in, and draw shotguns on the surprised checkout tellers who were running their registers for the shift total. The police watched as the store manager was pistol-whipped before opening the store safe. As planned, the stakeout team called for backup, and three cruisers converged on the holdup team as they exited the store with the night's cash receipts. The police ordered the men to halt. The men opened fire, blowing out the van's windshield, and ran to their car, an ancient rust-eaten Lincoln that concealed a well-tuned V-8. The police returned fire, and one man was hit in the buttocks. He hobbled to the getaway car, was kicked aside by his compatriots, and fell to the ground when the car lurched away. The police followed the car, which overshot a turn and crashed against the brick corner of the local African Baptist church. The three men escaped on foot. Meanwhile the stakeout team summoned an ambulance and began attending to the wounded man lying on the oily parking lot. This man was Wayman Carothers, who only six hours before had been released from custody.

Later—long after EMTs discovered and gingerly removed a loaded handgun from the deep pockets of his wool coat—a team of emergency-room residents took out the slug from Carothers and concluded he had narrowly missed being paralyzed from the waist down. A second slug was found lodged in the thick slab of muscle that wrapped around his left thigh. Though painful, the wounds were essentially superficial.

On Carothers, the detective said, was found a small address book, which listed a number of women, but no relatives or friends. Nearly every woman contacted said, when she realized she was talking to the police, that she no longer was in touch with Carothers, and thank the Lord for that. Except a woman named Vicki. The police met with Vicki and found that she and Carothers shared a $350-a-month apartment different from the one they had searched when Carothers had been brought in for the Whitlock murder.

All this had happened that morning. When the police searched the second apartment, they found a semi-automatic AK–47 assault rifle, three more pistols, several hundred rounds of ammunition, assorted switchblades, eight thousand dollars' worth of China White synthetic heroin—which suggested by its purity and packaging of blue tape and star label that it was from New York City—a crack pipe, several syringes still in their sterile wrappers, and an unopened, duty-labeled crate of whiskey stolen from a Philadelphia warehouse six months prior.

"Wait a minute," Peter interrupted. "You said before he was wearing a wool coat?"

"Yeah."

Carothers had originally been arrested in his mover's uniform. But it occurred to Peter that he may have been more likely to be wearing a heavy wool coat the night of the murder—in fact, the drunken woman who had identified Carothers had said he was wearing such a coat.

"Were you actually at this new apartment?"

"Yeah."

"Any other coats there? For cold weather?"

"Don't remember."

"See any bloodstains on the wool coat he was arrested in?"

"Sure, in the back where he got hit and—"

"I mean bloodstains elsewhere, a day or two old."

"Don't know."

"Where, exactly, is the coat?"

157

"At the hospital, I guess."

"All right," Peter said. "Get him blood-typed and have them check out the stains on that coat, see if any match the Henry girl or Whitlock. And do it before the coat is lost or the stains decompose. What else?"

The detective continued to narrate. The fact that Carothers was obviously a bad character would normally reinforce the original suspicion that he was the killer of Whitlock and Johnetta Henry. But in this case the opposite was true, because the police had found a well-drawn road map showing the ways to exit a local 7-Eleven convenience store. Even the streets were labeled. This store, police knew, had been held up two nights prior—the night of the double-murder in West Philadelphia. The 7-Eleven store clerk was shown mug shots of Carothers and easily identified him as one of several perpetrators.

Forgetting for a moment the incidents of the previous night, it now seemed impossible that Carothers had knocked off a convenience store, then driven across town straight to West Philadelphia to murder a college student and his girlfriend. The new information explained why Carothers was mum about his whereabouts on the night of the double-murder. It showed that, despite all else, he was a man of prodigious energy, having pulled off armed robbery at night and reported to his moving job early in the morning, been briefly arrested, and then committed armed robbery *that same evening*. But the new information did not explain who had killed the West Philadelphia couple and why the finger had been suddenly pointed at Carothers in the first place.

Peter decided, within the midst of this shower of information, that there was one more thing he wanted to do before turning his energies to the case. He called Vinnie.

"Peter, you're a busy man."

"I need something else done, Vinnie. This one may involve a number of basketball games between the Sixers and the Knicks."

"I'm reading you loud and clear."

"I want you to get me some information on a John Apple, works as a carpenter in South Philly. Big man, white, about twenty-six. Just run a basic printout, police file, FBI, service record, whatever comes out, if anything."

"This is risky, my friend."

There was a knock on the door. Melissa, the office secretary, poked her head in.

"I'm sorry, Peter, there's a man who demands to talk with you. I told him you're on another line but—"

158

"No sweat, I'll hold here."

The door closed.

"Vinnie, I'm going to put you on hold for about a minute."

Peter punched the buttons on his phone.

"This is Peter Scat—"

"Scattergood, this is Ronald Brackington, your wife's lawyer," a voice exploded at him. "I'd planned to give you a call later in the week, but circumstances have moved that up. I *can* file for a restraining order, Scattergood. Your wife comes home early and the painters say the *real*-estate man was here and she says there *is* no real-estate man, we finished the paperwork four *months* ago, and they describe him and she *knows* it's you. Then I have a very distraught client on *my* hands and for *good* reason. You are *not* to harass her in any way. *No* phone calls, *no* contact—"

"I know what a restraining order is. It's unnecessary." Peter said this calmly. "Janice and I get along fine."

"Look—what*ever* you're up to, Scattergood, keep away from her. You're a *pub*lic official and I don't have to, nor particularly *want* to, remind you that we can make it very embarrassing—"

"That won't be necessary." Peter switched lines.

"Vinnie?"

"Yeah, I was just saying it gets risky—"

"I know," he responded quickly.

"Risky especially for *you*."

"I realize that."

"If I find out where he is, should I make some calls?"

"No, no questions, just run a file, just keep it a piece of paper I can look at. Put it on the routine sheet, no special attention. Let me know when you have it."

An hour later came the information, relayed in unmistakably bored tones by a police ballistics technician, that the unfired bullets in Carothers's gun used in the supermarket holdup were the same caliber and brand as the bullet retrieved by the medical examiner from Whitlock's shoulder and brain. Furthermore—conclusively, the bore marks on the retrieved bullet matched a bullet that had been test-fired with the gun. Peter hung up and charged into the hallway.

"Who ordered the Carothers gun be test-fired?" he asked Melissa. "How was it done so quickly?"

She looked at him fearfully and it occurred to him that in the

159

context of always-shifting information, it was the secretary who sometimes was in the privileged position, for she knew who called and when, who came and went.

"I think—you should ask Mr. Hoskins," she protested.

"Well, of course I can and will do that, Melissa," Peter snapped, "but since you are right here, I am wondering—"

"I ordered it done," Hoskins said behind him, slipping a firm hand under Peter's arm, guiding him into a private office.

"Why the hell didn't you inform me, Bill? I'm running this investigation, on your orders! You tell me to go ahead, move with autonomy, and then you pull shit like this, dealing me out of the information loop."

"Peter," Hoskins said in a placating tone, "the word came in while you were out this morning. The gun was a caliber match and I told them to go ahead and get it checked out right away. They know how important this is and so the paperwork wasn't a problem. I was going to tell you. You've been tied up a hell of a lot today, and frankly, I didn't expect the report till tomorrow anyway. Can you fault any of that?" Hoskins stared at him, perhaps coldly, perhaps being reasonable. "You got a problem with that?"

"What do you think? Of course I do."

"We're a team here, Peter. Don't forget it."

He was torn between telling Hoskins to shove it up his wide-ride butt, or apologizing.

"All right." Peter backed down.

Hoskins smiled and opened the door, throwing an arm around Peter's shoulder. It felt good.

But not so good that right before five, after Hoskins had slipped away early, Peter asked Melissa if the Mayor's office happened to have called during the day.

"Somebody named Gerald Turner, an aide to the Mayor," she said as she clipped some papers together. "Twice."

"Who took the calls?" Peter asked.

She looked up at him, and caught within the blue eye shadow and black mascara around her eyes was fear. "Mr. Hoskins took the calls."

Angry, angry with everything, doubly betrayed that day, he worked straight through dinner in his office until eleven that night, burning through the paperwork, checking in with detectives on other cases, dictating memos and letters, calling witnesses at home to remind them to be in court next week, leaving instructions for Melissa, absorbing a foot-high stack of case files. There was a small amount of refuge in simply doing the work. When he realized he was no longer thinking clearly, he stood up, grabbed his coat, took the elevator down to the street. *I did everything I could to please him and I liked doing it.* In Janice's prim code, that was practically pornography, implying the steamiest, sweatiest, gone-to-the-devil-and-loving-every-second kind of fucking, the cosmic, obliterating fuck. He imagined her sucking away on big old John Apple, John Apple banging her from behind.

He could take the subway or walk. He decided to walk, and did so with the brisk pace of a man who, despite good parents, the many years of expensive education, the influence of a cultured, beautiful woman, despite all the civilizing institutions and experiences that he had been channeled through his whole life, knew that only physical activity eased his anger. It was the only acceptable outlet for the desire to punish and do violence and to murder, murder being the thing he wanted most of all to do now, take John Apple and, while explaining to him that nobody else could have Janice *ever*, beat the man senseless, truly beat the shit out of him long past the point that he had ceased begging for forgiveness, until the blood seeped from his ears and nose and mouth, until his ribs had splintered into slivers and pierced every internal organ, until his eyes had been gouged out by the rapid, repeated, and unhesitating jab of Peter's thumbs, until he had ripped Apple's heart from his chest, doing Robinson one better, and hold the warm, dripping, still-pumping and throbbing meat above his head, preferably in front of the entire population of Philadelphia, do it in fucking Veteran's Stadium for God's sake, and take that lump of bloody muscle, shove it in his mouth, and eat it.

He walked for nearly an hour, then stopped in a bar, had a drink, ate a plateful of potato skins, started to lighten up, even cracking a smile at himself. He watched the other patrons laugh and tried to laugh a little himself. He could be philosophical about Janice. Everybody got lonely. In a far-off way, the fact that she was lonely made him sad, and he could even work up a small amount of gladness that she was less lonely now. It was her right to do as she pleased. He certainly had gone running for comfort himself, hadn't he? He had another drink and asked the waitress her name. She granted him a professional smile and gave him the tab.

Back on Delancey Street, the house felt tranquilized. He stepped

161

over the mountain of mail piling up in the foyer, ignoring it. It was all junk, bills, or bad news. He clicked the lights in the hall and stairway, but they had burnt out in the past weeks. He didn't have any new bulbs and was no longer shopping. Yet he continued to flick dead switches on the walls at night, expecting light. He turned down the heat and got in bed. His brother Bobby's letter sat unopened on the night table. He tore it open.

Dear Peter,

Sorry we did not get back east for Christmas. I've been working on a new tectonic study for the U.S. Geological Survey. It's due in March and I had to spend January crunching the data.

Anyway, I called Mom two days ago and she said she hadn't heard from you in over a month. She told me she was afraid to call you because the last time you talked you got so angry with her. I think she's pretty upset about it, and that's basically why I'm writing. I know you're incredibly busy, aren't we all, but seriously she misses you and Janice and doesn't understand why you are so short with her. I know Mom can be a pain, but give her a call sometime. You don't need a lecture from your little brother, so I'll leave it at that.

What else. Carol and I went down to the Grand Canyon last week, took the burros down the trail. I shot a couple rolls of film. We both took off time from work. She's very happy being an obstetrician. She's pleased with the hospital and they are pleased with her, so looks like we'll stay here. They are working on some new fetal diagnostic techniques in her unit.

I guess the other news is that it looks like she's going to have a baby, in the fall. I'll tell you more when I know more. Give my best to Janice.

Bobby

When they were boys, Peter would stand in the doorway of his little brother's bedroom. Bobby possessed the ability to make a room odorous just by sleeping in it, from a combination of sweat and old breath.

162

Peter had always loved his brother's smell; it was the smell of innocence, the benign stink of a boy's forehead against his pillow. Peter
would make a preparatory whoop and fall on top of his brother,
crying, "Man Mountain McGhee goes for the takedown!" And his
little brother would groan happily and pretend to be annoyed. Peter
would agitate further, knuckling a fist into his brother's ribs, making
him writhe under the blankets. "McGhee is undefeated in four hundred and sixteen bouts!" And then Bobby would start to fight back.
"But he may have taken on just a *little* too much . . ." His brother
would be pulling his legs up, trying to establish position. ". . . the
young upstart *claims* to have the strength of nine Titans!" Then the
real battle would begin. Later, when he and Bobby were both in
college, the ritual continued on vacations. Except now Peter would
feel his brother's larger shoulders and superior strength under the
covers. Eventually his brother would say, "Lemme go, I gotta take a
piss." When Peter did not make a move, Bobby, who had grown to
weigh almost 230 pounds, would throw Peter off in a great sudden
release of stink from the blankets, staggering in his ratty underwear
toward the hallway and bathroom, his hair a bird's nest that when
combed was the color of teak, his shoulders wide as a door. He loved
Bobby for his uncomplicated goodness, a quality that back then Peter
already sensed he would never have.

He felt better now, his affection for Bobby bringing him closer to
himself. He switched off the light, smiled in the dark. He was almost
asleep when the phone rang. He hoped it was Janice.

"Yes? Hello?"

"Mister fucking D.A.! My brother is fucking rotting in prison and
it ain't—"

"Wrong number, buddy."

Peter slammed down the receiver, his heart kicking in his chest and
washing in his throat. He flicked on the tape machine next to his bed,
and while waiting for whoever it was to call back, tried to place the
voice. He had heard it before. His chest throbbed. He wished he had
an unlisted number, but as a public official felt an obligation to be
reachable.

The call came. He let the phone ring three times.

"Oh yes? Hello?" Peter spoke in a faintly effeminate voice to further enrage the caller into betraying himself.

"Yo, Mister fucking D.A.! You fuckin' recommended my brother
be denied bail and so he's rotting away up there in the prison! There

are a bunch of fucking homos queering him up the ass in the showers. He took seventeen stitches in the goddamned asshole last week. This week he got the shit beat out of him by the bastard prison guard for doing nothing! It's on your fucking head, Mister D.A.! It's on your fuck-ing *head* . . ." A pause. Peter heard conversation and a jukebox in the background, a bar somewhere. "So you listen to me, you son of a bitch! You hear what the fuck I'm saying? One of these days soon when you're out in front of your house washing your Mercedes or BMW or whatever fucking piece of shit you drive, me and some of the boys are going to make you wish you were selling candy corn at Woolworth's, instead of—"

"You just broke the law, Robinson." He flicked the tape machine off. "Section 4702, paragraph A-3, Title 18. Threat to do unlawful harm to a public servant with intent to violate known legal duty, a felony of the third degree. I'll let it go this time because fools like you deserve more than one chance. If anything happens to me or to my property, *Robinson*, you will be the first one visited by the police. This call has been recorded, *Robinson*, so it would be useless denying you made it. Your voice will be identified by the very able voice experts we employ from time to time. Let me repeat what I have just said to you, *Robinson*, you dumb shit. If you call, threaten, or harass me again, your life will become even more miserable than it already is."

He hung up, brushed his teeth a second time, decided not to floss, castigated himself for not doing so, told himself he could sleep soundly, drank a glass of milk, and, in the middle of the night, reached out his hand and found the phone. He wanted to call Janice, knew he couldn't, and wondered if John Apple was over there banging her, slipping it in and out. Maybe a mile away. By the glow of that dangerous kerosene heater. He pictured her giving Apple a blowjob, slow and wet and huge. The idea made him sick. There had to be a way to hide it from himself. He had not been thinking of Cassandra that day but now he called her. He didn't know if he wanted her to answer, but on the second ring she picked up her phone.

"I'm alone, Cassandra. I'm tired and alone."

She would be over in thirty minutes, she said, and he instructed her that he'd be in bed and would leave the house key taped inside the storm door, under the handle. He didn't like getting out of bed again, but the city, unfortunately, was not safe enough to leave a door unlocked—and of course he knew that this was the same key that Janice had given him so recently, but the irony didn't bother him; he was too horny and tired to care.

When Cassandra came in, he heard her re-bolting the door, the jingling of her car keys, and then her pumps on the stairs.

"Peter?" The bedroom was dark.

"Right here," he said, face turned toward the window.

He listened to her undress, the clatter of earrings in the ivory dish on the dresser, a gift to Janice she hadn't taken with her. The air smelled sweet, perfumed, now. How did Cassandra know to put the earrings in the dish?

"I appreciate your coming over, Cassandra."

"Don't be silly."

She slipped beneath the covers, matched her curves to his. Oh, did he like this; he was grateful. Her thick nipples pressed against his back and one leg nuzzled between his. She kissed his ear and ran her hand over his chest. He was immediately erect and desirous of her yet did not want to be pleased, even vaguely despising her for being so adoring and attentive. His anger was also a brutal lust, and as he turned her onto her back and pushed apart her legs, he knew that there was a great meanness in him. Cassandra had just washed between her legs, smelled soapy clean, and he began to pay attention. It seemed clear to him, his tongue now beginning to flick and dance over Cassandra's clitoris, that we must suffer in order to achieve love. But how much? What price wisdom? Peter felt the heat of Cassandra's thighs, remembered Janice and the women before her, flicked and teased and built up rhythms he riffed away from like a jazz musician, slowing into a tiny, insignificant flickering of pleasure, a minimum pulse that he would redeem sooner or later with a compensatory blast, building and choosing to fall back, Cassandra harder and fuller by the minute, until he decided that he would settle into an aggressive rhythm that she could not stay abreast of; it overtook her until the muscles of her stomach lifted into a knotted ridge and she contracted like a fist, her head and thighs pulling together, and when this happened he paused but did not stop. With one eye he watched the digital clock. She came five times, in nearly perfect minute intervals, and just before her hand crawled down to his forehead to beg him to stop—the pleasure apparently so intense it was nearly painful—he slowed the pace, wily and devious lovemaker that he was, and her hand lingered indecisively in the air for a moment before falling helplessly backward, his tongue apparently having slowed to a wide crosswise fluttering such that she could catch her breath. Yes—this was all good, what they both wanted, these precious, fleeting seconds. She inhaled, beginning to relax. But then a momentum began; there was a slightly faster speed and Cassandra's body tensed. Her hands spidered their way across her breasts and grasped his head, and when his tongue settled into fast, light flicking, *though not the fastest*, her fingers dug quite wonderfully and painfully into his scalp, and for this he was pleased, because in all honesty with himself and with the stadium of demons who watched over him, he loved the intimacy he had right now with another human being. He smiled into her flesh, knowing that she was open to him and that she trusted him and that he would take her where she wanted, give to her what he could. And he cared for her truly. He was in the safe real place where certainty has overtaken expectation, connected to someone now, and that meant that at least in some way he was not lost completely from himself. The muscles in his neck and back loosened, and his penis surged against the sheet. Cassandra's hands pushed and urged his head, tearing a little at his hair, which was curly and wet from sweat. Her thighs quivered independently of all conscious intention. When she came, she cried *yes* in a hoarse whisper and stabbed her fingernails into the cartilage under the skin of his ears. He whispered with her. Her strong arms pulled him up on top of her lean ribs. She spit into her hand and wet him.

"C'mon, Peter," she whispered in a hoarse growl that filled the room. "Hard as you can."

"That's going to be pretty hard."

"It doesn't scare me."

He began, then, with his palms under her buttocks, crushing her against him.

"Good," she whispered.

A few minutes later, as his heart slowed and Cassandra's contented breath washed in his ears, part of him—he swore it to himself—kept vigil next to the bed, standing absolutely still in the corner of the room. Now dressed in a plain black suit and plain black hat, arms folded, judging him. Was he a good man? If he wasn't, how severe would his punishment be? The figure's eyes glowed fearfully and angrily at the way his promises to Janice and hers to him were being lost.

SEVEN

Saturday, the weather cold again, Peter caught the Paoli Local commuter train on the Main Line. He'd gotten a first-degree conviction of Robinson at three o'clock the previous afternoon. The forewoman, an insurance office manager, had read the guilty verdict. Of course, Peter had known, as had Morgan. He could tell by watching the jurors as they came into the nearly empty courtroom; they avoided looking at Robinson and his bizarre expressions, which by now only appeared pathetic. Instead, they maintained the precious, fleeting objectivity they had constructed in isolation long enough for their judgment to be passed. Robinson's brother sat in the back while his younger brother heard the verdict. Peter gave the man a long, unmistakable look. Judy Warren's family gasped, looked at one another, and clapped in satisfaction and relief, but the moment was by definition anticlimactic, for it only reconfirmed her death. Robinson, in perhaps his first moment of public lucidity during the trial, suddenly looked down, eyes shut.

The big mob trial downstairs had broken up at the same time and Peter had run into several reporters on his way out. They asked him about developments in the Whitlock case and about the second arrest of Carothers. Were the crimes linked? Did he have new evidence linking Carothers to the murders? The reporters pushed at him, and he used the opportunity to discuss the Robinson conviction. One of the papers briefly noted the conviction the next morning. He hoped Janice had seen it.

Late on such a Friday afternoon he might have taken off a little early, but he'd headed over to the office and on the way in Melissa told him that a Mrs. Banks had called. The name meant nothing to him. "She didn't say why, only that she needed to speak with you. Wouldn't leave a number."

Melissa had stared at him expectantly then and this was unusual, for she had no reason or right to know why people called.

"Is there something you want to tell me?" he asked quietly.

She had only shaken her head.

Now he settled back in his seat, riding the Paoli Local for at least the thousandth time in his life, knowing without thinking that the train had cleared the great yard outside Thirtieth Street, feeling the long passenger cars roll into each wooden station and the hypnotic cadence beneath the seats slow to a rocking stop. The conductor called out, a few Saturday commuters departed. The train lurched forward again, hurtling past houses and leafless trees, slowing rapidly as the conductor called the next station; all this had been the same since Peter was very small, going into the city with his mother, Christmas shopping perhaps, carrying the large Wanamaker's bag, his mother searching her purse for the tickets as the trainman clipped holes in tickets or checked the watch connected to his belt by a gold chain. On weekday afternoons the outbound train was full of private-school children in uniforms and—at the other end of the same class trajectory— attorneys and businessmen with ruddy faces and blue eyes and graying hair; it had been this way for fifty, seventy-five years. They read the *Wall Street Journal* usually, and greeted one another and asked about work and the family. He was about ten when he understood why thick-ankled black women carrying plastic bags (containing work uniforms and low-heeled shoes) rode the train into the city while at the same moment these men in Brooks Brothers suits hurtled by in the opposite direction. There used to be a time when only men, more or less, rode the train in the morning, and the conductors, men of comparable age, union lifers in the old Penn Central company, would greet them, ask about the family. That was twenty years ago.

His grandfather had ridden this train for half a century, neck straight in a pressed shirt, the train ticket tucked inside his watchband; he was a man who conducted himself with the pride and disdain of one who felt he was seeing the last rotting moments of civilization. For a man who believed so fervently in God, he had very little faith in the nature of man. Whether this came by way of personal experience or historical perspective, Peter didn't know. Grandfather Scattergood's ancestors had been in Pennsylvania more than three hundred years. While William Penn had been drafting the laws of the colony named after himself and the vast tracts of forest King Charles II had granted him, his grandfather's ancestors had been chopping oak stumps from their fields. In the years when Benjamin Franklin, that unreconstructed bachelor, advised that older women remained sexually desirable because their lower parts had yet to dry up, his great-grandfather's great-grandfather was surveying Western Pennsylvania—which was more or less on the edge of the known world—and beginning to finance its exploration. Penn's idealized vision of a prosperous, tolerant city in a wilderness was under siege by human nature from the very start; during Revolutionary times his grandfather's ancestors confronted a depressed city that reeked of horse and human shit, where dogs, pigs, and chickens rooted through the quagmire for spoiled vegetables, fish heads, the guts of butchered animals, and rotted oysters, where shackled black children praying in African dialects sold quickly at auction, where merchant ships carrying silks, rice, tea, and other goods disgorged sailors who mingled in the bars with prostitutes, boozers, vagrants, and criminals, and where the framers of the Constitution, while perambulating around the brick State House, confronted a fetid jail where prisoners thrust begging poles from the dark recesses of their barred windows, crying and singing and roaring out their suffering. And then, after the Civil War, and toward the turn of the century—the great gilded age of electricity, streetcars, typewriters, and department stores—his grandfather had been born the son of a banker. Back when money was loaned at a laughable three percent per annum. As a child living in old Philadelphia, Peter's grandfather had collected horse dung from the cobbled streets for the family garden behind the house. He became an immensely stern man, but the repression was not so great that he didn't forcibly bed his fiancée before the wedding, so it was said. He became a prominent Philadelphia lawyer. Peter stared out the window, caught in a brief, compressed awareness, thinking of his grandfather riding the train, coming to the same stops for all those years, into the late fifties, while Ike was playing golf and Peter's parents were busy birthing two sons, and America slept happily in the somnolence of immense and ever-greater wealth, and the flickering black-and-white eye of the television suddenly appeared in more and more households, and the French still believed they could control Vietnam, and Elvis Presley wasn't dying his hair black yet or taking drugs, and Marilyn

Monroe was just another beautiful movie star, not the static image nobody would let die forty years later, and JFK was still a young Senator and Reagan a faded actor on the stump for General Electric—while all this happened, his grandfather became a heavy-chested cigar smoker who steadily worked himself toward death. By the time Peter knew him, he was an elder at the Meeting, a wealthy man who did not give freely of his money, but who nonetheless donated funds to Quaker activists giving medical aid to the North Vietnamese and setting up work camps for college students in the city's ghettos. That he could do so and vote for politicians who continued the policies these activists opposed was not a troubling fact for him, for he was that strange combination of a man who is socially progressive in belief, morally judgmental, and, in matters of economics—both personal and national—deeply conservative. The Philadelphia of the 1990s would have filled him with profound disgust. Here was a once-great city that no longer could support decent civil services, whose school system produced legions of illiterates, whose judges and police were corrupt, whose businessmen borrowed hundreds of millions of dollars to build bizarre towers of glass, whose unprecedented violence and drug-dealing had absorbed seven years of his grandson's life, and where the Mayor's family was no longer safe from violence. Which reminded Peter that he would get the blood test on Carothers's coat on Monday. Just a few specks of Johnetta Henry's blood on that coat would do.

The stations flew by, and Peter recalled their order from the irreverent sentence Bryn Mawr College girls had used for decades: "Old (Overbrook) Maids (Merion) Never (Narberth) Wed (Wynwood), And (Ardmore) Have (Haverford) Babies (Bryn Mawr) Rarely (Rosemont)." Every week a young mother or father killed their newborn, unable to restrain their frustration over the baby's crying, unable to address the true causes of stress in their lives. "A baby," Detective Nelson had once testified in court, "is an easy target." They had been discussing, he recalled, a dead boy found by a garbageman in North Philadelphia. The baby, stuffed in a whiskey carton, had been frozen solid. Each year perhaps one hundred newborns died mysteriously in the city. It was the norm, expectable.

He watched people get on and off the train, half-attentive for attractive women, aware that he had no plans for the evening. He missed the many parties he and Janice used to attend, for the best nights with Janice had often been after a large dinner party, after they had mingled and smiled and talked and laughed with other young professional couples, discussing with fraudulent intimacy any number of topics—politics, the city, the problem of the homeless. Then they would drive home and undress and Janice would complain about the smell of cigarette smoke in her hair and he would brush his teeth and realize he had eaten too many fat cocktail sausages or chips with avocado dip and then they would get in bed and lie there and gossip happily about the other couples. About who was saying what and why, speculating about the couples who were not happy and why it was they were not happy and what it was that would make them happy or forever keep them from being happy. For years this went on—in his mind the parties blurred into a generic tinkle of laughter and music, and they lay, all those nights, in that protective cocoon of smug and innocent certitude that their lives were more complete and happier than so many others'. Wherever they turned, so many people seemed to be unable to love happily, and the fact that he and Janice were happy then had made them feel unusual. Sometimes Janice had held him and said, "That will never happen to us, will it?"

And then of course it did—the habitual arguing and then the creeping readjustment of the definition of happiness; it was no longer contentment but relief at the absence of conflict. Then—part of the organic continuum of rot—the real unhappiness came, the palpable misery of always worrying about when he and Janice would fight next. He would see her bang the colander in the sink, or hear her sigh with a particular tone of public suffering, and he would know with the same conviction of knowing his own name that within an hour or so their carefully spontaneous conversation would conform to the groove that led to argument, resulting in a Machiavellian catalog of argumentative technique: verbal assault, denial, denial with counteraccusation, primary accusation with secondary retroactive accusations, rejection of opposing version of reality, admittance of one's own colored version of reality, accusation disguised as denial, guilt trip as apology, accusation as therapeutic analysis, apology as discouragement, and finally, recanting of apology in disgust, anger, and bitterness until he reached a moment of soul-engorging hate that made him need to lie on his back lest the ticking pains in his chest explode. Yet still he would shake his fists above his head and let the tears drain laterally across both cheekbones. Meanwhile, Janice, whose reaction was always to flee, roamed the South Street cafés trying to look happy, walking briskly in anger, wishing her life might suddenly change, hating herself for apparently not being lovable, and also for the stupidity of such insecurity, and then simultaneously comforting and punishing herself by eating some overpriced, revoltingly sweet confection. Eventually, perhaps hours later, she would return, and he would berate himself before her, hoping she would take mercy on him and offer forgiveness. But Janice, despite all of her professional training, was not good at reconciliation. Everything she had learned growing up suggested that truces were temporary maneuvers of the aggressor, and perhaps she was right. And so there was no real momentary happiness, only a waning, flickering, ever-thinner flow of affection. They ceased to make love every night, dropping off perhaps to once every several weeks. He coped during these dry spells by miserably masturbating in the shower in the morning—savage, soapy strokes before washing all evidence into the shower drain. He found he concentrated on his work rather well on those days. Eventually Janice would drink a couple of glasses of wine, becoming glossy-lipped and heavy-lidded, allowing of his advances, enjoying the confused fusion of nostalgia and present reality. On such nights they made love with a reverence for their past, a vengeance toward the present, and to feed their trust in a more loving future—kissing, sucking, squeezing, whispering darkest truths and deepest affections, knowing that they alone were loved by and did love the other, experiencing a drunken, lust-driven synethesia of sheets and skin, breath, shadows, fear and joy. He had made love to enough women—way back when—to know that with his wife it was best.

He came to his stop. There he stepped down to the platform and the smell of carbon from the train brakes lingered in his nose. The train cleared the station, and the low, cold afternoon sun sprawled across the bricks.

His mother stood at the edge of the outbound parking lot. She appeared to be exactly what she was, a sturdy-hipped sixty-year-old woman in wool coat and running shoes who had dropped off and picked up husband, sons, relatives, husband's partners, friends, and strangers many hundreds of times.

"Hey, Mom."

He put his arms around her for a hug that became lost somewhere in the thick coats they both wore. The sight of his mother's face comforted yet pained him; it was his mother whom he had wished to please as a child, it was his mother who had been his first great love, whom he had lost as a boy and then painfully rediscovered as a man. The longer he knew her, the more fragile she seemed. Someday, perhaps in ten years, he would have to care for her, and with this future in mind, and the anxiety over her operation, he looked appraisingly into her face. Her eyes remained clear and bright, but overall she was not aging well, time pulling sharply at her cheeks and the skin under her chin, her hair—once thick and dark like his own—now gone to that short, shapeless gray that most women, it seemed, eventually adopted in their fifties or sixties, when darkly dyed hair finally looked so painfully artificial that the guise was given up once and for all.

She was aware of his detached scrutiny, just as he was aware of her awareness of it—mother and son knowing each other too well—and she spoke to break the silence: "It's about time, you know. I'd just about given up." Her affectionate complaint comforted him. They got into his parents' car, which after their sons had been gone awhile, was no longer a station wagon. "I feel very sad for the mothers of that black Penn student and girl who were murdered. Don't you get tired of all this? I don't know how you get any kind of rest, Peter."

"I don't rest, Mom, I slowly decompose."

She pursed her lips in quiet reproach. "Your father said Ed Cohen told him the Democratic Party has you on some list now. Dad says they like what you stand for."

"The law and order issue is a no-lose issue, that's all." Eddie Cohen was part of the local Democratic machine, a burbly family friend who was always glad-handing at Peter's parents' Christmas open house. Sometimes Peter wondered if he was becoming a Republican, along with the rest of the country. "What do I stand for, anyway?"

"You better ask him. I want to know why you took that terrible, terrible case. That young man was so talented. They said he was one of the brightest biology students in the university. Can you imagine who would have done such a thing?"

"I didn't have much choice. I was ordered to do it."

"You always have a choice, Peter, you know that." She found her keys in her purse and started the car, as usual racing the engine unnecessarily. "I saw you on the six o'clock news the other night. Your forehead was wrinkled."

"I was probably trying to sound intelligent, Mom."

"You only do that when you're scared."

"Try to sound intelligent?"

173

"I'm not going to say any more, Peter. You always wrinkle your forehead like that when you're anxious."

He looked over his shoulder and saw three fifty-pound bags of peat moss and potting soil in the backseat.

"Dad hit a sale?"

"I think the sale hit him."

His father was the type of benevolent man who would lovingly fertilize all of eastern Pennsylvania if only he could. Like many men in their early sixties, he had given up on understanding the problems of the world and had retreated to symbolic yet satisfying acts, such as trimming his hedges faithfully and growing exact, healthy rows of tomatoes each summer.

"Right. I'll help him move them."

He cringed at the questions his mother was likely to ask. Better to divert her to another topic. "Mom, when Dad and I talked on the phone the other day, he said you're going to have an operation."

"Oh, I wish he hadn't mentioned that," she complained. "It's a small thing."

"You don't have to be demure about this, Mom. I'm used to stuff that's worse."

"Well, several of my friends have had it."

"Did you have tests yet?"

"Let's not go into it."

"I want to know, Mom. I need to know."

"I've had some. Early Monday I have the surgery."

"I want to know if you're feeling scared, Mom."

"Don't be silly," she told him. "I was more scared by your father's hernia operation two years ago. These are very routine things for people who are more than one hundred years old, people such as your father and me."

She did not look at him and smile, which meant that these words were not just a mildly sarcastic rebuff—perhaps she was angry about his lack of contact. But how was he to get his mother to talk about her feelings? For years she had swallowed her own self in sacrifice to her children, and as he grew older he appreciated this more—his mother, he had come to see, was one of those many intelligent, overeducated women who came of age in the fifties and who could have done almost anything with their lives, knew it, but had no answer to their frustration. Of course, she had finally gone back to work with what amounted to a real vengeance, and he and Bobby had suffered both

174

her frustration at having to care for them and her guilt for not doing so. It had been a chaotic childhood, with his mother's motherliness a changeable presence. He could not help but think his being such a difficult child had something to do with her unhappiness. When he was twelve and finding that the ability to be obnoxious was growing in along with his new pubic hair, he had once run into their house, screaming that Bobby had been hit by a car outside. His mother, who rarely lost her composure, had dropped a cookie pan on the floor and raced outside, leaving a smear of Crisco on the glass of the storm door. He had watched her frantically search the road for the body of her second-born, her eyes watering in frustration and anxiousness. Then she heard the steady whack of Bobby hitting a tennis ball against the garage. The horror on his mother's face did not come off when she looked back at Peter. He had not needed to be slapped for his act— such was the sudden power of his mother's gaze upon him—and yet later he had wished for severe punishment from her. Because he had never been punished, he felt he had never been forgiven. And yet, why had he needed to test his mother's love, see her reaction? He had always understood his mother's vulnerabilities in a way Bobby hadn't. He and his mother were harsher and more direct with each other than she was with Bobby. Bobby could be angry, but Peter had learned how to be cruel to his mother. Age fifteen, dancing in the kitchen like a speed freak, screaming at his mother, *I hate you categorically and wish you would die;* age sixteen, telling her she had failed as a mother and he did not her coming to his basketball games; age seventeen, on the day he entered college, insisting she leave as soon as she had arrived, not allowing her to enjoy the moment (this while other mothers did things his mother would never have put him through, such as laying paper down in drawers and spraying the dorm room with air fresheners); age nineteen, missing a dinner with her downtown in order to hump some now-forgotten freshman girl, knowing his mother had made a special trip into the city and was sitting in the restaurant checking her watch patiently. It was no wonder, he decided guiltily, that she did not allow him to comfort her.

"Should I press you for facts or should we just pretend that you're not undergoing major surgery?"

"Why is it that people must fuss over this?"

"Maybe you don't want to believe this is a serious thing, Mom, and maybe all this attention is impinging on your carefully constructed version of the facts. That what's happening? Mom?"

He watched her blink.

"Why must you push me?"

"Because I *know* you. You're my *mom*. I know just the way you're going to deal with this. Bobby's in Arizona, Dad's solemn but totally unable to talk about fears, and so I'm the guy who's supposed to ask these questions, right? Work this stuff to the surface. Brought in for the job, the number-one draft choice, the specialist in getting his mother to talk about—"

"Oh, Peter." She was laughing and crying at the same time. "Your father *has* tried. . . ." She smiled, loving his father, crinkling the crow's feet by her eyes.

"He's scared."

"He started cleaning the house, the poor man. The doctor said it wouldn't be unusual for me to be depressed afterward and that there are often aftershocks—I mean aftereffects. How silly. I guess I do mean shocks. It will be very different."

This would be about as well as he could do, to get her to admit this. They drove on, past what once was prime Pennsylvania farmland, now infected by a plague of real-estate developers, condo contractors, and the like. Once-fertile cornfields, farmed with contour plowing and crop rotation and dotted by old stone farmhouses, had been divided and subdivided into gentrified tracts of boxy three-bedroom homes and strange multi-level condo apartments that rose over hills like an advancing geometric wall. The growth outside the city was absurd, chaotic, and ugly: Historic old highways had been transformed in twenty years—within his memory—to schlock technoburb corridors of fast-food joints and office parks. He rode with an expression of disheartened disgust on his face, for he remembered what had been lost in his own life, past bulldozed swatches of denuded land with tiny red surveyor's flags flickering in the breeze, erosion gullies filled with a flotsam of plastic lids, foam burger boxes, man-made scum. His mother turned off the main road and passed old horse farms splintered into tract housing. He knew the back roads of the Main Line with a sad longing, for he had learned them as a boy. They passed the few old estates not yet broken up, coming from time to time to a crossroads, then down the lane past the house where the Declaration of Independence had been hidden from the British, and on toward his parents' home. He enjoyed the dark, wet woods as they blurred by, the warmth of the car. One of the bags of peat moss had a tear and he smelled its dark sponginess.

They parked in front of the large stone two-story house his parents had purchased when they moved out of the city proper twenty years prior, getting with the house an acre and half a dozen sizable elm and red oak trees, and enough lawn for the neighborhood boys to play tackle football on. His mother went in while he lingered outside. The yard had been the patch of the world he and Bobby had known better than any other. He had mowed it hundreds of times, knew where the grass grew in smooth, tall blades, where the plantain weeds thrived, where the clover had choked out the grass, where the mower had to be raised. For a short lifetime, he and Bobby had littered the bushes around the house with old tennis balls, Frisbees, broken tennis racquets, forgotten outfielder's mitts, punctured soccer balls, sneakers, tools their father had been unable to find, toy trucks, bicycle parts, skis, and pots stolen from their mother's kitchen. A special place, that irregular quadrangle behind the house. Many times Peter had found coffee cups his father had left behind while walking around the yard at dusk, listening to his boys holler at each other and at him—*Dad, watch!*—musing privately about his vegetable garden and the other things fathers thought about—not that Peter now knew what those fatherly things were. Perhaps someday he'd have an opportunity to find out. He liked to believe he would make a good father.

After eating a sandwich in the kitchen, he found his father in his study with neat piles of papers on the floor circling his desk.

"Pushing the paper, Dad?"

His father shook his head at the clutter.

"I walked around this house last night and estimated that there are thirty thousand individual bits of stuff here. It's crazy. We hoard junk, Peter, your mother, especially." He opened a desk drawer full of string, old stamps, pencil nubs, pennies, rubber bands, and cracked family photographs in faded Kodacolor tones. His father, who still retained the lean jaw lines and earnest scruff of hair over his forehead evident in those ancient photos, flipped the drawer shut. "There must be two hundred items in that drawer alone."

"What're you saying about me?" his mother called from the dining room.

"I'm *saying*," his father sang back, "that this *house* should be *do*nated to the Smith*son*ian Institution so that *someday* anthropologists will be able to study the cluttered habitat of Americans in the waning decades of the twentieth century."

His mother came into the study.

"Last night," she said to Peter, "your father drank a little too much wine and seriously proposed that we attempt to throw out half our possessions. I told him—"

"It's entirely reasonable," his father interrupted good-naturedly. "I was in the attic and I found baby clothing thirty years old! Keeping such junk borders on the *perverse*. I am *not* an Egyptian, needing to be buried with all that stuff."

"I told him that he would have to part with all his love letters from his old college girlfriends before he was allowed to throw out the letters I wrote him from France the summer I was twenty-two," his mother teased. "Your father was once in love with a very buxom young miss. In love with her buxom, more than anything else, I think."

"Your mother's a jealous woman, Peter. And I've made good use of it over the years."

"I'm not jealous at all. I pretend to be."

"Of course. Women love rotten men."

His mother scowled. Peter loved her playfulness with his father. Were they being that way to reassure him or to avoid each other's fears? He'd never know; that was between them. He hoped they would both live another thirty years in good health. Odds were his father would konk out at about seventy-five, and his mother would hit ninety, ossifying from osteoporosis and arthritis as her mother had. Hysterectomies increased the chances of osteoporosis along with a number of other ills, including decreased sexual interest.

"Speaking of women and rotting men," he said, wanting to avoid thinking about his parents' love life, "I'm sorry Janice isn't with me. She's busy today."

"I haven't spoken with her in ages," his mother answered absent-mindedly. "I miss her."

"I can ask her to give you a call."

They moved to the kitchen to do the lunch dishes. His father's shoulders, once large like Bobby's were now, no longer filled out his clothes. Time, of course, waited for no man, not even as decent and dependable a man as Peter's father, who somewhere early on had known he would never be a fiery or dramatic kind of man, and opted for quieter virtues. Nonetheless, there had been passion. Peter remembered the summer morning he was six and had wandered into his parents' bedroom. His father was standing naked next to the bed, fiddling with the air conditioner in the window. His mother sleepily reached out and swung a lazy slap at his father's rear end. She was naked and for a moment one breast hung free from the sheets. She fell back into bed and smiled. "All the heat in this room is due to *you*," his mother had told his father. Peter had then bounded onto the bed, screeching for attention.

Dishes done, he and his father went out to the porch, where a couple of Peter's high-school team trophies stood on the bookcase.

"Did you ever wonder about the other lives you might have had if this thing or that had been different?"

His father nodded. "Everybody thinks about that."

"You?" His father's life had always seemed ordered, progressing along the logic of his habits.

"The day I met your mother I was supposed to take a train to New York. The train was delayed and I went in to get a doughnut at a coffee shop. This was in Thirtieth Street Station in 1955."

"You mentioned this once maybe."

"I handed the woman a twenty-dollar bill. She gave me change for a ten. Twenty dollars was more then, it was more unusual to use one to pay for a doughnut, like using a fifty today. I knew I was running late, but I needed every dime for the trip. I said the change wasn't right, and she went back to the cash register to count bills. The manager came out and I explained and he didn't believe me. I was worried about the train but also about the money. The woman was no help, she was a refugee from Europe and obviously worried she might lose her job. The man knew I was thinking about the train. His teeth were bad, he plainly needed the money as much as I did. He fumbled around in the cash drawer, saying there was no twenty. The announcer called the train for the last time. I spotted the twenty in the back of the drawer and pointed at it. The man just shook his head. Did I argue with him or not? No. I dashed down the stairs to catch the train and sat down next to your mother. Half an hour later, I was in love. That's why I always say, I lost ten dollars and found my wife."

"Mom said you once told her you think you could have been happy with different women."

His father paused.

"I did say that, because I think it's true. But true of everybody, including her." His father was finished with the topic. "Mom mention I talked to Eddie Cohen?"

"What'd he say?"

"He asked me how politically inclined you were. I guess he saw you on TV the other night. I told him I wasn't sure."

"Mom said they liked what I stood for."

179

"Like Eddie said, you've got a law-and-order record of public service. You're liberal on all the right issues, as far as I can see. We talked a few minutes. He said he'd call you."

Peter wondered if losing Janice would hurt his political value. Of course it would. And what did this say about him, if he cared?

His father inspected the plants in the window.

"What's the trouble, Peter?"

He shut his eyes, then opened them.

"Janice and I are having a difficult time, Dad." Telling his father first was supposed to be easier. "She's moved out."

"Moved out?" His father lifted his glasses up, easing the pressure on the back of his ears.

"I hope it's temporary."

"Any reason to believe it might not be?"

He rushed to fill the silence, but could not mention the divorce lawyers. "I don't know how serious she is about it. Pretty serious, actually, I suppose. I can't face Mom with this now. . . . I wanted to just talk a little with you."

They sat there quietly.

"I want Janice to come back and for us to give it another chance. I think we could do it."

His father put his socked feet up on the sofa arm. He always did his most serious thinking lying down.

"Your mother and I *have* worried. It's not like we've been blind to what's been happening. You've been difficult to live with ever since you were fifteen. There's nothing more tiring than endless conflict."

"I'm tired of it, too."

The room was silent.

"Don't tell Mom until afterwards," Peter said.

His father was a man of priorities.

"I'd already decided not to," he said. "Now, let me just ask, did Janice leave because of someone else?"

"No."

"Good."

"Of course by now she might have met somebody."

"It's possible," Peter hedged, hurt by his father's accurate consideration that Janice might be unfaithful.

"You want her back, son?"

"Yes."

"Then go tell her that," his father said firmly, though his eyes were watering a little. "She's a wonderful woman, Peter. She's worth going to the wall over. She's worth going *over* the wall, whatever that means."

What would Mastrude say? He didn't care; his father knew him better than Mastrude, anyway. "I want to do something about all this, I want to fix it."

"I mean go to her when you've figured some things out. She's not going to forget you. Get your life in order, be honest—and realistic. Present a choice. And don't try all this until you're ready. Give it time."

"How much time?"

"I can't answer that. Whatever it takes."

Later, while his parents went shopping, he prowled the house as he always did when he came home, searching absentmindedly for that elusive secret that explained who they were and what held them together. In the self-written myth of his life with Janice, he was the one who had enjoyed the perfect childhood. But nobody enjoys a perfect childhood, and for all the suburban bliss, in his most honest moments, or those moments when the power of remembrance overcame the desire to forget, he knew that for years he had come home to his mother's note on the kitchen table that instructed him how to cook the meal. Gotten off the school bus, walked from the corner, pulled his key out of his lunch box, unlocked the side door, and then encountered the quiet loneliness of the absence of his parents. Of course Bobby was there, too, but he had several friends down the street. By age twelve Peter could cook a full meal, put chicken in the oven, make a salad, set a table, boil some rice, whatever. Sometimes, especially as they got older, he and Bobby would sit alone at the table eating the meal he had prepared while their mother was stuck on the Schuylkill Expressway. He would end up taking it out on Bobby. There had been several terrible brotherly fights in the backyard, once with steak knives meant for the evening dinner. One time, being chased by Bobby through the laundry room, he had run out the side door, flinging the glass storm door open. The door banged shut just as Bobby—running as fast as he could—placed his palm against the glass. His arm went through the window. Peter had calmed his terrified brother and told him to lie down. Blood spurted from Bobby's forearm and tiny daggers of glass disappeared into the skin. He wrapped kitchen twine tightly around the arm just below the shoulder. He called the ambulance, crisply rattling off street directions, continuing to hold Bobby's arm up in the air. When the paramedics arrived, the arterial bleeding had slowed. Neither of their parents could be reached from the hospital.

Later, the long shadows of private-school expectations began to reach him. It was understood that there was no reason he should not get A's in school. His mother insisted he take Latin, three years of it, and there were many evenings that she drilled him on his declensions and endings. *Amabo, amabis, amabit, amabimus, amabitus, amabunt.* "Now give me the ablative absolute," she'd say, staring into his Latin book. And he had joylessly performed for her, confusing praise with love. Perhaps he had started to become a lawyer right then, back in the seventh grade. His father was usually not home on these nights, and Peter had learned to fall asleep with the light on, waiting for his father to come home, and when he did he would climb the stairs heavily and turn off the light. "The electricity bill last month was sky-high," his father would complain. "These boys must learn to turn off lights." He thought he remembered a time when his father or mother would bend over and kiss him good night, and he hadn't understood why that had ceased.

Years later, it was Janice who restored his parents to him. He was easier to be with, less raw. His mother—quite inexplicably at the time—had suddenly come forth with family china and silver and paid for every cent of the wedding. In this he saw the goodness of his mother, and loved her freshly for her acceptance of Janice. Within a few years he had started to loosen up with them, make his return. The four of them would sit around and talk, and he felt that they knew him now, or as much as they could know of him, and he saw, too, that their affection for Janice had helped to heal the wounds caused by her own lack of parents, and so he'd seen, somewhere in his late twenties, the redeeming power that is family.

The light was fading from the day. He quietly shut the door of the study and phoned Janice. His father was right about taking the issue back to her, tell her how much he wanted to be with her, but wrong about waiting. This time, he decided, he knew more than his father. As the phone rang and she answered, he wondered if John Apple had spent the night there.

"Janice, before I say anything, I apologize for coming over to the new house. It was insane to do and I won't do it again."

"I knew you'd find me."

She said these words softly, which was good. It meant she didn't know about the journal. If she had found out he had read about John Apple, he wouldn't have a chance.

"I have no excuse, Janice. It's just that—"

"I'm glad you called, Peter."

"I miss you. That's not a helpful thing to say so abruptly, but I have to say it. I miss *us*." Would she acknowledge John Apple? "Janice, sometimes I wish we had done it differently."

"Sometimes," she responded, her voice slurry and confessional, more intimate than he could have hoped for, "I think about us being together again. It's like we're going along still *connected*, just not *together*. Like you're right next to me."

"I'd like to still be right next to you Janice. . . . You're the one I wanted—"

"Hey," she said happily, "let's have dinner tonight."

"Where?"

Where they usually ate on their anniversary. Quiet and dark, impeccable and fantastically expensive. The French waiters watched like statues from the corner of the room and made you feel catastrophically ill-mannered. But he liked the anniversary symbolism and, like any trial attorney, knew to quit when he was ahead. The answer was yes and he'd make the reservation.

Later, readying to leave, he asked his mother if he could take home a couple of light bulbs.

"Of course," she said.

"Actually, I need more than a couple, Mom."

"Take whatever you need." She smiled.

He kissed her and held her shoulders with both hands so that she would look straight at him.

"I'll see you Monday morning, Mom, after the big bad surgery that everybody is terribly afraid to discuss because it scares them, which they don't like to admit to anybody, least of all themselves."

His mother looked at him with love, eyes wet.

"That's unfair." She smiled tearfully. "And you know it."

Walking from the subway to Delancey Street, carrying the light bulbs stuffed in the pockets of his wool coat, he believed he had good reason to hope. He cleaned the living room and kitchen and replaced the burned-out bulbs on both floors—there was a genuine satisfaction in restoring normalcy. If Janice came back to the house, she would feel comfortable if the place was in order; she would think he wanted her back for other than housekeeping purposes, which was true. The mail had continued to pile up, so he attended to that, too, setting the bills on his desk, tossing out the junk. Phil Mastrude had sent a letter outlining the steps he was taking, and included a second Xeroxed sheet:

Dear New Client:
What you are going through is difficult. But you will find a way. Over the years I have gathered a number of aphorisms which, though they may seem trite or reductive, actually have the ring of truth to them. I send them to clients in the hope they may be helpful. If these words are useful to you, good; if not, give them the toss.

Humbly yours,
Phil Mastrude
Counselor-at-Law

THE ETERNAL TRUTHS

1. This is it!
2. There are no hidden meanings.
3. You can't get there from here, and besides, there's no place else to go.
4. We are all already dying, and we will be dead for a long time.
5. Nothing lasts.
6. There is no way of getting all you want.
7. You can't have anything unless you let go of it.
8. You only get to keep what you give away.
9. There is no particular reason why you lost out on some things.
10. The world is not necessarily just. Being good often does not pay off, and there is no compensation for misfortune.
11. You have a responsibility to do your best nonetheless.
12. It is a random universe to which we bring order.
13. You don't really control anything.
14. You can't make anybody love you.
15. No one is any stronger or weaker than anyone else.

16. There are no great men or women. If you have a hero, look again: You have diminished yourself in some way.
17. Everyone lies, cheats, pretends (yes, you too, and most certainly myself).
18. Progress is an illusion.
19. Evil can be displaced but never eradicated, as all solutions breed new problems.
20. Yet it is necessary to keep on struggling toward solution.
21. Each of us is ultimately alone.
22. We must live within the ambiguity of partial freedom, partial power, and partial knowledge, and all important decisions are made on the basis of insufficient information.
23. But we are responsible for everything we do, for no excuses will be accepted; you can run but you cannot hide.
24. All the significant battles are waged within the self.
25. You are free to do as you like. You need only face the consequences.

Peter confidently dropped the Eternal Truths into the wastebasket and left the rest of the mail on the hall table. Then, like an athlete preparing for a big game, he forced himself to lie down and take a ninety-minute nap. When he woke he shaved, inspected his face. Was he getting heavier and more tired-looking? He showered, finished Janice's shampoo, and stepped out steamy and relaxed. In the bedroom, he replayed his answering machine for the first time in a day.

"Peter? Cassandra. It's Friday afternoon and I think it's time for a little diversion, don't you?" Her voice lilted out of the answering machine, assuming more than it should. Did she see sex the way some people viewed drugs? There seemed an improvident eagerness in Cassandra that suggested some undernourished aspect of her personality. The other night, as she whispered obscenely into his ear, he had wondered if she actually remembered who was on top of her. She was one of those rare women who moaned while her partner was still on the other side of the room.

"Your line's busy at work," Cassandra's voice continued, "and I have to go into a meeting for the rest of the day, so I thought I'd leave a message here. There's a party Sunday night. I've been invited and told I should bring"—whatever poor sap is currently dicking you, he thought—"you. Talk to you soon."

No, you won't, he thought, I'm bringing my wife home tonight. He erased the phone messages. He removed all obvious signs of Cassandra, every cigarette butt. He vacuumed the rug in case she had left some distinguishing shoe mark; women, he knew, saw things men could not, and this reminded him that Cassandra had left the diaphragm in a tissue upstairs. The tissue had dried and hardened. He washed and returned the diaphragm to its original spot. He put new sheets on the bed and washed the old ones, not knowing what Janice might be able to smell; he threw open the windows to the winter cold and aired the house. He checked the bathroom drains for hair, under the bed for panties or stockings. He wondered if Cassandra had done the dishes. He checked, and she had. The silverware in the dishwasher rack was arranged by forks, knives, and spoons. He removed them. Janice knew he just shoved them in any old way. When Cassandra had made toast recently, she had carefully put the twisty piece of plastic around the bread wrapper. This, too, he removed. He vacuumed the bedroom a second time, and searched on his hands and knees for—what? A foreign brand of toothpaste, a hair, a kind of bobbypin Janice didn't use? Women see everything. He wiped down surfaces for fingerprints, though of course they couldn't be seen. An eyebrow pencil, an earring stud—and the game would be lost. What he needed was the mobile crime detection unit. And what he really needed was for them to find a little bit of Johnetta Henry's blood on Wayman Carothers's coat. That wasn't too much to ask.

Done with cleaning, he considered what to wear. Janice liked him to look his best, so he pulled out his last fresh suit, the blue one she bought him two Christmases ago, a clean shirt, and red tie. If he drove the Ford, that would give them two cars, reinforce their separation. If, however, he took a taxi to the restaurant, then the issue of her driving him home had to be considered. He checked his wallet—he'd use the American Express—made sure a light was on, locked the front door, and left.

By the time the cab dropped him before the restaurant awning, he had decided that spending over a hundred and fifty dollars for dinner was ludicrous, a crime. Then he saw Janice. She was waiting for him just inside, wearing the tight blue dress she knew he liked and her pearl necklace, a gift from his mother. She wore new shoes and her hair was up in a French braid.

"There's my date," he said to her after coming inside. Her eyes were excited, willing to play. He wondered if her mood was due to John Apple. He could cut that fruit in two and get different answers: One, Janice was bright and perky because Apple's attentions to her put her in a more confident position in respect to Peter, or perhaps, two—something he could never ask—things had gone sour with Apple and Janice was becoming more accommodating.

They ordered dinner and a bottle of wine. He told her about his mother's upcoming surgery. Janice smiled sadly.

"She's the mother I lost."

"I know. I always knew that."

"We picked out my wedding dress together. It was—"

"It was," he interrupted boldly, "a full-length, off-the-shoulder, lace wedding dress, with tiny hooks in the back, size six. It had to be let out just a bit in the bust"—he tossed back his wine—"and the dress and alteration cost a total of five hundred and sixty-six 1983 Reagan dollars."

Janice looked away, distracted.

"You know these things about me no one else will ever know."

"Of course I do," he responded, sensing the opportunity. "I know where the three fillings are in your teeth, not that that's such a wonderful detail. I know you rode a camel at the circus when you were six. You were hit by a car when you were riding your bike on your fifteenth birthday, and the driver was a fat, hysterical woman in her fifties. I know your left ankle aches in wet weather as a result. You sleep on your stomach and always have. And, *of course*, you peed in the cat box in the bathroom when you were three years old."

"That was an experiment." She tasted her food. He waved at the waiter for another bottle.

"I know that you are one of the very few people who can tie a maraschino cherry stem in a knot using only your tongue and teeth. What else? Your mother never would explain why the dates on her birth certificate and her driver's license didn't match. I know you're a better driver than me and most men. I know—"

"Peter, I don't like the way you figured out where I live." The tone shifted; he should have realized Janice would want to scold him. "Snooping around there was pretty sleazy."

"I'm a desperate man. That is said in truth, not in jest."

"What did you do, go in the bedroom and read my journal?"

"I went in there, but there was no time for that."

"You would have," she asserted.

"Probably," he laughed.

"Well, I was pretty upset. My lawyer is, too."

"Berger predicted you'd get somebody tough like him."

"Berger never liked me."

"Sure he did," Peter said with a full mouth.

"He said I was the kind of woman men loved but didn't like."

"I like you, and I love you."

She wasn't interested in this response. "So often men are only interested in women who present a *challenge*. If a woman is simply decent and loving, the man will tire of her. I see it at work. These women are trapped in patterns. No matter who they talk to, they still go back to their abusive man. Or *another* abusive man. It's what they *know*." She squinted and tapped her head. "Their *universe* includes a man like that."

They ate quietly. He wondered if the evening could be redeemed. Janice, he noticed, was enjoying her wine again, tasting it against her lips with her tongue, and, after the main course was cleared, when he ordered a third bottle with dessert, she smiled at him, sharing an unspoken secret.

"Well?" Her eyes were bright, her voice soft now.

"I can't decide. Part of me wants to take you home with me tonight, and part of me thinks it will only cause trouble."

"I feel that way, too."

They looked at each other.

"You seeing anyone?" Peter risked.

"Jealous?" Janice tasted her chocolate torte.

"Of course," he said quietly.

"It's too soon. You should know that about me."

He grunted credibly, amazed at the smoothness of their lies. He would not be depressed by it, however.

"You?" She looked up. "I'd imagine you'd get pretty itchy pretty quickly."

"I itch."

"Sure," she teased, her tongue on her bottom lip.

He leaned forward. His head felt loose on his neck. Janice, he saw, was completely drunk.

"I'm crazy about you, you know."

"How crazy?"

"I've got deep reserves of affection for you, stored in fifty-five-gallon barrel drums."

She laughed and pretended to scowl.

"No, it's true. A big warehouse near the river. I've got a man running a forklift twenty-four hours a day, stacking drums up to the ceiling. Rows ten high and five hundred long."

"His name please, for our records."

"Joe Cupid. He has lavender eyes and a tattoo on his chest, a wild riot of roses." That actually described a rape defendant he prosecuted several years back, but Janice didn't know that. "He was trained and handpicked for the job."

"Stop. It's not fun anymore. You're making fun of me."

"I'll stop, Janice," he said quickly to erase the moment.

They were quiet for a minute.

"I don't want any kind of answer now," he began. "Just think about what I'm going to say." The wine filled him with hope. "This is the proposition: You move back into the house. I quit my job now—"

"In the midst of this big case?"

"Yessiree Bob, and we go somewhere, anywhere. I'll get some quiet work, something with reasonable hours, and we'll start having a family. We've got about five years left to have a family, Janice. You'll be a great mother. I've always said that to you. We have a lot of things to work out, and I'd just like another chance to work on them. I mean, Jesus, Janice, it's been so many years together and you're my life, you know what I mean? We grew up together, Janice. We were *kids* when we met. I'll be honest with you—I can't throw all that away. A person can't throw away everything. Any psychiatrist will tell you that. I'm going a little crazy without you, Janice, I'm doing things—"

"What *have* you been doing?" she said, worry in her voice.

He remembered the nude, still form of Johnetta Henry. He did not want to know why he was thinking of her.

"What are we going to do?" Janice asked.

"Let me say what I was going to say." Peter had heard an open door in her voice. "I want you to consider coming back. Like I said, I'd get a different job, we'd move somewhere out of the city if you want, or stay. You could start having those kids, the whole deal. Damn it, why can't we have a hell of a good shot at it? We're the kind of people who should be able to make a go of something like this. Aren't you a little burnt out on dealing with all these other people's problems? I am. I don't think of myself as the same as the average guy out there, getting a divorce when the first problem pops up."

"I used to imagine you holding a little dark-haired girl in your arms," Janice interrupted happily. "I used to think about things like that."

"Well, keep thinking about them," he said softly. "They're damn good things to think about."

"You tip the waiter?" she asked.

"Thirty percent."

"Peter," she scolded happily.

"I've had a great night. I'm thankful."

She handed him the car keys. "You drive."

In her Subaru—the license of which was recorded on some computer file within Vinnie's empire—he flipped on the heater and rummaged through the cassette box, pulled out an old James Taylor tape, and popped it in the machine. Sweet Baby James crooned songs of love and suffering and loyalty. He drove slowly, conscious of how drunk he was—they had killed the third bottle with Janice going heavy. It was easy to get a DWI, and the papers invariably picked up on city officials caught drunk. He timed the green lights on Market Street. Bulky specters of men stood on billowing steam grates, silhouetted before the bright glass lobbies of the office buildings. They didn't scare him—they could all go to hell, or to the piss-stenched, rat-infested tunnels under the subway, which was the same thing. Tonight he was warm. Janice held his free hand.

"Hey, you," she murmured. He watched a flashing police car cross two blocks ahead and slowed. Janice pushed her forehead into his shoulder. "Why do I love you?"

" 'Cause that's the way it is," he concluded drunkenly.

"Am I doing the wrong thing now?"

"No," he said. "I honestly don't think so. I'm very happy about what you're doing."

He turned off Market. Cobblestone thudded beneath the tires, a sound that meant they were home. There was an open parking space under a streetlamp two doors from the house.

"I love this street," Janice whispered, shaking her head sadly. "I always have, long before we ever moved here."

"Well, we're home now."

He saw fear—a trusting fear—in her eyes. It was the same fear he saw in the families of murder victims, fear that the world had been torn apart and could never be put together again, trust that he would reassure them, offer them something to help.

"You love me?" she asked.

"Yes, Janice. Yes."

He reached for the door.

190

"Wait," she whispered. "Let's just wait a moment here."

He pulled her to him and made an affectionate whistling noise against her eyebrow.

"Hmm?" she said.

He kissed her nose, dabbed his tongue against its tip. She smiled sleepily. He was glad they had made it home safely.

"I want it again," she said as in a dream, gathering his hand to her breast.

He complied, then kissed her on the forehead and gently on the cheeks and nose again, then the lips; a deep, open kiss, then nuzzled in the private place behind her ear. He didn't care if she fell asleep and they didn't make love, just as long as he could hold her. That was all he asked. If she fell asleep in their bed, he would feel that God loved him. That was silly and hokey, but he believed it. Maybe he would start going to Quaker Meeting again, out of gratitude. Janice would fall asleep and he would curl up with her and hold her and know who he was again.

"It's cold out, too cold for sleepy ladies," he whispered, tucking in her scarf. They locked the car and walked toward the dark house. Janice touched her finger to the iron railing that ran up the beveled granite steps to their door.

"You sure you love me?" she asked him. "You want me?"

"Yes."

Inside, Janice dreamily walked up the stairs, heading straight down the hall. "It's clean," she said. He followed her. She let her fingernails trail along the wall. "Oh, my." She smiled when they were both inside the bathroom. "You are not allowed in here now, mister—sir." She checked the box beneath the sink and found her old diaphragm and the curled-up tube of contraceptive jelly. Deep within some sober sector of his brain, Peter guiltily rejoiced that he had replaced the diaphragm in its case. Was he evil for doing so? Of course he was.

"This will come in handy," Janice said.

"Don't use it," he told her. "Don't."

"No?" Her eyes filmed and her lip quivered happily.

"Have to start sooner or later, right?"

They embraced and she kissed him, pushing her wine-soaked tongue deep into his mouth. "I do love you, Peter Scattergood, and I do wish to be your wife, forever. Now get out of here so I can do my business."

Before he left her, he looked into the bathroom mirror, and what he saw—it was too good to be true—was his wife in his arms, her silky brown hair falling across his fingers, her nose buried into the wool of his suit, the youthful, eager flush on each of their cheeks and his own dilated, glad eyes defying the harsh light in the mirror. And wouldn't it be wonderful to make love knowing that this might bring a baby? Finally, after thousands upon thousands of copulations, with the sense that something truly wonderful might be created? The possibility was profoundly erotic.

"Okay," he whispered, hugging tighter. "I'll do the door and the heat and the lights. Be back up in a minute."

Then, having floated goofily down the stairs, something about the sound of the front-door lock as it turned made him pause. He realized that when he had passed the bedroom on his way down, the door had been closed. A minute ago it had been open.

Worried about an intruder, sweating suddenly, Peter tried to climb the stairs. But the wine made him sway from the wall to the banister. He fell forward and crawled stupidly on hands and knees to the top step. What he saw there made him stop. Janice paused naked with her hand on the door to the bedroom. She stood radiant beneath the soft hall light, her shoulders and breasts and arms gilded. Her nipples were hard, perhaps from the cool air. She was completely familiar to him. He knew all of her, every line. The sight of her naked seemed the most natural and wonderful thing in the world.

"My bathrobe's not here." She stuck out her bottom lip in mock sadness, then smiled at him. He was unable to talk, for he knew that smile and had craved it for weeks—it meant their history together was cherished, irrevocably intimate, that she forgave him all and forgave both of them, that her best hope was renewed. She turned the handle and walked into the bedroom.

The naked woman who walked out of the bedroom and shut the door five seconds later had been hurt so badly that she was unable to speak. She stiffened her back and looked into her husband's face with eyes filled not with anger—though doubtless that would come later, in greater proportion than ever before—but with simple incomprehension, brute shock. Her mouth was small, her eyes wide. Peter felt a crushing pressure on his head, as if two massive hands rubbed his skull between them. Janice peered into him and well beyond toward the unfathomably horrible trick that had been played on her. He tried awkwardly to move toward her, fumbling his feet on the stairs. *No!* she mouthed. She held her hands out in front of her, motioning at him to keep his distance. She wanted no comfort from him.

Neither of them spoke.

Janice retreated to the bathroom. He heard a muffled choking noise. He sank to the carpet, somehow knowing what she had seen. Janice emerged with her dress on and carrying some clothing. Cold sober. Her polished pumps touched the floor in front of his eyes. Janice hurried down the stairs, found her coat and purse in the living room, and slipped out the door she had walked through not ten minutes before. The car engine roared to life, and she gunned her way out.

In time he stood and lurched into the bedroom. A cigarette tingled in his nose. Janice must have known immediately. The room was dark, save for the red pin light over the bed.

"I guess I fucked things up," Cassandra's remorseless voice came to him. He was dead-dull inside his mind, guilty as charged, no need for a confession.

"Please," he murmured in a low shocked voice. "Please leave here, please."

EIGHT

In the hospital, the shift nurse asked him to wait outside while she checked his mother, saying she had lost more blood than expected because of the growth of the tumor. Peter checked his watch. Ten minutes was all he could afford. The new week was coming at him like the Market Street subway, one second a bright light in the distance, and the next, eighty tons of noise and violence about to run him over. The events of Saturday night had more or less trashed Sunday. Cassandra had gotten out of bed, the glow of her cigarette floating through the dark. Standing in the doorway—determined to crush out any semblance of romance—he'd flipped all the bedroom lights on. She stood naked, her bony chest meager and sad.

"Your wife is a very beautiful woman," she'd said then, either in self-deprecation or in anger, he didn't know which. She'd walked to his closet, where she'd hung her dress, then put her jewelry back on and brushed her hair. He'd watched the muscles in her arm. She was not attractive, not now, and yet a little jolt of misplaced sexual desire ran through him then. Cassandra had turned and met his gaze. Her voice was direct: "Remember, two women were disappointed tonight, not just one."

His response: "This time, leave the key here." And she did.

Sunday night, the local networks, desperate to scare up some sort of new twist on the Carothers case, had provoked the Governor into looking grimly into the camera lights and saying he was "taking a particular interest in this case." The D.A. had also been chased down in Washington and had uttered a few sonorous words to the cameras

194

about his faith in his staff. This activity was, of course, a nonstate-ment but it added another concentric ring of media coverage, another piece of grist for the daily news cycle, and would make Hoskins levitate in anxiety. Lying in bed, Peter had watched the newscasts. How stupid and meaningless the speculation! A trial would be months away, yet the anchors frowned and shook their heads gravely. Soon, Peter hoped, maybe even that morning, he'd get some proof that Carothers had killed Johnetta Henry. Just a dime-sized speck of blood would do.

He was due at work an hour ago but had called in to explain where he was. Hoskins had been unforgiving, even suspicious. "Tell every-body in your family to get better real fast, Peter. We got the Governor watching us." As if there weren't other cases going on that the hom-icide unit didn't have to worry about. Carothers had rightfully been denied bail and so was safely in custody, yet Hoskins would surely have his foot jammed on the gas, ordering further forensic tests at the sealed apartment in West Philadelphia, hollering from his desk to various innocent passersby, and acting for all the world as if his day in the sun was approaching. Using Peter as the tunnel rat while he carried the torch from a safe distance.

The nurse let him into his mother's room. There she was, alive, apparently, on her back, a tube into her wrist. Though she was not going to die, she seemed, if not dead, then suspended between her past and the several remaining decades of her life. He pulled a chair to the side of the bed and listened to the even whisper of her breath. Above her closed eyes rose arched wrinkles. They suggested not sur-prise but attention and decision. Her nose, once smooth and sharp, was rounder and heavier, the pores larger and not at all clear. The lines that started above the nostrils curved heavily down to the corners of the mouth, where there was no indication of mirth. Her upper lip and chin revealed a growth of hair not there when she was younger. The lips, which had always been thin, retained a patch of lipstick, and he knew that before the operation his mother had faced herself in the mirror and, with habitual perfection, puckered, applied the stick, sucked her lips in, then dabbed away the extraneous gloss with a tissue. Applying lipstick would not deliver her safely across the void she was to travel, and yet she was unable to do otherwise, for it was one of the small badges that ordered her life. The stern, sleeping mask of her face seemed to challenge the forces of dissolution. Life had been maintained, a family kept whole. "And in these times," the lines of

195

her face seemed to say, "a family kept whole is a mighty act." A legacy few accomplish. His father, wise yet not strong, amiable yet not passionate, had needed Peter's mother for the architecture of daily life as his career ebbed and secretaries and subordinates and business associates had fallen away from him. How they had all depended on her.

Janice, he realized, had sensed this strength and moved toward it tentatively, still needing a mother. She had been just young enough, at nineteen, to reseed the trust of a child in his mother, who, naturally protective and forever in a houseful of men, found in Janice something she had missed in never having a daughter. He checked his watch, bent down, and placed a silent kiss on his mother's forehead. On the table he left a spray of irises, her favorite.

Coffee and sugar in his bloodstream, papers piled on his desk, he dumped out his legal briefcase, which had remained unopened since Friday afternoon. The phones rang everywhere, and for half an hour he caught up, talked to everyone, got back up to speed. But the office tedium, the small intimacies at the watercooler, the arhythmically submerged tones of phones ringing close and far away, the men's room strategizing by attorneys on adjacent toilets—all this which once was the familiar offstage structure, supporting his onstage efforts in court, now tortured him with its oblivious tedium. Did no one realize the pain he was in? His mother was in the hospital, his wife *gone*. Why did they all mock him by not consoling him? And yet the tedium offered, by dint of its disconnectedness to his own heart, a refuge. At work he could lose himself for several hours at a time.

And still, the tide of paper and people did not reduce his worry about what had happened with Janice; the passing of every hour filled him with the apprehension. His father had counseled that he wait awhile—why hadn't he listened? Why hadn't he gotten the key back from Cassandra after she'd first used it? Maybe he *had* dawdled in that respect, stringing her along for convenience' sake. He should have suspected she might show up unannounced, based on her previous behavior—he could spot bums begging quarters, he mused, so why couldn't he spot a woman begging for love? Had he allowed events to slip toward this sort of outcome because he wanted to punish Janice? That was plausible. He was angry with her, angry at the rejection, but he had to believe he had not meant to hurt her. He believed himself able to temper his anger with reason and charity and perception. He had argued in court hundreds of times—clutching his fists before the jurors' faces, reminding them to search courageously for justice—that men and women have the right to be angry but have the responsibility for how that anger is expressed.

Unless Janice and John Apple were sleeping late these days, she had arrived at work about ten minutes ago, had skimmed the overnight log, checked to see that no crises had come up, and made sure all the women in the house were accounted for. Then would begin the day of writing grant applications and solicitations and outreach coordination. At a miserable twenty-six thousand! She could be making twice that easily in private practice! He called her. Janice answered on the first ring.

"We need to talk—I'd like to talk," he said.

Alarmingly calm: "About what?"

"What happened the other night was an accident. I, uh—"

"Involuntary behavior, Peter? Is *that* your defense?"

"Look, I had no idea—"

"Peter, I'm having a very hectic day," Janice said with infinite control, "and my responsibilities lie elsewhere, not with crazy-gluing your ego back together, so let me say this as best I can: I don't care if you didn't know *that woman* was going to be in what used to be my bed—it happened and it hurt." Her voice was neither bitter nor apologetic. "It's finished. I'm tired of talking and negotiating. Let me go without a fight, okay? We'll just get all the papers signed and then we can get on with our own lives. That's not so much to ask. I don't hate you, Peter. I still do love you very much. But we're finished."

These were the kind of words a man in his position could not afford to hear, so he didn't. "How about the way you felt and what we talked about?"

"I'm trying to pretend it was just the wine. Bye."

She hung up.

Hoskins was down the hall, in a good mood, which meant he was waiting to rip Peter's head off—but still Peter couldn't get started. He sat frozen, hearing and seeing nothing, though his eyes had been fixed on the window and his ears had heard the whoodling of pigeons on the cornice outside his office.

"I don't care if he won't cooperate!" Hoskins's voice boomed happily, savoring any shred of conflict as an opportunity to crush another soul. Peter flipped open a police report, gave it the five-second memorization. Officers had found a middle-aged man on the third floor of

197

one of the city's skel hotels near the Reading Terminal train sheds. The victim, one P. J. Delmonico, had been found on his hands and knees with over twenty stab wounds in his back. The man was known to police as a regular he/she prostitute who worked the east side of Market Street.

"Mr. Scattergood!"

Hoskins's fat head poked through the door, his skin so shiny he must have scrubbed it with sandpaper.

"Good morning, Mr. Scattergood, good morning! This is a big day, everybody is having a good, productive day, you included! What's that you've got there?"

"It's your basic transient homicide—"

"Good, good. Iron-fist control. You've caught up on Carothers, right? I expect you have. Get those blood tests pushed through. Let's get this wrapped up so we can put the Mayor at rest and get the reporters out of our hair. We'll talk later!"

Boom, and gone. Peter was safe for another half hour, perhaps. He returned to the file. Delmonico had been servicing a customer who, apparently, in the moment of climax, had whipped out a knife and started stabbing. This kind of thing happened all the time. Posing as either a gay trick or gay pickup, a robber would gain access to a man's apartment or hotel room, do him in. The police had plenty of evidence: semen with blood type, bloody fingerprints on Delmonico's back, hair samples, a witness down the hall of the hotel who saw an unidentified somebody running out and buckling his pants. The police—some of whom were no doubt masking their own homophobia—liked to tell stories about Jersey kids, tough mother-fucker football players in their varsity letter jackets, coming into the city for a blowjob and suddenly realizing that the lovely brunette they'd just paid fifty bucks was a man. The really good he/shes would lure a man into a car and get screwed in the ass without the customer ever knowing. Most just had the breast implants, leaving the external plumbing intact. Many drifted up to midtown New York City, Forty-second and Broadway. They made better money up there, had other friends, a subculture, specialized bars, etc., to combat the massive loneliness of being a transvestite.

He phoned his wife again.

"Hello, this is the women's shelter. My name's Janice. How can I help you?"

"Janice, let me just take a minute—"

There was only the sound of the phone being put gently on the receiver. He called a third time. Another woman answered in an upbeat voice.

"May I speak with Janice Scattergood, please?"

"She's in a meeting," the efficient voice said. "May I take a message?"

"Thank you, no," he whispered.

There was no time to think about this further. The phone trilled almost immediately.

"This is Lieutenant Snyder down at the desk, sir. There's somebody who wants to talk with you."

"These people want to see somebody or me in particular?"

"You, Mr. Scattergood."

"Just send them up, seventh floor."

"*She* won't come up, sir."

"What's her name?" Maybe it was Miss Donnell.

"It's Mrs. Banks."

He remembered somebody by that name had phoned recently. The world was full of nuts, and many of them liked to call up or visit the D.A.'s office, claiming to have important information. The police usually followed these leads up, but this was an opportunity for him to duck out of the office for a few minutes. He took the elevator down and turned left and out toward the desk detective. The lobby of the building was little more than a gray space that led from the outside door to the elevator, but visitors had to get past a detective.

"Counselor—" The detective motioned.

Outside the door, facing the street, stood an elderly black woman wearing a fox fur hat. She stooped over a cane.

"She wants to talk."

"She say about what?"

"No. You want me to get rid of her?"

"Yes, but I better go see what she wants."

He pushed outside into the noise and air of the street. "Ma'am, may I help you?" he hollered.

She turned her wrinkled face toward him.

"My name's—" he began.

"I know who you are, Mr. Scattergood. I appreciate you seein' me."

"How can I be of help?"

"Nobody thinks an old woman knows nothin', Mr. Scattergood. That I lost my hearin', or my mind. Well, I got both."

If she had anything to tell him, he realized, it wouldn't be directly in front of the D.A.'s office, with detectives and prosecutors and cops passing in and out. So he suggested they step into the restaurant a block down. She shuffled along, testing each groove of the sidewalk with her cane.

"I can make it. I made it all the way down here," she complained, working her tongue in her mouth.

In the restaurant she moved slowly to a table by the window, and with a series of small movements succeeded in sitting down.

"I saw you on the television news," she began. "Looks like you scared they gone see somethin' inside of your head," she crabbed, removing her gloves.

"Maybe you're right."

"I have dealt from time to time with the police. I can't feel I can trust them, and so I saw you up there squirmin' and sweatin' and I thought, that young man is very nervous that he do the right thing."

"Well, you're right." He took out a pad of paper and pencil. There could be a hundred reasons she was there. "Why do you want to talk to me?"

"No, none of that." She waved a bony, arthritic hand at the paper. He noticed a wedding ring trapped between the immensely enlarged knuckles of her finger. "No, you just listen to me."

He put the paper away.

"I have known that child since she was a baby," the woman announced. "And I have lived in my neighborhood for forty-two years."

"Who, ma'am, who do you mean?"

"Johnetta."

Instinctively he moved closer, spoke in a quieter voice. He wished they'd gone somewhere less public.

"Go on, uh, Mrs.—"

"Mrs. Banks."

"You called earlier—"

"Yes, and that girl just about asked me every question she could, includin' where the pearls are hid," she cackled. "My husband and I married in 1922 in the church in Tupelo, down south. I still got my sister there and a whole mess of family. Bet you don't even know where that is."

"Oh, I might."

She smiled at him. They had business to do but they also liked each other.

"Then tell me, Mr. Scattergood."

"Small town in Mississippi, Mrs. Banks."

She grunted. Yet she also appeared to sense his impatience.

"I'm gettin' to it, directly."

The waitress came and he ordered two coffees. She rubbed her hands absentmindedly.

"Now then, Mrs. Banks, you've got something to tell me."

She nodded gravely, with her eyes down.

"I know who killed Johnetta."

"Was it the same person who killed Darryl Whitlock, the Mayor's nephew?"

"Nuh-uh," she hissed.

"What makes you know?"

"Because the ones who want her dead didn't want him dead."

"Why're you telling me this, Mrs. Banks? Usually people in your position are sure to get assurances before they talk."

"I don't need no *assurance*. I'm eighty-eight years old. Nobody gone do nothin' to this old bag of bones that ain't been done before."

"All right. Who killed Darryl Whitlock?"

"I don't know," she said with a dismissive pursing of her lips, as if the question were unimportant.

"How about Johnetta Henry?"

"I can't say, exactly." She stirred creamer into her coffee.

"What do you know?"

"Maybe some people didn't like that girl, you understand what I'm sayin'? He was a mighty fine young boy and he had himself a future. That young man had been accepted by the Harvard University to become a doctor. Maybe they said some bad things about her, some mighty bad things that would make Jesus himself shudder." She shook her head, apparently remembering those awful things. "I get so *tired* of hearin' the way people talk, Mr. Scattergood, it goes against God. Some people—maybe you should ask some people up around Fifty-second Street. Why, she was just a little mixed up, never eat enough. I used to ask that child why she was so skinny, and why she never eat nothin'. But she went to church. Her little child, Tyler, he sing so *sweet*. My little Tyler, I'm his great-grandma. I been takin' care of him for two years now, ever since he had a little heart operation. They said he might be weakly but he *strong* and healthy. The people at the church donated blood, that's why. Johnetta my granddaughter, Mr. Scattergood. I know that gal, I raised her after her mother died and

201

her father went to prison. Maybe she run around some, but she real steady with this boy."

"Who was the child's father?"

"Johnetta, she never tell me that."

"Did she know?" Peter asked.

"Of course she did." The old woman glared, tossing his insinuation back into his face. "She just never got around to tellin' me."

Here were a couple of facts the police hadn't turned up. It didn't surprise him.

"Who was saying these bad things about your granddaughter, Mrs. Banks?"

"I can't say exactly as I remember."

"Was it somebody in the neighborhood, somebody in the boy's family?"

"I just can't say that."

"You told me you weren't too old to remember things, Mrs. Banks."

She lifted her birdlike shoulders and stared at him angrily. "Johnetta tell me Darryl ain't supposed to be seeing her. His father say Darryl made to be a doctor, and had no place for that kind of gal. They thought she was too black," the old woman said bitterly, considering the irony of this prejudice. "They decided she was just the worst kind. They kept tellin' that poor boy that over and over until he was just about crazy."

"What kind of girl was she, Mrs. Banks?"

"Oh, she run around some when she was younger." He extrapolated: She fucked whomever, took drugs, followed her desires, like most of humanity. "She liked the men for a time, but then she had the baby and started to settle down."

He remembered the autopsy report observation that she had undergone childbirth. "What do you know about this man Wayman Carothers?"

"He just some fool, far as I know from the papers."

"Go on, please."

"There was some talk about how when Johnetta worked in the campaign she heard some things—"

"What campaign, the Mayor's campaign?"

Mrs. Banks stared with a dead calm right into his eyes. The woman had a palpable force of will.

"Uh-huh."

The promises and noise and slurs and money of the campaign still

202

hung in the collective consciousness of the citizenry who watched the dangerous edge of political change. A campaign was a short-term civil war, and the new Mayor had won by capturing the white liberal vote and by having a bigger army of grass-roots organizers who delivered the black vote. Cars with loudspeakers slowly touring the crazy-quilt pattern of black wards of North and West Philadelphia, exhorting everyone to vote the black Democratic candidate into office. Polling places in little corner groceries, public schools, church basements, even private homes. The white candidates—Democrat and Republican—didn't even try to gather votes there; they just slapped up a few campaign stickers on the telephone poles and concentrated on the Italian and Irish neighborhoods. In Philly, the black voters made the difference when they turned out in high enough numbers.

"She answered the telephone. Everybody know how that new Mayor had to get his money from somewheres. Johnetta, she say a man would come in every day with a whole mess of money, cash money, and the man would come and go that quick, and she could hear them counting in the back office."

"How much?"

"She said she thought it was maybe ten thousand each day. And they used it sometimes, to go buy food for everybody or to put gasoline in the Mayor's car or somebody's else's or something. Or if they needed something done. She just kept her mouth shut," said Mrs. Banks. "You know what I'm talkin' about, where that money came from."

"Where?"

"Oh, you know what I mean."

Every big campaign had its distinct web of financing, much of it legal and reportable, but some of it not quite legal or from contributors who would rather remain nameless or who the candidate preferred not to be associated with in public. "She decided not to tell anyone?" Peter asked.

"Well, I expect she wanted to stay with her young man and didn't say nothin' about who was comin' and who was goin'."

By instinct he slowed his thinking; she had only given him shadows of facts, nothing substantial, nothing he could have corroborated. "You're saying—let me be sure I understand this—Johnetta knew something about the Mayor's campaign, she knew about some particular people who gave money?"

The woman clucked in impatience at his white man's stupidity, and her anger at him released her deeper outrage: "What I'm tryin' to *get said* to you is that gal knew she had found a good man and they was in love, but the family was too high and mighty and *they* thought she was a trashy nigger from North Philadelphia when they was long-time business people—huh!—and they saw she knew about certain things. They always preachin' about co-muni-ty, but them people don't care nothin' about nobody, exceptin' they own. Now, I can see some of their worry, if you want to know the truth. She had a mouth on her, I admit it, and—Praise God! Oh, praise God!" She stared at the window outside, rose out of her seat, and moved surprisingly quickly to the door. "Tyler!"

Peter turned in his seat. A black man, his face hidden behind sunglasses and hat, was holding a boy of about three under his arm like a bag of laundry. The boy was packed into a snowsuit and knitted cap, and cried tentatively at the sight of his great-grandmother. The man pointed to the boy and beckoned fiercely to Mrs. Banks as she exited the restaurant.

"Mrs. Banks!" Peter called. "Wait!"

Peter followed and flung himself toward the door, but not before another black man leapt in front of it. At the same time, the man in sunglasses hurried the old woman and child around the corner. Peter shoved with all his might, from the knees and thighs. The door did not move. The cold glass was heavily fogged from the heat of the restaurant and he couldn't see through it well. He swiped at the glass and pressed his eye to the cleared spot. On the other side of the door—six inches away—was the face of the second man, expressionless and yet—in the eyes and around the dry, pressed lips—sadder than any face Peter had ever seen. His eyebrows were broken by long-healed gashes and beatings, the nose long ago punched in. Below the man's mouth arced a thin, dark scar—an absurd smile of damaged tissue. The man checked to see that the others were gone, looked back at the solitary eye staring at him through the fogged glass, and silently shook his head: *Don't mess with me*, the man's sad eyes said, the gray moons beneath them testifying to unutterable sufferings endured and, perhaps, inflicted. In this face was the deadened quality of one who has been furious for a lifetime. Then, as if yanked backward by an unseen hand, the man leapt away from the door. Peter stumbled into the street. He tried to give chase. The man slipped through the crowd of midday shoppers and was gone.

*　　*　　*

"Hey, Mistah Scatter-God, I gotta show you something."

Back in his office, Peter looked up from his desk, where he'd written down all he remembered about what had just happened with Mrs. Banks. There was no quick way of judging the worth or truth of what she'd said. Here was Berger, carrying a stack of files.

"I saw Stein over in court at a pretrial," Berger began, wiping his hands over his scalp. "You have to hand it to him, he takes the cases no one wants. He was defending some guy who shot at a crack dealer for not getting exact change."

"Exact change?"

Berger tossed his files on the desk.

"This guy's from Chester. Drives up twice a week to buy coke at the Dewitt Park housing project. Not that he can't get it in his own neighborhood, of course. This is a total bullshit case. Pisses me off, for once—"

"What about Stein?"

"Well, what I'm going to tell you will interest you, but first I got to tell you this story." Berger ran his thumbnail along the cracks separating his teeth. "This guy bombs up to the projects twice a week. He comes into the city because the coke's better and because he's got some girlfriend in the neighborhood. Makes you fuck better, cocaine. Five times in an hour, etcetera, etcetera. Not that I would know, of course."

"Of course," Peter answered pointedly

"What's that mean?" Berger said.

"I mean, pal, that some ass-wipe detective I talked to a couple of days ago asked me about your recreational use of pharmaceutical substances."

Berger rotated his head toward the door and gave it a soft nudge with his toe until it shut. "Okay, Peter. That's over with. Done. It's been a problem but no more, and I don't want to discuss it."

The small room was silent. The police were routinely tested for drug use. Those who refused to be tested could be fired. Berger frowned at Peter, waiting for his reaction.

"I owe you a hell of a lot, Bergs. I want—"

"You don't owe me a speech, Peter. I can't take one of your moralizing speeches. Save it for the jury. It works better on them anyway."

"Fine." Peter shook his head in disgust.

205

"If I'm a hypocrite, just let me be one, all right?"

Berger gripped the edge of the desk with both hands and stared right at him; the man was plainly terrified.

"Suit yourself," Peter declared.

"If I'm going to fuck myself up, which I'm not, just let me do it without—"

"*Fine*," Peter snarled.

The room was quiet while the two men hated each other for caring so much. On the other side of the wall somewhere, a phone trilled.

"Tell me about this dealer," Peter said finally.

Berger slowly came back to life. "All right, this guy drives around in his car. Duded up with smoked glass, fog lights, initials on the door. This guy is a real stud, right? Roll down the window, get the stuff, pick up the girlfriend, have a time, right? Got it figured down to the last dollar. He doesn't make that much, but what he does make he spends carefully." Berger was into the role, shaking his head, jiving and shucking. "Got to have the best, yeah, motherfuckah. So he drives into the projects and they've got all these spotters and checkers and guys with radios and pagers and stuff. The neighbors say they see Jersey and New York plates around there, all the time, even Connecticut, Virginia. You know, these kids with about eight thousand dollars' worth of gold rope around their necks. And the earrings shaped like dollar signs. So the guy drives in. They wave him in and he makes the buy. He has a .45 under the seat. Turns out the kid selling doesn't have change for a fifty. Can't leave his post, there's too much business. The guy in the car either takes the junk and not get like three bucks back in change, or forgets the whole deal. These kids are getting used to dealing with hundred-dollar bills. Probably a status thing not to have little piddly-shit change like fives and tens. So this guy blows his top and pulls out a gun, takes a shot. He's got fucking dum-dums in there—"

"Exploding bullets?" Peter reacted, with a sense of doom.

"Yeah. Not even serious about it, figures he's bought a shot. I mean, if he picked off the dealer, maybe there'd be some sort of sick justice in all this, right? Well, no. He just squeezes one off, half-assed. The gun's heavy and he still has his left hand on the steering wheel. The dealer's running away from the car. It misses, goes through a window forty yards away. Forty yards! This twenty-eight-year-old mother of three is warming baby food. Her baby is sick. And her mother is a cripple with high blood pressure and this woman takes care of her, she's a fucking *saint*. We have a picture of how the pots were on the stove. Her kid's next to her. The bullet doesn't hit anything—not a tree, not a windowsill, nothing. Goes through the open first-floor window and *boom!* right in the neck. Practically fucking decapitated her. The oldest kid is standing there and sees the whole thing. The woman died in less than a minute. The kids are in a temporary foster, the old grandmother is in the hospital, the whole bucket of shit."

"Never'll go to trial."

Berger nodded in agreement. "I offered seven and second-degree. He'll probably take it. This is the kind of shit case that brings out the fascist in me, Peter. Prison is expensive. Nobody wants to pay thirty thousand a year of taxpayers' money for these guys. Hell, why not just round them all up, take them to the edge of a cliff, and blow their brains out and kick them over? The total number of casualties would be lower if that happened. You can call me any name you like, a Nazi-racist-fascist asshole, but I think the world would be a better place."

They both knew Berger didn't believe that. Though, on second thought, maybe he did, with the blind fervor of one who must burn off his guilt. The whole picture was much more complicated than blaming the dealers. It was guys like Berger who helped to keep them in business. And it was the nation's unwinnable war on drugs that made the price of drugs so high, thereby eliciting on the streets the violence over the profits.

"You feeling better now?" Peter didn't hide his disgust.

"No, and fuck you, too."

"What about Stein?" Peter asked.

Berger sighed, the tempest done. "He knows you and me are friends. He comes up to me and says that strictly unofficially he wants you to meet with him and Carothers soon. I said when and he said as soon as—he worried about his client's safety. Just you and me, too, if you need backup. Says he knows you're a good egg, that you don't dick over defense counsel. I said, he's just never been caught."

"Ha," Peter said in a dry voice.

"I just wanted to scare him a little. So he says that he doesn't want Hoskins in on this. I said, are you crazy, I can't guarantee anything. We don't do that kind of thing, even if we wanted to. Everything's above board. We follow procedure, etcetera, etcetera. He says he knows that. He says he's appealing to my higher instincts. I'm a sucker for those higher instincts, let me tell you. Okay. So I say, look, if there's something you think Peter should know, something you want to negotiate, there's no harm in that. He says he knows when Hoskins is over at the Union League for lunch every week, has been for ten years. I said fine, you could bring your man up at noon for forty-five minutes. He said why can't you guys come out to the prison and I said no way."

"We don't have the time."

"Of course."

"Has to appear harmless. Has to *be* harmless."

"Right. Just bring him up for forty-five and get him out again. I told him you'd call. I thought he could meet us in the conference room on the eighth floor. Skip the seventh floor entirely. Christ, it's lunch, everybody's out. We'll ask a few questions about the armed robbery, whatever. Hoskins will pick up on it sooner or later, but I say you could take that chance."

"Did they get through the hearing?"

"No, the room never turned over. Judge Kravetz is behind."

Berger had taken a risk by being the intermediary. But Berger liked risks—that's why he was a coke addict.

"Should I call Stein right now?" Peter asked.

Berger's eyes glazed and he took short, shallow breaths. This was how he did his best thinking. "No. Not yet. Give it a little time, let the pressure build. Let him call you."

"You do know there's something fucked about this case," Peter said in a quieter voice. He wouldn't mention Mrs. Banks. He didn't know if he still trusted Berger. "Don't you?"

"Of course."

"I haven't figured it out."

"You will," Berger said, looking at Peter. "Want to tell me what you were writing about when I came in?"

"It's nothing," Peter said.

"You lost faith in me?"

"Not as a lawyer."

After lunch, Mastrude wanted him to sign some papers. The secretary waved him in.

"What do you hear from Janice?"

Mastrude's fingers on fluttered on his belly as he sat back in his chair. "Your wife's lawyer has filed for a legal separation. He also informed me this morning of Janice's terms of the divorce. Seems your wife is taking the highroad, Peter."

208

"What do you mean?"

"She wants very, very little."

"She wanted a hell of lot when we still lived in the same house."

"No more."

This bothered him. Mastrude nodded, indicating he understood the psychology behind Janice's stand. "She's making it very easy on you. She wants this thing to be as smooth as possible, according to her lawyer, so smooth she's willing to cede a lot of ground."

"Hell, if we get divorced, I want her to be well situated—"

"She's not going to let you buy off your feelings of guilt."

"That's a bullshit position, you know that," he snapped.

"A lot of guys would think you were a fool. But of course you want to see that she's comfortable."

"By not taking *anything*, she's saying—"

He stopped, not wanting to say it, but Mastrude finished his thought: "She's saying there's nothing from the marriage she wants to take with her."

Well, he couldn't blame Janice. If she'd lured *him* into her bedroom and he'd found John Apple lying in bed with a hard-on and smoking a cigarette—the factual equivalent to Cassandra's presence—then he'd have plenty of hate for Janice, too, the kind of blind hate that distorted all information into fuel for anger. But Mastrude was wrong. Janice's denial of whatever he might be able to provide was not the highroad, it was the fuck-you road, the malice-aforethought, you-goddamn-bastard road.

"Could she be getting money from anywhere?" Mastrude asked.

"I don't think so. She hasn't any family left. There's a father who might live in Idaho in a trailer or somewhere." Another messy end, and perhaps Peter was just one in a series. "Nobody's heard from him in over ten years."

"Friends?"

"Her friends could help her out temporarily, but not in any long-term way."

"People in need don't usually *reject* financial assistance unless they have it coming from another source—that's my experience." Mastrude shrugged. "Righteousness is likeliest when it's affordable."

"I'm not surprised by her."

"That shows your inability to explain her behavior." Mastrude winked. "Do you think she's going into private practice?"

Peter looked toward the window, his mind struggling to find some small moment of grace, the kind of perspective one was supposed to acquire as one aged. He couldn't do it. "She'd have to disengage from the women's shelter, which I doubt she would do now since it gives her a community of people. And she's deep into a new project. Plus she'd also have to borrow first to set up a practice."

"Maybe she's making more where she works," Mastrude suggested.

He was familiar with the funding of the shelter; for years he had heard about its finances, and he'd often given Janice some general legal advice. "They operate on almost nothing, really—grants, state funding, a few contributions."

"Is she frugal enough to cut off your support?"

The answer was yes, and it made him sad to think of her counting every penny. The thrill of independence would wear off.

"Janice has been on her own since sixteen," Peter finally said quietly. "She's a survivor."

"Nope, can't buy that. A professional woman at thirty has different needs than a teenager," Mastrude insisted, "so I'm going to say it again—is there any other *possible* source of money for her?"

"I honestly can't think of any." Though maybe Big Bad John Apple had some cash.

"How shall I respond to her lawyer?"

"Tell him the offer of assistance still stands, in a general way, but that I would prefer she and I sit down privately and negotiate."

"She's communicating only through the lawyer."

"In that case, tell him to tell her that should she change her mind, then I'm willing to help."

Mastrude shook his head again. "No. I'll just say you understand and accept the terms. If she changes her mind later, which is what you want her to do, then if you have already shown your willingness to provide for her, she might still not take your help—in other words, if you tell her you *want* to help, then she may not accept it because she will feel like she's playing into your hand, like she has made no move spontaneously that wasn't anticipated by you." Mastrude's eyebrows lifted as he waited for Peter's recognition of what had just been said. "In other words, again, let her provide herself with the belief—or illusion—that she is operating autonomously. It allows her to maintain her self-respect, it allows you some self-respect, and it may get you what you want, too."

"You seem to have all the answers," Peter said.

"I have some of them. That's why you're paying me."

"Now I know." He scowled. "Why do I remain unconvinced?"

210

Mastrude knocked his knuckles together as if he were reducing many words to an important few. "If I told you, it wouldn't help."

Little match heads of stomach acid ignited somewhere under Peter's breastbone; he was miserable, beyond himself with unhappiness. He'd seen the same in Berger's face. "Tell me anyway."

"Nothing is learned that isn't experienced, including these very words."

So that was what they had come to. For *this* he was looting what available cash was left? "The essence of tragedy," he assumed dully.

"Yes!" Mastrude followed, enthusiastic at the turn in the conversation, away from the dirty details of yet another divorce case. "And there's a corollary to it: Nothing is believed until one figures out why one didn't believe it in the first place."

"Such as?"

"Come on, Peter. Don't be coy." Mastrude shook his huge greasy head in judgment. "You deal in drama every day."

This was true. City Hall was six floors of defendants arguing against the codified system of destinies, saying that it was not possibly they who stabbed the boyfriend, not they who broke into the warehouse or held up the convenience store, that their back property taxes owed were a mistake, or, in a slightly different form of argument, saying that yes, they beat and mugged five elderly people but that circumstances should ameliorate their fate, that if they pleaded guilty to possession of cocaine and not to the charge of selling it, they would finger the guy who distributed it. Or, if they were granted immunity for selling school-district heating oil to slum landlords, they would testify against the guy who doctored the city books and took the kickbacks. Plea-bargaining, necessary to keep the bodies moving through the system, was nothing more than disagreeing with the fate one knew one had constructed for oneself.

"You know, this is the thing—look." Peter laughed, watching Mastrude's waiting expression. "I believe the world is a good place and that most people are good. I do really. But then you have to be realistic, even if it hurts. You take the average guy out there, you can tell him that, say, if he does not quit beating his girlfriend every Saturday night, then pretty soon she's going to get angry and call the cops. You can tell him that if he keeps it up, he'll get picked up for aggravated assault. You can tell him this. I've seen it. People like to think that destiny is a question of intelligence and occupation, and upbringing. You know, that specific social norms will determine the outcome. I don't believe it. The point is—of course, I'm not telling you anything you don't know—you can tell and tell and *tell* a person how they are fucking up, and the fact remains so often that they won't believe you, or they will believe you but they won't change—" He had an idea. "For example, look at you."

"Me?" Mastrude frowned in surprise.

"You're fat as a goddamned house. The blood is probably squeezing through your arteries one molecule at a time, and you *know* what you could do to change that. So yes, I *agree* with you, more than you know. I could even sit here and tell you all this and act as if I were above this activity, and yet not be. Isn't that right? Isn't that what makes you worried?"

"Should I be worried?"

"It depends on whether you care."

"I care, but there are other people who care about you."

Peter hoped his remark about being fat hadn't hurt Mastrude. "Why do I feel like we no longer are acting like client and divorce lawyer?" he asked.

"Because we aren't."

Mastrude told his secretary to hold his calls. "I don't live for my work. I hate splitting people up—I'd rather help put them back together. But I recognize it happens and that I can't change the script of the marital tragedy, so to speak. So I help guys like you get back on their feet and heal and learn. Get it right the next time. To help a person mold the mess of their life back into something happy and worthwhile—that's an ideal to me. Ideals have a way of clarifying priorities. My priorities are to help people get on."

"That's why I wanted to be a D.A.," Peter jumped in. "I thought I would help—"

"Aaah, come on," Mastrude complained. "Being a prosecutor fit a lot of your other needs. Power, intrigue, knight on a white charger, the whole package. You're no better than the rest of us. Don't you see that?"

"You sound like my wife."

"I've never met her, but let me make a guess, based on my own experience. By helping others she reenacts the process of her own healing—"

"Yes, but so—"

"Listen to me, you're younger and more naive than you know." Mastrude scowled. "I blew it once, too. I truly screwed things up.

And she asked for a divorce. Not because she gave up on me, but because the natural strength of her character, her continued . . . *adherence* to an ideal gave her the ability to move on. I didn't learn any of this until long after the fact. But I got lucky. I met another woman, more attractive in some ways, less attractive in others. But she was a good woman, same high ideals. I cared for her. I forced myself to forget my first wife. I got married again. I was happy, for several years. My second wife and first wife even became friends. They went to that trouble for me. My second wife accepted my children. One day I flew to Chicago for a conference on some point of law that no one cares about. After the main speech I went to the hotel bar to think. I called my wife on the phone and she was a little down and I didn't want to listen to it. We talked, and I said the easy things you say when you'd rather not be bothered. I hung up, probably despised her a little for being down. Then I met a woman there, started talking. She was very sexy and in retrospect I see she thought I had a lot of money. Women can be stupid that way—it comes from lacking their own resources and opportunities. So, she made me feel good. Lots of men cheat because they think they're unhappy with their wives. Other men cheat for no good reason other than they're a little bored. When life is easy, your morals get fat. We went to bed. She was goddamn good in bed. I figured she'd disappear, that it was a temporary deviance. I remember lying in bed not a minute after I'd finished the sex figuring a way to ease this woman out of my life. Even as I kissed her I was thinking about how to dump her. But it didn't happen that way. She slipped her business card into my suitcase. Perfectly natural. I'm not blaming her at all. She was acting freely and so was I. My wife unpacked my suitcase when I came home and asked about it. I lied, said something about a prospective new associate at the firm."

"Did she buy it?"

"Yes, though maybe not in her heart. Then a couple of months later, the woman called my office. She was in town for the afternoon. We went out and had drinks, went to a hotel. I used the credit card. My wife kept our finances. I was working too hard and didn't remember to intercept the bill. Or maybe I wanted to be caught, relieve the tension. She didn't need to ask why I was staying in a hotel in my hometown."

"My problem is not fidelity."

"In a literal sense you're right, in a larger sense you're wrong," Mastrude said. "I'm talking about a process of revelation, not moral

213

bookkeeping. See, for our society to cohere, we have to realize that uncontrolled energy is disorderly—so, human energies must have forms. Marriage is a form. One can be indiscriminately sexual but not indiscriminately responsible, see? Irresponsible sexuality—like all these poor girls getting knocked up at fourteen because they don't know what the hell else to do with themselves, even when they know about birth control, that undermines society, not to mention their own lives—I know you know this, but I want you to apply it to your own life. Fidelity is the *discipline* of sexuality—you *choose* sexual responsibility. I know there are other aspects to what I'm saying—that some marriages really do go bad, and that gay people can be joined together, too—but in the main what I'm saying is true. When you decide not to fuck around with other people, you also preserve your vow, not only to your wife, but to society, to the people you *wanted* to sleep with. Let me tell you, when people start cheating they get very confused, because there is no form for cheating that we understand instinctively. Men and women who are married are united with their community, assuming they don't cheat. That sounds like I'm preaching, but I'm not, I'm just reminding you that people exist in communities of one degree of cohesion or another, and whether they know it or not. The community used to be married, in a sense. That's what we've lost, that's what people half remember and wish we still had."

Peter sat recalling the look on Janice's face as she backed naked out of the door to the bedroom: a moment of watching oneself being mutilated, knowing that in that very second one's heart was dying, at least for now. She had been betrayed too many times already: by her father, by her mother, who not only didn't protect her from her father but also abandoned her through suicide. How was it that all of his energy and time—*years* of his life—had led to a moment of betrayal? He looked at his watch. Was this worth it? Was he capable of learning anything?

"What I'm suggesting is that fidelity is more than sexual. Maybe if you consider the question of fidelity, you'll see—"

"What the *hell* are you talking about?" Peter hollered, filling the room with noise. "I *was* faithful to my wife! God fuck it all, Mastrude, you have your head up your ass or what? I *want* to be faithful to her. She left *me*."

"Because of a lack of fidelity—of some sort. Not just sexual. Why are you being so deliberately dense?"

Peter glared, yet felt confused.

"I'm saying that if you understand what you did not *do*, then perhaps you will let go of her more easily, and search for another opportunity to achieve fidelity."

He sat in silence. Put this way, his feelings for Janice seemed small and worthless, the pitiful strivings of an emotional dwarf. It scared him to think that after all these years, in some way, he had never touched her.

"I don't pretend I taught you anything," Mastrude whispered.

He had to get out.

"How do you feel?" the big man went on. "Ready to let your wife go, let this divorce happen?"

Peter stood. He wouldn't pay Mastrude's bill, not for this.

When he returned to his office, the bad news awaited him. Johnetta's Henry's blood type was BB. The blood all over the coat in which Carothers had been arrested was entirely his own, type O. There were further breakdowns of the blood type possible—technically, everyone had blood nearly distinct from everyone else, but the crude tests showed that Peter still did not have any evidence directly linking Carothers to the homicide of Johnetta Henry.

This was discouraging and it meant that Mrs. Banks might actually know what she was talking about. He imagined trying to put her on the stand. A defense attorney, someone like Morgan, for example, might very well be able to confuse her, get her to garble her information. She seemed to understand Johnetta's situation quite well, yet she lacked such basic information as the identity of the father of Tyler. He couldn't even be certain of what had happened in the restaurant. She'd left voluntarily. He had no idea who the two men were. It could be a family matter, unrelated to her talking with him. But how to find her? He didn't want the detectives to know about Mrs. Banks, and things were too hectic for him to do the work.

But he knew who could. Cheryl Yeager was like a lot of law students who did internships with the office: She was ambitious, extremely hardworking, and smart. But unlike most of the other interns who passed through the office, she was black. The murder of Darryl Whitlock meant something extra to her; more than the other interns, she understood what he had achieved. She was a quiet, solemn young woman who thought more than she spoke. Her father was a doctor and her mother an English professor at Swarthmore College. When

Peter had interviewed her the previous fall, she had told him that she doubted that she wanted to become a prosecutor; in fact, the reason she wanted to intern in the office was so she would know how the prosecutor's office worked so that she could successfully defend suspects. Peter had been impressed by her honesty and suspected that she would do a good job. Within a week of her arrival, she had proved herself so adept that Peter no longer had much opportunity to use her skills; too many other prosecutors already had claimed her time. But when he had had a particular job to get done that had to be done right, he gave it to Cheryl Yeager. This he did with the task of finding Mrs. Banks. Cheryl wasn't likely to discuss her work, and even better, Hoskins would not be interested in such a low-ranking member of the office. He wouldn't even see her.

The hospital's visiting hours ended at five o'clock, so he couldn't see his mother again. But he retrieved his car from the parking garage and headed toward his parents' house. Maybe he could eat a meal with his father, talk some. He pressed the gas, angry again suddenly, angry as usual. How obsequious he had been with Mastrude. What the situation needed was *control*, not half-assedly swinging a flashlight around the caverns of the psyche! The way he'd been letting Hoskins push him around made him sick. He, Peter, should be eating guys like Hoskins for lunch! Control! Clap and the world freezes, waiting for the next command. Why didn't he have it? Just wrap your fingers around whatever it was and hold it and know you *had* it. He wanted Janice back, and he wanted to control her emotions so that she would be fucking happy and satisfied for once. He really wanted to control the fact that she had a shitty childhood—yes, he'd *really* like to rewrite history and get all the bugs out of her development so that she would come out happy and perfect like he wanted her to. He'd like to control good old John Big Dick Apple, too, maybe show him who the hell was boss. What would have happened if Cassandra hadn't been in his bed? Had he missed by so little, missed another forty years of life with the woman he loved because he let someone use his house key?

There was no car in his parents' driveway. He opened the front door with his own key and had just stepped into the living room when the phone rang. He answered the closer phone in his father's den. It was Bobby.

"You're home? I was sitting here and thought I'd call and check how Mom is."

"Dad's out. I just walked in. You know about Mom."

"Dad said not to worry."

"Well, don't," Peter said, hoping to calm his brother.

"Carol was examined by another obstetrician. She's right on the weight-gain curve."

"That's great, Bobby."

"I'm scared of only one thing."

"Birth defects?"

"No. Yeah, well, of course I'm scared of that, too."

"What's scaring you, then?"

"Seeing her in such pain. I hear that no matter what kind of crap you learn in the childbirthing class, it's still a lot of screaming and crying and—"

The line changed hands.

"Don't listen to this," came Carol's sweet voice, laughing. "The pain will be a *pleasure*. I've waited years for this."

"God, I hope so, Carol."

"How's Janice?"

"I never see her anymore."

"Poor *Peter*. You've always been so dependent on Janice." Her laughter tinkled in the phone again and he understood again why his brother found Carol so attractive. "Tell her I said for her to come home and give you a back rub."

"Okay," he whispered.

"Here's Bobby."

"So everything's okay back east? Everybody's okay?"

"Don't worry, Bobby. Just think about the baby."

He hung up and settled back into his father's armchair, hating himself for lying to his brother, knowing it couldn't be any other way. He would rather lie than be shamed. The chair smelled of his father. How many times had he watched his father hunch over his desk writing out figures in pencil on legal pads? Now the papers and bills seemed discouragingly familiar; he was gaining on his father, reducing the distance between them, knowing now what it was like to write out check after check each month for years at a time, watching the bank statements, keeping medical records in order, a Rolodex of phone numbers, stock newsletters, insurance forms, loan agreements, pension reports, credit-card bills, useless warranties for household appliances, stacks of canceled checks in case the IRS descended. He pulled out his father's middle drawer: keys, stamps, pens, a few letters, paper clips, a broken garage door opener, a faded matchbook, random family photographs. These papers once enclosed a mystery about his father, proved he served as the intermediary between the real world and the insular space of family.

He noticed his parents' checkbook and idly picked it from the papers on the desk. He flipped to the beginning of the register and noted a series of repetitive entries for gas, food, insurance, and so on. His mother wrote nearly all the checks, and yet each week his father would total the balance, which usually fluctuated around three thousand dollars. Each entry was flagged at the end of the month, as his father compared their record against the bank's. It had been this way for years, a steady harmony, literally a system of checks and balances that promoted trust and stability.

He flipped further and saw Janice's name.

There it was, written matter-of-factly in his mother's handwriting. A check for ten thousand dollars, written four days prior. A deposit of the same amount was written in next, indicating that monies had been deposited into the account for this very purpose, probably from a savings account. The date corresponded perfectly with Janice's decision to be independent of his income. He flipped through every page of the register and found no more record of payments to Janice. The pattern of entries—simple numbers, simple words—was reestablished as if nothing had happened and all was normal, not as if his parents were helping their daughter-in-law leave their son, betraying him as he had never been betrayed before.

He retreated, perhaps from shock, into the cold analysis that had stood him in such good stead and which had destroyed so much of his life. He would have to consider the motivations of three individuals in their decision to individually and collectively deceive someone they loved. He assumed Janice and his mother had communicated. Janice, out of pride and a sense of what was right, would not call his mother. His mother had asked about Janice repeatedly and then, as was her character, decided to contact her independently, perhaps calling her at the women's shelter during the day. Janice would not ask for money, but she would be frank with his mother. His mother would never probe him for details of his separation, in respect for his privacy. If Janice had decided to leave him, then his mother would assume, in her respect for Janice's character, that this was a considered, intelligent move. His mother would know that Janice would not do such a thing rashly. As an assertive and intelligent woman, she would have a keen sense of Janice's needs and expectations. She therefore would decide to support Janice, with the understanding that if the divorce were to occur, it might as well happen as smoothly and easily for all involved. No hard feelings, make the transition to the next phase of life. Perhaps meaning, *I apologize for what my son has done to you.*

Then he saw his options: He could either explode, thereby snarling all of his relationships, or he could play along. When he convinced Janice to return to him, and the payments were eventually revealed, he would win points by appearing relaxed and accepting of this necessary fibbing. Perhaps they would all laugh about it someday, how his mother had to help Janice stay away from him, so he would wise up. Son disciplined, husband chastened. Ha. He felt like torching the den and all its papers. But instead—for he was a man in control, wasn't he?—instead, he replaced the checkbook, got his keys from the kitchen counter, and left.

When he pulled onto Delancey, he saw Cassandra parked in front of his house. She got out, severe and dangerous in a long black coat.

"Peter."

She was a striking woman, and against his will, or perhaps not, he remembered her legs wrapped around his back. He shook his head, avoiding her face. "I'm in a rotten fucking mood."

She moved toward him.

"Don't, Cassandra. I don't want you, goddammit it. My wife and I were about to make love. We were . . . together, closer than you or I could ever be, and then you and your goddamn cigarette smoke were there, fouling my *life*. It was totally inexcusable, totally. Immoral."

Her words came through the chill air: "Peter, I'm still here."

Was she insane? The thought was remotely intriguing.

"Forget it," he snarled, cutting around her toward the door. "You've met a fucking stone wall." He knew who she was and he wasn't going to become one of *them*, one of the lonely shades, chasing after life, pursuing death. "Go on, get out of here." But she stood there like a statue, waiting. "Go on, leave me. Go read trashy romances and cry your eyes out. Go masturbate with a vengeance against all the men who never loved you. Whatever it is you do, scrape yourself off *me*."

Inside his house, he turned the heat up, made a couple of sandwiches. He needed something to calm him down. Cassandra had extracted the worst from him.

The phone rang, and Vinnie's thick, bored voice announced itself.

"Hey, I saw you quoted in the paper about the kid who got shot."

"Sad."

"Yeah, very very sad." Vinnie didn't give a damn.

"Hey, I owe you on that bet."

"Don't worry about it," Vinnie said. "That's not why I called."

"What do you have on John Apple?"

There was hesitation on the other end of the line.

"That's why I needed to speak with you, see. Peter, I think it's going to be . . . ah, a little time before I have anything on this individual and I'm, ah, running into some overhead."

"A search doesn't cost you."

"Well, Peter, you're right about that. It doesn't cost me directly, not a thing, actually. But this is, of course, a service, see."

Peter didn't like this.

"There's going to be a charge, Peter. There's going to be a big charge, because this is an extraordinary service. You right now are a very hot property in this town and so that makes it an extraordinary service. Ten thousand is all right. That's the charge."

"Then forget the service."

He hung up, pissed at his own stupidity. The phone rang.

"Peter, don't hang up again. I can't accept disrespect from any person. Don't *ever* do that again."

"Vinnie, if you're going to bleed me for running a search that costs three dollars of computer time, then forget it."

"I can't forget it."

"What do you mean?"

"I mean I can't. I want that money whether I run the search or not. Don't get short arms and long pockets on me, neither."

"Forget it, Vinnie. In fact, fuck off."

"Peter, hang on a minute. I want you to hear something." Vinnie's voice was fainter. "Gimme that thing, Jimmy, no—the goddamn tape, give me that." There was a click, then a rasping noise. Then: " 'Just get what you can get. I want it fast and quiet.' "

Peter's own voice. As he had taped Robinson's brother.

"You made your point, Vinnie. That why you had me call you at a certain number?"

"I'm tired now, Peter. This bullshit tires me. Want some advice? Don't fuck with me. Don't think you can talk your way out of this. Remember how dirty I used to be under the boards? I haven't changed."

220

"Look—"

"I'm gonna look at you giving me some money, that's what I'll look at. Meet me day after tomorrow at nine A.M. in front of the old Bellevue-Stratford. That used to be one of the greatest hotels in the world. They had to go and chop it up. I don't even know what they call it now. Say, Peter, we haven't seen each other for a while. I've gotten very fat, very big."

"This is a threat?"

"No. If I really wanted to threaten you, I would, you punk asshole lawyer. I'd tell you things, you know? I'd tell you that you should have picked up the fucking peanut-butter sandwich on the floor next to that dead boy.

This fact had not been released to the media.

"I'm not giving you a damn cent, you fucker."

"Think, Peter. *Think.*" Vinnie hung up.

He lay down on the sofa, sick with anxiety and suddenly over-whelmingly exhausted, yet knowing he had to analyze the problem. Maybe Vinnie was a bluffing small-time nobody, but then again, maybe not. The corruption in the city was like a pervasive organic slime; crooked careers sometimes flourished overnight or grew steadily with little notice. Because Peter had never done anything like this, and because his prosecution speciality wasn't organized crime and unions, he didn't know the latest arrangements. Vinnie could be work-ing under the aegis of somebody genuinely powerful. Structures shifted, friendships occurred, disputes realigned enemies. This was how the system went bad. How could he afford to pay Vinnie's blackmail? His money situation was a mess. He was locked into a huge mortgage. The interest payments were like a heartworm, wrig-gling into one's financial system, unnoticed at first, then causing slight discomfort, then panic, finally choking one to death. The only way to get money out of the house without selling it was through a home-equity loan, which took weeks and which would require a signature from Janice. But even if she somehow allowed him to get the money out of the house, he'd never get her back.

The mail had piled up and he took all of it to the computer and slipped in the financial spread-sheet disk. There had been previous times when he feared he lacked control, and through diligence he'd found a solution. He flipped through the mail for bills while the computer creaked as the magnetic head searched for the boot-up pro-gram. In the last few months his bookkeeping had been nearly non-

221

existent. But perhaps he could scare up a thousand dollars and get Vinnie off his back for a little while. He opened his bills and made a neat stack of indebtedness before him. And here it was: He owed Mastrude a $750 payment. The monthly mortgage was overdue by two months: two payments totalling $3,113.56. Soon the bank would start hassling him, threatening to foreclose. Some of that was tax-deductable, but he wouldn't get that money back until spring of next year. The MasterCard and Visa totaled $1,785.34. He could pay the minimum amounts, but that was lost in interest immediately, almost as if he hadn't paid anything. He owed American Express $423.86. Where the hell had that come from? He looked over the bill. A microwave for Janice's apartment and automatic quarterly billing at the health club. Luckily, the telephone bill was reasonable, $63.39. The car, life, and home-owners' insurance were due. There was a notice that his personal liability insurance was overdue, now in the grace period. He'd gotten something in the mail recently, detailing a liability insurance rider. Took you up to $2.5 million in liability for only a couple of hundred bucks a year. It seemed like a good idea then, a way to feel safe. People would buy anything to feel safe.

But it was the heating bill that broke his spirit: $389.34. How could that have happened? He had been so careful. All the windows had their storms—he had done it at halftime of an Eagles game on TV last fall. According to his bank statement—luckily it had arrived only two days before and was therefore fairly current—he was down to about three hundred dollars in his account. And—thanks in part to his mother—Janice hadn't even written out any checks. Anyway, he was running thousands behind the pace, as best as he could determine, with another mortgage payment due in three weeks. Vinnie could ruin him, easily and forever. A leak to the right reporter, anything. What was money compared to what Vinnie could do? His paycheck would arrive at the end of the month, but it was already spent. Insanity! He had not recorded his checks or the frequent money-machine withdrawals he was making.

If only he could freeze the chaos in his life and untangle each piece one by one. He looked at the figures of income and expenditure, and decided to root out the cause of his $389.34 heating bill. The basement was the first place to look, and past the old bicycles and moldy boxes of papers he found, to his horror, that the door leading to the old coal chute was wide open. He had been heating an unsealed airspace, for the chute also opened to the street via a pair of loose-fitting steel ground doors. He couldn't remember having gone down there recently. The typical winter month bill should be two hundred dollars. He knew positively that he hadn't been down in the basement for over a week. He looked at the bill. The meter read date was three days prior, on Friday. Because the door was still open, that meant two things: One, he would have to pay for three days of open-door heating on his *next* bill, and two, that it was at least five or six days ago that the door had been opened. What was happening then?

He put on his coat and walked outside to inspect the ground doors of the cellar, thinking he could tell Vinnie to go screw himself if he and Janice could get together. He could string Vinnie along for a little while longer, then duck out and deal with him as a private citizen.

Peter brushed back the winter-dead forsythia bushes and found the fat padlock that locked the chain fed through the loops of the doors. It appeared untouched. He gave it a yank.

The chain came flying off the doors. Someone had cut the narrow links of chain, then arranged them carefully to look unchanged. Nothing had been stolen, that he knew of. Had someone been in the house and left quickly when he arrived home? Who? The elder Robinson and his evil, drunken henchmen, "me and the boys"? Someone else?

When he returned inside, his answering machine was blinking.

"Listen, Scattergood, listen very carefully." It was Stein, Carothers's lawyer. "My client Mr. Carothers two hours ago was attacked by two other prisoners who are complete strangers to him. He was very lucky, very lucky indeed, for the guards broke it up immediately. Nobody was even scratched—it was over in fifteen seconds. These men are well-known drug dealers and they appeared ready to kill him. There is no motive for this, do you understand? I'm appealing to you because of your reputation. This was a setup. There was no altercation, no grudge already there. My client hasn't been in prison long enough to make enemies, and whatever my client's short-comings, he's not a dealer. There are no old scores being settled. I'm going to put it to you straight. Somebody's trying to get to my client before he tells his story. I don't know who or why, but I demand action or I go to the papers."

Berger had been right, and now Peter could squeeze Carothers, force him to talk. The pressure was on, and soon Peter would have to decide if was going to play against Hoskins or with him. The same could be said of Vinnie, and Peter headed back to his study to figure out when, if ever, he could pay his former basketball teammate. On the screen, DISK ERROR flashed at him. He tried to open the file again. The disk drive spun and clicked and screeched, trying repeatedly. He pulled out his manual, searched through it. He hadn't cleaned the disk drive in a long time and the disk contained a year's worth of financial information. DISK ERROR flashed rhythmically at him, producing a sense of crisis. He hit one of the keys and saw $Z$$$$Z$^^^^****WHA??????^^^#HAOOH@@@@!!!hhkWHA????snjtRR~~~}{%%2 qflZ$UUUUU^—strings of thousands of senseless characters confronted him.

"Fuck! Fuck this machine!"

He yanked the disk out and flung it across the room.

That night, sprawled feverishly on the tangled sheets, he dreamed he had rewritten the entire Pennsylvania civic and penal codes, thousands of pages encompassing all the state's laws, bound in leather. He could open any of the fat volumes anywhere, and inside before his eyes was the law, written to perfection. In his dream he breezed through these books, reading sections that in waking life he didn't remember. Each word was his, heartbreakingly beautiful. When he woke, there was the lingering sensation that something great and miraculous had happened, that for a brief instant his brain had been engorged to its fullest power, making the regular operations of the conscious hours seem pale flickerings of the smallest wattage.

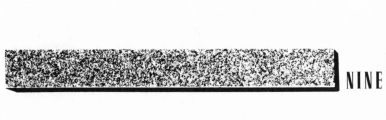

NINE

Philadelphia was about to get hit, about to be dumped on as a snow front two hundred miles wide blew across the Great Lakes, Ohio, West Virginia, West Pennsylvania, Pittsburgh, and east. Specks of storm swirled around the stained bronze cheeks of the impassive five-foot face of William Penn atop City Hall, the whole tower lost within a low gray ceiling of unnatural darkness. Time to gather in and protect oneself from natural elements, and, doing just that, Peter had on his thick-soled hiking boots, long, one hundred percent wool black Brooks Brothers coat, black leather gloves, two scarves stuffed around his neck, and an L. L. Bean's Irish Tweed "Thatch" Hat, with tapered "Bucket" crown with two-layer brim, size 7⅝. It was time, he had decided, to take care of himself.

He stepped into the hunting goods store. A small electronic bell chimed as he crossed the threshold. Displayed in locked glass cabinets was an arsenal of deer knives, pistols, rifles, and shotguns. Gazing into this case stood a large man dressed in camouflage survivalist gear and command boots. On his arm was a patch that read OUTLAW GUNS AND ONLY OUTLAWS WILL CARRY THEM. Peter moved to another case. A short balding man in wire-rim glasses looked up from a gun he was rubbing with a cloth.

"What can I do for you?"

"I'm from the Philadelphia D.A.'s office."

"Everything's in order here," the salesman replied. "Every gun's registered, and we don't sell to questionable customers. We'll turn down the scale, in fact. Sometimes have to do it."

"Good," Peter smiled. "I'm here on personal business. Somebody broke into my house. They cut a heavy-duty chain that went to my cellar. My wife's pretty upset. I've also gotten threatening calls from relatives of felons I've convicted."

The salesman nodded sympathetically, pursed his lips with avid concentration.

"I see your problem. You'd be surprised how often this less-than-optimal thing happens. You don't know *who* is out there, walking around. I had an insurance investigator in here yesterday. Nice guy, mild tempered. Checks burned buildings for arson. Gets all kinds of calls. Many less-than-optimal calls." The man rubbed the muzzle of the gun energetically. "People like you and me and this other guy, we get backed to the wall. We can't have a world like this—now, sir, that's a fact. Look at what happened to that mailman that was on the news, that got shot. Those young nobodies just came into the train and shot him. Didn't know him. Thought it was fun. You try and mind your own business and . . . No, sir, sometimes you just gotta—"

"I *have* fired a pistol, once or twice, but not much more," Peter interrupted, having heard this speech many times in the past from cops, legislators, and well-intentioned madmen who thought they could tell the good guys from the bad and that gun control was a mistake.

"Know what you want?"

"I don't care what kind of gun it is, as long as it won't misfire or jam. I want something I can put in a drawer in the bedroom and forget about until the moment some asshole is messing around downstairs or trying to get in."

"*Yes*, I see it that way myself." The salesman nodded vigorously. "I've got kids and a wife, too. It makes you see things differently, when you're threatened. You get worried."

The man unlocked the glass case and drew out several pistols, placing them reverently on a thick felt pad.

"Basically, what I think you want—if I may suggest it—is a firearm that is light enough to handle easily—say, for you and your wife." The man looked up, it being understood between them in an unspoken male language that in Peter's absence the wife would have *only seconds* to blow away the big bad motherfucker set on raping her in the bedroom, set on stealing that which belonged to Peter, and Peter alone. He thought momentarily of John Apple, who, though not an intruder in the usual sense, certainly had taken something from him.

"Something," the man was saying, "something with little maintenance. And adequate at short range. Very important it be comfortable. Something comfortable in the hand. Okay, there're basically two theories at work here. The snubby short-range revolver"—he pulled an ugly black short-barreled gun from the case—"keeps it simple. Anybody can understand how it works—you don't need to practice with it to use it. You pull it out, point it, and pull the trigger again and again until the problem is gone." He pulled out a square-barreled semi-automatic pistol. "But then again, maybe you want some security features, like a safety, which you flip this way, or a magazine disconnector. This is a .380 pistol, eight shot. Plenty of stopping power. Takes about four seconds to load a clip. About twenty-eight ounces—less than two pounds. Runs about two hundred. You remove this . . . and it won't fire. Also you got a slide-mounted safety that locks the firing pin like this. The firing pin can't strike the cartridge primer."

The man's hands blurred over the gun, flipping small levers, tapping at the trigger, assembling parts, clicking them out again. He had seen cops do this in the courtroom when explaining how guns were discharged. "You pull the trigger and nothing happens. You could keep this one in a drawer with the chamber unloaded and the magazine dropped. And put the hammer on half-cock. And flip on this manual safety lever, like this. You gotta practice all this, though. This takes a while to get it straight. Otherwise the guy is gonna be in the bedroom and your wife is going to be messing around with this stuff and not be able to use the gun."

The man looked up, expectantly.

"Let's say I need something," Peter asked, "like you mentioned earlier—that I just want to grab and fire." He pictured somebody— Vinnie, Robinson's brother—breaking into his house at night; he would hear them and stand in the dark and be ready, and no matter what happened next, he could say he'd been defending himself.

The man had produced another gun. "*This* is the ultimate .357 snubbie. Fires the 125-grain Remington semi-jacketed hollow-point. That's a top load. Real man-stopper. There's a vicious recoil and muzzle jump with this weapon—you're gonna feel like you have a cannon in your hand. The kick comes more into the hand, see, less upward muzzle flip."

"Why is that important?" Peter humored him. He had called Stein and was due to see him with Carothers that afternoon while Hoskins stuffed himself at lunch. The homicide chief, Peter had seen, ate with a vengeance, as if someone were about to yank away his plate.

"No matter how much your hand stings, the barrel comes back down faster, back on target. See? This magnum is spec'd for thirty-three thousand copper units of pressure, which means you can use this man-stopper SJHP ammo with confidence. Has a very nice single-action pull, can't be thumb-cocked. You can put a guy in a body bag from a hundred yards with this mother," the man breathed, the edge of excitement unmistakable in his voice, "so you can imagine what it does from ten feet."

"How much is this?" Peter asked.

"That'll run you about three hundred and fifty. You'll need a couple of boxes of ammo, too. We can do the bill of sale and the permit and federal form simultaneously. Since you're in law enforcement, I don't anticipate any problem."

The man sucked at his lips in concentration.

"Say! You're the guy that's been finding the killer of the Mayor's kid? And the girlfriend or something? Sure! I seen you all over the news!" The helpful salesman tone and diction was gone, replaced by a dark enthusiasm. "I'm telling my wife, just the other night, I'm telling her, 'this guy, he really knows how to handle them!' I was watching you. Well, it's a pleasure, a real pleasure. Name's Sam." The man stuck out his hand, as if the pleasure should be Peter's. "Now, you ask me, just between the two of us, I don't think the Mayor is worth the shit he craps every day but that don't matter. I didn't vote for him. What matters is you got another one of them killers off the street. Aaah, this used to be a great city! I'm glad to see the story on TV, even if the Mayor ain't worth shit. We haven't had a decent Mayor since Rizzo! How many Mayors ago was *that*? Three, four? So, I'm tellin' the wife, I like this guy, *informing* them TV faggot newsman with the blowdry-blowjob haircut you ain't telling him any more 'at this present time.' Half the city's expecting to hang that guy. Yaaaah!"

The worst kind of gun nut. Who might brag to all his friends about to whom he'd sold a gun. Peter left without a weapon, offering no explanation. The snow was falling now, the storm coming.

The killer also knew about guns. Dressed in a new suit and shackled in back, Wayman Carothers silently bit the tip of his tongue as he and his attorney Stein emerged from the elevator, followed by two cops attached to escort the defendant. Carothers was taller and thinner than Peter had expected, looking almost as if he hadn't eaten enough recently, or ever. He moved stiffly from his wounds, which were healing well. Peter led the men to the conference room. He put his hand on the cop's shoulder.

"Unlock him and wait out here."

"Yeah?" one of the policeman said.

"We're okay."

The cop clicked open the cuffs and sat down outside the door, which Peter then shut. It was a room with a long table, chairs, an ugly dropped ceiling, and a dead coffee machine.

Peter had seen many defendants in his time, all variety of men, from the most despicable to rather likable, talkative fellows; either type could be remorseless or weep with guilt. Carothers possessed a handsome, watchful face and the strong, loose-limbed build that conveyed, like a middle-weight boxer, the ability to move fists quickly through air when angered. He stood rubbing wrists with the quiet detached cool meant to counterbalance his powerlessness in the situation.

"Have a seat, Wayman." Peter nodded.

He was stepping into territory without rules. He would have preferred Berger had been there, but he didn't trust him anymore. If Hoskins found out about the visit, Peter would have some explaining to do, and possibly would have to give up the case. With Hoskins and most everyone else at lunch, however, he could stray along the edges of whatever it was Stein had hinted at. Hoskins, feared and respected in the courtroom after over a decade in the office, would not tolerate ambiguities served up by the defense. Alternative arguments, conflicting information, countervailing statements by witnesses—these were impediments to the version of reality by which Hoskins guided his prosecution, flies buzzing around the buffalo logic that he used to pound out one conviction after another. It was true, moreover, that Hoskins often had been right to dismiss these attempts to have him reduce or withdraw charges, since defense attorneys could be amazingly unscrupulous and creative. But occasionally Hoskins missed the truth as it darted past him, and now Peter was glad to be free of the man.

"Okay," Peter started. "I haven't much time. What do you gentlemen want?"

Stein opened his file. "My client is prepared to offer important information in return for immunity from prosecution for the Whitlock homicide."

"That's bullshit," Peter said automatically, "and you know it. "We don't trade down on homicide cases. Our evidence's too good. Why should I do it?"

"Because my client's not guilty of the girl's death."

"You're trying to beat a death sentence by splitting off one of the homicides. We've got too much." He would leverage Stein. "We have a witness who says she saw him outside in the hallway that evening. Now we have phone calls back and forth from the second apartment where the detectives found all the guns and stuff. We've got the bullets in Whitlock, which match perfectly. It looks like Wayman here strangled the girl, waited, then *boom*, hit the boy. Why in the world should I listen any further?"

"There's a lot you don't know, man," Carothers muttered.

"Wayman," Stein interjected quickly. "I'll remind you that *anything* you say can be used against you. If you have a question, we can talk privately."

Carothers shook his head. "Way I see it, Mr.—uh—Scattergood, is like this. You got me on both robberies and you pretty much got me on the shooting that night—"

"Hey, Stein," Peter interrupted. "I don't want you saying later that I coerced any of this. This came freely."

Stein nodded, and smiled dutifully at Peter's insistence that all be fair. They were playing by the rules in order to ignore them.

"Wayman," Peter said, "I must ask you this: You understand that we're making *no* deals here, that no agreements have been reached, that I am *not* promising to drop charges or reduce a charge—not a thing. Sometimes we work with defendants on a charge if they're willing to make a plea, as I'm sure Mr. Stein knows, but we're not there yet, and maybe we won't get there. So I have to say this to you, out of respect for your rights, that I am making no promises and that anything you say here can and will be used against you. Understand that?"

The defendant nodded. And exhaled. Perhaps he was finished with something, moving on, betrayed by his fellow bad actors, shot and narrowly missed being paralyzed, no doubt reading the papers that trumpeted his guilt, and finally, aware that the black community was in no way interested in his defense. Shorn of all constituencies, a man will make overtures in the ways he can. Peter checked the defendant's face, searching for resolve, signs of decision. Chronologically, Carothers's skin and tissue were young, but there existed within his countenance the grave look of a man who had found that life was nearly always a trial. This was just the latest face, however. Philadelphia was full of them, boys who received chaotic, minimal schooling, and who by the age of twelve or fourteen had been so damaged,

230

it was unlikely they would ever read properly or be able to question their behavior in terms other than those they had learned on the street. These thousands upon thousands of poor ghetto boys were an army marching toward a cliff. The city's social services agencies composed a fragile net. Many were rescued in other ways, some found decent jobs, some stayed in school. But the rest—those like Carothers—found themselves closer to the edge. The waste of life was immense, and nothing new.

"You're saying this of your own accord?" Peter asked.

"Yeah."

"All right."

"Frankly, Counselor," Stein began, trying to bring the conversation back to an amiable tone, "Wayman insisted we meet. We had the attack on him just the other day, and we need to start giving you a reason to want to see him healthy. Also, he says he knows the armed-robbery charge will result in a conviction, which I'm afraid is probably true, given everything, and, since he does have an extensive record—"

"Four charges for agg assault, twice arrested for armed robbery." Peter referred to his file. "Plus the old murder charge he beat."

"Yes, we're looking at the same piece of paper—it's all right there," Stein went on. "And, uh, we've got the murder charges, too. Why don't you say what you want to say, Wayman," prompted the lawyer softly.

Carothers looked up at Peter, then down again. He's scared, Peter thought, poor motherfucker. I'd be scared, too.

"I didn't kill Johnetta," Carothers exhaled. "It not like everybody be talkin'. They don't understan', you know what I'm sayin'?"

"What Wayman means—" Stein began.

"Wait a minute, I can say it. You just *told* me to say it."

"Okay—right. I'm sorry, Wayman," said Stein.

"I'm sayin' I *did*n't kill Johnetta. I *loved* Johnetta, man."

"Did you kill Whitlock?" Peter shot back.

Carothers looked at Stein for direction.

"My client would like to explain some of the details of the homicide of Whitlock, with the understanding that the second murder count—"

"No deals, Stein! I can't promise a thing. I won't do it and the D.A. won't back me up." Peter looked at his watch. Had Hoskins ordered dessert? "I'll listen to what you have to say, I'll compare it to what I know. But no promises, no deals. Got it? You decide."

Carothers looked at Stein, who nodded silently.

231

"All right," Carothers responded, his voice catching. "This is the way it's gonna be. I got somethin' to say. I know what I got comin'. Maybe like you say this ain't goin' to help me. That's all right. I understand that. I understand my prerogative, right? I'm sayin' this on my own. I killed that dude Whitlock, he surprised me. I didn't have no choice. But that ain't that I want to say. I *did*n't kill Johnetta, man, I loved that girl, we was tight, we was close to one another, you know what I'm sayin'? Maybe we had some problems, maybe I messed around, but she and I go way back. We grew up in North Philly together, man. That girl—she had somethin' special I never saw before. No way I could kill her."

"What were you doing over in that apartment?"

"I got back home—"

"After you held up the convenience store."

"Yeah. We drove off and split up the money and I was goin' to go out for some celebratin'. That's when I went to that bar I was tellin' them detectives about. We was thinkin' about picking up some yellow tape—"

"Coke?" Peter asked. Sweat had gathered over Carothers's brow in the exhilaration of telling what perhaps was the truth.

"Right, right. But I went home. I got a machine, and when I come home the little red light is blinkin' and the counter say I got six messages. I played them and every one is Johnetta. She's callin' 'cause she's upset—"

"Where was she calling from?" Peter asked.

"A pay phone somewhere," Carothers answered.

"That's why the detectives haven't turned it up," Stein said, anticipating Peter's thoughts. "If she had called from the apartment, then we'd be able to show that Wayman had been contacted."

"That wouldn't prove anything other than that they'd spoken," Peter said. "In court I could argue that they were probably fighting and *that's* why he came over."

The room was quiet.

"Go on," Peter said.

"Well, anyway, she in West Philly at her boyfriend's apartment. Somebody had been tellin' her she in trouble. Somebody say she been messin' with the wrong people and she better leave good enough alone, all right? Now, I don't know if that was on that same night, or if it be some other time. She starts explainin' to me how they don't like her and how somebody done already broke into her apartment once and messed her shit up. And she say she can't call the police because

232

she don't know exactly what they goin' to *do* when she does, like where all the *connections* is, you know that I'm sayin'? Like, she know the people you would normally trust she can't trust. And she say she think somebody been followin' her in a car that night when she walk home. It's real late and she thinkin' she see the same car outside on the street, and each time she on the phone she *more* upset with everythin', like it's comin' *at* her, like she know even *more* than she sayin', you know. Then the last call is maybe ten minutes before I got home and she say she's scared to go into her apartment."

"You have all this on your phone machine tape?"

"Fuck!" Carothers exploded, staring vehemently at Peter.

A cop knocked on the door.

"We're okay!" Peter called.

Carothers glared at him. "Do I fuckin' *look* like I got a fuckin' tape? No, I ain't got no tape, that's why I'm tellin' you this." Carothers rubbed his temples. "I *erased* the motherfucker soon as I heard it, 'cause it was *proof* I ain't been home." He shook his head dejectedly. "So I didn't even call her, I just drove over to West Philly fast as I could."

"You have a key to her apartment?"

"Yeah, she give me key. We got a deal that maybe she be seein' another guy, whatever, she always let me have a key to her apartment, you understand? We tight, we go way back."

"How far back? You have any proof of this relationship?"

Carothers wagged his head back and forth unhappily.

"Oh, man, you bustin' my chops over nothin'. I got—man, we had a *baby* together. Tyler lives with his great-grandma."

"What's her name?"

"Her name is, uh, Mrs. Banks."

"We've been looking for her, hoping to get some kind of statement," Stein interrupted. "We think she could shed some light on what was happening, but we're told she's down south somewhere with relatives. My investigator was told she left a day or two ago. That's extremely convenient for somebody."

"Go on, Wayman," Peter directed.

"Johnetta and me, we was never married, just you know—"

"Yeah, okay," Peter said. "So you go way back."

"Yeah, so I get there—"

"You had the gun with you? You hung on to it?"

"In my coat. I go to the building. That woman saw me. She drunk, axed me for a dollar. I said, 'Woman, get out of my face.' "

233

"Wait," Peter interrupted. "Where did you park?"

"They was some kind of delivery truck blockin' the driveway, so I pulled in down the street. The buzzer was busted on the door. I just went in with the key and up. I got inside and it was quiet and I axed, 'Baby, where are you?' and I got no answer. Then I thought maybe she sleepin', so I was real quiet. Then I go back into the bedroom and I saw the bathroom door."

"Wait a minute," Peter said. "Was her front door locked?"

"Yes."

"What time was this?"

"Maybe three o'clock. She was dead, man. And naked. I saw her, she was dead. But she was still warm, still limp. I carried her over to the bed, thinkin' maybe she all right. But somebody hit her on the head. She break easy, man. I just—" He bowed his head, shaking. "I couldn't believe it—she was lyin' there. I knew that it just happened. I touched her face. She my son's *mother*. You know what I mean? I just sat there and was fucked up."

"You get any of her blood on your coat?" Peter asked hopefully.

"No. I took that coat off before I moved her. There was a little blood on the shirt, but I threw that away. I seen a lot of homeboys messed up in my time, you know? Fucked up bad, shot. I'm not puttin' on no attitude 'bout that. But seein' her was different. She help me keep it together through the years, somethin' not right, my mind messed up about somethin', and I'm havin', like, problems with somebody, or get depressed about how bad everythin' is, then I called her and she axed me what was the matter. I'm always connected to her, you know? No matter what happen, we connected to each other. In the hospital and all, back before I went to jail the first time. And I'm thinkin' about how I want to say this to her. I want to tell her and I can't. She always knew me and now she in front of me dead and I can't do *nothin'* about it. I just robbed a fuckin' store and got seven hundred in my pocket and then I'm here and I can't do nothin'. Then I'm *mad* at the motherfucker who did this and my anger is in effect, word, and I know why it was done. The boy's family didn't care for her. They thought she dirty. She no good for this boy. She from the ghetto, not *upwardly mobile*. I can understan' that, my brother works for the post office and he think I'm just a god-damn homeboy. He won't talk to me. Soon as I saw her there I know why she killed. In my heart! An' I'm mad, real mad. They thought she was goin' to fuck up their boy."

"Who thought that?"

"Fuck, man, the Mayor's people, and who that be exactly I don't

234

know. He got all kind of people. They all over and you don't mess with them. I just wish I—" Carothers made a fist. But he didn't have the conviction to continue with the threat.

"Evidently Darryl was very much in love with her."

"Yes he was, and I don't blame him. She an angel, you know what I mean? I got nothin' against him, man. Nothin' personal. In fact, the man got my respect all along. But when I hear him comin' in maybe a half hour later I didn't think of that. No I didn't. All I could think of was that *he* the reason she dead. He shoulda protected her, called off his people. It's *on him*, see. He was in the kitchen and I waited a few minutes. Then I just walked in and gave it to him, I couldn't take it. He never knew what hit him, man. So yeah, I did it. I didn't think about it ahead of time. I didn't plan to kill nobody. I just got so fucked *up* from what happened and seein' her like that, so angry with everythin' and unfair—how unfair it was and how she never had a chance and the same people preachin' about the black man coming up and jobs and no discrimination and all that shit nobody really believes is going to happen—they the *same* people who did *this*. They was too good for her, and I just—"

"Three shots?"

"Yeah. Twice across the room and then in the head."

Peter remembered the gun salesman: *You point it and pull the trigger again and again until the problem is gone!* Like most methods, guns were a messy way to kill, assuming you wanted to get away with the crime. A gun sent particles of powder all over the place, including on the person who fired, and left a bullet that could be matched to the barrel, as in Carothers's own case. Knife and other instrument stabbings were trickier, but usually the forensic pathologist could count the wounds, determine the type of weapon, and often the angle, height, and pattern of the attack. And even if the attacker was right- or left-handed. Carothers, of course, had never thought about this. Nobody did. They just pulled the trigger. That was the awful beauty of guns. You don't touch the victim. A tiny muscle in your finger contracts and across the room someone's head explodes.

"What time was this, exactly?"

"Maybe three-thirty."

Peter glanced at his papers. This time was within fifteen minutes of the medical examiner's assessment of the time of Whitlock's death, based on the temperature of the body and the degree of uncompleted digestion of the food in his stomach.

"What was he doing when you shot him?"

"Eating."

"What, what was he eating?" Peter asked, remembering that Vinnie knew of this.

"Sandwich, maybe. How the fuck am I supposed to remember shit like that?"

Peter glanced at Stein. Attitude problem here, Counselor.

"Wayman, Mr. Scattergood has agreed to *listen* to us. He doesn't need to do us a favor."

"Yeah, I know. I'm sorry, man. This thing—that guy, he all right, he doin' it, you know—doin' the college thing, gonna make it, so yeah, it was too bad. But you had to know Johnetta, man. You had to know her."

"What else?"

"He was just standin' there in his underwear. He had undressed, wearin' some designer shit, the colored kind."

"Okay. What time was it, now, after you shot him?"

"About a minute later, I wasn't gonna stick around."

"But you picked up the shells. You had the presence of mind to do that."

"Yeah, I did."

"How'd you leave?"

"I knew the gun was loud, so I opened the kitchen window. There's a fire ladder. You stand on the ledge and you reach it and then you're on the roof and across the back, and you come down on the fire escape on the next building."

"How'd you know?"

"I didn't, man, I just opened the window and it was there." Carothers waved his hands. "If it wasn't there, I would have gone some other way."

Silence, and anxiety. In the restaurant, Hoskins was signing the charge-card receipt, making sure to shred the carbon paper.

"Is there anything else, anything at all, you might know that could help us find the person who killed Johnetta?"

"Nuh. She and I tight on the phone, you know, but I don't know those people over in West Philly she runnin' with. Never met nobody, never saw nobody. Just a lot of the Mayor's people."

Peter nodded to Stein.

"Okay. I'm interested. We'll talk, see what we can do. Maybe we'll get a statement from you. Give me a couple of days." He jerked a finger to the door. "Now try to get out of here in about two minutes."

*   *   *

In City Hall three hours later, after a preliminary proceeding for another case, Peter pulled his papers together. The courtroom door opened and Berger came in, all smiles.

"Hey, there you are, I gotta tell you something." Berger waved at the legal case on the floor. "Talk to Stein yet?"

"He hasn't called," Peter lied.

"He will," Berger asserted. "Anyway, listen to this, this is great. This sums up the whole place. I was in recess for the bench trial I'm doing. Down the hall is some bullshit rape case where the girl traded sex for coke and then decided it had been against her will, the usual stuff. The defendant is this guy from Upper Providence, big insurance guy. The guy is outraged and will not bargain, and so on and so on, so he's here in court finally, and like an asshole, doesn't want a regular defense attorney. He hires a big-firm partner who hasn't been in a courtroom in about thirty years. Maybe the guy did some defense work a long time ago, I don't know. I saw the guy earlier in the day, not your regular City Hall attorney, his suit must have cost a couple of thousand. He's maybe sixty, gray hair, very distinguished, everybody's idea of a, uh, *barrister*, you know? So it's the recess and I happened to be following him down the hall. I can tell by the way he's walking he doesn't like being here."

"Right," Peter said, watching Berger move his face.

"So we're both headed to the men's room. The big one on the southwest corner. We go in and the guy steps up to the urinal. He's taking his time—you known how old guys always take longer to piss? So I notice that there's somebody in the toilet stall, there's clothes on the floor. I hear all this splashing in the toilet. It's some guy, you know? Some bum. He's drunk, he's singing to himself. So just as this old barrister is about to piss—you can see he knows it's finally coming—the other guy comes out of the stall. He's totally naked with lather about an inch deep all over him. Looks like a skinny abominable snowman or something, and he stumbles over to the guy and scares the hell out of him. 'I got soap in mah eyes, can ya help me?' That's what he's saying. He keeps coming and he's all drunk and the other guy says, 'Stay away from me, sir,' and the drunk guy just keeps coming and fucking *falls* all over the other guy and knocks him down and there's piss and soap all over everything, and the older guy is down under the urinal with all the fucking pubic hair and cigarettes and old piss."

237

Berger smiled so hard that his skin shone, looked ready to tear, even. He was sweating, and a vein snaked its way over his eyebrow. He sniffed once or twice, and then he looked up at Peter, his eyes wide.

"I'm going to make it, Peter. I'm fine, I'm going to make it."

"Bergs—"

"No, no. I know what you're thinking, but I'm in control, great control. You should have seen me in there, I was great, really on top of the whole thing, just flipping the witnesses over, getting them to say what I needed, bing-bing-bing, just getting through it really fast." Berger's smile was huge, his eyebrows arcing madly up—his face a living mask.

"Peter, hey, hey! I forgot something. My wife saw Janice yesterday, having lunch at that place off Rittenhouse Square."

"Where?"

"That place, that little expensive place. Where all the waiters are real waiters, not college kids."

"Who was she with? A man or a woman?"

"I forget, maybe I didn't ask her."

"Oh, come on, Bergs, you know how important this is to me, you know what I'm going through, and you didn't ask? Where's your wife now? I want to call her."

Berger put his hand up.

"Wait a minute there, big guy, you don't need to call Stephanie. It was an honest mistake. I've got many, many, many things I'm dealing with, so just hold off there, all right, just re-lax, okay?"

Peter stared at Berger, angry. He had confided in Berger as he confided in no one, and Berger had missed a chance to help him. If it was a woman, he could relax; that meant Janice was probably doing business, meeting with a foundation officer perhaps. Or an old friend. If it was a man, then that could be the same thing of course, but maybe it wasn't, maybe it was John Apple. But it couldn't be John Apple. He was a carpenter who spent the day in work clothes, who couldn't afford some fancy place. If it was a man, it was *another* man, perhaps some older guy who made big bucks.

"I really wish you could remember if it was a man, Bergs."

"Sorry. Hey, really."

"Right," Peter said with a small mouth. "Really."

"Hey. Come on." The big smile again. "No big deal."

"What the fuck is happening to you, Bergs?" Peter looked hard into Berger's eyes and thought about grabbing his friend by the neck. Instead he just walked away.

*   *   *

The day was limping grayly toward its end, and finally he remembered what he had forgotten. He slipped inside a phone booth at the end of the hall. The light didn't work, but that was fine; he didn't want to see anybody he knew. In the half-darkness, he inserted coins into the slot and called his broker.

"Saul? Peter Scattergood. I want to sell IBM today, now."

"The market closed already, you know that," came back a voice. "But, Peter, hey, you haven't held it long enough. They have some great new stuff coming out in a couple of weeks. We're expecting a great quarter."

"I don't care," he responded. "I do, but not that much. Sell it tomorrow, all of it. I'll at least come out even. When can I get a check?"

"Well, the credit to your account—"

"A check, when can I be issued—"

"Five business days," Saul answered. "But tell you what, if you really want to sell off the IBM," Saul continued, "let me get you into something with a little higher dividend, something you're going to feel happy with in the short term. We got some great cyclical stocks paying up around eight percent, so we could turn the IBM around into that, or split some off into a money market, what do you say?"

The broker was trying to work out a double commission, with a sell and buy order, as well as keep Peter's capital on his books. Fuck him—did he think Peter was an idiot?

"Saul, I want to cash out, not churn the portfolio. Do you have any sort of in-house deal whereby you buy client's stocks immediately for them and resell on the next day the exchange is open?"

"Why should we?" came Saul's irritated voice. "So we could watch the stock drop? We'd eat the loss."

"Not if you agreed to buy at the next day's price or lower."

"Theoretically, I suppose—"

"And pay me a reasonable portion up front."

"Sounds nice, Peter, but you're forgetting that legally we can only buy IBM stock through the New York Stock Exchange—"

"You don't deal in cash, of course."

"Of course not, Peter. Sometimes we do presell orders, which can involve a credit line, but your customer account is not—not of a sufficient, uh—"

"You mean I'm not *rich*, and so I don't get any special treatment?"

239

Peter exploded. "Is that what you're stumbling over yourself to tell me, Saul, even though I've been a loyal customer for five years? Well, hell's bells, Saul, maybe I should take my tiny little mouse-shit portfolio elsewhere."

"Peter, I gotta tell you—my hands are tied on this, chained behind my back." Saul's voice slowed to patient, patronizing reasonableness, the voice of a man trying to preserve a profit. "What you got is the national office in New York has delineated certain guidelines we follow, a particular set of privileges for each, uh, level of portfolio, and—"

Peter hung up. There was no time to listen to Saul's backpedaling. Five business days was an infinity, what with the weekend. He was due to see Vinnie the next morning. What could he do, assuming he took Vinnie at his word? He couldn't get to the police, for a variety of reasons. He couldn't go to the FBI or the Justice Department—there couldn't be any scandal, any official information. The Police Department was a sieve of information, and Vinnie *worked* there, knew people. Who could say what people Vinnie was connected to? The man knew about Darryl Whitlock's peanut-butter sandwich, which meant he could know just about anything.

Besides, Peter couldn't tell anyone, for what he had done was wrong. Any official action would require an investigation into his own doings. At the best, he could only cut some kind of deal for immunity. That ran into other problems, like being wired, providing grand-jury testimony, and so on—an ever-deepening morass of problems, all of which, when publicized, would absolutely finish him, not only in the office of the D.A. but in Philadelphia, even in the state. Every scandal was delicious, as long as you weren't involved. Calling Vinnie had been a momentary, unfortunate indiscretion, but nothing more, really. Yet others wouldn't see it that way. The cleaner you are, the more the dirt shows. No, by all means he had to avoid any kind of scandal. There were a lot of people out there who would lick their chops to see a promising A.D.A. go up in smoke—a definite career builder for the right person. Sells newspapers, too. He could be disbarred. And he could lose forever any chance he had with Janice.

No, he reasoned, it was better he deal with Vinnie quietly and try to minimize the situation. Keep the lid on, make the payment, string along the situation until he could work it out. If he went into private practice, he was a much less interesting target, especially if he and Janice moved, say, out of the city to a nice country house. Defuse the problem that way. Hell, he had bar exam reciprocity in Washington,

D.C., and a couple of other states—they could move if necessary. Vinnie would see he no longer had much leverage over Peter—that was a good plan, wasn't it? He clasped his hands tightly. He'd finesse the problem.

So the next step was cash. There was nothing at home he could sell on such short notice. High-tech stuff like stereos and televisions went for a fraction of their original purchase price when sold secondhand. He owned no gold jewelry other than his wedding ring. His parents had money, but they were now the last people in the world he wanted to ask—besides, they didn't keep much cash around the house. A check from them would take several days to clear. Janice herself probably had some of her parents' money stuck in an account somewhere, but of course he couldn't ask her to pay blackmail on his behalf. She would think his life was becoming totally unraveled and it would confirm her decision about leaving him.

Few people, even the very wealthy, could put their hands on ten thousand dollars cash in a matter of hours. He could borrow a few thousand on his credit cards, but he needed a bank to do that. He looked at his watch—quarter to five. The bank closed at three, and the automatic teller machine wouldn't let him take out more than five hundred dollars in any twenty-four-hour period. Maybe he could overdraw the account in some way—take the remaining money out with the machine card, and then write a check and cash it at one of the check-cashing operations. But they only cashed paychecks and government checks and Social Security—otherwise, every drunk in the city would cash personal checks. He could go over to the specialized loan sharks who worked the courts, but someone might recognize him; besides, he didn't have any bail papers. There were other guys, who charged ten percent vigorish a week, but he didn't know exactly who they were, and besides, if he dealt with them, they could blackmail him, too.

Berger spent every dime he made keeping his little girl in the most correct private nursery school in the city, keeping his wife happy, and keeping his nose full of junk. Peter needed someone else, a discreet friend.

In the booth, next to I LOVE PUERTO RICAN COCK etched in the wall, a dirty, well-thumbed phone book hung chained to the underside of the phone, and he flipped to the B section. He dialed the main office of Cassandra's bank, not knowing how he would begin the conversation, or if he even dared. The operator transferred him to her division and a secretary answered.

"I need to speak with Ms. uh—Cassandra, the Vice President."

241

"I'm sorry, she's in a meeting, sir. May I take a message?"

"It's a matter of importance."

"I'm sorry, but she is—"

"Miss!" Peter barked. "I am with the District Attorney's office of the City of Philadelphia. This is an urgent matter, extremely important, and it supersedes whatever meeting she is in. Do you understand?"

This got results.

"Peter? I really didn't expect to hear from you."

"Yeah, well, I was pretty angry, wasn't I?"

"I'm glad you called."

"Why? I was a complete asshole the other day."

"I don't hold grudges, Peter. Just tell me what you need."

"I'm in a jam, and I'm wondering if you as a bank officer can facilitate an overdraft for me this afternoon. Quickly."

"I don't—what's the problem?"

"Between you and me, I need ten thousand dollars cash tomorrow morning. For a personal problem."

"Oh." Then, in a cold voice: "Is it your wife?"

"No. She has nothing to do with this."

"Okay . . . I'm thinking, give me a second."

He felt impelled to fill the silence with explanation. "For various reasons, I don't have the money myself. I can't get it until next week."

There would be few papers on her desk, a desk made of chrome tubing and glass, perhaps. Cigarette in hand, breath smelling like death, masked by the smells of soap, shampoo, cologne. Something made of hammered gold around the ever-tanned skin of her neck. Oh, he had fucked her and she had tightened and squeezed herself around him at the right moment, fucking back at him—these were the things he wanted never to remember, these were the things he would forget when he was back with Janice.

"Ten thousand?" Cassandra's deep, velvety voice mused, having found the answer. "I can lend it to you."

"You can?" Again, as in their first meeting, he felt she had been waiting for him to lunge forward, into her grasp.

"I'll bring it over tonight. You make some dinner in that kitchen I like so much, and I'll bring you ten thousand bucks. Okay? I have to get back to my meeting."

He hung up and stared through the phone booth glass. Down the hall, a silhouetted mass of jurors herded out from one of the courtrooms. Hours passed in this terminal dead zone, punctuated by the occasional crowded explosion of TV camera lights, a moving, yelling serpent with wild bright eyes and boom microphone antennas that squeezed from courtroom to elevator. He stood up and started to move, feeling suddenly that he had walked hundreds of miles down these halls, worn out too many shoes carrying the file folders of Philadelphia lives that fed the machinery.

"Mr. Scattergood!"

A figure hurried through the shadows toward him. It was Miss Donnell, the *Inquirer* reporter. She stopped and moved close to him. They stood in a dark corner, almost conspiratorially.

"I can't—" he began tiredly.

"One question," she said in a low voice. "Just one."

He stared exhaustedly at her, his silence an assent.

"After the first nine-one-one call, the police took over an hour to get to Whitlock's apartment, right?" She whispered her words.

His mind was too numb to consider exactly how he should answer. He admired her resourcefulness. She was a few days behind him, no more, and maybe they were on the same side.

"They were late. They didn't respond to the first call when Johnetta Henry was in trouble. I'm not saying it was purposeful, I'm just saying it happened," she said. "Right?"

Outside the courtyard windows, snow danced madly in all directions, confused by the drafts caught within the four walls. Flakes of white adhered to the crevices and ledged surfaces. Down the hall, policemen rocked on their heels, passing duty, chopping the time down until they were free of this dark, large place. He looked into the reporter's eyes and nodded, just perceptibly.

The men outside a church soup kitchen shook their arms and stomped their feet, all lost in a blizzard tonight, with the new skyscrapers disappearing within the low white pall. The temperature was dropping, with snow expected to fall most of the night. The Mayor, eager to prove his compassion, had ordered the police and social service organizations to sweep the streets and put the homeless in the municipal services building for the night. There, amid desks and filing cabinets and protected by a duty of cops, they could sleep in warmth. And tonight Janice would light the kerosene heater next to her bed and the soft color would flicker across her face as she slept. He could imagine this quite clearly, having seen her sleep in front of the fireplace in their house. That kerosene heater worried him. It could fall over and spill fire across the floor.

Tonight, too, in search of warmth, he would take the subway. He descended the stairs, the cold following him, invading him. He moved more quickly and dropped the change in the slot, pushed through the turnstile, boarded. A group of gangly black youths got on, biker caps and big sneakers, ghetto boxes, pulsing rap music coming from a Walkman—maybe young Carotherses in the making, maybe harmless kids. Thank God for the SEPTA transit police. The subway car flashed through the tunnel with a rackety, tubular velocity. The other commuters seemed mesmerized by the jarring roar; some folded their newspapers, some smoked illegally, tapping the ashes to the floor, while others simply stared into space, lids half-shut, mouths open, oblivious to the recurrent rumbling wind-whipped roar. Peter, doing his best not to think about anything, especially his wife, turned his head in time to see a train pass on the other side; it was identical in every detail to his own, and the blurred gallery of faces could well have included his own.

Then he was home. He checked the basement door and all the first-floor windows, running on the adrenaline of fatigue. Maybe he should have the locks changed, upgraded to Medeco, maybe install a security system. Motion detectors on all the floors. Cassandra was coming over; what did that mean? He inspected the backyard for footprints with the flashlight, finding only the tiny forked marks of some hungry bird. But somebody could have gotten in, somebody could be watching him, maybe even the police. Though they made mistakes sometimes, the police were actually pretty sophisticated at undercover work. Cassandra was coming, he'd get the money. He needed to tell somebody why he was fearful, test reality with somebody he trusted. Nobody at the office. Needed to call his mother, find out how she was. But he was angry at her, both of them, too angry to call. Why had he left his files out at the office? No, that was okay, that showed people he was not suspicious, did not fear that they would be tampered with, inspected. He pictured Hoskins waiting until everyone had gone home and then quietly looking in Peter's desk. Would he find Vinnie's phone number in the Rolodex? Hoskins was smart enough to realize that if Peter meant to conceal something, then he *would* leave the files out. The awareness of another's awareness of you. No, he thought, that was silly, Hoskins had a million other things to think about. Like Berger, who acted stranger every day, picking and scratching at his nose even. Could he talk with his father about this?

244

Perhaps, but that would only confirm his parents' conviction that helping Janice had been the right thing, just what he didn't want. *My God, the woman is having lunch with some well-heeled banker or executive.* Who else would take her out to lunch there? Some old guy who smiled too much and endlessly flattered her—ah, that was okay, he wanted Janice to feel good, he really did. He wished he'd complimented her more. But she was susceptible to the charms of money. Not that he blamed her for it. Some old guy who would take his time, just move in inch by fucking inch. His chest hurt when he thought of that. An accepting father figure—some women were made helpless by it, craved it. Maybe more of a threat than a young stud like John Apple. Maybe John Apple somehow knew Robinson's older brother, put him up to the breaking of the padlock in the basement. He was sure something was going to happen, that things were connected in some way, some pattern, that he was on the brink of understanding. Maybe Vinnie knew the Mayor. Unlikely. Vinnie was more likely to know Hoskins or somebody who knew Hoskins. Vinnie had police contacts all over the city. Everybody knew everybody, and somebody had broken into his house once—when were they coming back? Maybe he should have bought the gun that morning. There you are asleep and a man is in the room and he kills you while you are asleep and you never know. Then he drinks a beer from your refrigerator and leaves. It could happen. There was no food in the house. No way could he make dinner for Cassandra; he'd order out for Chinese instead. Perhaps the gun nuts knew something he didn't. How was that possible? He was an Assistant District Attorney in the homicide unit in the D.A.'s office of the country's fifth-largest city. *Of course* he knew the world was dangerous, but dangerous, he'd always thought, for other people. Not him—the world is not dangerous for a healthy, well-educated thirty-one-year-old white man who stands six-two. That was true, wasn't it?

He called the Chinese place, told them what to deliver. The Chinese in America were getting rich, they and the Koreans, leapfrogging over the blacks. Johnetta Henry and Darryl Whitlock had been moving out of the dangerous world, moving up and out, toward money and education and professional work. Then Carothers came along, and whoever else had been in that apartment. It was time to get all the relationships straight. He sat in the kitchen, making notes. Where does the sad man fit in, he wondered, the one he'd seen outside the coffee shop? Who is he? One of two men who knew who Tyler was, knew how to dangle him before Mrs. Banks. He reminded himself to ask Cheryl Yeager the next day to look for Mrs. Banks in Tupelo, Missis-

245

sippi. The sad man was crazy or confident enough to threaten Peter, if only with his eyes. Maybe the man was unrelated to the Mayor. Maybe Carothers was a slick liar and had a pile of cash somewhere and Stein was going for the money, setting him up, using an everyday prison rumble to sell a story. Carothers could even be fooling an experienced defense attorney like Stein. Yet, Peter had to admit, Carothers's story held together and had the stink of truth. But why hadn't the police told him that he was the father of Johnetta's son? Such a fact would tie Carothers to the murders more concretely. Peter could have a detective look into that, find the hospital records, but then he would have telegraphed his knowledge of Carothers's paternity. The cops who escorted Carothers might or might not be connected to the Mayor's network, and this was true too of the prison officials. But he had to assume that the Mayor's people would be right behind him. There were so many questions: Why had the relatives of Whitlock hated Johnetta Henry so much? Why did she represent such a danger to them? How did one penetrate the secrets of a family? Families, especially the damaged ones, adhered to a certain logic, which either kept them together or ensured their destruction. Peter couldn't just go out to West Philadelphia and start asking around. A white guy in a suit standing under the elevated tracks at the corner of Fifty-second and Market was helpless in a situation like this, the fluke of Mrs. Banks's appearance notwithstanding. As a prosecutor, he usually interviewed the witnesses the police developed, in his office. Why had Stein and Carothers come forward so quickly? Stein could be planting the seeds of doubt in Peter's mind in order to undercut the whole prosecution. Maybe Carothers really had killed his old girlfriend—gone over to celebrate, taken her out to party, and she'd told him to leave. Maybe he had been jealous—there was no doubt that he was violent. Whitlock would have been confused or angry if he had come home and found Carothers standing in the doorway to the bedroom, with no sound from inside indicating that Johnetta was all right. They could have gotten into an argument. That could be it, that could be the truth. But he doubted it.

The bell rang, startling him, and he opened the front door an inch, feeling the air.

"I'm here!"

Cassandra, cloaked in an immense black mink, swept in, her heels clicking on the floors, and before he could shut the door, she gave him a long kiss on the mouth. He smelled perfume. Cold fur touched his skin.

"Hi," she whispered. "Your private banker arrives."

He pulled back into the warmth of the house. Cassandra's lips were strangely red. She had probably changed from work; her dress was cut deep and tight. Tightly circling her waist was something made of brass and bone.

"I really appreciate this," he apologized, already erasing the ashy taste of Cassandra's tongue from inside of his mouth. "I happen to need cash for tomorrow and I don't have it—"

"No need to explain, Peter." Cassandra looked appreciatively at him. "I think we're finished with these explanations, don't you?"

She handed him her fur to hang up; it was thick and exceptionally heavy. How Janice would love such a coat, despite her protestations that she didn't want one, didn't believe in killing animals for warmth.

"Well—I *do* appreciate it. Were you able to draw on your account at work?"

"I keep a small safe at home."

"Ahh," he said, wishing he knew why.

During dinner he told her about the Carothers case and took satisfaction in her pleasure in hearing the inside account. Despite his eager audience, he remained careful, however, to omit any suggestion that he was circumventing Hoskins.

Then Cassandra presented dessert. "This is a complicated recipe," she announced. "Each step is simple, but you have to do everything in the right order."

Yes, he thought, half listening to her, he needed to complete a sequence of events from Carothers's arrival at his apartment to the moment he was arrested. Compare the police events minute by minute with the Carothers version, find the holes.

"Hey," he said as Cassandra spooned out some heated concoction of pudding and pie, "that looks good. But I should tell you that I need, in not too long, to get some work done."

"You're forgetting one thing." Cassandra smiled, brandishing the pie knife. It flashed in the light. She possessed a crumbling beauty. "You're forgetting why I'm here."

Her presence in his kitchen seemed absurd.

"No-oh, I'm not. You came over to lend me some money. Which reminds me, I'll pay you back, with interest, of course. I'm selling some stock, and—"

She lit a cigarette. "You don't have to pay me back."

"That's ridiculous."

The room was quiet. Cassandra's presence pushed at him, drove him toward another mood.

"But you do need to do something for me."

The pie was on the plates, nobody looking at it.

"Name it," he said. "You're doing me a hell of a favor."

"Take me to bed tonight."

"Ha—come on."

She said nothing, didn't blink, didn't breathe.

"You're paying me ten thousand dollars to take you bed?"

She looked at him. He laughed too loudly. "Cassandra, there are ten thousand *guys* in this town getting drunk in bars *now* who would happily pay *you*."

She shook her head ever so subtly. He sensed an unnatural determination in her, a potent, controlled rage. "I scare most men, Peter. That should be clear."

The tendrils of smoke curled from her nose, lifting, spinning, weaving, above her head.

"Yes or no, Peter."

"I need the money, but—Jesus, what does that say about me?"

This seemed of little consequence to Cassandra. She shrugged. "You're the one who needs the money. Loans must be repaid. Here's a chance to pay off your debt immediately."

He pictured Vinnie's fat, expectant paw open before him. *"I've gotten very big,* Vinnie had said.

"Why are you doing this? You don't *need* to do this. Cassandra, I'd rather—assuming you're not playing some joke on me—I'd rather we just forgot it. I can get the money some other way. I—" He stared at her. "You're kidding. This is ridiculous. You're pissed at me—"

"What is it that makes you resist me, anyway?" she asked bitterly. "I want to test that."

"Why? Why be angry at me? Jesus, I'm just some guy with a lot of problems. . . ."

She shook her head, unwilling to listen to his filibuster.

"Peter, I deal with men all day long. I know how they think. I saw right away that you're a good man. I'm not so good a woman, not really. I'd like to be happy for a night." Her voice remained abstracted, smoke around her head. "This is a nice house, you're a good man. I find you very attractive, the kind of man who doesn't want the kind of woman I am, understand?" Her voice held a zombie precision. "I know men like you—you live by a certain code and expect to be rewarded. You *expect* that your wife will be happy with you, because she's the kind of woman who you want to be with. But there's something else." She exposed again a savage smile that glinted dental work. "I know there's something about me, something that attracts you to me—otherwise we never would have met. There's something in me you want. You don't want the softness." She was right. "It's not sex, exactly, because I'm sure you had *nice* sex with your wife. It's something else."

"What?" he said, half knowing what she meant.

She smiled and tapped her purse. "Ten thousand dollars is nothing, Peter, *nothing*." She bit on this word as she said it, for that nothingness had cost her a great deal. He could stand up and give her one swat and she would be out the door. Maybe she saw this in his face, for she sat down, stubbed out her cigarette, and put her cool hand against his cheek.

"Listen to me," she said. "I like it when I'm in bed with you. You're a big man, you make me feel good." She put her arms around his neck. He felt revulsion at his own desire, but this time he knew what he was doing was beyond stupid, palpably wrong. Yet if he could stall Vinnie off long enough to finish the case and get back with Janice, then he could blow town if he had to. Vinnie's potential blackmail was a lot more powerful as long as he was in office. And he wanted the information on John Apple. He needed to figure out who he was dealing with, competing against. Essentially, he could fuck Cassandra while being fucked by Vinnie—he wished he could just slip out and let them do it to each other, especially since the money transfer was exactly the same. Yet trying to sort out these questions—trying to get an idea if it really was *worth* it—was difficult. Cassandra was pulling at him, cooing in his ear, suggesting they move upstairs to the bedroom. And he had been lonely lately. She pulled a fat white envelope from her purse and laid it softly on the kitchen table. They left the dishes. In the upstairs bathroom, looking into the same mirror where he and Janice had held each other, he brushed his teeth. Cassandra removed from her purse a pill that looked like an oversized aspirin and swallowed it.

"What is that?" he asked tightly.

"A pill."

"No kidding." He imagined punching her.

"I call them fun pills. Everything slows down, feels better, deeper."

"Well, I'm tired, so don't expect too much."

She turned off the bedroom lights, whispered to herself.

"What?" he said irritably. "What did you say?"

Then, long minutes later, in the dark, Cassandra pulled him toward her, forcing him close to her.

"C'mon," Cassandra demanded. "Do it."

He turned toward the window. Impossibly, the snow was still falling. They all would be buried soon. He turned back. She moved beneath the covers and had him in her mouth. Her hand pushed his chest down and he hated his own lust, saw it for what it was, small and distracting. But what she was doing was very expert—all the nerves were attended to, around and down, and flickered over and stroked. He clutched the bedposts with both hands. This is what men over the centuries craved and were stupid for. He shut his eyes. Then Cassandra came up from the covers, keeping him in her hand, tightly.

"Let me see your ring," she said.

"Why?"

"Let me see it." She squeezed him. "You can trust me."

He pulled it off with a humoring sigh and held it up. She snatched it with her other hand and put the gold circle against her mouth and slipped the red tip of her tongue through it. She knelt over his groin and pushed the tip of him against the ring.

"Give it back now," he called uneasily.

Cassandra smiled. He lunged for the ring. She put it in her mouth, and with a quick, forceful nod of her head, swallowed it.

He grabbed her mouth, jammed his fingers in. She bit them, laughing. Instantly, he understood her game: He was supposed to be filled with hate for her and in doing so give her the fucking of a lifetime. Well, maybe that would happen, maybe it just would. He pulled her out of bed violently and lifted her upside down by the legs into the air, his waist against her head. His body was suddenly sweaty, shaking, and he had forgotten he was this strong. She laughed more and took the opportunity to lick his penis mockingly.

"Throw it up!" he demanded. "Throw up that fucking ring." He tossed her back on the bed, pinning her with one arm.

"C'mon, Peter, come here," Cassandra sang archly. Her gaunt face leered up at him, teeth large. He did hate her now and, with the pressed lips of someone who must complete some wretched task—the removal of a long-dead animal, perhaps—he pressed his hand against her neck.

"C'mon," she growled wildly, using her last breath. She grabbed his head and pulled him forward and their teeth cracked painfully. He hovered above her, silently, still erect, his hand heavily at her neck.

She didn't struggle, and instead pulled him into her, keeping her hand on him, grinding him around. He removed his hand from her neck and started to move with her. It neither hurt nor felt good, and his eyes moved toward the window.

The snow fell gently, begged at the windowpanes. The plow trucks would be out, traffic snarled. And in this he remembered the words he had heard earlier that day, somewhere lost to him hours before. Carothers had driven to the apartment house. How frustrating it must have been to try to park with a delivery truck blocking the entry to the parking lot. Cassandra was scratching his back with her left hand, urging him to moan, shiver, or otherwise display awareness of her, but the image of a delivery truck parked outside the apartment house intrigued him infinitely more. A truck, a driver, somebody who knew the streets. Cassandra tilted her pelvis forward and lifted her knees up around his ribs and was sucking and licking at his chest, and he knew instinctively that he was driving very deep into her. The truck had probably been on a routine stop. Why hadn't it been mentioned in the police report? The neighborhood patrol cars would know every delivery truck in their sector. The police always asked questions of delivery men, gas-meter readers, mail carriers—anybody who routinely passed through a scene could notice something different. Now Cassandra rolled them over, her on top. Should the truck have been there? If yes, perhaps the driver remembered something. Or perhaps the truck itself was related to the homicide. The truck was there, Carothers parked, and found the body still warm, he'd said. The absence of a report indicated either oversight or purposeful omission. Peter wished he remembered if there was a back staircase. Carothers might have been coming up while the killer of Johnetta was going down the back of the building. A man in a truck might tell him who was coming or going in the minutes before Carothers arrived.

He glanced at the clock: nearly two. Carothers had seen the truck before three. There was enough time to dress and drive across town. Like a seven-foot center going for a jam to the hoop while harassed by a pesky guard, he flicked Cassandra away from him, stood, and yanked on some clothes.

"Hey!" Cassandra yelled. She saw he was leaving. "Goddamn you!"

Downstairs, he found his coat and hat and car keys. In the kitchen he paused and thought about taking the money just to be sure. He ripped open the unmarked envelope. Inside was a stack of grocery store coupons—breakfast cereal, cookies, dish soap, nothing more. He tossed them into the air and the colored paper fluttered to the kitchen floor. He considered going back upstairs and doing something unmentionable to Cassandra. It seemed only just. But he couldn't waste the time.

Thirty minutes later, Peter stood outside the apartment house, checking his watch, staring at the windows on the fourth floor, and enjoying the dead calm. The windows above him were dark, indicated nothing more than their existence. He had prosecuted cases where bodies had been found in burned-out warehouses in the Northeast, in the rail yards of West Philly, in the elevator of a parking garage, in the backseat of a trolley, in the washroom of the national headquarters of an insurance firm. But those were the exceptions; most murdered people lost their lives in their homes or in the street. It was the intimate spaces that were most vulnerable to moments of rage or greed or jealousy: hallways in apartment buildings, bedrooms, stairwells, front stoops, places people knew, places so intimate people forgot themselves. The window above led not only into the bedroom but into a set of lives that now included his. That he had told no one of all he had discovered made him feel like an accomplice, part of a chain of guilt, and this compelled him; something more—he knew not what— lay at the end of it.

The cold air burned the inside of his nostrils. He spewed great shadows of steam and watched the occasional car pass, worrying he'd made a mistake, but convinced, somehow, that he hadn't. He thought again of Janice and the heater. She seemed always to get cold easily and she would love the radiating warmth, the bright hiss of the flame. He moved his feet, paced.

Then headlights turned the corner—a delivery truck, slowing as it neared him. He slipped out of the lights. The truck slowed, then stopped before the neighborhood grocery next to the apartment building. The driver parked, keeping his engine on, and disappeared for a moment within the truck. He emerged carrying two large flat pallets of what could only be bread, given that they were light enough that the man held them with one arm. He wore baggy pants and a thick jacket, and carried the pallets around the back of the building, probably, Peter thought, to drop them off inside a delivery door to which he had a key. The truck was red, green, and white—Italian bread.

Peter waited. He was a good eight inches taller than the other man, and wished not to frighten him.

"Excuse me," he said when the man returned. "Sir?"

"Ain't got time for drunks." The man brushed by him.

"Wait!" Peter called. "I'm not what I seem."

He explained who he was, what he wanted. Did he remember that particular night exactly a week ago?

"Yeah, but I already told the police what I knew, just after it all happened," the man said doubtfully.

"They asked you?"

"Sure. A detective asked me what I seen and when I was here."

Whoever had been sure that Peter never saw the report knew he couldn't know of the existence of each and every potential witness.

"So, what did you say?"

"Ah, geez." The man shook his head. "I told them I deliver, all the little stores early in the morning. It's a five-hour run. Most of the stores, they open around seven."

"Usually pretty quiet?"

"I like it that way, Mr. . . . Scattergood, you say your name was? No traffic. See, I drove an eighteen-wheeler for twenty years, Philly to Chicago, via New York, round trip twice a week. Load up medical supplies to New York, then men's suits to Chicago—"

"Okay," Peter interrupted, "that was a while back. But what about that night? Remember what you told the police?"

"Probably, but not in this cold."

They climbed into the truck, and the man reached for a Thermos of coffee under his seat.

"Got the best goddamned heater in the city."

"Okay."

"I drive this route three days a week and my other route two."

Peter saw he would have to take his time. The man was a loner with an itch to talk and in no hurry to say his piece.

"See, bread prices are based partially on delivery. That's why your cheapest bread is in a bakery, because it don't have to be delivered. But it's harder and harder to make a profit, these little mom-and-pop places. It's all money, everything's money. So the bigger companies deliver. Every time you go to these little stores, like the one here"—he thumbed his hand backward—"you pay more because of they have to take delivery more often, they don't have the storage space, and because they don't do the same volume. I drive the truck this route here every Sunday, Tuesday, and Friday—"

"The night I was asking about was a Wednesday."

253

"That's right, it was," the man continued, pausing to sip his coffee. "I start my route on Tuesday at eleven and I don't get here until Wednesday morning. The only thing I remember that night was some guy parked in my parking spot, which is actually illegal. I always park in the same spot, all the legal spots are taken. Everyone's home, what're ya gonna do? Some guy was parked there, that's all I remember."

"When was this?"

"About now, quarter of three."

"He was parked."

"His engine was running. Right now where we're sitting."

"What happened?"

"Nothing."

"All right, anything else about that night?"

"Wait a minute, I'm still telling it. I went around the block once, thinking he was going to pull out at any minute. When I came back he was still there. I double-parked and tapped the horn quietly. I had six racks and I didn't feel like making three long trips. Then—"

"Racks of bread like tonight?"

"Exactly the same, all of them."

"How did you hurt your left arm?"

The driver stared at him, mouth cocked to one side.

"Shit, man, that's scary. How did you know that?"

"Just now you carried two pallets with your right arm," Peter explained. "That means you should be able to carry at least three, maybe four, with both arms. Which means you could easily carry six pallets in two trips, not three."

"You got my vote, buddy." The driver shook his head. "Yeah, some guy slashed me bad one night, truck stop just over the Indiana line. Coming from Ohio." He pulled back his sleeve to show the scar on the inside of the elbow. "Guy had a ponytail a foot long. Got all the tendons. He took my truck. The county clinic sewed it up, but what're ya gonna do? Couldn't drive, couldn't barely make a *fist*."

"That's why you deliver bread—it's light."

"I made good money with my rig. Got to have both hands. Hated to give it up."

"I'm sorry."

"Yeah, well."

They sat a minute, looking at the snow.

"Tell me what happened after you saw the guy parked in your place, after you honked," Peter said.

254

"Nothing happened, so I got out and went up to the window of the car."

"What'd he say?"

"He said he was moving on in a little while."

"What did he look like?"

"Some black guy."

"Could you see his face?"

"Easy. I have night vision, after all these years."

"What'd his face look like?"

"Not much, heavy."

"Heavy?"

"Sad. He looked like a sad guy."

Peter stared up at the window, remembered Johnetta's still body, the tight, attractive slit of her belly button. Had the man who snatched the baby boy also killed her?

"In his thirties maybe?" Peter finally asked.

"Yes."

"Built well, strong?"

"Didn't see."

"Anything else?" Peter pressed.

"It was mostly his face. Just looking at me, and sad. The bottom part under the eyes were droopy. And some kind of bad scar on his chin."

"Curved like the letter C?"

"Yeah—right. You must know him."

"You told the detective all this?"

"Just like I'm telling you."

"Okay, then what?"

"He looked like he meant it, like he wasn't going to discuss it no more, you know what I'm saying? I had plenty of time, so I got back in the truck with my heater and waited. I could have carried the bread a little further, but that would leave the truck blocking the street while I was taking the bread around. So I just sat. He went in and came out maybe ten minutes later and drove off. I pulled in, did the delivery, and left."

"Did he *run* out of the building?"

"No, he just walked out, just like anybody."

"You see another guy hurry into the building a few minutes later, tall skinny black guy?"

"No."

"What's your name?"

255

"You don't need it, do you? Call me the bread man. Here." He reached back and handed Peter a package of fresh sticky buns. "I gotta go."

Back in the car, he ate his breakfast bun listening to the radio croon rock songs so old nobody under thirty knew them any longer. Everything Carothers had said so far appeared to be true. Peter tried to see it all from his point of view. Carothers must have thought about Johnetta and Tyler, the child they brought into the world. Surely, he had stood in the hospital room, looking into Johnetta's face as she held their child. Seen the wrinkled eyes and the clutching chubby fingers working at Johnetta's gown. The hope of it all! The immense hope that springs from the most evanescent of emotions! Certainly Peter understood that. And yet, never married, together only a short while, before circumstances—what? boredom, fights, lovers, family, crime, drugs—had pulled them apart. Peter started the car and pulled out, picturing Wayman moving others' furniture—happy family rituals repeated each week before his eyes. The big three-bedroom apartments overlooking Rittenhouse Square, the mansions in Chestnut Hill, the estates on the Main Line. *Please take that into the bedroom. Thank you! . . . Oh! Those boxes are the china—careful!* A big quiet black man watching this, nodding to the aerobicized blonde who tells him this, seeing the children examining the big moving truck.

He must have wondered about his child, his *boy*! The tiny body that had come, in part, from his. Even a killer can be moved by the sight of a baby's toes, no? How had Carothers felt as he saw Johnetta dead before him? Wouldn't he, Peter, have killed anyone if he thought, even for a second, that person threatened Janice? Wasn't it just basic human nature? Of course—idiotic to expect otherwise. A man like Carothers would have cursed himself for not being present to protect Johnetta! She had *called* him! And what was he doing? *Knocking off a supermarket with three low-life, coked-up motherfuckers.* Carothers must have thought some of these things—who wouldn't? Who wouldn't question the way things had turned out, sought to know why? Peter drove on, vaguely heading back the way he had come. Carothers, he saw, was begging now. He had suffered enough, in his way, and deserved every sliced corner of law coming to him.

The sad man, Peter saw, had probably killed Johnetta and then snatched Tyler, the baby boy, in an effort to get Johnetta's grand-mother to keep quiet. According to the grandmother, it was Whit-lock's family—the Mayor's family—who wanted Johnetta out of the picture. The sad man was tied in somehow—close enough to be picked as the one to either threaten or kill Johnetta, close enough again to be assigned to keep an eye on Mrs. Banks, the grand-mother. But what did Johnetta Henry know? What knowledge was worth her life?

The police—or one or two people in the department, someone who the Mayor no doubt controlled through the Police Commissioner—had made only two seemingly small mistakes. The first, if in fact it was planned, was letting just a little too much time pass before send-ing a car to respond to the neighbor's first call—an oversight that resulted in Whitlock's death at the hands of Carothers. The second mistake was not reporting the interview with the truck driver, which by its absence became conspicuous. The driver's account corrobo-rated Carothers's account and presented an alternative scenario and suspect—of course, it had needed to be purged. And it was probably just a couple of paragraphs. Among other definitions, the Police De-partment was a huge bureaucracy, one that often lost documents, evidence, and information. The police, at the street level, were not likely to wish to protect the Mayor. Most cops, by far, were not corrupt. It was dazzlingly simple—all that was necessary was that one detective be told or paid not to file a one-page account of the interview with the delivery driver.

Strengthening the reported version was the woman who had seen Carothers while emptying her trash. Somebody had spotted her use-fulness and whisked her down to the Roundhouse hoping she could identify a suspect from the books. That she actually did so correctly was amazing. That she happened to be drunk was bad luck for who-ever was pulling the strings. Carothers then had to be released. That Carothers was stupid enough to then go out and stage armed robbery seemed ludicrous—luck had capriciously cut back and forth between the two sides. Once Carothers was back in custody, and with more evidence found, the police could blamelessly cease looking for other suspects.

Of course, neither Carothers nor Stein had any idea of the sig-nificance of the delivery truck. Nor did they know about the sad man. And because Peter did not officially know about the truck and the driver's recollection, then that fact never became part of the of-

257

ficial record Stein would probe to build a defense. If Carothers hadn't blurted out what seemed to him an extraneous aggravation, Peter could not have connected the sad man to the night of the homicides.

Where had Hoskins come in? he wondered. The irony in all this was that man didn't give a pea-sized shit about the death of Whitlock but had apparently used his death to attach himself to the Mayor. Hoskins, who each day seemed to metamorphose further into a dense, evil bullet of a man, would fight Carothers every step of the way, twist every angle, tweak his own mother's nose with his meaty fingers if it would bleed evidence that supported a conviction and his own career.

Driving aimlessly across the city, it occurred to Peter that Hoskins had selected him for exactly the opposite reasons as he had told him the morning of the murders. The praise and encouragement! How could Hoskins *not* have noticed that Peter had been in trouble these last few months? The occasional lapses, having to depend on Berger from time to time, the problems at home? The man was not stupid, and he had been in the game far longer than Peter.

Hoskins made his decision thinking he had the killer in hand. If he hadn't known about Johnetta Henry at the time he'd called Peter early that morning, then that might be proof that he himself hadn't gotten the whole story, at least not initially. But Hoskins had made a mistake: He'd never complained angrily about the fact that he'd been informed of only one homicide, not two. Such an oversight usually sent him into a rage. But he'd been complacent about that fact, never bringing it up. That suggested he did not want to emphasize the differences between the homicides, did not want Peter thinking that they had different causes. Was it possible Hoskins felt Peter's attention would be scant and hoped that he would groove on the media attention that came with quickly having a suspect, and *not* do a thorough job, *not* dig behind the facade of facts the police provided him? Is this why Berger hadn't been chosen? It was conceivable Hoskins was way ahead of all of them—somehow making sure Berger was in Harrisburg the morning of the murder, putting heat on Berger all along, maybe even planting the comment on coke-snorting by the detective at the murder scene. But that would mean that he'd known the murders were coming and that was impossible, since Carothers had acted spontaneously. It was more likely that Hoskins had been called by the Mayor in the early hours after the murders, and had seen an opportunity in Berger's absence and Peter's unsettled state.

Figuring backward and forward, getting caught in knots of logic and speculation, Peter circled past City Hall and down Market and over to Delancey. He wouldn't be able, he realized, to deduce everything that had happened. His house was dark and Cassandra's car gone. A night such as this was no big deal to her; she would find other men, he supposed. He would let his membership at the club expire and never see her again. As for the ring, that was, he supposed, lost. Unless she had somehow regurgitated it in a soupy puddle of vomit, an unlikely effort.

Across from his house, he saw two men sitting in a car. Dark shapes behind the windshield, almost invisible.

They, somebody, were watching him and meant him ill will, wanted to make sure he did what they wanted him to do. He receded into the shadows, returned to his car and drove down to the big industrial sites by the Delaware River, parked, and walked along a high chain fence. He knew exactly where to go to get what he needed. If not here, then somewhere else, one of the all-night bars. He kept walking, turning up the thick collar of his coat to cut off the sides of his face. The L. L. Bean hat came down far over his forehead.

Two cars were parked within a triangular shadow of a brick warehouse. As Peter neared, one of the cars started and drove off. Once within the shadow, his eyes adjusted. Two men lounged on the trunk of the car, smoking. Peter checked the cash in his pockets.

"Yeah?" greeted one man, recognizing Peter as an unlikely customer. "We got a sale on, mister. This here is John Wanamaker's, Strawbridge and Clothier's."

The man slapped a gloved hand on the other man's hand.

"You are a *mother*fucker, man." The other smiled. "Gimme that shit there." A confetti of colored crack capsules littered the asphalt.

Peter spoke in a dead, unrecognizable voice: "What do you have to show me?"

"Depends on what you want. Lingerie on the fourth floor."

Peter waited for the men to stop laughing.

"Something small."

The man unlocked the trunk and opened it.

"Okay, okay."

He pulled a small flashlight from his coat and swept it over a

259

wooden crate. Inside lay dozens of different handguns. Pistols and semi-automatic assault rifles—Chinese-made AK-47s, Uzis, MAC-10s, semi-automatic guns with collapsible stocks. Revolvers. Cartridge clips. Enough for a small army. The man pulled out an assault rifle.

"The President says it's illegal to import these motherfuckers," he cackled. "But we ain't importin', we just keepin' them in circulation." He held up the gun. The bullets from these guns penetrated policemen's vests, brick walls, even municipal garbage trucks.

"No." Peter shook his head.

"Fuck, man, this thing fires two hundred fucking bullets a minute!" The man pulled out another gun from the crate. "Semi-automatic, hair-trigger. This one's forty. With a clip, forty-five."

Peter was silent.

"What else you want to know about it?" came the man's irritated voice. "It'll shoot."

"Safety on it?"

"No. You want safety, don't carry a gun."

The two men cracked up. This was the funniest thing they had ever heard. Peter handed the man two twenties and a five. The other man rummaged around in a smaller box, pulled out a few clips, tested them until he got the right size, loaded the gun, and handed it, barrel down, to Peter.

"Tell your friends about us!" the first man called after Peter. Their laughter followed him.

Stuffing the gun under the car seat, his mind deadened from lack of sleep, he felt compelled to figure the situation further. The District Attorney, an elected official, could not be fired by the Mayor. The D.A. was a smooth-talking man, a good man in his forties given to gold tie pins and stern law-and-order statements to the press. Perhaps Hoskins wanted to be the next District Attorney. As Chief of Homicide, he was in excellent position to run for the position. But if Hoskins wanted to rise politically, he was going to have to consider the black leadership of the city, which controlled the black voting base. This was tricky: There were the old black leaders who had been around a long time, who knew their constituencies, who were considered men of the utmost honor. Then there were the younger leaders, such as the Mayor, who were steadily changing the power relationships in the city. Once he had jockeyed his way through the intra-party struggle of the primary, the Mayor had utilized the black

Democratic machine to its fullest, as could be expected. His appointments were everywhere. He had an excellent organization and appeared to have strong if silent financial backing. He had moved into office with great vigor and was the pole around which the power in the city was slowly magnetizing. The Mayor could use a man in the District Attorney's office, for the office traditionally operated autonomously and even in conflict with the Mayor's office. There were plenty of incentives for the Mayor to develop a relationship with someone such as Hoskins who knew the legal community well and who had ties to all the big firms in town. And if Hoskins decided—however stupidly—to run for the D.A. office in the future, and was running a cover-up, then he already had a favor coming from the Mayor. It was conceivable that the Mayor would then support a candidate for D.A. who offered only token resistance to Hoskins. Or, more likely, after the current D.A. moved on, Hoskins might not actually run for the office but would be in a position to deliver it to whomever the Republican machine assigned as its candidate. Assuming that the Mayor was at least indirectly culpable, all of this would have been feverishly reasoned as soon as the Mayor knew of the murders. A phone call in the early hours, then some fast decisions, a call put in to Hoskins. The back-door possibilities were endless. Both the Mayor and Hoskins would be in positions of power in the city for the foreseeable future.

If Peter told the D.A. what he knew, the man would have a choice to believe him or not believe him. If the D.A. believed Peter, then they could either act or not act. If they dropped charges against Carothers for the murder of the girl, they would have to answer to the Mayor, the police, and to the press, which would seize on this event as a major twist in the story, since it implied that someone else killed the girl. All this seemed unlikely, considering the evidence of fingerprints, witness testimony, ballistics match, and the obvious motive of the ex-lover. The police administration—also ambitious—would know the D.A.'s office was on to something, and might be unhappy at the public embarrassment. The Mayor, who also knew how to strum the strings of the media, would understand that the investigation was dangerously close to his own family. The Mayor could allude to the D.A.'s political aspirations. In short, to go public and drop the second charge against Carothers with what amounted to meager evidence would put the D.A. in a precarious public position.

That was only one option the D.A. had if he, Peter, was believed.

261

The D.A. could believe yet ignore what Peter had to say, which meant Peter would have to decide whether he was able to go along with the office. *That* meant prosecuting Carothers for a murder he didn't commit. Stein, whom he respected, would be furious and quite willing to march into court, and, with nothing to lose, might blow the whistle on their secret meeting. Peter would either be isolated within the office or knowingly be prosecuting a man for a murder he didn't commit, which was probably the best way to lose a trial, not to mention one's soul. A second murder conviction could easily be the difference between life in prison—which Carothers was going to get anyway—or electrocution . . .

. . . because two murders, one of a promising young man, following an evening of armed robbery, were just about a lock for a death sentence. The murder and the robbery charges would be tried separately, but it was stupid to think that the homicide jury wouldn't know about other charges. If, however, the homicides were separated into two cases, and it were shown convincingly that Carothers was responding to a *cry for help* by rushing over to West Philadelphia, then one had a very different story. The homicide of Whitlock would be seen as the unfortunate result of grief: second-degree murder.

He drove on. Perhaps he should resign before having to go to trial. Carothers would be tried by someone else, maybe Hoskins himself, while Peter sat at home. Quitting was cowardly; he'd save his neck but not Carothers's. But should Carothers be saved? Really? The guy *had* killed Whitlock, had been involved in armed robbery, was more or less fated for prison. Was he just another scumbag no different from the rest of them?

It came down to how much Peter believed in the law. The pure law. By the *law*, given the aggravating circumstances, such as the fact that he had been carrying a concealed deadly weapon, and the mitigating ones, such as the fact that he had just found the mother of his son brutally murdered and had no idea that Whitlock would enter the apartment, Carothers should go to prison but should not die. The law, at the moment, was the only thing Peter could believe in. Furthermore, Carothers should not pay for someone else's crime. Whoever killed Johnetta—he assumed it was the sad man—should do the time. The first murder was premeditated, the second spontaneous.

Inside all these choices, Peter decided, there existed an improbable outcome called justice.

If Peter went to the D.A., there was the possibility that the D.A.

already knew of the situation or would not believe him. In that event, he would be removed from the case and possibly even asked to resign. Whatever happened, the machinery would go on and he'd be shut out from helping Carothers. But, and this prospect attracted him in a secretly righteous and prideful way, if he did *not* go to the D.A. right away and continued to oversee the case, he could also continue probing what he had discovered, in effect prosecute *a priori*. No one would know about this—except, of course, if the sad man knew Peter had been with Mrs. Banks and told the Mayor. He assumed the old woman wouldn't tell whom she had been talking to. No—that was stupid. They would get it out of her—and probably that had already happened, since the two men were now outside his house.

There had to be a way out. He could play along with Hoskins and, before going to trial, present the information to the D.A. and threaten to go to the papers if he didn't cooperate. They would both know that Peter could blab about a cover-up and ruin the man's chances for the Senate. This might work, no? No one else in the office would know the case as thoroughly as he, and the D.A. would be in a tough spot, what with all of the city waiting for the trial. Perhaps by then he could offer the D.A. a proverbial "yesable proposition," an alternative course of action—in this case another defendant, such as the sad man. Perhaps the D.A. *then* would separate himself from Hoskins's version of the events and see Hoskins as a threat to his reputation, garner a little righteousness for himself. Whether or not Peter accomplished that would be a matter of luck, what with the police controlling the evidence and names of witnesses. But if he could locate Mrs. Banks on his own and then get her to give him some more names, that was a start.

Beyond this architecture of analysis, something else drew him toward altruistic action—there was the self-serving aspect to all of this. Which he freely admitted to himself. Yes, that was the beauty—the necessity—of it. Once the papers found out how he alone had fought so diligently to uphold the law and spare a man's life, then the Mayor would be powerless to seek retribution. The media would paint him as a man who walked the lonely path to truth. Most important, Janice and his parents would know; they would see that he had undergone immense risk to seek justice. How could they not help but admire him? They would see that their betrayals of him were unjust and that they should return to him.

TEN

Four-thirty in the morning. Preserve thyself, Peter Scattergood chanted under his breath, get some sleep, just a few hours. The hotel, a squat four-story brick building, stood tucked underneath the north side of the new glass office towers, a remnant of the old city. It was frequented by hookers working the area and cost only thirty dollars a night.

And thirty dollars was nearly all that Peter had left in his pocket after buying the gun, having left his wallet and credit cards on his kitchen counter and Cassandra sitting up in his bed. Hours ago, decisions ago. The old man behind the bulletproof glass didn't give him a second look. Cash only, out by noon. He could rob the place now— but, of course, he didn't wish to do that. He pushed bills through the window slot, scrawled illegibly on the register card, and asked for an eight A.M. wake-up.

Everything was bolted to the floor. Rotten mattress, laundered pillowcases. He pulled off his clothes, careful to hang them, since he'd be wearing them to work. With breakfast, he'd be broke. On the bed, peering up at a water-stained plaster ceiling, he tried to calm himself. *How could he have just bought a gun?* There was this fear. Don't worry about Vinnie, he thought, the guy's a hustler, a nobody. The key was the important things: Remember Janice, and the work toward the truth in the Carothers case, *seek justice wherever you can.* . . . He sat upright, his mind tugged by childhood—there it was, coming back to him when he least expected: the Quaker queries he'd heard as a boy, sitting on the long, uncomfortable wooden benches in Meeting for

264

Worship. *Do you seek justice in your daily tasks?* With his grandfather holding his hand, eyes shut, aging veins pulsing in his forehead, a man plumbing his own mystic depths while communing to Peter through the slightest variations in the grip of his fingers that there were ways that one must live one's life. He had feared and hated and occasionally loved his grandfather. Never did he suspect that his grandfather had actually *struggled* to behave justly; it had seemed, always, quite the opposite, that the man who clung to the plain speech of "thee" and "thou" while American B-52s napalmed Vietnamese children did not experience difficulty in *restraining* himself. Yet, of course, Peter reflected, the man must have warred against himself, as was evident from the veins straining in his grandfather's forehead as he sat rigid as a gravestone, the moments of anger, the judgmental pronouncements at the way the world tended. Grinding his teeth till the day he died. Temperamentally, his grandfather had been a violent man.

And so was he, but that did not mean—oh, what insanity to buy a gun! A moment of small-hearted fear. The world would come to an end if every Peter Scattergood bought a gun the first time he was scared. He lay on the greasy blanket, arms outstretched. How psychologically blind, how impotent! It was almost a joke that he'd bought a gun! A man with his education and upbringing—ridiculous. He turned off the light. He would get rid of the gun in the morning.

But the sound, puncturing his thin membrane of certainty, was of a woman getting the screwing of her life, emitting an unending throbbing of moans, cries, testimonials to technique and rhythm, and exhortations to the gods. *Oh jesusjesusjesus. Oh-ho-oh, that, yes, oh jesus.* She was superb and she drove Peter crazy, and his mind, inflamed with a distracted lust, flipped in hallucinogenic clarity from Cassandra (his crotch still smelled of her) to Janice (*must not think about John Apple*) and then to Johnetta. The sounds insinuated into his mind, wrapping around him, touching a polished fingernail to his ear. It was too late for this kind of crap—he was almost sick with exhaustion.

"Where's that shoe?" a man's voice muttered.

"Here. This is a well-made shoe, a *nice* shoe. How come you buy good shoes like this and you don't give me nothing extra?"

"Always the same," the man exhaled. "I'm going."

"It's a reasonable question."

"Fuck off, woman."

"I just did."

"Yeah, right."

265

"Ah-ha, you loved it," she protested playfully.

"Do you always believe everything you imagine?"

A bitter silence.

"Throw that away. I hate wearing those things. I don't have to wear them with my wife."

"She so good, how come you here with me?"

"Don't ask me that," the man croaked. "I can't take it." They laughed together.

Good morning, City of Brotherly Love—good morning to the insurance men and lawyers and bankers and senior vice presidents and office managers and systems engineers and receptionists and marketing specialists and communications coordinators and all the soldiers of America's new economy marching into the towers and offices, showered, shaved, perfumed, brushed, combed, dry-cleaned and pressed, fed and ready, with newsstand radios spouting the latest scandals, the garbagemen finishing up their morning runs, and last, and in most respects least, the homeless, shaken awake from subways and shelters, making their way into the snowy sunlight, carrying filthy bundles of clothes, shoes, papers, items of curiosity and survival.

Peter watched from a coffee-shop window, chewing at a doughnut, reading the story by Karen Donnell that carefully raised the possibility that the police might have arrived late to the murder scene. She'd quoted "unnamed officials." The Mayor would want to know who that was. He and Hoskins would see their control of the situation unraveling hourly. Perhaps, Peter worried, he had been seen talking to Miss Donnell the day before, even though they spoke for no more than a minute. Someone down the hall could have seen and stopped and made note of it. His chest ached. The regularity of the day was sliding by him. He craved it now, just to have a normal day facing him, the usual problems, the usual phone calls and paperwork. It seemed like days since he'd been in the office. Perhaps he could call Janice or his parents. If only he had gotten more than a few hours' sleep, this nervousness would be gone. Police cars cruised by the window every minute or two. Peter imagined they were looking for him. Had those men really been waiting outside his house? He'd left the gun in his car.

The rest of the newspaper was full of tragedies, to be forgotten tomorrow. A big plane had crashed. The Middle East was on fire, Congress monkeying with budget problems. The Japanese had bought some more real estate in New York. But he couldn't concentrate, for the day pushed at him—it was almost nine A.M., and the sun cut the cold air and lay broad stripes of light across the ledges of the office buildings, brightening the already-dirty snow. He bought a paisley tie from one of the Korean sidewalk venders. With his suit and the new tie, he was fine—he'd shave in the office men's room with the electric razor he usually used before an afternoon session in court. No one would suspect he'd been anywhere but home that night.

He was to meet Vinnie in five minutes. There was, of course, no money, but he wanted to see if the man would show. He slipped into one of Cassandra's money-machine booths near the Bellevue, as it was now called, just as a waxed, black Cadillac eased in next to a fire hydrant and stopped. The sun dashed itself against the glass, and so, even though he was a few yards away, no one would see him. Vinnie sat in the back of the big car, spooning something into his mouth. He had, as he said, gained weight; his head appeared to lack a chin, and through a transition of shapeless flesh became his chest. He ate methodically, swiveling his head from time to time toward the facade of the old hotel to see if Peter had arrived. Minutes passed. The plastic spoon went out the window. Vinnie spoke to his driver, drumming the fat fingers of his right hand on the outside of the car. A paper ice cream container shot out the open car window. Vinnie looked straight at Peter. Had he been seen? The window glass rose in a smooth electric glide, and rising with it was the curved reflection of the city. The car pulled out, headed down Broad Street. Peter watched, knowing Vinnie would eventually find him.

Mrs. Banks had told Peter that she and her husband had come to Philadelphia from Tupelo, Mississippi, so many years ago. Cheryl Yeager already knew, from her early attempt to find Mrs. Banks, which church she attended in Philadelphia, and in her quiet, methodical way began to talk to church secretaries both in the city and in Tupelo to find out where Mrs. Banks might be. Cheryl was unfailingly polite, and her voice, soft and calming and black, masked the fact that a very anxious man waited and paced in his office, eager for her to succeed. Peter occasionally checked on her, saw her scribbling new phone numbers down on her pad of paper, hearing her say, "Yes, that's very helpful, and I do appreciate your willingness to help. . . ."

He looked at his watch, feeling that he was running blindly in a race, with the distance and his opponents unknown to him. Vinnie was sure to get in contact with him sooner or later. He shut his door and drank more coffee, yet remained exhausted. He thought about Janice and how she loved snowy mornings like this. If the police were looking for him by looking for his car, they might find the gun. Vinnie certainly could find his car, having found Janice's in a short time, and Peter's was parked in Center City, the worst place to hide a car. He called the hospital but was told by a nurse that his mother was asleep. Thoughts crowded him, pushing, worrying him. What had happened with Janice the previous Saturday night would only send her deeper into John Apple's arms. It was human nature. Stein would be calling before too long, wanting to know what was happening. So would Karen Donnell, who surely had sensed his vulnerability.

Then Cheryl knocked and came in.

"I found her in Mississippi," she said, "but she said she won't talk to you."

"You have her on the line?" Peter asked.

"Yes."

"Tell her that I know who killed her granddaughter, in case she's interested."

Cheryl stared at him.

"Tell her that, and tell no one else."

A minute later, his phone rang.

"Can you hear me, Mrs. Banks?"

"Yes, I can."

"Good morning."

"They just trying to scare me, that's all."

"Did they hurt Tyler?"

"No, he's okay. He's down here with me, singing at the church."

"Is anybody else there, listening to you?"

"No. I'm in my sister-in-law Celie's kitchen washing the breakfast dishes."

"Now, listen to me carefully, Mrs. Banks. I'm going to ask you a couple of questions and I want straight answers. You're safe and sound in Mississippi, but I'm dealing with the problems back here. I'm still trying to find out what happened to Johnetta. Don't you care about that?"

"Of course I do."

"Who were those two men that had Tyler in the window at the coffee shop?"

"Now, Mr. Scatterblood—"

"Scatter*good*, Mrs. Banks. Don't play with me now."

"They was two men who wanted me not to talk to you."

"Of course I know that."

"So I can't."

"Did they know who you were with?"

"No."

"Are you sure?"

"They kept askin' me who I was talkin' to, but I never told them."

"You do know them, right?"

There was a pause. "One of them was Charlie."

"Who is the man with the scar on his chin?"

"That's Charlie."

"Who is he?"

"Well . . ." she stalled.

"Mrs. Banks, I believe this man Charlie killed your granddaughter."

"Lord!"

"Tell me, Mrs. Banks. Tell me what Johnetta can't say now."

"Oh . . ."

"Mrs. Banks, listen to me, please. I've seen something you haven't—I've seen what this man Charlie did to Johnetta. Do I have to tell you what he did?" He would let Mrs. Banks imagine the worst. "Tell me—"

"His name is Charlie Geller, and all I can say is that I think he used to work for the Mayor. Maybe he drove him around, I can't rightly remember."

"That's it?"

"All I know is he works for the Mayor."

"Is he down there with you?"

"No, he still in Philly."

"Are you sure he doesn't know you talked with me?"

"They know I talked to somebody. But he looking at it the other way around and he confident."

"What do you mean?"

"The other man asked Charlie if the man in the restaurant, you, seen Charlie's face, and Charlie say the glass too fogged up for anybody to see him. He say he couldn't see you, so he pretty sure you couldn't see him."

Her tone carried fear in it. If the Mayor had people in this small

269

town, then it would only be a short matter of time before they found about the inquiries from the D.A.'s office.

"Who is the father of Tyler, Mrs. Banks?"

"I told you, I don't know."

"I thought you knew everything about that boy."

"Everything else. Of course I do."

"Everything? Absolutely? Do you remember the heart operation you said he had?"

"Yes, of course I do."

"What's his blood type?"

There was a pause of silence and the low wind of static blew over the line.

"It wasn't the same as his mama," Mrs. Banks said tentatively, warming to the question. "I remember that it was the kind that—he had some transfusions and we had to ask people in the church if they had—"

"A certain type, right?"

"Yes, how did I remember? I used to say, 'The baby, we have to ask for blood, the baby . . .' " wondered Mrs. Banks. "*Yes*, AB sounds like 'baby.' Tyler has type AB blood."

"You're sure?"

"That what I used to say, 'Type AB for the baby.' "

Peter fumbled with Johnetta Henry's autopsy report and found the page he needed.

"Johnetta had type BB?"

"I can't say that I know. I have to go now, they're coming back."

She hung up, and he held the receiver, thinking. He called Cheryl back into his office and asked her to find Charlie Geller immediately. He told her that he lived in Philadelphia and might work for the Mayor. Finding him would be much less difficult. Then he called Arizona, where the time was two hours earlier. His brother answered.

"Bobby, I'm terribly sorry to bother you. I need to ask your wife a question."

Bobby's wife came to the phone.

"Carol, please listen to me quickly. I'm sorry it's so early. You're the only obstetrician I can call this fast to get answers.

"Well, we're about the leave the house, Peter. What is it?"

"If a baby has type AB blood and his mother has BB, what kind does the father have?"

Carol laughed lightly, almost a groan.

"Well, it's not quite that simple."

"I know that blood types get complicated—"

"Okay, first, the ABO blood groups and the MN groups are different ways of typing blood," Carol said. "Generally, a BB mother with an AB child means the father is AB or AA. But these are just crude blood types, Peter. You can string twenty letters together and describe a blood type."

He knew that. Captain Docherty had said something very similar during the Robinson trial.

"But can the father be an O?"

"Absolutely not."

"Sure?"

She yawned agreement.

"Are you absolutely positive?" he snapped anxiously.

"Peter, excuse me, I know what I'm talking about," Carol answered. "Remember, it's easier to *disprove* paternity than to prove it."

"You're positive?"

"I better be. I have nurses type newborn blood every day."

"Thanks, Carol." He said good-bye and hung up. He now knew—within a reasonable degree of scientific certainty, as Captain Docherty liked to say—that Wayman Carothers was not the father of Tyler Henry.

It was then that Melissa knocked on the door and came in and handed Peter a memo. It said:

> To: Homicide Unit and Staff
> From: William Hoskins, Chief of Homicide
>
> It is my duty to inform you that for reasons of a personal nature, Harold E. Berger has been relieved of duty from the unit and office, effective immediately.
> Reassignment of Mr. Berger's caseload will be made shortly. His change of status has been communicated to the Court of Common Pleas. Defense attorneys affected by this event will be advised this morning.
> All questions regarding this matter should be directed to the Chief of Homicide.

He could only imagine that Hoskins had confronted Berger with evidence of his coke use, and told him he was fired. Peter looked about the room and at his desk, wondering if Hoskins had been poking around. Berger's office was probably already cleaned out. What was most disturbing here was not that Berger was gone—that, clearly, had been an approaching event. What was disturbing was the way it was done, without his being given the chance to enter a recovery program, without even a grace period in which to find a new job. No, Hoskins had not cared for Berger the man, nor that he would lose an experienced attorney. He had sacrificed even the operational advantage of creating a caseload transition. Berger had been chopped out with precipitous haste, which suggested tremendous pressure on Hoskins. In respect to the Whitlock and Henry killings, it left Peter alone.

So, barely suppressing his paranoia, he attended to the paper on his desk. The sun pushed a brilliant slant over the desk blotter and in this brightness he saw the lighter, soft skin on the fourth finger of his left hand, indented still, though the ring was gone. That same hand remembered holding Cassandra's neck, her chin tipped up, mouth leering at him, eyes bright sick fires delighting in a grim contest. But it was difficult for a man, any man, he knew, to simultaneously consider a near fate and a far one, so he forgot Janice and Cassandra and made the usual phone calls, lined up witnesses, ordered reports, sucked information toward him from all directions. Hoskins hadn't showed up yet, and this worried him. He went out to the reception desk, where Melissa took the messages and screened the calls the homicide unit received.

"Where's the boss?" Peter asked.

"He called in and said he'd be late," she answered.

"Do you know where, exactly, he is?"

"No, Peter."

He wasn't sure he believed her. "No number where he can be reached?"

"He can't be reached," she said firmly.

With the last of his dollars, he bought a cheesesteak, which he wolfed down, then checked on his car and his gun. Not wanting to return to the office, he stood anxiously outside City Hall, numbed with exhaustion and worry, a tall man wrapped in a thick coat, thinking in the cold. Perhaps Hoskins was huddled in the Mayor's offices that very moment, figuring a way to finish off another errant Assistant District Attorney. He turned away from the building and looked west. The skeletal framing of another huge office tower had climbed

272

over the older buildings; in a generation he would be an old man remembering a city that no longer existed, a city of the previous century. It seemed clear to him that he and Janice would be together, perhaps having moved out of the city, or maybe even still living in the Delancey Street house, the mortgage paid off, kids through college, his parents near the end. It was this conventional future he craved now. *Concentrate, you motherfucker*, he swore to himself, *get it all back.*

And so he marched back into the office ready, again, and it was then that Cheryl slipped through his door and told him she had found Charlie Geller and that he wanted to come in and talk.

"What?" Peter exclaimed. It seemed impossible that Johnetta's killer would walk into his office. "You sure you got the right guy?"

"Positive, Peter."

"How in hell did you find him?"

Cheryl gave him an affectionately sarcastic look. "He was in the phone book. Most people are. I reached his wife and she gave me a number."

"Okay," Peter said, "okay, just let me have his number and I'll give him a call. Wait a minute. Better yet, you make the call, see when you can get him in here."

Then Cheryl was back.

"He says he's got an hour free. He wants to come in now. That okay?"

With Hoskins out of the office, at least for the moment, this was an opportunity. So he told Cheryl yes, still not understanding why the sad man would willingly visit the District Attorney's office. Only the innocent were usually so forthcoming. It might mean Geller was giving himself up, perhaps in return for protection from the Mayor. That seemed unlikely; a deal like that would be negotiated through intermediaries who translated across race and class. It was more probable that the Mayor knew what Peter was up to and had ordered Geller to march in and lie if accused, or otherwise provide false information. Maybe Geller had been told to find out what Peter was thinking.

He couldn't accuse Geller without a prepared warrant nor detectives ready to make an arrest. There was no official awareness of Geller as a suspect. Peter began to list some questions to ask Geller and then the phone rang. It was Mastrude.

"How are you?" Peter asked absentmindedly.

"Really want to know?" Mastrude wheezed in contentment. "My

wife says I ramble too much, she says I just buzz. Ha! She told me I'm 'blowing on the kazoo of senility.' That's a quote—very poetical, my wife. Look, Peter, I've been thinking about this—I think maybe you should try to see your wife. I rarely change my mind about these things, but I also don't usually find somebody who is so determined—"

"Right," Peter said, cutting him off. "That's nice, thank you very much."

"Actually—"

"I can't discuss this now, I need your help this very minute. You're the one who studies human behavior. I got a guy coming in very, very soon. I'm pretty sure he's killed somebody. He's got to know that we suspect him. He's probably protecting some very powerful people. Why in hell would he agree to come in, when asked, just like that?"

"Was it a professional killing?" Mastrude asked.

"No. He beat a young woman to death."

There was silence on the line. Peter looked at his hands.

"Is he a subordinate, a true subordinate?"

"Yes," Peter said, hearing Mastrude make eating sounds.

"Is there great pressure on the people he represents?"

"Yes."

"Then the group may be coming apart," Mastrude suggested.

"There's no evidence of that."

"He may want to confess."

"I doubt that, too."

"He may hate the group he's with, he may hate what they make him do. This can happen even to men who feel themselves absolutely loyal. It's surprising what we come to hate. And remember, your man may not even be aware of this."

"Okay. But what if they put him up to it?"

"Then you have to figure out how strong he is and see if he'll reveal himself anyway. You have to find your way into the man's beliefs. I have to do that when I cross-examine my clients' spouses sometimes. It can be nasty."

"Yeah," Peter said, thinking of what Mastrude could do to Janice.

"I was thinking about our conversation about the causes of tragedy," Mastrude continued. "I was thinking that the very causes that make it occur also bring judgment. People crave the release of judgment, the end of their private guilt."

"But this guy may be a totally amoral psycho," responded Peter. "I have no indication that he has any desire for this kind of judgment. I think it's something else."

"Well, I can't say, then," Mastrude concluded. "I haven't met the man and I need to do that in order to understand his motivations."

"You understand my motivations?" Peter challenged.

"I was wrong about you," Mastrude answered, "though not in the way you think. But I've got the answer, my friend. I believe very firmly that you need to see your wife again soon. I think that is the way this is going to be resolved. I think you need to see her and I think you need to see your own self—"

Peter had another call. "Wait a minute," he said, switching lines. It was from the Mayor's office.

"I've got an important call," he told Mastrude.

"Remember what I said?" Mastrude asked.

Peter wondered if Geller was in the Mayor's office that very minute.

"Remember?" Mastrude repeated.

"Go see Janice, get her back."

"No," Mastrude answered in discontent, "that wasn't exactly it. . . ."

There was no time for this chatter, and so Peter simply cut off Mastrude, switching to the Mayor.

"Yes, sir?"

The Mayor came on quickly: "Peter, I'm calling to get a new sense of how things are progressing in respect to the murder of my nephew. I've seen the papers."

This was an outright command for information, lubricated by power into the smoothest of requests, and in it Peter understood that the Mayor's early insistence that Peter only talk to the Mayor and not to other members of the deceased's family meant that Peter had received no chance to probe them for the cause of the killing and perhaps trigger an emotional outburst of information. "Don't forget Johnetta Henry," he finally answered.

"Of course not. Bill Hoskins and I were talking just yesterday, and I was remarking to him that beyond what I read in the papers I haven't much idea of what's happening in the case. We've been quite busy, as you can imagine, trying to get some of our new job programs implemented and I haven't had an opportunity to call."

"Yes—" Peter began.

"And Bill assured me you were running the investigation quite comprehensively at this point in time and that the case against this fellow, Wayman Carothers, was developing nicely," the Mayor continued, as if he were describing a tropical plant grown in unnatural conditions. "Indeed, I might say Bill added that he expected your investigation was nearly *complete*." Anger leaked into the Mayor's tone. Maybe the man was standing there in his expensive wool suit, twisting the watch about his wrist and looking at Charlie Geller. "I understood there to be no other suspects, no other scenarios, Mr. Scattergood. I thought my information was good, do you understand? So this morning, when the paper—"

"There are still a number of things I'm—"

"Excuse me, I was talking. Now then, I'm assuming that little article is just journalistic speculation. Indeed, I must say that when I expressed to my sister this morning that we might have some kind of resolution to all of this, she seemed—"

"Mr. Mayor, what exactly do you wish to know?"

The line was silent at this direct inquiry.

"I was hoping"—now the voice had returned to its measured, for-public-consumption tone—"to get your estimation of the nature of the evidence against Carothers for these two vicious murders."

"The murder of your nephew seems pretty straightforward, sir." He wouldn't mention the unusable confession in the private meeting with Carothers.

"And for Miss Henry?"

The Mayor had put the question to him, inside of two minutes, and Peter could feel the man's power reaching at him through the telephone, cornering him with his hidden conclusions and off-the-record investigations, daring him to thwart the city's highest official. How much did the Mayor know?

"Well," Peter stalled, "our evidence is very limited in that respect, sir. There's some question as to whether Carothers even killed Johnetta Henry."

"That *is* interesting," came the calm voice. "I was under the assumption from Bill that the evidence gathered thus far included both victims and excluded other participants. So you're suggesting the newspaper article might be right and that perhaps Carothers and someone else *together*—"

"I'm not suggesting that last idea, no."

With just the slightest irritation—a fist imperceptibly tighter—the voice of a man riding the edge of control: "Then what are you suggesting, Mr. Scattergood? Why are we playing guessing games? I have always disdained such psychological tactics. It appalls me to think that this is what we have come to. What is it, precisely, that you see here?"

But before Peter could say anything, a voice in the background apparently drew the Mayor away from the receiver. "Excuse me," the political voice said, perhaps with masterful timing, perhaps having knowingly *not* forced Peter to answer, perhaps creating a last opportunity for Peter to change his mind, "but I have another pressing matter. You and I will discuss this later today or early tomorrow. I have several calls that have come through. In the meantime, I trust your investigation continues satisfactorily. I am interested in this new information. Please keep me up-to-date about this second-assailant theory of yours. I will be eager to know what new information has yielded this development."

The phone clicked. Before Peter could evaluate whether he'd made a mistake—he had contradicted the Mayor and officially represented the office with Hoskins's approval—there was a tentative knock on the door.

"Yeah, what?" he called.

Cheryl came in, followed by a short, strongly built man in his thirties with pomaded hair. He wore overalls and a thick jacket and moved with the rigid pride of one who has once been very badly injured, perhaps beaten to a whisper of his life. He did not limp or show any particular weakness, Peter noticed, but as Cheryl silently directed him to the chair facing Peter, he held his body with ready stiffness; it was a body that knew punishment and had been forced to conform to its damage. He did not take off his jacket.

"Thank you, miss," Geller said in a hoarse voice. He wore no gold rings or a watch or any mark of status that would indicate one who might receive favors from the Mayor. He raised his face to look at Peter, silent and seemingly watchful from a great depth within himself. His eyes, which did not blink, lived in his face not as bright, moving windows to the soul but as an expressionless surface, like that of stone. Beneath the pressed, quiet lips arced the rough smile of a scar. This was the sad man, and Peter—despite his anxious exhaustion—sensed that the man was wholly unperturbed by Peter's presence.

"Thank you for coming in on such short notice, Mr. Geller."

"No problem." Geller shrugged in a deep whisper.

Geller didn't seem to recognize him, but of course the man would

277

not communicate this, for it implicated him in the snatching of Tyler. Peter forced himself to breathe slowly and concentrate, a trick he'd learned at the foul line when the crowd was screaming for blood.

"I guess Cheryl called you."

"She say you wanted to ask me somethin'." Geller knitted his hands together and waited.

"About Johnetta Henry and Darryl Whitlock, yes."

"Right," Geller mumbled. "She said that."

"Just a couple of routine questions. Frankly, we think we have a pretty good case against the suspect, Wayman Carothers," Peter said, leaning forward and smiling in a manner suggestive of the notion that his own lust for Carothers's conviction might be just the kind of blindness that would allow him to miss Geller's guilt. "We have a pretty good case against him and so we're just trying to ask some of the people who knew Johnetta a few questions, just more or less get the whole background picture. We have to get everything on the man, you understand?"

"Right," Geller said.

"We appreciate your cooperation."

"Right," Geller agreed in a calm voice, neither sarcastic nor aggressive.

Peter looked at Geller, expecting him now to say something about how he knew that if he hadn't come into the office, then he might be suspected for that very reason. Very often a suspect would insist with the obsessive energy of the guilty that he was coming in to get his name cleared.

"You've been associated with the Mayor a long time?"

"Almost ten years."

"Now, I also understand that you do a little work for the Mayor, during his campaign and whatnot, drive him around. And Johnetta Henry did, too, right?"

"That's right," Geller said without expression.

"Since you were in contact with her, maybe you could tell me what her duties were and so on."

Geller stared at him.

"What she did in the office, that kind of thing."

"She talked to everybody on the phone," Geller said, eyes moving little, the information coming from a mouth unlinked to the muscles of his face.

"Yes?" Peter responded after a moment, wondering if Geller had been told to stonewall all questions. "What else?"

278

"I think she did some, you know, accounting, where they took the political donations and counted them and put them in the safe."

"She was pretty, wasn't she?"

No answer.

"She popular with the men? You had a woman running around the office, a strong-minded, good-looking woman."

"I didn't care for her, if that's what you're askin'."

"Okay." He had to bring Geller to life, get him talking. "Tell me about when this was, what was happening."

"This was a couple of years ago when he was gettin' ready for the election. Gettin' everybody together, you know."

"Okay. What else? What else was going on?"

Geller stared. "Not too much, far as I remember."

The man was not hostile or even actively concealing information. Peter's questions simply hadn't activated Geller's personality. There had to be a way in, as Mastrude said, to expose the man's beliefs.

"Are you religious, Mr. Geller?"

"I been thinkin' about God a long time, Mr. Scattergood."

"You believe that there is a right and a wrong?"

"Yes, I most certainly do." Geller's voice was more animated.

"Would you say that you have moral beliefs?"

"Yes," Geller responded, his eyes now coming back to his face. A murderer, Peter reflected, might need to believe in redemption. "If I know somethin' is right, then I will do it. We are all in great trouble, you know what I'm sayin', and we must do the right thing."

"You've worked for the Mayor a long time. You must believe in him, in his methods."

"For a long time." Geller closed his hands before him. "The Mayor is a very great man. The Mayor is a man who believes. He is a man who will help the people of this city, Mr. Scattergood. He believes we can have a great city, a city where people are good."

"What have you been doing for him all this time?"

"Anything the man thinks is important, anything he asks—drivin', runnin' little jobs, anything."

"Why so loyal?"

"That man has a vision, he has an understanding, you got that? Back when he was a councilman he had it and some of us saw it and we wanted to work with the man."

"You grow up in the city?"

"Yeah, North Philly, here and there."

"Good childhood?"

Geller stared at him, and the coldness passed again into his face. "You'd rather not say?" Peter jabbed.

Geller's lower lip tightened and pulled back from his teeth. The anger, thus, was very near, always.

"Why didn't you like Johnetta Henry?" Peter said.

" 'Cause I didn't think she was good for what we was tryin' to do. She was a bad girl, just tryin' to get some attention," Geller blurted. "Here you got people who work twenty years to get where they're goin'."

"Was she still seeing Carothers when she was involved in the campaign?" Peter asked.

"Yes. And after she moved in with Darryl they was goin' around Darryl's back," Geller said in a rigid voice, his eyes watering ever so slightly in concentration. The man was serious as death. "She was that kind of woman, always behind somebody's back—she knew we knew and she didn't care. That Carothers boy used to come over there while Darryl was away."

This seemed unlikely to Peter, but he couldn't be sure. After all, Carothers had possessed the key to the apartment. "What did they do?"

"What you expect?" Geller said.

"Why didn't anybody tell Darryl she was cheating on him?"

"He wouldn't of believed it." Geller looked at Peter. "That boy trusted everybody."

"You know him well?"

"Of course I did!"

"Didn't the family care that their favorite son was in this situation? Didn't the Mayor want her to marry into the family?"

Geller seemed to have some trouble coming up with an answer. If the family didn't care for Johnetta, as Peter had been told, then that created a motive to scare or hurt her and get her out of Darryl's life.

"You just told me that nobody would tell Darryl that Johnetta was cheating on him. Why would you know it and not him?"

" 'Cause I'm tied in there, I know everybody."

"Did you care for Darryl?"

"I watched him grow, I saw what he was goin' to be." Geller's hands opened now and grasped in frustration at the air before him. "I saw the wonder of that young man, and what he meant to the Mayor and his family—"

"You're bitter?"

"Very bitter, Mr. Scattergood."

"You blame it on Johnetta?" Peter shot across his desk.

Geller glared at him and Peter peered back, seeing that of course Geller blamed Johnetta, for without her there was no Carothers, the murderer of Darryl Whitlock. Geller must have seen with those same yellowed, watering eyes that he, too, and more directly, had caused Whitlock's death.

The phone rang. Peter picked it up, expecting Berger. "Excuse me just a moment," he said.

"This is Gerald Turner," a harsh voice ran at him breathlessly. "Let me talk to Geller, now."

"Who?"

"I understand that Mr. Charles Geller, one of our staff members, is over there, Mr. Scattergood."

"I don't know who that is," Peter said, nodding at Geller that the call would be brief.

"He received a telephone call from your office not an hour ago. Don't bullshit me."

"Look," Peter responded icily, "if your information is so good, you would know that I have just come from my attorney's office, where I have been negotiating the sad end to my marriage. Get out your Yellow Pages and look under lawyers and you'll find one named Mastrude, specializing in divorces. *That* is what is on my mind, Mr.—" He almost said Turner's name, which Geller undoubtedly knew. "Completely on my mind, not your own office difficulties. This is a big staff and I don't know exactly what everybody is up to, but I'll be happy to ask around when I get the chance."

"Then tell your staff Geller is to call me as soon as he comes in," Turner demanded. "Got that?"

"Fine," Peter said.

"You and I need to understand some things," Turner said in the same panicked voice. "The Mayor has decided that he is to be apprised of all developments in this case as soon as they occur. Do you understand? You are to report to me on a daily basis."

"That is a remarkably unlikely arrangement. You have no jurisdiction in this case—"

"I do not understand your *tone*, Mr. Scattergood. We all desire the same outcome to these events, I trust."

"I trust. I remind you that you have no ability to dictate—"

"Listen to me," Turner growled. "Bill Hoskins will get it straight through your head if I can't. Every witness, every lead, every bit of evidence. I want the whole file on my desk tomorrow morning."

Turner hung up. Now Peter knew Turner had lost track of his unpredictable, true-believing executioner; Geller was operating on his own.

"You tell the Mayor you were here?" Peter asked.

"He trusts me," Geller stated solemnly, raising his eyebrows.

"Okay," Peter responded casually, "you were telling me about Johnetta Henry. Was she dating Carothers or Whitlock back before her son was born?"

"Well," Geller said, "not Darryl yet, but she was spendin' time with a few different men back then."

"She got pregnant sometime back then, right?"

"Yes, she did," Geller stated.

"What was it about her?"

The sad man nodded knowingly. "She had this way of playin' with you, tryin' to make you pay attention. But to my mind it just wasn't right, it wasn't right that she was messin' up what so many people had tried to do."

"Who was she seeing?"

"Oh, well, it was a busy office, phone callin' and so on, and she was messin' around with Carothers and maybe some other people, you know. Far as I can actually remember, Darryl didn't come into the picture until later. She got pregnant from Wayman Carothers and it was later she moved in with Darryl."

But Carothers, Peter knew, was not the father of Tyler. He didn't know how to respond; he'd use one of Janice's counseling tricks, the nondirective response that repeated information.

"Other men?"

"Sure, you know."

"Men in the Mayor's group, the campaign people?"

"That girl, well, lotta them wanted her—"

"But who got her? The Mayor?"

Geller stared at Peter, then looked away, caught. "Everybody knew she started seein' Darryl after she had that baby. It used to make me mad, you know? How everybody had worked so hard. You're askin' me, mister, if she fucked the Mayor. Now, I find that to be an insult. That's an insult to a man I care about and know deeply. The Mayor and I go back a long way, so I'm not sayin' what you want me to say, you understand? All I'm sayin' is she and the Mayor, they was friendly

282

and that she liked to laugh. Far as I'm concerned, she was just a distraction to the man. She might have wanted the man's attention. I'm willin' to say that. But after a couple of months it was pretty clear that gal was goin' to have a baby, you know, and everybody heard how Carothers was the father but she didn't want to see him no more maybe, and then there was no more jokin' and huggin' with nobody once she was pregnant—you see, Mr. Scattergood, what you don't understand is that the Mayor is a man who *respects* the sanctity of life—and then one day after the baby come she walk into the office with Darryl and tell everybody she and Darryl were thinkin' about gettin' married, and then she got another job and never come into the office no more. After that nobody talk about Johnetta, and then after about a year everybody forgot about what she was doin' and nobody knew where she went. And then she was livin' with Darryl and nobody see her with her baby. Everybody be askin' about where she put her baby, and of course her grandma had kept it the whole time. So that's all I can say, you know what I'm sayin'?"

It sounded like Johnetta had gotten pregnant by the Mayor and then sought the relationship with Darryl for protection from the Mayor's disapproval. By fooling Carothers into presenting himself as the father of Tyler, she let the Mayor off the hook. Geller didn't seem to know that the Mayor might be the father of Tyler. His devotion to the Mayor seemed to depend on such a blindness. Who knew what twisted rationale Geller had contrived for himself? The question was whether or not Geller had been working independently the night of the murder or whether he had been ordered by the Mayor to do something— maybe only to scare Johnetta Henry or maybe even to kill her. Upon reflection, Peter decided it was unlikely that the Mayor had asked Geller to kill Johnetta. By all accounts the Mayor was a decent man— though devious and power-hungry like any politician—and his message of compassion and city unity seemed too genuine to come from a man who could order a murder. What was certain was the fact that while alive, Johnetta Henry could destroy the Mayor in several ways, claiming perhaps truthfully that he was the father of her baby, or that his election was funded illegally. Perhaps he only expressed frustration with her and Geller had heard. What was even more certain was that, even if he hadn't ordered the murder, the Mayor had panicked and tried to cover it up.

"How come you've told me all this?" Peter asked.

Geller stared back at him and in this moment Peter saw that the man who had suffered innumerable beatings had no fear of arrest.

"Because I feel this great righteousness of what we are tryin' to do. The Mayor is a very, very great man. He would not mind me tellin' you these things, Mr. Scattergood. His mind is above these little questions that you and I are talkin' about. He has a terrible sadness about losin' Darryl. And anything I can do to help the man get past that is somethin' I'm goin' to do. I don't need to be asked to help the man. I don't need people pointin' out to me, 'Oh, this would be a nice thing to do for the Mayor.' He knows that his way is right and that I am only followin' him. We have our way. This is our way. We are goin' to overcome."

"I see," Peter responded in a respectful, considering voice—the same anesthetizing tone he used when listening patiently to the Jehovah's Witnesses and Mormons who came to the door in conservative coat and tie and politely tried to engage him in discussions of doctrine. He knew that he was nearly out of time, that he had to get Geller out of the building.

"Who killed Johnetta Henry?" Peter asked.

Geller's hands closed.

"Somebody who decided that it was the right thing to do."

Neither man spoke. Perhaps, Peter wondered, Geller had mumbled his pathological dogma even as he threatened Johnetta Henry, hurling his judgment of her danger to the Mayor at her, backing her into the bathroom, and, with the means of his thick, well-preserved body, bludgeoning and choking her until she conformed to his truth. Geller, Peter concluded, was deeply sick, the kind of man who found a way to express his rage within a morality scheme, a man who justified murder with the highest of ideals. Most men who killed did so out of bravado, anger, jealousy, greed, and panic—the most petty, human motivations. There were the few men who planned murders with the exactitude of a gem cutter and the few whose understanding of reality had been destroyed—Robinson fit into that last description. And then—moving toward the most ominous and cruel—there were the men whose sexual happiness demanded a corpse. And last, perhaps, there were the men who, save for a fractured moral cosmology, seemed to have no reason to kill, whose interior lives had compressed the memory of ancient abuses into a dense stone of hatred. It was in this small unknowable space that these men existed much of the time, even while performing their day-to-day functions with plodding ability; these were the unredeemable wretches who decorated their prison cells with bizarre slogans and practiced private and unknowable rituals. In order to survive, they followed those who provided acceptance and interpreted society for them. They knew themselves to be not quite of this world, their rage to be a quiet, flat thing that only found its penultimate expression rarely, and that normal people did not have much use for such men as them, that the world condemned their behavior and had only suspicious compassion for them. These were the men who leave a cold hand over the heart and these were the men who see death—someone's, maybe their own—as a possibility of each moment.

"My wife expectin' me," Geller uttered, breaking the silence. "So I had better—"

"I've got one more question," Peter interrupted.

Geller stood up, zipped his coat, and waited.

"If you don't mind, how'd you get that scar on your chin?"

Geller's face hinted at a smile for the first time. "My wife and I had a little misunderstanding about ten years ago. She handy with the razor. This was back before I was doin' much."

"Same wife?" Peter asked with true curiosity.

"Same wife." Geller nodded. "We all right now."

An hour later, with Hoskins still not around, an elderly couple walked in.

"Hey, hello, Mr. and Mrs. Warren."

"We come to pay our respects, Mr. Scattergood," said Mrs. Warren, the mother of the girl Billy Robinson had murdered. They were a couple in their fifties who appeared older. "We know you're a busy man, so we won't stay more than just a minute." Mr. Warren, who looked like a coat hung on a stick, quietly squeezed his gloves, unable to make eye contact.

"After the trial we was just so relieved that I didn't get a proper chance to say to you . . . See, it's *unnatural* to lose your child, Mr. Scattergood. It's unnatural and it makes you sick. You wish you died. Because your time is closer, see? My husband, he ain't the same, Mr. Scattergood. I don't know if he'll ever get over it. We felt you found something for us, Mr. Scattergood," the wife said, seeing her husband's discomfort. His eyes burned brightly but uselessly. "I can't exactly tell you . . . what I mean. You found it and now we—" She stammered, blinked, then caught herself. "You never think something like this is going to happen—"

The door opened, and in stepped Hoskins. For a short man, he looked huge, his yellow suspenders tight against the pressed cotton wall of his chest, his neck pinching out from his collar.

"I'm going to have to interrupt this meeting," he announced.

"Oh, I'm terribly sorry." Mrs. Warren blinked. "We'll go, I'm sorry."

"Wait," Peter commanded. "Wait right where you are." He turned to Hoskins.

"These people, Bill, are Mr. and Mrs. Warren, whose daughter Judy was murdered last August. You remember we convicted her murderer last week, and the Warrens are here to pay their respects to the office."

Hoskins looked quickly at the couple, turned back.

"We need to talk," he said to Peter. "Very soon. About where you were last night and what the hell you've been saying to the Mayor."

"Why don't we set a time?"

Hoskins stared at him, evaluating his face, he knew.

"Ten minutes."

"That's fine."

"I'll meet you here. Ten minutes."

Hoskins left the door open.

"Sorry for the interruption," Peter said. "Can you hold on just a minute? I do want to talk to you. Just sit tight."

Peter called Westerbeck, the young detective out in West Philadelphia who had been at the murder scene.

"Was it you or Jonesy who interviewed the bread truck delivery man?" Peter asked.

"Who wants to know?"

"I do."

"Jonesy talked with the guy."

"Why didn't I get the report?"

"He said the guy didn't know anything, that it wasn't worth typing up."

Westerbeck, Peter hoped, only wanted one thing: to solve the murders and win the respect of his peers.

"Remember that you got a couple of prints off of the bathroom mirror that you couldn't identify?" Peter asked the detective.

"Yeah, but we got Carothers."

"Only for one body, Mr. Westerbeck."

"Maybe," the detective said irritably. "So?"

"I know what you think of me, but I'm going to do you a favor."

"I don't usually let assholes do me favors, Counselor."

"What's the problem, Westerbeck? You seem like the kind of guy who—"

"The word on you is that you brought Carothers in and nobody else got to talk to him. Is that how you expect people to help you out?"

Peter ignored this. "There's a guy named Geller." He gave the address. "Why not pick him up and get a print? No big deal. If the print matches—"

"C'mon."

"If you need a reason and if you're not afraid Geller will disappear, then run down the driver of the delivery truck that's on that route and ask this guy what he saw on the night of the murder and put Geller in a lineup and see if the driver can identify him. See for yourself."

There followed a silence during which Westerbeck realized he'd been handed an immense gift.

"You mentioned this to anybody else?"

"No. It's yours."

"Right."

The detective hung up.

"We'll just say good-bye, Mr. Scattergood," Mrs. Warren said. She looked toward her husband, who sat twisting his gloves. The man remained speechless, and though he did not cry, his eyes watered like the lip of a dam, as if he suffered a constant grief that overflowed from time to time.

"It was a terrible shock to him, he's not the same after it happened," Mrs. Warren told Peter again. She leaned forward. "He blames himself. He thinks that if we raised her differently she wouldn't have fallen in with this boy. . . ."

Mr. Warren moaned and shook his head.

"You got flowers, Peter." Melissa stepped in with a big package. "They just come?"

"Just now." She looked in the wrapping. "They're sort of ugly, actually."

He opened the card. *Get Well Soon!* exclaimed the printed lettering. Inside was a many-folded note in Berger's handwriting, which he read as Mrs. Warren began talking again.

Peter—

By now you know Hoskins dumped me last night. I had no

chance, I was working late and there was a knock on the door and Hoskins was there with a cop and a German Shepherd. I had a small stash in my pocket and the dog found it in about five seconds, practically pawed my leg off. I don't expect you to be sympathetic and if you were, I'd be pissed off, because it meant you were going fucking soft. By the time you read this I'll be at Philly International booked to Bermuda. My wife and I are going to be there for a week and see where we stand.

But this is the other thing—Hoskins sent the dog and cop away (at least he didn't fucking arrest me) and told me I was finished and that I had an hour to clean out. He left and said he'd be back in one hour. So I wondered how I could use the hour best—nothing more could happen to me. I tried Hoskins's office; it was locked. I know you're in a jam, buddy, and I was trying to think of some way to help. I know you've dealt me out of the information and that's okay. You sensed I was due for a fall and you were right. So now Hoskins can't bully much out of me. You're getting smarter. So I was thinking about this and just poking around, and then I saw Melissa's message book. You know, she tears off the white slip, but keeps the yellow carbon, and she usually has about three days' worth of carbons so she knows who's called, and I went through her book and counted four calls from the Mayor's office to Hoskins, and the last message said, "Car will pick you up at 4 P.M. That was yesterday. There's too much contact going on there, Peter—they're working something out, and getting rid of me was the first step. They're scared, I think, starting to shake the tree.

My advice to you—this is the best goddamn advice I got, Peter—is stop fucking overanalyzing the situation and make your move *now*.

Bergs

P.S. I put the spare can of racquetballs back in your office.

". . . and so anyway, we been over it and over it, Mr. Scattergood. We thought we raised that girl right. We thought we knew her. But we didn't. She ran off with this boy because she didn't have the values we thought we had gave her. She wanted the money and the thrills and this is what she got. I hate to say it, but that's what happened."

The couple stood to leave.

"You're busy, Mr. Scattergood," Mrs. Warren finished. "We just came in to let you know we appreciate—It's not easy, we could all see that. We all feel you're a good man helping people, all of us."

He murmured a vague thanks, and before they were out the door picked up the phone and dialed the *Inquirer* city desk and asked for Miss Karen Donnell. This would be the enormous breach that put him in direct conflict with Hoskins. But perhaps the editors there could save him and Carothers, and not let the Mayor protect Johnetta Henry's murderer.

Of course they put him on hold, the earpiece clicking every few seconds. Hoskins, in the hallway and talking to one of the new young A.D.A.s, saw he was on the phone. What momentary consideration stopped the man from entering Peter's office? He'd have to say each sentence with absolute precision, since Donnell would transcribe his words onto her screen as quickly as he said them.

But this was not the place to make the call, not with Hoskins in earshot. He would have to get out of the office. Perhaps a minute remained of his ten—not enough time to take his coat, schmooze casually with the secretaries, and wait for the elevator. Hoskins would call downstairs before he reached the first floor.

"Yes?" someone answered. "This is Karen Donnell."

"One moment please," Peter said. Hoskins was still hovering outside his door with bulky impatience.

"Yes," Peter continued in a quiet voice. "This is the D.A.'s office."

"Is that Mr. Scattergood?"

He ignored the question. "I have Bill Hoskins, Chief of Homicide, on the line for you, Ms. Donnell. He is prepared to make available to you important new information on the Whitlock and Henry murders. Please hold."

Peter rang Hoskins's number and Melissa answered.

"Important call for Bill."

The secretary rang Hoskins's phone and he reflexively lumbered the fifteen feet back to his office and picked it up. Ms. Donnell, Peter knew would quickly ask many questions and keep Hoskins tied up for a few minutes while he was caught on the defensive. And that was all Peter needed. He took the entire Carothers file and left.

In his haste he'd forgotten his hat, and it was another killer winter night in the making, the sun starting to die, air freezing. Where would he go tonight? His house was the most obvious place anyone would look for him, including Vinnie. He retrieved the gun from the car and slipped it quickly into his coat pocket. He jammed the thick file into the wheel well of the spare tire. Back on the street, he dialed the *Inquirer* from an open phone booth. He got the metro desk.

"Karen Donnell, please."

"She just left," a voice responded. "She'll be back later."

"Okay. I need to talk to somebody . . ."

"Who? We're all on deadline here."

"This is an anonymous source," he muttered in a low voice, feeling stupid and stagy about his words. He looked down the street. The Mayor could have somebody following him *now*. All he had to say, he knew, was his name and title, just whisper it, and the half-attention of the editor on the other end would change. And things would never be the same.

"Yes? We have anonymous sources with all kinds of stories all over the place, pal."

"I've got, uh, a big story. It concerns the murder—"

"What? Who is this? Look, I'm on *deadline*."

"This is for real. About the two murders. The girl was killed by someone else. Somebody—" How unclearly he was thinking! His mind grinding words out in broken sentences. "—and they know about this and maybe have somebody in the police running the investigation there. It's all inside, see. There's enough proof—"

"Okay, okay," came the voice, "slow down here. Before this goes any further, I gotta have some kind of identification, some kind of verification. Who is this? Wait a minute." The phone was put down. Peter heard the clacking of computer keys, phones trilling in the background. "What case are we talking about, who got murdered? We're going to have to verify these charges." More clacking. "Shit, I'm on a *terrible* deadline here, maybe if you could give me more to go on."

He took a breath, deep enough to expel several sentences.

"See, the Mayor is—"

He couldn't say it. Not yet, not before he told Janice and explained it all to her, laid it out at her feet and showed her the pressure he had been under. Made her understand! Once he went to the press, he'd be caught in a wave of controversy without a chance to talk to her. If they spoke first, she would be able to see the whole catastrophe unfold from the inside, feel for him. He could wait a few hours to tell the press. What could happen in a few hours?

"Yeah, bud, still got that story for me?" came the editor's impatient voice.

"Oh, *yes*," Peter crooned, finding the voice of a lunatic. "The Mayor and I own the same bird, called Smiley the Bird, and Smiley can talk to anybody, and I asked Smiley to ask—"

The editor groaned and hung up. Peter left the booth. He walked five steps, spun on his heel, and looked behind him. Two men walked in the same direction. Had he imagined a problem? He would stay on foot. It was an odd feeling to have the solemn weight of the gun in his pocket. He'd get rid of it, but where? He couldn't just throw it in a trash can. He crossed Chestnut Street and reversed direction, slipping through the revolving doors of John Wanamaker's, past mannequins and women with impossibly bright faces—faces the color of hard candies—past thin, faggy men trying to entice passersby with skin bronzers and facial scrubs and colognes and all other manner of junk, watches, shirts, shoes, past the perfume counter where he had once bought a Christmas gift for Janice, and then outside to Market Street, where the XXX-rated peep shows had been pushed back a block or two by the urban renewal sweeping toward the river. The old buildings were being rehabbed, the great Reading Railroad Terminal, the huge columned facade of the Lit Brothers store. Big dollars, big deals, young guys making serious money. This time of day, Billy Penn was just a dark silhouette in a knee-length coat and flat-brim hat, the eyes hidden and the grave cold lips shadowed in judgment. And somewhere directly beneath Penn's immense cold feet, where the window lights shone in the darkness, the Mayor sat now in his plush suite of offices, pondering his own fate.

Peter wondered where the Mayor and Johnetta had gone for their rendezvous. Certain accommodations can always be made; it was really only a matter of checking into a room in a motel—near the airport would be easy, at night. Perhaps a few bills changed hands, perhaps Geller himself had driven the couple and even gone in and rented the room, then sat outside in the car listening to the radio. Peter could certainly understand the Mayor's appetite—if, to Peter, Johnetta Henry had been sexy *dead*, then it must have been quite another thing when she was alive. Women like that had a way of gravitating toward light and power. And the Mayor, yet to be elected, was in the flush of ascendancy from City Council member to mayoral candidate. The attentions of an attractive woman might only be expected. And so it happened between them, maybe only once, maybe dozens of times. What was certain was that for a brief moment the Mayor had gazed into Johnetta Henry's lovely black face in passion, certainly—like all men—knowing in his heart the precise degree of his affection for her. But for all of his wisdom—and there should by now be plenty of it, for the Mayor was well into his fifties—the man could not have known that in this moment—a brief cry, a grimace of pleasure—a son would be brought to life, nor that this woman whom he held close, if not quite dear, would pursue him beyond the grave.

Looking down, Peter noticed a man standing huddled against the wind in a doorway. The cold did not cut the man's stench.

"Hey—what's it going to be?"

"You again?" Peter smiled.

The man thumbed a nickel high into the air. It caught the last of the sun. Spinning, a piece of light.

"Heads," Peter said. "Heads will definitely be up."

The man snatched the nickel, slapped it on the arm of his coat, and glanced at it.

"Well, what the hell is it?" Peter barked.

The man burst out laughing. His teeth were rotten, every one. Loose-limbed, he shuffled away, flipping the coin.

Running a sweat, walking the blocks toward her house, the sky winter-dark already. He would not push at Janice, just sit down like a reasonable man at the kitchen table and talk. The women's safe house would be finished soon—he remembered a March date in Janice's papers—and she'd be moving again. He needed to talk to her. Berger was gone and she was the only one he trusted now.

It took a while, but finally he turned the corner of Sixth and Christian. The house looked appreciably better, with fresh paint and a new door. The door harmonized with the rest of the exterior, but had no windows, appeared to be heavy oak, and was studded with several new brass locks—a door meant to keep out angry husbands and boyfriends. Janice and the others had been careful not to make the house more noticeable than those around it. He knocked on the front door. No answer.

Just as he stepped back to the sidewalk, a man turned the corner and saw Peter standing in front of the house under a streetlamp. The man was four or five years younger, an inch shorter, and was in a vague way similar in appearance to Peter—yet working class, no doubt, as was apparent from his clothes and boots and curly, unbarbered hair. His face was large and readable, and he examined Peter's suit and long wool coat.

"Help you?"

"Ah, no," Peter replied. "Don't think so. Thanks."

Peter saw keys in the man's hands, which were thick with callus. He knew, then, who this was.

"Live around here?" The man squinted, thinking.

"Not far."

Had John Apple seen pictures of him? Maybe on television. Apple unlocked the three new locks and looked back at Peter.

"Sure you don't need something, bud?" Meaning, *Move along if you don't have any business here.*

"Positive," Peter replied.

"You *look* like you're looking for something," Apple argued. "Or somebody."

Apple must know; how could he not? Peter didn't say anything, only glared, thoughts and violent possibilities arising in his mind. Apple shrugged and disappeared behind the door, although not without giving Peter one last, obviously scrutinizing look. He didn't care if Apple was there or not, he had to see Janice. Apple could simply leave while they talked. He wanted to talk. Just that.

And, a few minutes later, right on schedule, came Janice in the Subaru, expertly backing it into an open spot. He heard her yank the hand brake back, he heard the buzz of the door as it opened, and as soon as he saw her heel appear on the sidewalk, he knew he had done the right thing in coming here this evening. She wore the Icelandic wool sweater he'd given her. She was a very pretty woman, his wife— this woman whom he had set his course by, who with a momentary smile could drain him of all malice, hatred, and small-mindedness.

He crouched behind a car, peering intently at Janice, thinking forward and backward, his mood shot through with anger and yet a nervousness as well, almost giddiness. He could not resist the idea that all this despair and difficulty was the very dear price that he had finally paid in order to get Janice back. They would start again. He'd cut back on his hours and they would spend more time together. Just find a job in some cushy law firm a couple of blocks from City Hall, maybe work with Berger, the future ex-addict; the hours would be better and he'd start out at about one hundred grand a year and the work would be cleaner, not so much blood on his hands. Finish the Carothers case, end with a bang, and get out and have a houseful of kids. He honestly believed that he had paid the price of understanding and that now he could rededicate himself to her and to all they had. After all these years, still he was obsessed with her; he knew this and knowing it intensified the obsession. That he didn't have her made him want her all the more. He loved her and would do anything for her—she looked ever so beautiful *now! this moment!* in her blue skirt with its crisp pleats and the pearls around her neck. Her hair, the beautiful dark hair he used to run his hands through, was piled up above her neck, and this was the way he had always liked it best. She stood before him finding her house keys, unconscious of him. She didn't know about Vinnie and the Mayor's threats and what the bread man had told him. He would tell her and then call the newspaper reporter tonight. He knew that everything in his life would fall into place if he just stepped close to her and their eyes met. He would be set free.

Janice stopped at the house, dipped her head as she unlocked the door, then disappeared inside.

Peter Scattergood, estranged husband, mutinous Assistant District Attorney, former mediocre high-school basketball player, lousy son to a mother recuperating from surgery, turned the corner and walked up the alley behind the house. The kitchen window was lit, and he remembered standing in his own small backyard back when he and Janice were happy, staring contentedly at the golden-lighted windows of his own house. He slipped inside the gate at the back of the plot and through the tangled brush by the rotting picnic table where the painters had eaten lunch last week. Janice was probably waiting until the weather became warmer before tackling the backyard. Maybe he could help her—yes, he would like that. He chrunched his way through the icy snow, keeping an eye on the windows. If anyone from the house on the other side of the alley were to look out their second- or third-floor windows, he might be seen. But it was still winter, after all, and in a few minutes he would be invisible in the dark.

Wrapped in the thick folds of his coat, he cut along the back of the house like a thief looking for a way to break in. The double-paned kitchen window opened outward and was set over the sink. One of the crank windows was open an inch and he eased himself next to it, close enough to spy a strip of gauzy curtain and a bit of kitchen wall. He heard water splashing in the sink.

". . . these in the market," his wife was saying. The water was turned off and the pipes creaked inside the wall next to him. "But I assume they're covered with insecticide," she continued.

Is this what new lovers talked about, chatted over happily, the small, easy things? He rubbed his ears with his gloved hands.

"Where *do* tomatoes grow in February, do you think?"

"California?" came Apple's voice—more throaty than when Peter had heard him speak before.

"You know, the ones you get in the supermarket are barely tomatoes anymore. They're bred for their shelf life and lack of bruisability, if that's a word."

"Doesn't surprise me, Janie," Apple answered her.

Janie?

"Sure," Janice went on, "they're picked green and exposed to some gas to make them ripe."

A knife hit a cutting board.

"Will you get the wine?" his wife asked.

Peter heard a refrigerator open and shut, the squeak of a cork being pulled. Then something garbled from Apple, then nothing. Thirty seconds passed.

"All right," his wife said happily, "enough of that for now, Mr. Apple."

"Enough of what?" Peter heard Apple say.

Janice used to stand at the sink, bent over a bit, which made her thrust her rump at him in an unconsciously saucy way, and he'd come up and put his arms around her, weighing a breast in each hand, giving her a lewd thrust from behind, maybe then drop a hand and get a handful of her crotch. She'd loved it, once. But the thought of that, or perhaps having stood for so long, tired him. He squatted beneath the window with a chill in his feet that reached his knees. His nuts were cold, too. The dark had come fully now; no one would see him. The water pipes rattled again as Janice rinsed her hands.

"Ready," she called.

Apparently John Apple had prepared the meal, for they moved into another room to eat dinner. He pressed his ear against the edge of the window but could hear only the indistinct sound of conversation. Janice's voice lifted from time to time in relaxed delight. Time passed, his feet getting colder in the snow. He studied the window hinge and concluded that he might be able to force the window further open. He grasped it and pulled. It moved half an inch—the amount of play in the crank mechanism. But half an inch made a huge difference, afforded him a wide angle of view. Now he could see the kitchen counter, on which stood an open bottle of wine and half a head of lettuce. The kitchen, recently painted, was full of new appliances, bought with funds from grants Janice had obtained.

He squatted down again, legs and ears aching from the cold. The gun bumped against his thigh; did the cold affect the firing mechanism? He waited.

Finally, Janice set the dinner dishes in the sink. He stood up soundlessly.

". . . he's a good man, John. I wish you hadn't said that."

His wife stood at the sink, gazing over the backyard. He could see her profile, the length of her eyelashes. She lowered her head, the pipes sounded a trickling hiss. "This warm water feels good." She shook her head aimlessly. Two arms appeared around her and she shut her eyes and let her cheek fall against one of the big hands.

"I'm sorry," she murmured, grasping one of the hands and giving the thick hairy wrist a slow kiss. "You've been very patient with me. This whole thing will take time."

They stood there rocking. Peter repeated Janice's words. She was talking about him. Didn't this mean that she remained ambivalent? Now, then, was the time to talk to her. Yes! He darted quickly out of the yard up the alley, around the corner to Christian Street, and as he set his bare knuckles hard against the door, his heart hurt, as if his blood had reversed direction, the ventricles in there confused, flapping open and shut excitedly. He gave it a good rap. This was the confrontation he craved, wasn't it? Hadn't he known all along that he must do this?

He knocked again, this time harder, with unmistakable urgency. But there was no answer. He looked down the block, where under the cone of streetlights boys tossed snowballs at each other. *Hey, yuh motherfuckuh! Can't hit shit!* He and Bobby had always wound up like big-leaguers—this was back when Steve Carlton had just won twenty-seven games in one season—and shelled the side of their house until it was pock-marked with powdery white explosions; once his father had lifted a window to tell them to stop and an ice ball flung by Peter had passed through the open space and across the room, knocking a hairbrush from his mother's hand.

He rapped one last time. No answer.

Back around the side of the house again, he peered in and saw nothing. And no sounds. Were they upstairs? He clawed at the cold, dead grass in the backyard, remembering the trash he'd seen before. His hands passed over nails, screws, cans, and other unidentifiable junk until finally he found some sort of old file. The idea was to not make any noise. He *knew* they were upstairs. He took the steel shank and ran it along one of the four windowpanes in the back door, cracking the dried putty from the pane that kept the glass in. He meant to get the metal under the edge of the glass and quietly wedge the pane out of the frame. It wouldn't go—too much old hard putty remained and he couldn't see well enough. Fuck it. He tossed the metal aside and, positioning himself with his back toward the door, gave a quick, sharp elbow to the glass, the kind of sudden jab he once learned as a basketball player to discourage a defender—a secret foul. The glass popped into several pieces and fell inside the door.

He froze, waiting for alarms and discovery, his limbs stiff, ears alert, breath muted. Should he run? But nothing happened to dissuade him from the next step, which was to reach carefully through the broken pane and unlock the door.

He slipped in the door, knowing as he passed over the threshold that this was as wrong a thing as he had ever done, but that he must do it and that nothing in his nature could stop him. He was exquisitely alive in his torment, and after the weeks of inactivity and confusion he felt clear-headed and aware of every sound and of every muscle and bone and vein inside his body. He was inside the house where upstairs his wife lay with another man. This was movement, a vector, this was an intersection of desire, the moment when a man executed a vengeful will upon the world.

Now the kitchen. It looked different, painted, lived in, full of cooking utensils. The house would be a wonderful place to live, a haven, thanks to Janice. He surveyed the remains of what looked like an excellent meal. And stopped: On the counter was Janice's German chocolate cake. Her specialty, *his* favorite! He found a heavy butcher knife on the counter and messily cut a piece of cake and wolfed at it from his hand. How hungry he was! The icing, the chocolate. He stuffed another piece in his mouth. The taste was entirely familiar: exquisite. So perfect was Janice's German chocolate cake, and she knew it. They had eaten it at dinner parties they'd given, she had made it for his parents, she had given it to their friends, she had made it each year for him on his birthday. He had made love to her with the taste of that cake still in his mouth, the chocolate mixing with the taste of her. He slipped the big knife into his other pocket.

Now, onward to the stairs, where he heard music, jazz perhaps, floating down from the second floor. The stairs were constructed from wide oak boards, pegged into place, smooth and bowed irregularly with age. The wood creaked, and in that sound, repeated once again, he froze, knowing beyond himself and with ancestral sense that ghosts of Quaker ladies trundled up and down the stairs, a candle and brass candleholder in one hand, their long, gray wool dresses brushing the wood, while below, slaves ate soup and waited, talking about Canada, glancing up from their bowls at the slightest sound. Then, ninety years later, Italian immigrants slept here three to a room, happy that war had broken out in Europe and that the shipyards and locomotive works needed labor. He tried another step, staying on his toes.

Top of the stairs. Louis Armstrong, razz-voiced, romantic, a trumpet, a smile. Through the music, he heard them talking. The door to Janice's room was open. It was dark.

"What are we going to do when the house is done?" asked John Apple.

"I'll get a place not too far, someplace nearby."

A moment of silence, filled with the last strains of Louis Armstrong. Peter sank to the top stair with infinite quietude, holding his breath, still tasting chocolate. The sweat was soaking his clothes through, and he breathed rapidly, yet he was a genius of quietude, slowing each inhalation. Every nerve wired in to silence. He crawled along the floor until he was squatting only five feet away from them. As he lifted his coat so the gun would not knock against the floor, the cassette deck clicked to a stop in the bedroom.

"I see my lawyer tomorrow," Janice said.

"Mmm?"

"He says Mastrude is taking too long on everything."

"He's a bad lawyer?"

"No, it's probably Peter," Janice answered. "He's got a lot of stuff going on, what with this case. I saw him on television the other day, on the news."

"Yeah," came Apple's unenthusiastic reply, unwilling to grant Peter's importance.

"I saw that boy they've charged with the murders." Janice's tone was one of sympathy for Carothers. "He looked so *scared*. I'd be terrified, too. I *know* what Peter's going to do to him, I've seen it. He can be absolutely vicious. He's going to turn him inside out and go for the death sentence."

"I don't believe in it."

"Neither do I. Maybe that was a basic problem, John." Her voice sounded sad, reflective of her own shortcomings, too. "Peter's probably at home right now, trying to think up ways to get that poor man executed."

Peter laughed wickedly to himself.

"Hey," Apple soothed. "Someday you'll look back on this—"

"You're right, John. I just wish . . ."

There was the sound of bedclothes rustling.

"Hmmm?" Apple asked.

"Feels nice."

More loud silence.

"Again?" Janice asked in mock surprise. "You're Mr. Energetic."

Fucking a second time—they'd done it once to the music while he was running around outside, knocking on the door, and breaking glass. No wonder they hadn't heard him. The man would screw Janice twice in Peter's presence?

Yes—the sound was unmistakable. Fragments of words, pieces of breath. He shut his eyes. The bed creaked.

"Here, just move down a little," Apple told her. "Okay."

A rhythm began. Peter stared at the wall before him. Did he dare to stand up and enter the doorway, to *see*? Could he do that? To them or himself? He did want to see, didn't he? Oh, God, yes. To see—to find out if he could take it, or if he couldn't. To feel the full power of his anger. Wasn't that it? Janice was having a good time, the bed creaking faster. Her breath was shortening, her voice uttering broken cries, rungs on a ladder. Peter had taught her to make those sounds. Didn't they *belong* to him? And Apple was making some sort of ungodly swinelike groaning and snorting and growling, the bed about to fly apart, *Oh God, I love to fuck you, Janie*, he was slobbering, and then, right there, a happy determined madman, Peter yanked the gun from his pocket and held it out from him, aiming toward the bedroom, nodding his head forward with the rhythm of the fucking on the other side of the wall, faster and faster, and then he aimed the barrel at himself, actually putting his finger on the trigger and staring his right eye into the barrel, looking into the tiny black hole an inch before him, wondering if the gun might go off accidentally—it was a cheap gun, maybe even faulty—listening so well, wondering if he could hear the shot or feel the impact of the bullet as it splintered through his skull, hearing so clearly as Janice began to contract in pleasure, every rasping breath singing a shut-eyed lush world of pleasure—he could see and feel and taste her and he could not stand to hear another man make her make these sounds.

He slipped the gun back into his pocket, stood up, and stepped into the doorway. The sheets were gone and John Apple's hairy, muscular ass pumped high, then deep—quickly—and Janice's legs were lifted and bent. Apple's moaning heightened suddenly and Peter recognized this sound.

"Stop!" Peter roared, filling the room with a huge, violent sound.

Janice screamed. The couple tore apart awkwardly, grabbing sheets for cover. Peter flicked on the wall switch.

"Peter!" Janice screamed.

He towered over them in his dark coat. They were absolutely terrified, gulping breath.

"Janice," he breathed slowly, letting each word slip from his lips, "I need to talk with you. Now."

"Hey!" Apple exclaimed hoarsely. "You're the guy outside the house. Before dinner."

Janice looked to Peter.

"You've been here?"

He nodded.

"You've been here *all along*? Why, Peter?"

"Janice," he said, "I'm in a lot of trouble. I need to talk. Now, to you."

"Oh, Peter." She pulled on her nightgown, which had been crumpled on the floor by the bed, dressing quickly and modestly under the sheet, as did Apple, who struggled into a shirt and shorts. Janice's face did not hide her concern for him. He was desperate, and there was something touching in that—sad, dangerous, but touching, her eyes seemed to say. "You *know* this is impossible."

"Just send this guy home for a while so we—"

"I can't do that." She shook her head.

John Apple stood up, ready to change events. Peter immediately shoved his hands in his pockets.

"Listen, if she doesn't want you here, you've got to leave."

"Shut up," he snapped, anger starting to leak into his words, "this is between the two of us. Don't think you're a part of this. This is about things you don't know about and never will."

"Wait." Janice held her arms out. "Why couldn't you have called

300

me at work, Peter? This isn't fair. You know that." Her eyes were wet.

"Just tell your pal to hit the road for the night." Breathing hard, still shivering, he looked at Apple. "You can tear yourself away from my wife for just one evening, can't you, big guy? It's pretty good, though, isn't it? Hard to leave stuff that good, right?"

"You don't have to deal with this crap, Janice," Apple responded, helping her stand. "This guy's fucked in the head."

"You're wrong," Peter interrupted. "It's me who doesn't have to deal with you. Why don't you just get the hell out of here and let us talk?"

Janice's eyes darted from one man to the other, her mouth twisting in dismay.

"I'm not leaving unless Janice feels comfor—"

"I'm not asking, you, I'm *telling* you to leave," Peter stated. "Janice, tell this guy he has to leave. I don't want any trouble, but he's got to drag his ass out of here, now."

He had to get rid of Apple. She'd understand everything he'd done as soon as he could explain.

Janice unconsciously hitched her hand against her nightgown, shifting in unease. She had just gotten out of bed, he realized, and she usually washed herself afterward—now Apple's semen was leaving her, crawling down her thighs, making her uncomfortable. But this sensation seemed to help her find a measure of control. She shook her head. "I can't talk with you tonight. We can talk about everything, but not tonight. Okay?"

The room felt smaller. "No. I've come here."

"Hey, Peter," Apple said, holding his open hands out, attempting a mediation. "I appreciate that this is a tough situation for you. I mean, no hard feelings. I've been there before. No shit, man. But—I mean, we're all responsible adults here, so let's work this—"

"Be quiet," Peter ordered. "Janice, we have to talk. Now, tonight."

She was shaking her head, one anxious hand gathering in the material of her nightgown.

"I can't, Peter. I really can't."

"Okay, you heard her," Apple said firmly, stepping so close that Peter could see the wetness in his beard. "Let's go."

He fingered the revolver— his hands were warm enough now to feel the cold metal—then pulled the gun out of his coat.

"Oh, shit." Apple jumped back.

Janice stared at him, her mouth small, watching him, he knew. Good. She saw how serious he was. He had her attention.

"Peter, put that away."

He only stared angrily.

"Put it down."

They didn't believe how serious he was, they thought that they could just sweet-talk him out of the house. Be nice to him, he's acting crazy. John Apple stood in a slight crouch, ready to spring or run, yet also by his expression scoffing at Peter. The gun was now a terrible, potent weight in his hand, and he was conscious of the thin arc of the trigger that cupped his forefinger. And with this awareness came an idea: If he fired the gun away from them, then they might realize that he was angry and that he was to be respected. This was only half an idea, carried by a fragment of conviction.

"Put it down, Peter." She examined him, made a decision—he saw it in her eyes, just as he had seen it the moment she'd told him she was leaving. And, with a grace that looked nearly practiced, she took a long step toward the stairs and touched a red button on the wall.

"Don't do that!" he yelled.

She turned, her eyes sad and yet resolute.

"You fucker," Apple snapped at Peter. "That's a police call button, a silent alarm."

"Call them back," Peter ordered. "You have maybe half a minute to call them back."

"No," Janice said.

"I will, then,"

"There's a code."

"Call. Tell them the code."

"I won't, Peter."

"Hear that?" Apple said.

"You!" Peter stepped toward Apple and pointed the gun at his head. "God, I'd like to blow your head off, you motherfucker. Get down, now. *Now! I mean it!*" Apple collapsed heavily onto the floor and this angered Peter even more. Apple lay at his feet; Peter raised his foot and jammed the sole of his shoe into the man's back.

"Peter!" Janice screamed. "Stop!"

He pointed the gun at Apple's head.

"Call, Janice."

Apple had risen to his hands and knees. Peter kicked hard, in the fleshy part between the hipbone and the bottom rib.

302

"No," she cried, weeping, "I can't."

He touched the gun to Apple's head.

"Please, man, I'm fucking begging you," Apple cried. "Janice, please call."

Peter began, slowly, to squeeze the trigger, knowing that it would take a deliberate contraction of his finger to pull the trigger to the point that it offered no resistance such that the gun would go off. As he watched their faces, frozen in anticipation and anxiety, this minute increment of space widened in his mind, and as he held the gun and the obvious danger of it—the muscles in his forearm drawn tight—he pressed the trigger ever so slightly more, experimenting where the resistance changed. There would be a great noise, the jerk of motion, a bloody spray against the wall. He felt the string of control running from his brain to his finger. Apple lay rigid.

"You lied to me and planned it for months." He looked at Janice. "You took my parents' money, you thought you could just cut me out. You lied to me as carefully as you could."

She nodded, weeping.

He clutched the gun tightly, and with the means of destruction at hand, the impulse was great. He checked that John Apple did not move. It seemed most natural that he kill Apple, and the desire to do it was unchecked by further thought. Apple had impeded his plan to get back his wife. Janice sank to her knees, her cheeks wet now, a grieving tenderness in her face, and he resisted the sight of her, resisted the meaning of her torment, for it confused his resolve to destroy the both of them.

"Peter, you have to go. They're coming."

"What the fuck do you care?" he responded.

"I care. About what happens next."

He stared at her.

"You can't, Peter," she whispered.

"Listen to her," Apple cried hoarsely.

Without answering, he put his foot heavily on Apple's head.

"You're not this mean, Peter. Not this mean to anybody. Not even to yourself."

Janice wept quietly, her eyes locked on his. He felt clearer, cleaner. Always her crying had done this—shocked him, drained him of malice—for her tears came from the deepest part of her, where she saw a world torn apart again. He hadn't the heart for any more. He lowered the gun.

"I loved you, Janice."

She nodded, again and again, wordlessly. The siren neared.

"Go, Peter," Janice whispered. "Please go."

Outside, having laid the knife next to the chocolate cake and hurried through the back door, Peter lingered at the window. The siren ebbed directly outside, the light spinning noiselessly across the leafless trees and alley. Apple came to the door, holding both arms around his middle where he had been kicked, but Janice motioned to him with a violent, insistent waving of her arm to go upstairs and not be seen. Apple left the room. Now car doors slammed, and inside, Janice heard this, as did her husband. She wiped her eyes quickly on her sleeve and pulled on a coat from the closet. The knock came. She opened the door and invited the patrolmen in, pretending to shake her head in embarrassment, quite obviously explaining the accidental alarm, apologizing at the stupidity of what she had done.

Minutes later, running in his long coat and breathless, Peter reached Penn's Landing on the Delaware River, across from the lights of Jersey on the other side. The water moved blackly before him, the wind whipped the sweat from his face. It was upon this old shore that the city was born with the force of hope. Behind him rose the low brick row homes, then City Hall and the glass towers of the future. He would, he knew, have to find his way back through the old crooked streets, and figure out how to get out of the mess he was in—set his mind to it, and at the very least tell the people of Philadelphia what he knew. The city must know about itself, and he was ready to carry to it what he held of the truth. This was the only way to continue. He was still poisonously angry, almost to the core, and filled with a full wretched vision of his guilt. Thus, there was some small satisfaction in heaving the gun as far as he possibly could toward the black swelling water, grunting with the effort. His arm ached immediately and this was good.

Peter Scattergood sat alone in one corner of the old meeting house, a large and austere room of white plaster and unfinished wood where for several centuries Quakers had sought answers for their questions in the compelling silence of worship. The meeting house stood in a compound of trees behind a brick wall at Fourth and Arch streets. And now, with a blustery, wet April morning washing in gusts against the windows, Peter sat motionless in the shadows of natural light on the hard, wooden bench, seeking in his silence to know just why, eight weeks prior, he had been so lost to himself and to those whom he loved as to point a loaded gun at Janice and John Apple.

The other worshipers had long since left the room, disappearing after the regular Sunday meeting had finished with a handshake by the elders, as was the custom. No one had chatted with him. Peter leaned forward on the bench just as he had done all his life whenever problems needed thought. He felt heavy and tired, another year older, changed by this winter. Just this morning he had caught a sideways glimpse of himself in the mirror, seeing not himself but someone who looked a bit like his father, more time in the face, the first real wrinkles pulling at the eyes, the squint of experience resting in his expression.

The days were brutal now, spinning past in a whirl of lights and public argument, with Peter assuming the grotesque proportions of a man who suddenly everyone knows. The newscasters already had pasted the usual descriptions to his name: "embattled prosecutor Peter Scattergood" and "the suspended Assistant District Attorney who alleges," and so on. And this sudden transmogrification of his identity was just one of many, for the city now watched all the actors in this latest scandalous drama with disgusted judgment on their faces. No one was innocent and no one would come out of it clean. Peter pressed his fingers to his face and closed his eyes. On Friday he had received official notice from the District Attorney that he had been fired. On Monday he was to be questioned by the U.S. District Attorney's anticorruption office about the extent of his activities with Vinnie. The bank had informed him that it was initiating foreclosure proceedings on the Delancey Street house due to missed mortgage payments.

He sat motionless, seeking revelation as to how disaster had resulted from the best of hopes. On the night he almost killed Janice and her lover—and that, he decided, was really the truth; he had wanted to do it, he had been as close as you could get without actually pulling the trigger—he had found it in himself to seek justice, as he had been taught. All other avenues seemed ruinous and so he had called Karen Donnell, the *Inquirer* reporter, who happened to be working late that night. Standing in the cold, he had briefly explained that he needed to talk to her and she had responded guardedly, as might be expected when a city official tries to feed information to a reporter. But still she agreed to meet him at a public place in an hour. She would hear him out, she said, but make no promises. He had retrieved the Carothers file from his car and they met in the Greyhound bus station, where amid sleepy travelers and the homeless, he outlined the cover-up being engineered by the Mayor and Hoskins, about Tyler Henry's real father, all of it. He gave her Detective Westerbeck's name and told her to call him to confirm the arrest of Geller. This was the end of his legal career in the city, but the reporter didn't seem to care. He dumped the whole file on the bench. "There it is," Peter said. "Take it."

The next day, soon after Peter was notified that he had been suspended immediately without pay, it was revealed that Detective Westerbeck had matched Geller's fingerprints with those in the apartment and arrested him. Geller, it soon became apparent, had lost touch with reality and in a videotaped confession described the murder of Johnetta Henry. Inevitably, the television stations—which now gorged themselves on the scandal—soon got a copy of the tape and played it on the news.

That night Peter dialed half a dozen hotels in Bermuda, hoping that Berger hadn't made a pass at one of the hotel waitresses and caused a huge fight with his wife, resulting in their fleeing the island in crisis.

Finally, listening past the low humming crackle of the phone lines, Peter had reached Berger and explained all that had happened.

"It's going to be hard to find a job," Berger said.

"You'll find me one," Peter answered. "Right?"

Berger's laugh came through the line.

"What's happening with Janice?" Berger asked.

"Last night I found her in bed fucking some guy and I had a gun and just about blew them away."

"Yeah, right," Berger said sarcastically.

And the next day, even as Karen Donnell's story hit the paper, quoting an unnamed Assistant District Attorney at length, the Mayor's office announced that the D.A.'s office was suppressing information that would disclose that Wayman Carothers committed both murders. The spokesman called for "full and immediate disclosure." And then came the countercharges by the D.A.'s office, which had closed ranks and was set to wage bureaucratic war with the Mayor's office. Hoskins started to appear on television making statements about the investigation. Peter's name was never mentioned. The District Attorney, fresh from huddling with his media guru, decided after all that he had better jump back in front of the public eye, get a fresh scalp on the pole, so to speak, and catch the battle on the upswing.

It was only a matter of time before the hounds of the media identified Peter as the source in Karen Donnell's story and wanted to know if and why he had been suspended when in fact it was he who had turned up the crucial information. Then Peter found himself outside City Hall in the late afternoon, speaking from the wool warmth of his muffler and coat, spewing shadows of steam at the reporters and cameras, some of them from the networks, the bright glare making him feel he was looking into the sun, and he again recounted the story, carefully explaining how it was that a young black woman named Johnetta Henry, whose desires were typical—a safe life, hope for her child, and marriage to a promising young man—had been killed by a man who no longer was sane, a man who worshiped the leader whom the public had so recently elected, and how this tragedy was compounded by simple error on the part of the police and by the impulsive and sickening violence of Wayman Carothers, and how the Mayor and his allies had panicked and sought to suppress the truth.

It was a grim and depressing story and the papers and the television stations spent weeks corroborating it, putting the Mayor in a desperate position, forcing him to backpedal and countercharge, saying that "this fellow Peter Scattergood" was a demented and desperate man, unstable with grief at the breakup of his marriage. Suddenly Peter's association with Vinnie became known, and Vinnie's unsavory activities surfaced in an undercover investigation—the Mayor's power brokers had cut various deals with the party to turn up Vinnie, thereby sacrificing the fat man in the effort to discredit Peter. Vinnie's sudden appearance spawned fresh inquiries into his activities and other scandals came to light, all of which tended to make Peter guiltier by association, especially when it came to be known that Vinnie had received a $25,000 kickback for his role as middleman in the purchase of a thousand defective police radios. That a young Hispanic policeman—a churchgoing father of four children—had recently been gravely injured while trying to call for backup on one of the faulty radios immediately was a heartbreakingly perfect twist of fate and sent Vinnie into a friendless hell. The charges about Vinnie created rumblings about state bar association disciplinary proceedings for Peter, and he received formal notice that a preliminary investigation was imminent.

The fact that Peter had been in the midst of a disastrous marriage was endlessly fascinating to the newspapers, of course, because fractured love relationships seemed to be the theme running through the entire affair. And, relatedly, what everyone wished to know was the mind of the Mayor, for until the scandal it was generally agreed that he was a good man, a man who might lead the city with grace and passion. And what people wanted to know was whether in his heart he was still a good man and if it pained him to have hidden his fatherhood of Tyler Henry and if his wife forgave him or not. The newscasts showed the Mayor and his family grimly attending church each Sunday, with all comments about the case coming through the Mayor's spokesmen and his attorneys. And had he loved Johnetta Henry or had he only felt great lust at the sight of her, the same body Peter had seen naked on the bed in the West Philadelphia apartment? No one knew these answers now, or if they did, then they were not forthcoming.

The black community was undecided about the issue, half believing with understandable distrust that Scattergood and other white officials had framed the Mayor, others disgusted and angry that they had been betrayed so quickly. The Mayor's office, trying anything it could to restore the public faith, also went after Hoskins, alleging that it was in fact he who had sought to cover up the facts of the murders while engaged in an open struggle for power in a city agency that was now adrift, due to the political aspirations of the D.A. But either these charges were too abstract or Hoskins had too many allies packed away in the Republican law firms of the city because the charges weren't sticking. It was rumored that Hoskins would turn in his resignation and be asked to accept a lucrative job in one of the private firms in order to keep him out of harm's way as the D.A. continued his bid for the Senate. Thus Hoskins would be kept busy at the luncheons in the downtown hotels, on the dinner circuit in the Rittenhouse Square townhouses, and at the weekend parties out on the Main Line. He had, it seemed, escaped public judgment.

As for Carothers, he had been banished to the endless wait for his various trials, and no one believed that his cause merited public consideration. When the facts showed that Carothers was not the father of Tyler Henry, it became known through Stein, the defense attorney, that Carothers was despondent and uncooperative; the problem was that Carothers had loved Tyler and now, this too, his fatherhood, had been taken from him. Soon thereafter Carothers was involved in a prison fight in which one of his lungs was punctured. The man was lost, Peter knew, and could never come back.

Peter looked up. The rows of empty meeting benches seemed gathered in silent contemplation of him and of his sins. It had been in this very room that he and Janice had been married. He still hoped that he would get his ring back someday, wrapped in a tissue and mailed in a small package, but he assumed that Cassandra had not gone to the necessary trouble of retrieving it. She had not called him and when he had finally returned to his house, the shopping coupons—the phantom money—still lay on his kitchen table and floor.

And neither had he seen Janice, despite the fact that their divorce now proceeded in a normal and almost dignified manner—Mastrude and her attorney arguing over nothing, conducting a calm and orderly transaction. Yet no matter what the inevitable fluttering of legal documents, the foreknown entry into the ledgers of the men and women no longer betrothed, the many decrees and judgments, always they would be linked in the most difficult of ways. After the charges about Peter's arrangement with Vinnie surfaced, the press quickly found Janice, eager to see just what kind of woman a promising young prosecutor would wreck his career for. The *Daily News* photographer caught her off guard as she left work, and her alarmed and frozen expression had flitted across the newsstands one day just last week with the caption SHE WON'T TALK ABOUT SCANDAL beneath the photo. Janice had called him from her lawyer's office to assure him that she would respect his privacy if he respected hers, and he wished to hear forgiveness in her voice. They both knew that he lived now at a very far remove from her, by his dangerous and inexcusable actions and by his position in the sprawling public crisis. She was no longer seeing Apple, she mentioned without being asked, and yet there was no hope in this for either of them, their passion long burnt out by torment, leaving only a residue of memory and an uncertain desire never to become strangers to each other.

The light of the day had crossed the wide planks of the floor and in this reminder that time would push all events into the past, that stone was even now being melted by the rain, and that a man's fate was a small thing, Peter rose and thrust his hands into his pockets, feeling the familiar and comforting shapes of coins and keys. He passed through the empty foyer of the meeting house and out the large heavy doors. The drops touched his head and face. Daffodils had pushed their green fingers up through the earth, and he recalled that his father's seasonal labors were now just beginning. His mother was feeling better and would be able to help. Under the wet, budding trees near the gate he thought again of Janice, wishing with sudden great hope that she might be waiting for him in the car, holding a cup of coffee warm in her hands perhaps, knowing somehow that he was there. He would slip in and lean over and kiss her and smell the coffee on her lips and she would ask him to hold the cup as she started the ignition. He would check to see that they both had on their seat belts. In such a mundane act would be genuine and eternal redemption. But as Peter looked, it came to him that Janice was not there and that she would not be there in the future.

And so, on that day in April, with the dark and old city besieged and in turmoil, Peter Scattergood walked, the wind flapping his long black coat as he found his way past the many places he knew, and it was somewhere in those hours—the first moments that he seemed to be himself again—that he suddenly remembered Tyler Henry, the small boy who knew almost nothing of what swirled around him, who only later in life would come to see that it was for him and for his doomed mother and her young lover, and for his powerful father, that a city of millions had stopped and taken pause, had examined the newspaper photographs of him, shaking their heads in amazement at the contrast between the boy's innocence and the evil that had beset those who had brought him into the world. And, as Peter recalled as he walked out of the shadows of the Walt Whitman Bridge and turned toward Independence Mall, one of the television stations had found Tyler Henry one previous Sunday morning in the West Philadelphia church that he attended with his grandmother and where he sang in the choir, and for a moment the whole city again saw the black child in his pressed collar, neat tie, and red choir robe, his small and perfect mouth forming the words to the hymns, singing in a clear and high tone, his eyes lifted upward with the trust and hope that only a young life holds.

DAHLGREN MEMORIAL LIBRARY
GEORGETOWN UNIVERSITY
MEDICAL CENTER
3900 RESERVOIR ROAD, N.W.
WASHINGTON, D.C. 20007

Leisure Collection